D0228873

LIVING WITH THE DEAD

LIVING WITH THE DEAD

KELLEY ARMSTRONG

www.orbitbooks.net

ORBIT

First published in Great Britain in 2008 by Orbit

A CIP catalogue record for this book
is available from the British Library.

ISBN 978-1-84149-732-7

Printed and bound in Great Britain by
Clays Ltd, St Ives plc

Papers used by Orbit are natural, renewable and recyclable
products made from wood grown in sustainable forests and certified
in accordance with the rules of the Forest Stewardship Council.

FSC **Mixed Sources**
Product group from well-managed
forests and other controlled sources
www.fsc.org Cert no. SGS-COC-004081
© 1996 Forest Stewardship Council

Orbit
An imprint of
Little, Brown Book Group
100 Victoria Embankment
London EC4Y 0DY

An Hachette Livre UK Company
www.hachettelivre.co.uk

www.orbitbooks.net

ACKNOWLEDGMENTS

With every book, I thank my agent, Helen Heller, and my editors, to whom I'm always indebted. But this one needs an unusually big thank-you to my editors. Writing multiple points-of-view had its challenges, primarily that more voices meant more blather . . . and a bloated first draft. A huge thanks to Anne Groell of Bantam US, Antonia Hodgson of Little, Brown UK and, particularly, Anne Collins of Random House Canada (who wields the most incisive blue pencil I know). Thanks for your support and guidance, which made the process so much easier.

Thanks, too, to John G. for his help with Finn's detective parts. Any errors in police procedure are mine. As much as John tried to help me make Finn's investigation realistic, sometimes the needs of story take precedence over verisimilitude . . . so I must take the blame for the errors.

Big thanks as always to my beta readers, who help me catch the little bugs that crop up in every manuscript. Again, any remaining errors are mine. They're readers, not miracle workers! Thanks to Xaviere Daumarie, Laura Stutts, Raina Toomey, Lesley W, Ang Yan Ming, Terri Giesbrecht and Danielle Wegner.

LIVING WITH THE DEAD

ADELE

To call Portia Kane a waste of space was being charitable. She was negative space—a vacuum that sucked in everything around her. An entire industry had grown up to service this spoiled "celebutante." Lives were wasted catering to her whims, feeding her ego, splashing her vapid face across the news.

And for what? She wasn't smart, wasn't talented, wasn't pretty, wasn't even interesting. Adele should know. She'd spent the last two years wallowing in the oatmeal mush that was Portia's mind. But soon she'd be free. If she dared.

Adele stabbed a ripe baby tomato. The innards squirted down the front of her shirt. The insanely expensive white shirt she'd bought just for this meeting. She grabbed a linen napkin, but only ground the pulp into a bloody smear.

A tinkling laugh rose above the murmur of the lunch crowd. Adele turned to see Portia leaning over the table, whispering to Jasmine Wills. Laughing. At Adele? No. To them, she was invisible. That was the goal—never let your prey know it's being stalked.

Paparazzi. An ugly word, with an uglier reputation. The kumpania never used it. They weren't like those curs, endlessly chasing their prey, trying to corner it, provoke it, snatching mouthfuls of flesh where they could. Kumpania photographers were clever foxes, staying out of the fray and getting the most profitable shots through cunning, craft and clairvoyance.

A man cut through the gathering near the restaurant entrance. Was that him? They'd only spoken by phone, but she was sure it was. He had *their* look—the thinning blond hair, the unnaturally blue eyes, the arrogant tilt of the chin, the razor-sharp cut of the suit.

And he was looking right at her. Smiling at her. Coming toward her. In that moment, Adele knew how a fox felt when it saw its first grizzly.

All sensible supernaturals feared the Cabals, those corporations run by sorcerers whose idea of severance packages usually involved the removal of body parts. For clairvoyants, though, that fear rose to outright terror. By the time clairvoyants finished working for a Cabal, they'd lost the most vital body part of all—their minds.

The power of clairvoyance came with the price tag of insanity, a fate the kumpania promised to save them from . . . in return for a lifetime of servitude. They also promised to protect their clairvoyants from the Cabals, which would woo them with promises of wealth, then drain their powers and retire them to a padded cell, drooling and raving, brought out only for horrific experiments.

And now Adele was willingly meeting with a Cabal sorcerer. Willingly offering herself to his corporation. Was she mad? She had to run, escape while she still could.

She gripped her thighs, squeezing until the pain crystallized her fear into resolve. The grizzly might be the biggest predator in the forest, but a clever fox could use that. A clever clairvoyant could use the Cabals, make her fortune and get out while she was still sane enough to enjoy it.

Adele touched her stomach. In it, she carried the ultimate bargaining chip. With it, she didn't need to flee the grizzly. She could run to it, hide behind it, *use* it to escape the kumpania and get the kind of life she deserved.

The man stopped beside her table. "Adele Morrissey?" He extended his hand. "Irving Nast. A pleasure to meet you. We have a lot to talk about."

ROBYN

The world was a shitty place; no one knew that better than Robyn Peltier. Every day for the past six months, she'd scoured the news for a story that proved it. She sometimes had to check two newspapers, but never more than that.

No common murder or assault would do. What Robyn looked for were the stories that made people call over their shoulders, "Hey, hon, can you believe this?" The ones you really didn't *want* to believe because they supported a sneaking suspicion that this world was an ugly, fucked-up place where no one gave a damn about anyone else.

The experts blamed everything from video game violence to hormones in the milk to the wrath of God. People wrung their hands and moaned about what the world was coming to, as if callous disregard for human life was some new phenomenon. Bullshit. It started back when the first caveman clubbed a buddy for his wicked new spear.

But it's easier to tell yourself the world is a good, civilized place, filled with good, civilized people, because that's what you need to believe to keep going. And it works just fine until the day the ugliness seeps to the surface and sucks your life into the cesspool.

Today, Robyn found her story on page two of the *L.A. Times*. A man had shot a kid for walking across his lawn and thought he was perfectly justified—because, after all, it was *his* lawn. She clipped the article, laid it on a fresh page of her bulging scrapbook, then smoothed the plastic over it. Number 170.

Before she put the scrapbook back on the shelf, she flipped back to page one and read the headline, as she had 170 times before: "Good Samaritan Gunned Down on Highway." She touched the face in the photo, tracing his cheek, where the plastic covering was almost worn through, and she thought, for the 170th time, what a crappy picture it was.

There was no excuse for picking a bad photo. As a public relations consultant, Robyn knew better than anyone the importance of providing the right picture to convey your message. She thought of all the ones she could have given the press. Damon playing hoops with his nephews. Damon treating his tenth-grade class to post-exam pizza. Damon goofing around with his garage band. Damon grinning at their wedding.

Damn it, any picture of him *smiling* would have done. How hard was *that*? The man was a born performer—stick a camera in his face and he lit up. After five years together, she had hundreds of photos of him, any one of which would have shown the world what it had lost that night.

But when asked for a photo, she'd been dealing with the press, the police, the funeral arrangements, everyone clamoring for her attention when all she'd wanted to do was slam the door, fall to the floor and sob until exhaustion blessed her with sleep. She'd grabbed the first picture she could find—his somber college graduation shot—and shoved it into their hands.

Robyn's cell phone rang. "Diamonds Are a Girl's Best Friend." Portia had set up the ring tone. Not that Portia needed her own special one. These days, if Robyn's phone rang, it was almost always Portia, who kept her busier than her dozen clients back in Philadelphia. In this business, the only job crazier than doing PR for Paris Hilton was doing PR for the girl who wanted to be the next Paris Hilton.

She put the scrapbook back on the shelf, then answered.

"Finally," Portia breathed. "It rang, like, ten times, Rob."

Three, but Robyn knew better than to correct her. "Sorry, I was in the other room."

Silence, as Portia contemplated the concept of being, even momentarily, cell phone free.

"So how was lunch with Jasmine?" Robyn asked.

She braced for the answer and prayed if cleanup was required, it wouldn't involve posting bail this time. The tabloids called Jasmine Wills a "frenemy" of Portia's, but if there was any "friend" in the equation, Robyn had yet to see it.

The two young women hadn't spoken since Jasmine stole Brock DeBeers, the former boy-band heartthrob who really had made Portia's heart throb. Robyn had warned Portia not to accept the invitation to a makeup lunch, but Portia had only laughed, saying Robyn didn't understand the game yet, and besides, she hadn't really liked Brock *that* much. She only kept his photo in her room because she hadn't found time to redecorate.

Apparently, Jasmine had spent the entire meal regaling Portia with tales of her wild sex life with Brock. Man's inhumanity to man. Sometimes it was shooting a helpful stranger, sometimes it was beating your BFF's dignity into the ground with a crowbar.

"But I'm going to get her back. I have a plan."

Portia's singsong cracked at the edges, and Robyn bled a little for her. She wished she could write Portia off as a vacuous twit who was sucking her dry with her neediness, but she supposed it would take another 170 articles in her scrapbook to drain her last ounce of sympathy.

Or maybe Robyn just liked to bleed. Maybe that was why she'd taken the job. Representing Portia Kane was the lowest, most meaningless form of PR work she could imagine. But after Damon's death, she'd had enough of representing not-for-profit organizations for a pittance. No one else cared. Why should she?

"Oh, and then, just before the bill came, Penny called and guess what? They can't make it to Bane tonight because—get this—they're going to the opening of Silhouette with Jasmine. How much you want to bet Jasmine told Penny to call at lunch so she could watch my reaction?"

Every dollar I have, thought Robyn. Portia wasn't stupid. That was the problem. It'd be so much easier if Robyn *could* write her off as a vacuous twit. But then she'd show some spark of intelligence, some proof that she could do more with her life than grace club openings.

"So what about that benefit concert tonight?" Robyn asked. "If you're skipping Bane, I can call and get you back on the list—"

"Benefit concert? Oh God, Rob, kill me now. No, I'm still going to Bane, and you're coming with me."

How lonely did you need to be to invite your PR rep clubbing? "I'd love to, but I have plans. Remember that friend I was with yesterday, when you came by?"

"The Indian girl?"

"Hope is Indo American."

Portia's put-upon sigh made Robyn press her fingertips into her temples. Portia never ceased to complain about Robyn correcting her gaffes, ignoring the fact Portia had asked for that "sensitivity training" herself, after she'd been quoted making a racist comment about the city's Hispanic population. Hiring Robyn had been her idea of damage control. She'd needed a new PR rep and someone mentioned Robyn, saying she was looking to relocate after her husband's death. *A real tragedy. He was trying to help a stranded motorist, but the woman saw a black guy coming at her on an empty highway and shot him.*

With that, Portia had seen the perfect way to prove she wasn't racist. Then Robyn showed up—blond haired and green eyed—and from the look on Portia's face, you'd think she'd never heard the term *interracial marriage*.

Portia was still nattering on about Hope. "So bring her and make sure she looks hot—but not hotter than me."

"We already had plans, Portia."

"It's *Bane*. Now, I know she works for *True News*, but under absolutely no circumstances is she allowed to report on our evening. Got it?"

In other words, Portia expected full coverage on the front page.

"Hope isn't a celebrity reporter. She's their weird tales girl, so unless you're going to sprout a tail or breathe fire, she's not—"

"Okay, tell her she can report on it. An exclusive. Oh, and make sure she brings that hot boyfriend, and tell him to bring some friends. Hot friends."

"He doesn't have friends here, Portia. They aren't from L.A.—"

Portia let out an eardrum-splitting squeal. "Finally. Jasmine's coming out of the restaurant. Tim, start the car. Move forward, slowly. Rob, hold on."

"What—?"

The line went dead. Robyn was putting the phone down when it rang again.

It was Portia. "Remember how you gave me shit for wearing that micro skirt last week? Wait until you see this." A split-second pause. "Well? What do you think?"

"Of what?"

"The photo I just sent you."

Robyn checked her mail. There, with the caption "Wait til tabs see this!!!" was a picture of Jasmine Wills wearing what looked like a baby-doll nightgown. A *see-through* nightgown. Gauzy pink, with a red bra-and-panty set underneath.

"Well?"

"I'm . . . speechless."

"You're going to send it, right? To the tabs? Oh! Send it to your girlfriend at *True News*."

"She doesn't cover—"

"Then tell her to make an exception. Oh, my God! There's Brock! Tim, pull forward."

Click. Portia was gone.

HOPE

It took a half-dozen tries to get the key-card light to work—long enough that Hope was tempted to practice her electronic lock-picking skills. When the light finally did turn green, she was leaning against the door, handle down, and it flew open under her weight, sending her stumbling inside. She listened for Karl's laugh and when it didn't come, felt a twinge of disappointment.

She shouldn't have been surprised. She'd told him she'd probably have to work late, so she didn't expect him back. Still, her disappointment smacked of dependence. Karl wasn't the kind of guy she should count on.

Hope went to toss her purse on the bed, but threw her laptop case instead. Too much on her mind, fretting about how to help Robyn, worrying about her relationship with Karl, fighting the nagging feeling that the two weren't unrelated. The more she watched her friend spiral downhill, the more anxious she got about where she was heading with Karl.

She kicked off her pumps and squeezed the carpet between her toes, luxuriating in the feel of it, inhaling the scent of . . . flowers?

There, on the desk, was a bouquet of yellow and purple irises. Hope read the tag. From her mother, hoping her first week of work was going well. It wasn't exactly a new job—she'd been at *True News* for four years, and this was her second L.A. work exchange.

She hadn't planned to return. Los Angeles wasn't her kind of city, really. But the chance for a six-week stint came right as Hope had been trying to schedule vacation time to visit Robyn, and it seemed like the perfect solution.

They'd been friends since high school, when Hope's private academy had been running a joint fund-raiser with Robyn's public school, and they'd been assigned to the same committee. Afterward they'd stayed in touch, gradually becoming friends. Then, in Hope's senior year, when the visions and voices started, she'd had a breakdown and spent her prom night in a mental ward. Robyn had been the only friend who hadn't slipped away, as if Hope's problems might be contagious.

Now Hope had a chance to help Robyn with her problem. When she'd come to L.A., she'd expected Karl would take the opportunity to do a "work exchange" of his own in Europe. Instead, he'd joined her. As good as that felt, she couldn't shake the fear she was getting too used to having him join her on business trips, and that the day he didn't want to come along, she'd be devastated.

"You're home early. You should have called."

She spun as Karl stepped inside. He'd changed since meeting her for lunch, trading designer chinos and a brilliant blue polo for a dark suit that looked like it came from a department store, well below Karl's usual standards. Not that it mattered. Karl could make Goodwill castoffs look good. The lowbrow attire was camouflage—Karl's way of blending into a crowd, and the moment he stepped into the room, though, the tie and jacket were off, cast onto the chair like a hair shirt.

"Good hunting?" Hope asked.

"You forgot to lock the deadbolt and chain."

He kissed the top of her head, cushioning the rebuke. She could feel the chaos waves of worry rolling off him. When Karl settled in a new city, he couldn't relax until he'd cleared out any other werewolves. Kill Karl Marsten, and a werewolf would instantly seal his reputation, guaranteeing for years to come that others would clear out of *his* way.

Hope knew that having her there made it worse. She was an easy way to get to him. So if he wanted her triple-locking the doors and taking a taxi to work until he'd finished scouting, she understood. The same way he understood the quirks and issues of a chaos half-demon girlfriend.

As he took off his shoes, she told him about Robyn's call and Portia Kane's "invitation."

"And, apparently, Portia insists I bring my 'hot boyfriend.' "

Karl snorted as he put his shoes aside. Not that he doubted Portia found him attractive. Hope knew his ego was too healthy for that. What he objected to was being called anything as common as "hot."

"Give it some thought while I grab a shower," she said. "If you want to get more scouting done instead, that's fine."

"If you're out, I'd rather stay close. I know you wanted to spend time alone with Robyn, though . . ."

"Not much use if Portia's there." Hope started unbuttoning her blouse. "In fact, it'd probably be better if you did come, keep Portia occupied, so she doesn't spend the night ordering Rob around."

"Using me as a distraction. I should be insulted."

"You aren't."

"True." He reclined on the bed, arms folded behind his head as he watched her undress. "She was wearing a lovely diamond bracelet the other day. At least ten carats. Platinum setting . . ."

"Don't you dare."

"If I'm expected to spend my evening charming a silly little girl, I think I'm entitled to compensation."

"Oh, you'll get compensation."

He plucked the hem of her skirt as she passed to the bathroom.

"It's a big job. I think I need an advance."

"And I need a shower."

"The two don't have to be mutually exclusive."

She paused, as if thinking it over, then lunged, skirt breaking from his grasp as she sprinted for the bathroom. She got the door closed just before he thumped against it, then she quickly fastened the lock. That would slow him down . . . for about ten seconds.

She smiled and tugged off her skirt.

ROBYN

As Robyn spotted Portia across the club, she was tempted to grab Hope and bail. Portia certainly didn't look as if she wanted company. She had the best see-and-be-seen spot in the club: a trio of sofas overlooking the dance floor. At least twenty people had squeezed onto those sofas, basking in the reflected glow of Portia's celebrity.

But even from across the dance floor, Robyn could tell no one was speaking directly to Portia. When she saw Robyn, she leapt to her feet and frantically waved her over.

"Oh my God. Finally! Rob, you look *amazing*."

She didn't and she knew it. She wore an unremarkable black dress and basic makeup, with her shoulder-length hair brushed straight. For Portia, that was perfect—presentable enough not to embarrass her, but in no danger of upstaging her. As Portia's gaze traveled to Hope, though, her eyes narrowed.

Robyn had neglected to pass along the "hot but not hotter than me" message. Why bother? With perfect features and long black curls, Hope looked great without trying—which was good, because she rarely did. Tonight, though, she'd put in the extra effort, wearing a pale green sheath dress and heels, her hair swept up, tendrils dangling.

"I love that dress!" Portia squealed, air-kissing Hope. "Where did you find it?"

Hope glanced over her shoulder at Karl.

"Vagabond," he said. "In Philly."

Portia swept past Hope and embraced Karl, giving him a kiss that definitely made contact. "I am so glad you could make it." She tugged him onto the sofa, scooting over so close she was almost on his lap. "Robyn tells me you're in the jewelry business, which is perfect, because I have a question."

"We'll let these two talk shop," Hope said to Robyn. "I think there's a spot over there . . ."

Karl's hand shot out, grabbing the hem of her dress and yanking her down beside him. She laughed and made room for Robyn.

Karl chatted with Portia, leaning over every now and then to whisper in Hope's ear, smiling as they shared a joke or wry observation. Just like Robyn used to do with Damon.

She remembered how she used to want that for Hope, with her endless stream of casual boyfriends. Someone to whisper and laugh with. Someone to lift the shadows from her eyes.

Karl wasn't what Robyn had in mind. Too smooth, too good looking, too old—almost a decade Hope's senior. She'd feared Karl was a gold digger, his eye on Hope's family money and social connections. But Karl had his own money and, she'd eventually conceded, his only interest in Hope was Hope herself.

As Portia monopolized Karl, Hope talked about work, making Robyn laugh as always with her tales of sewer monsters and alien abductions. Robyn used to worry that Hope's breakdown after high school had shattered her self-confidence, making her think she couldn't do better than tabloid reporting. But Damon had scoffed at that, saying Hope had the most interesting job of anyone he knew. It was like taking this position with Portia Kane. Sometimes, you just had to say to hell with relevancy and immerse yourself in the trivial. Not that it was working out so well for Robyn . . .

She gazed out over the club and saw a face that reminded her of Damon. She always did, finding him in the tilt of a stranger's chin, the curve of a face, the crinkle of an eye. She imagined him sitting beside her, getting a kick out of all the posturing around them. Peacocks, he'd call them, so busy preening and parading they never realized everyone else was too absorbed in *themselves* to notice.

He'd cut up the music, too, say they were warping perfectly good songs into dance versions for white boys from Nebraska. Then he'd lean over and sing in her ear. She could feel the tingle of his breath on her neck, the warmth of his finger sliding down her arm, the deep bass of his voice vibrating through her. He'd sing "500 Miles," their song—the one he'd been singing on the phone that night, driving home late from a conference in Pittsburgh.

When Robyn closed her eyes, she could hear him. Then he stopped and said, "Huh. Looks like someone lost a tire. Shit. Guess I should be a gentleman and offer to help."

Don't, baby. Please, please, don't . . .

She drained her champagne glass and refilled it. Hope didn't notice. She'd stopped talking and was staring across the club, eyes glazed over.

Gave up on me, I guess, Robyn thought.

She stared at the bubbles in her glass and allowed herself a two-second self-pity break.

She could imagine what Damon would say. *What did you expect, Bobby? She came all this way to help you, but she can't do it by herself. You need to give a little.*

Help her with what? Get over it? Get over *him*?

Robyn downed the drink. Hope was still staring out at the club, eyes unfocused. When Karl tapped her shoulder, she jumped. He whispered something. She shook her head, mouthed "nothing." He frowned, unconvinced.

Then Portia declared she was ready to move on. To another club, Robyn presumed, but Portia was chattering too fast for Robyn's booze-soaked brain to keep up.

She did know, however, that she had no intention of going anywhere but home. Hope and Karl decided to call it a night, too, and Hope offered her a ride, but Robyn insisted that Portia's driver would drop her off. Otherwise Hope would see how drunk she was and want to walk Robyn to her apartment. It wasn't ready for visitors yet. Robyn had been there three months, but still needed a few things. Like pictures for the blank walls. Dishes for the empty cupboards. Food for the bare fridge.

Portia barely waited until Hope and Karl were out of earshot before grabbing Robyn's arm and squealing, "Oh my God, he is so fine. I know he's kind of old for me, but I could use an older guy, don't you think? Someone more mature? He's classy and smart and funny." Portia sighed and Robyn thought she was going to swoon. "Can you imagine what everyone would say if I showed up at the premiere next week with him on my arm? What Jasmine would say? And Brock? You *have* to give me his number."

"I don't have it. But I do have Hope's. His *girlfriend's*."

Portia dismissed the reminder with a toss of her hair. Two weeks after having her heart broken by a stolen lover, and she was ready to do the same to another woman. No one gave a shit. It didn't matter who got hurt, so long as you got what you wanted.

"Portia, you can't—"

"Do I pay your wages, Rob?" The snap in Portia's voice made a few people look their way. "I'll expect that number in the morning. Now call Tim. Tell him to bring the car around. I'm going to touch up my makeup."

Robyn didn't argue. Her job was to get Portia out of public confrontations, not start them. Come morning, Portia would forget all about it anyway.

It took Portia fifteen minutes to make the rounds, saying her goodbyes and handpicking a few to invite to the next club. The moment she was gone, the uninvited dispersed, as if fearing they'd look like they were hanging out with Portia Kane's dowdy PR rep.

Robyn gazed around the club, at all the twenty-somethings, laughing and hugging, and she couldn't believe they were her species, let alone her generation.

Widowed at twenty-eight.

She thought of all the people who'd come up to her on the day of the funeral and said she was still young, as if she should be thanking God for taking her husband before she was too old and ugly to attract a new one.

Did they know what she'd give to have spent those years with him? If God had said, "I'll give him to you for six more months, but you'll never marry again, never fall in love again, never *touch* a man again," she would have screamed, "Yes, please, yes!"

Her own mother had hugged her, and in a whisper, asked whether she was pregnant yet. When Robyn said she wasn't, her mother had said that was for the best. A remark uttered in thoughtlessness not cruelty, but Robyn would never forget it. Just as she'd never forget that day three weeks later when she'd glanced at the calendar and realized her period was late and her knees had given way as she prayed. But even that scrap of mercy had been too much to ask for.

"How long does it take her to pee?" a plaintive voice moaned at Robyn's ear.

She looked over to see a red-haired waif. Some starlet whose name Robyn wouldn't waste energy remembering.

"Well?" the young woman said. "Shouldn't you go check on her? Isn't that, like, your job?"

Only if Portia was peeing in the hall and the paparazzi were snapping photos.

Robyn had a good idea what her client was doing and it wasn't a bodily function, unless that included "inhaling." Last year, Portia had spent a month in rehab. She hadn't been addicted to anything except publicity, and realized rehab had been a sure way to get it. There, she'd made new friends who'd expected her to snort the coke they smuggled in. So Portia Kane became quite possibly the first person ever to become addicted while *in* rehab.

Still, given the choice between checking on Portia or listening to this starlet whine . . . Robyn rose unsteadily and headed for the back rooms.

ROBYN

Portia wasn't in the washroom. Robyn even peeked under the stalls for her Jimmy Choos, ignoring the outraged chirps of the chorus line reapplying lipstick at the mirrors. That row of young women, shoulder to shoulder, gave Robyn a good idea where Portia was.

While her client didn't mind having her drug problems splashed across the tabloids, she wasn't nearly as open about letting people actually see her using. If the washroom was busy, she'd go in search of a more private place.

Robyn could just head back to the club and wait, but walking—and thinking—was clearing her head.

The first two doors she reached were labeled Private, which to Portia would scream privacy. But both were locked. Robyn continued on. As she neared the end, something clattered around the corner.

She froze, listening.

A low moan. She envisioned rounding the corner to see a couple.

She cleared her throat—loudly—and listened for muttered oaths or exclamations. A moment of silence, then running footsteps. She rounded the corner to see the exit door fly open, a woman's figure disappearing through it.

She started going after her, then replayed the pounding footsteps and knew they hadn't come from Portia's four-inch heels. She looked down the hall. There was only one door—half open, dark inside. She guessed that's where the woman—or couple—had fled from, but she should check it for Portia, just to be thorough.

Stepping through the darkened doorway, her foot knocked something. She bent, fingers closing around metal.

A gun.

Her startled brain gave the command to drop it, but she stopped herself. With her luck, someone would find it and use it in a crime . . . with her prints all over it. Better to find a staff member and hand it in.

As she turned to go, a moan sounded behind her. The hairs on her neck rose. She squinted into the dark room. A pale figure lay crumpled on the floor.

"R-Rob?" Portia's voice was a papery whisper.

Robyn raced forward and dropped beside her, letting the gun clatter to the floor. Her gaze snagged on the dark stain spreading over Portia's blouse.

"Cell . . ." Portia whispered. "Cell phone . . ."

"Right." Robyn fumbled for her purse, digging out a handful of crap and dumping it before finding her cell. "I'm calling 911."

"No, my . . ."

Portia's voice trailed off in a rattle. Then she went still. Robyn shook Portia's shoulder. She didn't blink, just stared. Sightless. Lifeless.

Robyn lifted her phone, fingers trembling as she dialed 911. Then she remembered the figure running out the back door. Portia's killer had just left. Robyn might still be able to catch her, or at least get a better look at her.

The 911 dispatcher answered. As Robyn ran from the room, she quickly explained what had happened—that Portia Kane was shot, wasn't breathing and needed an ambulance. She gave the location as she raced out the exit door. It was shutting behind her when she heard a scream.

Outside the room where Portia lay, a server was looking straight at Robyn. Their eyes met. The girl screamed again, backpedaling, her hands flying up.

"No!" Robyn called. "I—"

She lunged to catch the door. It shut with a clang. She grabbed for the handle. There wasn't one—it was solid metal. She banged a couple of times, but she knew it was useless—that girl wasn't about to open the door to a presumed killer.

Robyn remembered her call. The dispatcher was gone. She started redialing, then stopped. She'd given everything they needed. The best thing she could do right now was keep going and try to catch a glimpse of Portia's killer. She could explain the misunderstanding later.

She took off down the alley.

WELL, THAT HADN'T WORKED out quite as she envisioned . . .

Robyn stood at the end of an alley, looking up and down a road packed bumper to bumper with taxis and limos, all jockeying for curb space to disgorge their celebrity passengers. The sidewalks were just as full with people jockeying for a look at those passengers. A hundred feet away, a flashing sign announced the opening of Silhouette, the newest "see-and-be-seen scene" in L.A.

She scanned the crowd. Not a single bloodstained psycho killer in sight.

She shook her head, stifling a laugh. Ridiculous to think she actually could have caught Portia's murderer. The woman had a good five-minute head start. Robyn wasn't even sure it *had* been a woman. Maybe a slender young man?

Still, she kept looking down the street. The killer had to have come out here. Robyn had followed the first alley to a second, which led to a service lane blocked by a truck. The only other route had been a third alley . . . the one that ended here, at this road.

She started stepping out, then stopped herself. Speaking of bloodstained potential killers . . . Robyn's knees were red from kneeling beside Portia's body.

Portia's body.

Robyn took a deep breath. She hadn't always liked Portia, but there'd been something there, some spark of potential. If only she'd nurtured it, pushed for Portia to go to that charity event tonight instead.

If only she'd told Damon to stay the night in Pittsburgh instead of coming back so late . . .

Robyn took another deep breath. This wasn't about Damon. It was about Portia, and the best way she could help her was to get back to Bane and tell the police what she'd seen.

ROBYN TOOK HER TIME going back. She wasn't looking forward to explaining why she'd left the scene. She imagined the officers rolling their eyes at the dumb blonde who'd raced off, trying to catch a killer. She'd had no intention of catching her—just catching a better look. But it still sounded a little foolish. Okay, a *lot* foolish. File under "seemed like a good idea at the time."

As she rounded the corner, she caught a flash of motion. A black-clad figure darted behind a Dumpster. Robyn froze and replayed her memory of the fleeing killer. A slender, light-haired figure in black pants and a dark shirt.

Robyn took a slow step backward. Then she stopped.

Just a look, that was all she needed. Better yet, a picture. She pulled out her cell phone and stepped forward. Gravel crunched under her shoes. She reached down and tugged them off. Then she crept along the Dumpster until she heard the quick shallow breaths of someone trying to control panic.

Robyn turned her cell phone around, camera lens pointing out. Then, finger on the button, she reached around the corner of the bin . . .

Snap!

A choked gasp. As Robyn wheeled to run, she saw a shadow lunge at her.

Thwack.

Something hit the back of Robyn's head. She spun as a shadowy figure raised a chunk of concrete. It caught Robyn on the cheek. She stumbled back, tripped and went down. As she fell, the cell phone started to slip. She grasped it tighter, pulling her arm under her and landing facedown on it.

"Did you hear that?" said a distant voice. "Call for backup."

A radio squawked. Footfalls sounded in the next alley. Robyn's assailant let her go and ran.

Robyn scrambled to her feet. She slipped and recovered, but when she looked up, her attacker was gone. She heard an officer radioing for backup, saying that they might have found the suspect. Robyn almost called out, saying that their suspect was getting away. Then she remembered who those officers were looking for: her.

She looked down at herself, bloodied and battered. A bump on the head, a scrape on the cheek—proof she'd been in a fight, maybe with Portia. If those officers found her, they wouldn't keep looking for the fleeing killer; they'd presume they already had her.

Robyn took off.

FINN

JOHN FINDLAY—Finn since first grade when there'd been three Johns in his class—stared down at the body of Portia Kane, lying flat on her back, shirt ripped open, blood-smeared nipple rings glistening under the harsh light.

"This is one photo you wouldn't want in the tabloids," he murmured.

He lifted his gaze from the body and looked around the room for the ghost of Portia Kane, hovering over her body in disbelief or huddled in a corner, pulling her torn blouse closed. Nothing. Maybe she'd headed back into Bane to get in a few more minutes of clubbing before she was trundled off to the great beyond.

He snorted at the thought, earning a wary look from the new police photographer who circled wide, his looks saying he suspected what they said about Finn was true.

A hand slapped Finn between the shoulder blades and he turned to see the beefy figure of Mark Downey, one of the crime scene techs.

"Got that mojo working for us tonight, Finn?" Downey asked.

Finn glanced around, seeing no shimmer of Portia Kane. "Fraid not."

"Don't listen to him," Downey mock-whispered to the photographer. "This guy is a regular Sherlock fucking Holmes. I swear, crime scenes talk to him."

Not crime scenes, Finn mused as Downey wandered off. The photographer kept eyeing him warily. He wondered what the kid had heard. The mildest rumor was that Finn was a crack detective, but somewhat eccentric, and not really a team player—hence the "partner" who'd gone on leave five months ago and never been replaced. Worst were the stories that blamed his partner's absence on Finn—the stress of working with a wacko the department kept on only because of his clearance rates.

It didn't matter how careful Finn was. Every now and then, someone would see him carrying on a conversation with thin air and staring at things no one else could see. He wasn't psychic, he just saw dead people. Not like the kid in the movie, though. With Finn, they usually only appeared at homicide scenes, distraught and confused.

If he was lucky, he'd get a few questions answered before the ghost disappeared. And if he didn't? Then he was shit outta luck, because they never came back. This was, apparently, one of those times he wasn't getting any help from the dead. He took one last look around, then set to work.

ONE DEAD CELEBUTANTE. Apparent gunshot. Possible murder weapon lying beside her. After an hour's work, he knew no more than he had looking in from the doorway. He had a witness, but all she could say was that she'd heard something, come back here and seen a woman run out the exit door. As for what the woman looked like? Between eighteen and fifty, five foot to six foot, not fat, light hair.

She'd agreed to work with a sketch artist, but from the panic in her eyes when he asked, he wouldn't put much stock in the result. Eyewitness accounts were notoriously unreliable, and Finn knew the truth of that better than most. Twice he'd had ghosts give him a full description of their killer, only to have the evidence prove it was someone who didn't look anything like the sketch.

Finn didn't blame the ghosts. Both had been killed by strangers—one jumped in an alley, one catching a stray gang bullet. In that split second before death, they sure as hell weren't taking notes. And in those shell-shocked minutes after, their memory had shown them the face of a monster—bigger and uglier than the reality.

"Hear that?" Downey cocked his head, meaty jowls quivering. "The wolves are baying at the door. Think we should toss them a few scraps?"

Finn listened to the dull roar of the press firing questions to the officers guarding the perimeter. The club had been very helpful, even calling in off-duty bouncers to help them with crowd control. They must have had a few infractions on the books, hoping their cooperation might make those disappear.

He knelt beside the items that had been scattered beside the body. Women's things—makeup, a compact, tissues.

"I figure that belongs to the victim," Downey said. "Her purse was empty—dumped."

Finn surveyed the small mound of items, then glanced at Portia Kane's purse, barely big enough to hold a pack of smokes. "All this didn't fit in there."

"Hey, you should see all the crap my wife squeezes into hers. I swear, those things are magic."

Finn nodded, as if he understood. He wasn't married. No girlfriend, not for . . . well, it had been a while. It took all his time and energy to do his job—a life spent in service of the dead.

He could resent it, but he'd never really seen the point. He'd been given this gift, and it was his duty to use it.

Finn sorted through the purse debris with a gloved hand, looking for insight into the woman who'd left it behind. A young officer tapped him on the shoulder and said Marla Jansen wanted to speak to him. From the way he said it, Finn knew he should recognize the name, but he considered himself lucky to know who Portia Kane was.

He followed the officer—Tripp—into the hall and found a young woman with stop-sign-red hair bouncing on her tiptoes, trying to see into his crime scene.

"The body's been removed," Finn said.

"Oh!" Jansen's dark eyes widened with put-on horror. "I didn't want to see—" She shuddered. "Eww."

An actor. In this town, one learned to identify them at a hundred paces. From her exaggerated expressions, he would peg her as a wannabe—and likely to stay that way—but if Tripp knew her, she must be semifamous. Finn just hoped she didn't expect him to ask for her autograph.

"Officer Tripp says you saw something."

Jansen launched into a lengthy account of being in the club with Portia then sending Kane's PR rep—a woman named Robyn Peltier— to find her when she'd been gone too long.

"Portia Kane goes clubbing with her publicist? Does she expect to need her?"

"Of course not. Portia feels sorry for the chick. She lets her tag along with us sometimes. I always told her you shouldn't socialize with the hired help, and now look what happened. The chick flipped out and killed Port in a jealous rage."

"Was there an issue?"

Jansen fluttered her hands. "There's always an issue with people like that. They hate us. Finally it just bubbles over and . . . boom."

"Boom?"

"Or 'bang,' I guess. Anyway, they were fighting."

"About what?"

"How would I know?"

"When did this happen?"

"Right before Portia left us," Jansen said smugly. "The PR chick said something and Portia didn't like it. She told her to call the driver and went to the bathroom."

Didn't sound like much of a fight to Finn.

Jansen nibbled a purple-painted fingernail. "Do you think I should, like, get a bodyguard?"

"I doubt it's an epidemic."

Her brow furrowed, trying to figure out what he meant. Then she gave up and pulled out her cell phone. "I'm going to get one. Maybe two. You can't be too careful."

ROBYN

Robyn stood across the road from Bane. She looked down at her cell phone for the umpteenth time, as if the image she wanted was just slow in materializing, like one of those old Polaroid cameras. It was a great shot . . . of the blurred top of a light-haired head.

She looked at the club—at the growing crowd, at the reporters, the TV vans, the police cars, the ambulance . . . and she realized that every step she'd taken since finding Portia's body, as right as it had seemed at the time, had only made her situation worse.

She'd left her prints on the murder weapon. She'd been spotted fleeing the scene. She'd maybe even been spotted running down the alley. And now, to turn herself in, she'd have to pass the gauntlet of reporters and news cameras.

A primitive voice in her head screamed for her to run, but she silenced it. That would be the worst thing she could do.

She imagined a client calling her with this situation. She'd tell him to prepare for a trip to the station . . . just as soon as she'd made a few calls and gotten professional advice on how to proceed.

That's what she needed now: professional advice.

SHE DIDN'T CALL AHEAD, just showed up on Judd's doorstep and prayed he was home. Judd Archer was a contract bodyguard Portia hired when she needed extra security, or wanted to look as if she did. He was much in demand in Portia's circles, not so much for his security abilities—which were top-notch—but for the extra services he provided.

Judd was an ex-cop. Robyn wasn't completely sure what his story was, only that he'd been screwed over by the department. And he was mad as hell about it, which meant he was happy to exact some revenge by advising his clients on ways to deal with the law.

Judd answered the door on the second ring. Dressed in sweatpants, he rubbed his fist over his bleary eyes.

"Rob?" He blinked hard. "What's wrong? Portia in trouble?"

"Not her. Me."

He frowned, as if he must have misheard.

"Portia's dead," Robyn said. "And they think I killed her."

He backed up and waved her inside.

THEY WERE IN THE KITCHEN, Robyn on a stool at the island, Judd behind it making coffee.

Judd had loaned Robyn a sweatsuit. She'd changed into it and carefully folded her dress into a bag, so the police could test it for gunshot residue. Then she told Judd everything.

"Did you get a look at the detectives?" he asked. "I knew most of the homicide guys in that division."

"One guy in a suit came out to talk to the officers guarding the scene. Big guy with a craggy face. Dark blond hair in need of a trim. Early thirties, maybe?"

"Did he have an accent? Texan, I think. Or Oklahoma . . . No, I guess you wouldn't have been close enough to hear. But it sounds like John Findlay. Hopefully it is. He's a good cop. Might look like a cowboy, but he isn't, not when it comes to police work. Slow, steady and thorough. He won't jump to conclusions or railroad you into a confession."

Robyn stirred her coffee as she took a deep breath. "Okay."

"It's not like you have a lot of choice, Rob."

"I know. I just feel like an idiot. I ran from a crime scene."

"Trying to get a look at a fleeing killer. *After* you called 911. And when that girl saw you, you tried going back to explain. Even banged on the door. You've got scrapes and bumps to support your story, ones that wouldn't come from a run-in with Portia. And you have a photo."

"Oh, yes. The amazing photo." She took the cell phone from the table, looked at the blurry picture again and put the phone into her pocket as she shook her head. "I'm not even sure that *is* the killer. For all I know, I accidentally ambushed a street kid."

"But it still supports your story."

Robyn wasn't so sure. She knew Judd was trying to make her feel better. Like he'd said, she didn't have much choice. She had to turn herself in.

"Can you call the detective now?" she asked. "Get this over with."

JUDD HAD PHONED A CONTACT at the station and discovered that Detective Findlay was indeed assigned to the case. He left a message with the dispatcher. Findlay would call him back.

"So," he said as he sat again. "Do you have any idea who this woman might have been?"

"If it *was* a woman. I didn't get a good look. But I still wouldn't know. Portia didn't make enemies. People loved to hate her, but no one really hated her."

"Maybe someone wanted something?"

Robyn shook her head. "If they did, she gave it to them—she was so desperate to be liked."

"What about tonight? Did anything out of the ordinary happen?"

"I spent most of the evening talking to my girlfriend. And Portia was too busy flirting with my friend's boyfriend."

Judd's brows shot up. "Your friend couldn't have liked that."

"Honestly, she wasn't the least concerned. He stayed right beside us and didn't flirt back. Portia asked me for his number afterward. I said I didn't have it. She wanted me to get it. Not exactly a fight—she just snapped at me and—" Robyn looked up sharply. "Could they use that against me? Proof of a fight?"

"Just explain it to Findlay before he brings it up."

Judd prodded for recent incidents, but Robyn couldn't remember anything. Portia would have mentioned it—she told Robyn more about her personal life than she ever cared to know.

Eventually Judd said, "We'll leave the speculating to Findlay. He should be here in a few minutes. I'll start another pot of coffee."

ROBYN

Robyn was in the bathroom holding a cold cloth to her face, listening to Judd grinding more coffee beans, when she heard a bang. And the grinder stopped.

She froze, not thinking, not moving, heart slamming against her chest. It couldn't be what she thought. She had guns on the brain and her nerves were shot. She opened her mouth to call for Judd, but she couldn't get his name out.

She crept to the door and opened it just enough to hear footsteps. Heavy footsteps. Judd had been in bare feet.

A loud crack, like a door smacked open.

"Damn it," someone muttered. A male voice, young, and definitely not Judd.

She backed away from the door, clicking off the light. The footsteps and mutters continued. He was searching the house.

As she retreated toward the shower, she scoured the counter for a weapon. Not much to choose from. She grabbed an aerosol can of deodorant and a heavy silver toothbrush holder.

She set one foot in the tub and stopped. Hiding behind a shower curtain? Was she nuts?

Robyn crept to the door. Across the hall she could see a bedroom. There had to be better hiding places in there. She took one step . . . and the footsteps moved toward the hall. She darted behind the door and shrank back, the aerosol can lifted to eye level, her finger on the trigger.

The footsteps continued past the door, then squeaked as they turned into the spare room where she'd left her dress. Robyn slipped out. As she tracked the footsteps to make sure they stayed in the spare room, she hurried toward the kitchen. The front door was on the other side of it. Get to the end of the hall, make a left—

The footsteps squeaked again, coming back toward the hall. Robyn dashed through the nearest doorway. The living room. She spun, looking for a place to hide. As she turned, she saw through the hall to the kitchen. Judd's bare feet lay on the floor, sticking out from behind the island.

The footsteps kept coming.

Robyn tore her gaze from Judd. As she turned, she saw patio doors across the room. When she yanked the handle, the door hit the stopper with a *bump-bump* that sounded as loud as a crash.

The footsteps stopped.

Robyn dropped to a crouch. Hands shaking, she tugged out the stopper. As she straightened, she noticed a pair of old sneakers by the door. She scooped them up with one hand as the other pulled open the door as slowly as she could. The footsteps had started again, slow, measured, as the searcher listened for another sound.

Robyn almost got the door open far enough to squeeze through, then it let out a piercing squeal. She yanked it open and stumbled out. Running footsteps sounded behind her. She lurched across the deck and nearly fell off, missing the edge in the dark. As she jumped down, the door squealed again. She turned to see a slender figure silhouetted in the dark doorway, his hand going up.

Robyn dove as the gun fired. She hit the damp grass and skidded, almost dropping the shoes. The figure raised the gun again. She rolled as the second shot sounded. Lights flicked on in the house behind Judd's. The figure backed into the house.

Robyn pushed to her feet and ran.

THE PLAN, like all her plans that night, had seemed so simple. Get away from the gun-toting killer. Take cover. Call 911 to get help for Judd. Then go back, find Detective Findlay and turn herself in. But again, the universe conspired against her.

Judd's attacker had only retreated into the house for a moment. Then he'd come after her. He hadn't tried shooting her in the open again, but he'd chased and he'd chased until finally Robyn managed to fake him out by hiding and letting him run past.

Then she'd put on Judd's shoes, lacing them tight so they'd *stay* on, and found a safe spot to catch her breath and make that phone call. But her pocket was empty. Her cell phone must have fallen out. And it was at that point, as she told herself Detective Findlay would be at Judd's house by now anyway, that it hit her.

Robyn had just fled another crime scene.

FINN

FINN RANG THE BELL again. He imagined Judd Archer inside, trying to calm a suddenly panicked Robyn—he checked his notes again—Peltier.

He stepped back for a better look at the house. Small, maybe two bedrooms. A decent neighborhood. Not good, but decent.

He should buy a house.

He'd been saying that for three years, but hadn't so much as skimmed a real estate page. He supposed that unless the perfect house magically appeared—For Sale sign on the lawn, Realtor at the door—he'd never get further than wishful thinking.

Apartment living wasn't for him. The endless trekking up the stairs or elevator. The noisy, nosy neighbors. Watching his money evaporate with nothing to show for it. Finn told himself he didn't have the time to house-shop, but the truth was that he didn't dare invest his life savings in a place where he might discover he wasn't the sole tenant.

Though Finn rarely saw ghosts outside a crime scene, it did happen, especially in places where he spent a lot of time. Twice he'd had spectral roommates.

The first one, he'd only glimpsed. He'd walk into a room and see the faint outline of a middle-aged woman, who always faded before he could get a better look. She hadn't scared him, but it was like reading with someone hovering over your shoulder. He could always sense her there, was always waiting for her to interrupt him.

The second one he *had* seen. Another woman, this one young, lying naked in the claw-foot bathtub. Not such a bad image . . . if she hadn't slit her wrists and looked as if she'd been in that tub for weeks. Finn had worked a few floaters in his time, and it wasn't a vision he wanted to see first thing every morning. He'd moved out within two weeks, and lost a big chunk of cash.

That second one still bothered him. Even on crime scenes, the ghosts he saw appeared whole and unharmed as they'd looked before their death. And the drowned woman had never moved, never spoken, never opened her eyes. He'd wondered whether there'd been something he was supposed to have done. He'd researched the case, but never found anything. Just an anonymous death in an anonymous city.

Finn rang the bell a third time, then leaned forward, straining to hear a struggle or an argument. Archer said Peltier wanted to talk to him, but she could have changed her mind.

He should have brought backup. Under any other circumstances, he would have, but here he'd figured he already had it in Judd Archer. He didn't know the guy, but he'd heard his story—ex-cop turned celebrity bodyguard. Not true. Archer had never left the force. He was undercover, trying to break into an organized crime ring through their purported relationship with some glitterati types. If things went bad in there, Archer would be Finn's backup.

Finn wondered whether Portia Kane was one of those celebs who supposedly liked hanging out with young mobsters. If so, that could answer some questions about her death. And this Peltier . . . Jansen said Peltier hadn't been with Kane long. She could be a plant, maybe a mobster's—

Finn shook his head. He was daydreaming again. One foot in this world, one foot in the next, his mother used to say.

He gave the doorknob a tentative turn. It opened. When Peltier woke Archer, relocking had probably been the last thing on his mind.

Finn called a hello. No one answered. He took out his gun and started forward.

The lights were on in the front hall and what looked like the kitchen beyond. Finn stepped into the kitchen and saw Archer standing over a body.

Finn's gaze flicked from the body to the figure above it. The ghost glanced up. Their eyes met.

"Shit," Finn whispered, and looked away.

Gun poised, Finn began searching the house for Archer's killer. He made it through the front rooms and was heading to the bedrooms, when a voice behind him said, "You want some help with that?"

Finn hesitated then, not glancing back, continued on.

"I know you can see me," Archer said, stepping in front. "You looked right at me in the kitchen. You can hear me, too, or you wouldn't have paused when I spoke."

Finn lifted a finger, telling Archer to wait until he'd finished his sweep. Insensitive but necessary. He'd once been so engrossed in questioning a victim's ghost—and keeping the rest of the team from overhearing—that he'd missed the killer hiding behind the sofa. The only thing that saved him from a bullet was the guy's shock when he leapt out to discover the detective was talking to thin air.

So Finn continued his search, with Archer tagging along, calm and focused, as if he was just another officer on the scene. Finn met two kinds of ghosts: those too distraught to give a coherent account and those whose accounts were eerily coherent. They knew they were dead; it just hadn't sunk in yet.

They'd finished searching the spare room when Archer, heading out the door, went to pull it farther open for Finn, and his fingers passed right through. He stared at them, then did it again.

"Ah, shit." Archer's shoulders slumped.

"I'm sorry," Finn said.

Archer nodded. He kept staring at his hand, and Finn resisted the urge to pepper him with questions, knowing the clock was ticking and at any moment Archer could vanish.

"So what happens now?" Archer said. "Am I stuck here? A ghost?"

"You'll be taken to the afterlife." Finn had no idea where ghosts went when they disappeared, but it was something *after* life, so he wasn't lying.

"I guess this is how you solve all those cases, huh?" Archer managed a small smile. "Insider information?"

"It helps. Can you tell—?"

He stopped, remembering Archer's body lying on the kitchen floor. The longer he waited to call in the death of an officer, the more fast talking he'd have to do to explain the delay . . . and fast talking really wasn't his thing.

While he called for assistance, he asked Archer to explain what happened. Unfortunately, this was one of those times when having access to the most important witness wasn't going to help. Archer hadn't seen who'd killed him. He'd been making coffee and, the next thing he knew, he was standing over his body.

"Did you hear anything?" Finn asked after he'd hung up.

"Nah. I was grinding beans." He gestured to a small appliance on the counter. "Yes, I grind my own. I had a girlfriend who got me hooked. Anyway, those things make a helluva racket." He paused. "I may have heard the shot, but it was too late."

"Where do you keep your gun?"

Archer told him, and Finn went to check, motioning for Archer to follow and keep talking.

"Guess I left the front door open, huh?" Archer said. "That must be how the guy got in."

"If the killer wasn't *already* in."

"Huh? Wait, you mean Robyn? No way."

"You didn't see who killed you."

Archer seemed to consider lying, saying he'd caught enough of a glimpse to know it wasn't her. But the cop in him won out and he said only, "Rob had nothing to do with this, unless it was indirectly. If Portia's killer thought Rob was a witness, he or she could have followed her here. But my money says it's unrelated. Someone made me as a cop, decided to take me out."

Finn wasn't buying "tragic coincidence," but there wasn't time to argue.

"Was Portia Kane connected to your investigation?" he asked.

"Nah. She was just an easy client to cement my rep with, you know? She got me access to the people and places I needed."

"And Robyn Peltier?"

"Her PR rep. Not a drug supplier. Not a con artist. Not a mobster's girl. If you knew Rob, you'd laugh at the thought. She's a complete straight arrow. She doesn't smoke, doesn't drink—which is why those few glasses of champagne screwed up her judgment tonight. She treated Portia more like a little sister than a client. Tried to keep *her* straight, and was always there when she needed someone."

"I spoke to an actor who was clubbing with them tonight," Finn said. "According to her, Peltier was a hanger-on. Kane let her party with them, felt sorry for her."

Archer snorted. "Trust me, Rob was the one on pity-duty. Portia wasn't a bad kid, but she was needy, and what she needed most was a friend. She clung to Rob like she'd found her new best buddy."

"Did Peltier resent that?"

"If she did, she could have walked away. She had no ties to L.A. All her family is in Philly. She didn't need this job. She didn't kill Portia and she didn't kill me. My money's on—"

Archer vanished.

Perfect.

Finn waited, but when they were gone, they stayed gone. And Judd Archer was no exception.

HOPE

Hope awoke and rolled into the middle of the hotel bed. Karl's spot was empty. No surprise there. It didn't seem to matter how late they got to bed—or how long it took them to get down to sleeping after they got there—Karl was always up first. Even when he slept, it was never soundly. On his own since fifteen, he'd spent too much of his life on guard against other werewolves looking for an easy notch in their belt.

Last year, when he'd encouraged Hope to get back into rowing, he'd joked that he'd get up for her dawn practices . . . in time to meet her for breakfast after. But if he was in town, whether they were at his condo in Philly or hers in nearby Gideon, he always drove her. He'd drop her off, saying he'd grab a coffee and paper and wait, but when she was out on the water, she'd see him, apart from the huddle of sleepy partners and spouses, tucked into some dark corner, sipping his coffee and watching.

A guy doesn't stand in the cold November drizzle at 6 a.m. to support his girlfriend if he's not committed to the relationship. But after a life without family, friends, lovers, what was she to him? The beginning of a new stage in his life? The satisfaction of a suppressed urge to mate? Or a temporary diversion?

Hope told herself to enjoy it while it lasted. Nothing came with guarantees. But the more she saw Robyn spiral downhill, the more she worried about herself.

When her powers first started kicking in, bringing visions of death and destruction, she'd spent years struggling for sanity. Even after she'd learned she was a half-demon, it didn't solve the problem—it just gave it a name. She'd wobbled back onto her feet, but it was Karl who helped her stand firmly. Without him, would she be like Robyn, her world thrown off its axis again?

The hotel room door opened with the clank of silverware. She jumped up to help Karl with the breakfast tray, but he waved her back. He'd been to the breakfast buffet again. Though buffet-style eating didn't meet his culinary standards, he could fill two large plates and eat half of hers, which met his metabolic requirements. Taking buffet food back to your room was probably against hotel policy, but with a smile and a generous dose of charm, Karl usually got what he wanted.

Hope checked the clock. Nine o'clock. Any other day, she'd be late for work. Fridays, though, she usually spent at home writing. Or she did in L.A., where the *True News* office was the size of a boiler room, and twice as hot and noisy.

As Karl handed her a coffee, he said, "So, are you going to tell me what you saw last night?"

"Hmm?"

He stripped off his shirt and crawled back into bed. "At the club. You saw a vision or heard a thought that bothered you. And you conveniently distracted me when I asked."

"Ah. Right. Well, see, there was this jewel thief who stole a celebutante's diamond bracelet . . ."

"I put it back." He sipped his orange juice.

For Karl, Portia Kane's bracelet was a fat, lazy rabbit hopping in front of his nose, too tempting to ignore. Hope chased tabloid stories to satisfy her less civilized urges; he stole jewels to gratify his. They did what they had to and if when the phone rang late at night while he was out of town, Hope jumped awake with her heart in her throat, certain he was in jail, she wasn't ever going to tell him that.

"Something was bothering you last night," he said. "I'd like to know what it was."

"Just your typical niggling power blip. Everyone seems to be having such a great time at a place like that, but I'm picking up all the bad—jealousy, hurt, anger. Add alcohol and drugs and it's a chaos powder keg. I could feel my nerves twanging, waiting for the explosion."

"We could have taken Robyn and left. I'm sure she wouldn't have complained."

"But I have to get used to it, right? If my powers are getting stronger, *I* need to get stronger."

A low noise in his throat, a grumbling growl. Their major point of contention.

"It was only when Rob started withdrawing from the conversation that I couldn't help picking up other stuff," she said.

"And . . . ?"

"There was another supernatural there. That's not unusual in a big crowd—especially in L.A., with the Nast Cabal based here. But this felt weird. Wrong."

"What race?"

"That was part of the problem. I got a vision, but it was just random flashes of faces."

"I'd guess necromancer, but you'd recognize that."

Hope put her plate aside, barely touched. "I have no idea what the supernatural type was, but I know he or she was thinking about Portia Kane. Something about pictures. I thought maybe they wanted to get a photo of her, but there was a definite negative vibe there."

Karl eyed her plate. As she passed it to him he said, "I presume someone like that generates a lot of ill will. Perhaps another woman wanted her picture in the papers and was preempted by Portia."

"Maybe. Anyway, for the next twelve hours, we're off duty. Work for me this morning. Then I'm having lunch with Robyn, and afterward you and I are going apartment hunting. I might invite her to help us look. Otherwise, she'll just go home and work." She paused, coffee cup at her lips. "Is that condescending? Trying to get her out and about?"

"That's why we're here."

"But she's got family. Other friends. Am I being arrogant?"

"You got the job offer, so you came. Robyn is a side project."

Project? That *did* sound arrogant. But at least he was supporting her decision, even if it wouldn't be his. The world had never done Karl any favors, and he saw no need to treat it any differently.

"I'll ask her to come apartment hunting then." She took the *L.A. Times* and passed him the *Wall Street Journal*. "Then, you and I can kick back, maybe take in—"

Hope stopped. There, beneath the fold, was the headline: "Portia Kane Shot Dead." She skimmed the short paragraph on the front page, then flipped to the rest inside.

"Portia's dead."

"Hmmm?"

"Portia Kane. She was murdered last night, after we left."

As Hope reached for the phone, her gaze snagged on Robyn's name in the last paragraph.

She stared at the words. Read. Reread. Then she dropped the paper and scrambled from bed. She pulled out her clothes. The paper rustled behind her as Karl retrieved it.

Robyn was missing. Last seen at the club. Now sought by the police. Hope had caught that vision, known someone in that club had Portia on his mind, and she'd brushed it off, leaving Portia to die and Robyn to be kidnapped. Or worse.

Pants half on, Hope stopped and turned to the nightstand, where her cell phone lay. Karl got to it first.

"I'll call her," he said. "You get ready."

Hope was in the bathroom, brushing her curls back into a ponytail, when she heard him speaking.

"Who is this?" he said, voice sharp.

She threw open the door.

"Where did you get this phone?" he demanded. A pause. "And where is that? What's the nearest intersection?"

Karl finished with a string of curses and punched redial, but his expression said he didn't expect anyone to answer. They didn't.

"Someone found her phone, didn't they? Where was it?"

"He wouldn't say. Hung up when I asked for a street."

"I mean *where*? In a bathroom? A coffee shop? On the side of a road?"

He said nothing. Just hit redial again.

"Karl?"

"Behind a trash bin," he said after a moment.

Hope was out the door before he could stop her.

ONE ADVANTAGE to being a tabloid reporter was that Hope knew all the tricks for getting a cop to talk when the department was saying "no comment." It helped that she didn't look like an ambulance chaser . . . or a hard-hitting journalist. It also helped that she was under thirty, female and relatively easy on the eyes.

Hope wouldn't call herself a natural charmer, but growing up in high society—debutante season and all—gave her the basics, and Karl had taught her the rest. So after twenty minutes nursing a coffee in a shop near the police station, she managed to lure a young officer to her table.

She sized him up and debated her options. She considered the wide-eyed crime groupie routine, but this guy looked like a cop whose intelligence outweighed his ego, so she went for option two. She confessed she was a tabloid reporter. Even flashed her creds.

"But I'm new and I'm assigned to this Portia Kane murder and, well, it's just not like back home, you know? These guys totally play hardball, and they've buried me already. What I really need is a fresh angle."

A nod, not unsympathetic, but wary. "My best advice would be to attend the press conference. I can give you a few tips on how to get your question answered, but I don't have any inside information on Ms. Kane."

"Oh, I wasn't looking for that." Hope scooted forward in her seat. "I need a totally fresh angle, one they're all ignoring. The other woman. The missing PR rep. Are the police speculating on what happened to her? Kidnapped?"

"Kidnapped?"

"She's missing, right? And you're looking for her."

"Sure, but not as a victim. She's our prime suspect."

ROBYN

To say that running from two crime scenes was the stupidest thing Robyn had ever done put it at the top of a very short list. Robyn didn't make stupid mistakes. Her father had always said that he'd never had to teach her to take care before crossing the street, because she naturally looked both ways—twice . . . then reconsidered whether she needed to cross the road at all.

The biggest chance she'd ever taken was Damon. They'd met at the wedding of his sister, a casual friend of Robyn's. They'd been seated at the same table and talked through dinner. At the end of the night he asked her out, but she'd been seeing someone—Brett, an ad exec she'd been dating since her freshman year. He was a good guy who treated her well, and they had a comfortable relationship that both expected would lead to marriage, a minivan and a house in the suburbs.

When she'd turned Damon down, he'd gone to his sister for details. Was Robyn engaged? Living with her boyfriend? No on both counts. So he sent her an invitation to a club where his band was playing. She didn't go. He sent a card, asking her for coffee—no strings, just coffee. She said no. Then he sent her a CD of him singing "500 Miles." The band at his sister's wedding had played that and, after one and a half glasses of wine, Robyn had proclaimed it the most romantic song ever.

She'd listened to the CD. More than once. Then she called. He invited her to coffee again, but she couldn't justify meeting a guy she knew wanted more than friendship. Not when she was involved with someone. The only alternative was to end a good three-year relationship for a "coffee date" with a near-stranger. Madness, of course.

That night, she told Brett it was over and called Damon back. A year later, they'd been celebrating their own wedding.

As incredible as that payoff had been, though, she'd never seen it as proof she should take more risks. Just as a sign that she'd probably used up her life's allotment of good fortune.

Yet that potentially dumb move wasn't even in the same ballpark as this one. How did someone *accidentally* flee from not one but two crime scenes? In one night?

She hoped Judd was still alive, but she doubted it. His attacker had been shooting to kill. And who had his attacker been? Someone from his former days as a cop? A disgruntled current client?

No, Robyn was sure *she'd* brought a killer to Judd Archer's house. Whether it was Portia's murderer or a partner, it didn't matter. Robyn had run to Judd for help and she'd been followed. She'd gotten him killed. And then . . . And then she'd done nothing.

It was almost morning. She'd been sitting on a park bench for three hours. People passed. Some glanced her way. None ran screaming for the nearest cop.

She almost wished they would.

After hours of wandering, exhausted and shock-numb, she'd stalled on this park bench, wanting nothing more than to stretch out and sleep. If she did, would *that* make anyone notice? It might if she still looked like Robyn Peltier. But this bedraggled woman in oversized sweats and old sneakers? Just another homeless person. No one would care. From respectable to forgettable overnight.

She pulled up her legs and closed her eyes.

ADELE

Colm stared out Adele's bedroom window. Through his reflection in the glass, she could see his eyes, blank, his mental gaze searching for the woman. For Robyn Peltier.

He couldn't do it, of course. He was too young. But she'd let him try, let him feel useful.

A clairvoyant didn't read minds or see the future. Instead they got the power of remote viewing. They could fix on a subject and see through their eyes.

Unless the subject was nearby, fixing on her wasn't as simple as picturing her and jumping into her head. The clairvoyant needed either a personal object or a personal connection, built up through exposure and effort. It had taken Adele months of constant surveillance to establish a connection with Portia. There was no way Colm could fix on Robyn Peltier after chasing her around for an hour the night before.

They were in Adele's tserha, the house she shared with Lily and Hugh, Niko and his wife. There were four houses on the kumpania property, four tserhas—households. Colm and his mother, Neala, shared the neighboring house. Adele and Colm usually met here, away from Neala's watchful eye.

When a door opened and closed downstairs, Adele went still. If it was Lily, she was safe—they'd been raised as sisters and Lily would never tattle on her for being with Colm. But there was no way of knowing who'd come in without looking. Only the most powerful clairvoyants—the seers—could remote-view other clairvoyants. But the footsteps receded and the door opened and closed again, and Adele relaxed.

She moved up behind Colm and rubbed his back. He leaned into her fingers, eyes closing, like a cat being petted.

"It's not your fault," she said. "We'll find her."

"One minute," he said. "That's all it would have taken to grab her purse. I saw it there in the kitchen. Or her dress, on the bed. If we had that, we could find her now."

Adele said nothing. She hadn't mentioned that she'd been even closer to Robyn—having clocked her in the alley. All she'd had to do was wrench her up and grab that cell phone. But hearing the cops, she'd panicked and run. A mistake she would not repeat.

Nor would she make the mistake of admitting her failure to Colm. His resolve was shaky enough. The story she'd told him was that she'd been tracked down by a Cabal VP, Irving Nast, while Portia had been lunching with Jasmine. To avoid trouble, Adele had gone outside with Nast, promising to talk to him, planning to bolt at the first chance. Then, as she was remote-viewing Portia, she saw her snap a photo of Adele and Nast. She could only guess that Portia figured out Adele was the photographer selling those most unflattering photos of her to the tabloids. Adele couldn't risk that photo getting back to the kumpania—the punishment for speaking to a Nast was death. So she'd tried to get it back. A plan that hadn't gone quite as she intended . . .

Now Portia was dead. Adele had her cell phone . . . and had discovered that Portia sent the photo on to Robyn Peltier to be passed on to the tabloids. The same Robyn Peltier who'd seen her at the murder site. The same one who'd snapped her photo in the alley.

"We'll take something from her apartment," she said. "Then we'll find her, get her cell phone, get that picture, and I'll be safe."

Colm turned, his freckles bunching as his face screwed up with worry. "What if she's already sent it to the tabloids? If they print it, if the phuri see it—"

Adele lifted onto her tiptoes and pressed her lips to his. He pulled her against him and kissed her, hard from the moment their bodies brushed.

So young. So eager. So hungry.

That's what made it so easy. A fifteen-year-old boy, expected to mingle in the human world but keep himself separate. Look but don't touch. No friends, no girlfriends. Colm had never even been on a date. Nor would he. Not with anyone but her.

The elders—the phuri—had already decreed they were to marry when he turned eighteen. It didn't matter that Adele was five years older. It didn't matter that they'd been raised as brother and sister. Keeping the blood pure was all that counted.

Clairvoyants were the rarest of the races. Even within the bloodlines, there was usually only a 10 percent chance of inheriting the power. The kumpania boasted odds of 75 percent, through careful selective breeding. To most clairvoyant families, 10 percent was already too high, considering the eventual sentence of madness. But the kumpania's training methods virtually eliminated that threat. They promised all the benefits of clairvoyance and none of the disadvantages . . . except for the small matter of surrendering your free will, living in a commune, supporting the group by working as a "celebrity photographer," marrying whomever they chose, and breeding more clairvoyants.

Adele touched her stomach. She'd done the breeding part, all right. Just not with the right partner. Her child would be a more powerful clairvoyant than she could have produced with Colm—the Cabal was certainly convinced of that—but to the kumpania, what she'd done was an atrocity, her child an abomination.

Another reason for Adele to leave the group before they found out. But if she jumped at Irving Nast's current offer, he'd see her eagerness and take advantage.

Adele was supposed to meet Irving again that morning. She hadn't dared—couldn't risk him smelling her fear. So she'd called his answering service, leaving a message saying she couldn't make it and would call to reschedule. He wouldn't like that. The longer she postponed, the sooner he'd sense trouble and try to find her.

She had to get those photos and eliminate every trace of them. If that meant killing again—or having Colm do it for her—that was fine. After all, they were only humans. Outsiders. Inconsequential.

HOPE

After getting all she could from the officer in the coffee shop, Hope made a pit stop at the *True News* office. Checking in, getting her mail . . . Hardly critical under the circumstances, but if Robyn was a fugitive and Hope was her best friend in L.A., eventually the cops were going to find their way to her door. And when they did, she might need to prove she'd been going about her day, business as usual.

After that token appearance, Hope and Karl returned to the club. He stood watch as she circled the exterior trying to find the place closest to the crime scene. If she could find it, she might catch a vision of what had happened last night. It took some fine-tuning to pinpoint the spot, but eventually the vision came.

Hope saw a dark room, with Portia leaning over what looked like a table. Doing lines, it seemed. She was anxious, worried about being caught, feeling guilty, telling herself this would be the last time. At a noise, Portia had jumped, a small burst of chaos exploding. She wheeled to see someone in the doorway.

"Hello?" she said, forcing attitude into her voice. "This room's taken."

Whatever she saw, Hope didn't. A vision wasn't like the reconstruction of an event, where she could move around and see the whole thing. It was a single-camera scene. What she saw is what she got—whatever angle, clarity and length.

As usual, her focus was on the victim.

"I need to use your cell phone," the intruder said. It sounded like a woman, the voice pitched high with stress, the waves flowing off her twice as strong as Portia's.

"Like hell. There's a pay phone in the—"

"I need your cell phone."

"Buy your own, bitch. Now get the hell out before I call my body-guard."

"You didn't bring one. You only take one when you want to show off."

Portia inhaled sharply, chaos blasting off her. "Wh—what—"

"It's called a gun. Now give me the fucking cell phone."

Portia opened her mouth. Only a split-second shriek escaped. Then the chaos surged, so strong it blocked the rest of the vision. Hope had to replay it twice to see the ending. Portia started to scream, reeling back, then the first bullet hit and the scream died in her throat. A second bullet struck as she was already going down, the silenced shots barely more than loud puffs of air.

It was over quickly, the chaos surge brief but powerful, that final explosion . . . exquisite.

The first time Hope had seen a vision of a recent death, there'd been no pleasure in it. Too intense. Too uncomfortable. She'd taken solace in that. It was one thing to get a thrill from hearing strangers arguing. But to enjoy another's death? She wouldn't know how to deal with that.

Soon she had to. As her powers grew, she started to enjoy death. It was the purest, most perfect chaos imaginable. The ultimate high.

Even if she stopped chasing weird tales for *True News* and investigating rogue supernaturals for the council, she couldn't escape the experience of death. Passing the site of a recent car crash was enough. Short of locking herself into a room for life, she had no choice—she had to learn to deal with it.

With Karl's help, she was learning to accept the demon in her. She'd come to think of it that way: the demon. That didn't mean it was a separate entity—she could never make that mistake. It was as much part of her as Karl's wolf was of him. But it didn't need to rule who she was. She had to learn to appease it and control it. Accept the demon, master it and use it to her advantage, to protect herself and help others.

If it sounded like she had it all worked out, she didn't. Intellectually, she understood the lessons Karl taught her about acceptance and control. But that didn't keep her from feeling like a ghoul.

When Karl came looking for her behind the club, she was huddled against the alley wall, hugging her knees, forcing herself to replay the vision over and over, through that endless cycle of bliss and self-loathing until she'd wrested every last clue from it, fighting and cursing when he hefted her over his shoulder and carried her away.

So, no, she didn't have it worked out. And she was starting to think she never would.

ROBYN

There had been a moment, after waking on the park bench, when Robyn had reflected back on the events of the night and decided the answer was simple. She'd cracked.

After one too many glasses of champagne, she'd gone into that dark hall at Bane, and like Alice falling down the rabbit hole, she'd emerged in some hellish alternate reality of her mind's own making, where Portia had died, then Judd, and she was the primary suspect.

A shrink would claim the whole scenario was a subconscious manifestation of illogical guilt over Damon's death. Whether it was indeed a complete mental collapse or simply a drunken nightmare, she was relieved. A mental hospital she could deal with. Not like she hadn't expected to end up in one anyway.

Her relief lasted until she passed a newsstand outside the park and saw the newspaper headlines. It was like someone cut her power cord again, and she meandered for an hour, shocked, confused, lost . . . and thoroughly disgusted with herself for it.

A few years ago, when she and Damon had passed a poster for a book called *The Purpose Driven Life,* Damon joked it must have been written by Robyn's long-lost twin. She always had a purpose, a goal, a plan. Even on vacation, she never left without researching the locale and drawing up an itinerary. That didn't mean she scheduled every moment, but she'd hate to later hear someone talking about some hidden gem she'd missed.

In high school, she'd taken a test to identify where her strengths lay, and the answer came as a surprise to no one. Logical reasoning, organization and planning. Public relations might not have seemed the ideal fit for her, but it was. No matter what scrape a client got herself into, Robyn could say, "Give me a minute," and come up with a solution, usually two or three.

Now there was a citywide alert out for her, and here she was, wandering aimlessly, as if hoping someone would catch her and save her the trouble of taking action herself. When she heard a man call "Robyn," she turned to embrace her fate.

It was a testament to her mental state that it wasn't until the dark-haired man stopped three feet away from her that she recognized him.

"Karl?"

"It's all right." He moved forward slowly, hands outstretched, as if approaching a timid deer. "Hope sent me."

She nodded.

He took a cell phone from his pocket and held it out. "I'm going to take you to her. Do you want to call her? Check first?"

Robyn shook her head and let him lead her away.

THEY DROVE IN SILENCE to a motel. Karl parked right in front, checking to make sure no one was watching, then hustled her to the door.

Hope was inside. She closed and relocked the door as Karl strode past, scanning the dark, cool room, shades drawn.

You'd almost think they were harboring a murder suspect.

Robyn tried to laugh, but couldn't. Hope led her to the bed, where icy bottles of water, sandwiches and brownie bites waited. Robyn eyed the food, as if she could mentally will it into her hand. Hope handed her a bottle and told her to drink slowly. She did and it seemed to unstick her brain.

"How did you find me?" she asked.

"We found out where that undercover officer lived," Hope said. "Was he a friend of yours?"

Undercover officer? Judd? So now she was the main suspect in a cop killing?

When Robyn didn't answer, Hope went on. Something about knowing Robyn wouldn't have taken a taxi when she might be wanted for murder, so she couldn't be more than a few miles from Judd's place.

It was plausible, she supposed. But that was still a lot of area to cover. And why leave Hope behind when two sets of eyes and legs could have searched twice as fast?

"We need to talk about what happened," Hope said.

"I didn't kill them."

"I know. But you need to tell us exactly what happened so we can figure out what to do."

Well, at least someone was taking charge and making plans.

Robyn told them everything. As she talked and drank and nibbled on a sandwich, the deadening layer of shock lifted enough for her to look around and realize the situation was real, and she couldn't take refuge in fantasies of madness.

"I should turn myself in," she said finally.

"You will . . . just not right now. Karl talked to a friend. He's a lawyer who specializes in this sort of problem."

There was a specialty in this?

"He advised us," Hope continued, "and, if we need him, he'll come down. He's in Oregon, but he's licensed to practice in California. Anyway, the main thing now is to keep you in L.A., just away from your apartment or anyplace you could be recognized. That way, we can say you weren't on the run, just in shock. But that excuse will only work for a day or two, so we have to work fast. We need to give the police another suspect—preferably the real killer."

"You're . . ." She looked from Hope to Karl. "You're going to solve this yourselves?"

Hope smiled. "Hey, I'm *True News*'s weird tales girl, remember? Solving mysteries is my thing. Karl's helped me before. He used to be in security."

"I'm not sure . . ."

Karl spoke from across the room, his first words since they'd arrived. "You don't have a lot of options right now, Robyn."

Hope shushed him with a glare, but he was right, and his cold realism felt somehow more reassuring than Hope's bright optimism.

Hope cracked open a water bottle. "I can't promise we *will* solve it. But we're going to try, and if we're no closer tomorrow than we are right now, we'll get our friend's help, let you turn yourself in and keep on working. We have some leads already."

"You do? How?"

"Like I said, there's an advantage to having a tabloid reporter on your case. I have the perfect excuse for snooping, and people aren't nearly as reluctant to talk to the tabs as they let on." She took a long gulp of water. "There's a rumor that someone heard Portia arguing in that back hall. She was talking about a cell phone. And maybe something about a picture."

"Cell . . . ? Wait. Before she died, Portia mentioned her cell. I thought she wanted me to use it to call 911, but that didn't seem to be it."

"Her cell phone wasn't with her body. She had it earlier, didn't she?"

"She must have. I always swore it was surgically attached."

"What about pictures or photos? Does that ring a bell?"

"People were always taking Portia's picture. The only time *she* snapped shots was when she wanted to show something—a purse or an outfit she liked. She did send me one yesterday—from her cell actually—but it was just of Jasmine Wills."

"Jasmine?"

"In an ugly dress. Portia's been having this passive-aggressive feud with her, and she wanted me to send this picture to the tabloids."

"How big a deal *would* that be? I mean, I can't see anyone shooting Portia to stop her from getting a photo published, but maybe Jasmine tried to get it back, waved a gun and it went off. Sounds farfetched, but you did think the killer might have been a woman."

"At first. But Judd's killer was a young man, so maybe I was mistaken."

"That could have been a friend or someone Jasmine hired, after she realized you'd seen her." Hope shook her head. "Okay, that really *does* sound far-fetched."

Maybe, but people killed for less every day. Robyn had a scrapbook to prove it.

"We should look for more likely explanations," Karl said. "Was there anything else about the photograph? Was this girl holding something—drugs? Kissing someone's husband? Was there anything else in the frame? Something or someone Portia may have accidentally photographed?"

"I-I don't know. I didn't take a good look. It was just . . . Portia being silly. I filed it away, waiting to see whether she'd insist I send it."

"We're going to need to see that picture," Hope said. "Do you—? Shit. You tossed your cell, didn't you?"

"Lost it," Robyn said. "But I downloaded the photo to my laptop. I do that at the end of the workday to keep all my messages in one place."

Hope smiled. "As organized as ever. Now we just need to get your laptop."

FINN

FINN HAD NEVER BEEN TO A SPA.

No, that wasn't true. He'd once had a crime scene at a spa. The ghost claimed to have been bludgeoned to death by her romantic rival as they awaited some hot new treatment guaranteed to make them irresistible to the D-list actor they were both pursuing. As it turned out, the young woman had been pawing through a shelf of discounted hair products when a massive bottle of conditioner had fallen and hit her in the head.

Finn doubted the ghost had intentionally lied. She'd been bending over, felt a blow and made up her own explanation. If her version made her death feel less pointless, she was welcome to it.

Today he was tracking down witnesses. The death of Portia Kane was a high-profile case. The death of Judd Archer was just as big—at least for the cops involved. Whether the two were connected remained to be proven. A team had been hastily assembled, pulling in resources from everywhere. Other detectives would work the Archer angle, in case his death was related to his undercover work. Finn would lead the team working on Portia Kane, which included finding Robyn Peltier. Another team member was handling the press side—that really wasn't Finn's thing.

He'd also assigned a pair of detectives to look into Robyn Peltier's life—conducting interviews, checking her apartment, gathering background. Her husband had been killed six months ago in Philadelphia. Shot to death. Finn doubted there was a connection, but he had people working on it.

As for him, he'd spent most of the day tracking down people who'd been at the club with Portia Kane. He'd started with Marla Jansen, gotten three names from her, found them, learned nothing but got another name, and so on. Half the time, all they could say was that they hadn't seen anything unusual, but you should talk to their good friend Tina. Ask for Tina's last name, though, and apparently their friendship hadn't reached the exchange of surnames stage.

Finally, Finn's persistence had paid off. He'd followed a trail to these two young women who'd been with Portia's crowd at Bane. Madelyn and Kendra. And they had a lead for him. Robyn Peltier hadn't gone to Bane alone. She'd brought a friend.

As for details on that friend, though, that's where things got fuzzy. They agreed she was eastern—from the eastern U.S. by her accent and from an Eastern ancestry by her looks. Middle Eastern or East Indian? They bickered over that until Finn assured them a final call wasn't necessary.

As for a name, neither had caught it. And they got into another fight because their friend "Chas" claimed he recognized the girl from some high-society charity ball back east a couple of years earlier. He'd mentioned a name, which they'd forgotten, except that it was "totally Anglo, like Jill Smith," which Madelyn claimed proved Chas was too wasted to see straight and had mistaken the girl for someone else. Kendra disagreed about the "wasted" part, but admitted Chas might have just been angling for an introduction to an attractive young woman.

An attractive young woman who had come with her boyfriend, as it turned out. Now *him* they remembered.

"He was white," Madelyn said. "Older. Maybe thirty-five. He looked like a banker or a stockbroker. A money guy. Portia was all over him. Normally not her type, but he was very fine . . . for his age."

"Was that a problem?"

"His age?"

"Portia being 'all over' this other young woman's boyfriend."

"She didn't care. Probably used to that. The culture, you know? Arranged marriages, multiple wives . . ."

Kendra sighed. "The girl was obviously as American as you."

Madelyn dismissed the idea with a snort. Finn wrapped it up and jumped to his own dismissal after getting this "Chas" guy's cell number.

He was in the outer room when a deep voice behind him said, "Whoa. Those chicks were brutal. Me*ow*."

A man stood across the room. Finn's cop eyes assessed him, spitting out vital stats. Roughly thirty. Six foot two. A hundred ninety pounds. African-American. Dark hair and eyes. Short beard.

"Look sharp," the man said. "Corporeal being at one o'clock."

Finn turned as Kendra hurried from the spa room, still dressed in her robe and turban. She shut the door behind her

"I wanted to say I think Chas did recognize that girl. Madelyn's just jealous 'cause he was checking her out. But you might have trouble getting hold of him. He took off to Ibiza this morning, and he always 'forgets' his cell, so his dad can't bug him. If that number doesn't work, call me—I have his e-mail address somewhere."

When Kendra was gone, Finn turned back to the man, who was leaning against the wall, arms folded, humming under his breath.

"We done here?" He bounded forward, arms uncrossing. "Good. We have murders to solve."

He started for the door, then noticed Finn hadn't budged. "I suppose you want an introduction first. The name's Trent. I'd shake your hand, but we both know that's not going to work out."

So he was a ghost. The quip about corporeal beings should have been the tip-off.

Finn said nothing until they were in the car. The ghost—Trent—passed through the door and sat in the passenger seat. Finn never understood how they could do that. If you can walk through a chair, how can you sit on it? Whatever he'd learned in physics, apparently it didn't apply to ghosts.

"You are a hard man to get hold of," Trent said as he settled into his seat. "I've been following you all day. A couple times you glanced my way, like you saw a flicker, but that was it. That glow you've got, the one that says you're a necromancer? It's really dim. I suppose that means your powers aren't very strong. No offense."

"Necromancer?"

"That's what they call your sort, isn't it?"

Finn had no idea what his sort were called. The power to see ghosts ran in his family, skipping most, but hitting one or two every generation, to varying degrees. His mother sometimes caught flashes, but had never actually seen a ghost. His great-aunt saw faint outlines, but couldn't communicate with them. Supposedly her brother—his great-uncle—had been able to, but he'd died when Finn was in preschool.

His family presumed there were other people who could see

ghosts, but they'd never given it much thought. You heard about that sort of thing all the time—spiritualists, mediums, whatever—and his family didn't see any use in sticking a name on it. It was what it was, and you learned to live with it. Or you didn't. Your choice.

"What can I do for you?" Finn asked the ghost.

"The question, sir, is what can *I* do for *you*. The answer? Help solve this case."

Finn pulled out of the lot. "You know something?"

An enigmatic smile. "I know a lot of things."

"Specific to this case?"

The ghost reached for his seat belt, cursing as his fingers passed through. Then he gave a short laugh. "Not like I need that anyway, huh? Old habits . . ."

"Do you know something specific to this case?"

"About what those girls said, Detective— Can I call you Finn?"

"What do you know about this case?"

"This and that."

"In other words, not much. Look, if you need something from me, ask. I'll do what I can. But I don't like games. You don't need to pretend you can help—"

"You're right that I don't know squat, but that doesn't mean I can't help." He faced Finn as they idled at a light. "You like blunt? Okay, let's be blunt. I'm bored. I've been wandering around on the other side for . . . years, I guess. Eventually, I suppose I'll go wherever it is I'm supposed to go, but in the meantime, I'm bored shitless. So I see you, a necromancer, trying to solve this case, and I see a chance to have some fun and do some good at the same time. Maybe that's why I'm stuck. I did some time when I was a kid, ran with some people, did some shit I regret. If I do a good deed, maybe I can get wherever it is I'm supposed to go."

Speaking of shit, Finn could smell it a mile away and Trent reeked. Finn had met rehabilitated gangbangers. If this guy was one, Finn would turn in his badge and declare himself unfit for detective work. Not a scar or tattoo to be seen. Well spoken, obviously educated . . . Finn wasn't enough of an optimist to think it came from prison classes. And his manner was far too relaxed for anyone who'd had repeated run-ins with the police. But that didn't mean he hadn't done things that might keep him from passing over.

When Finn said nothing, Trent went on. "Think of what I could do. You can't get a search warrant? I'll pop in and take a look. You question someone who seems jumpy? I can hang around after you leave, see if the guy does anything, calls anyone. You need someone followed discreetly? It doesn't get any more discreet than me. Best of all? When you solve this, you get all the glory. I'm the perfect silent partner."

He flashed a smile that reminded Finn of his little brother. Whenever Rick had been trying to cajole Finn into doing something he probably shouldn't, he'd smile like that—a disarming grin that made Finn feel like a spoilsport for refusing.

Maybe it was the grin, but as Finn considered the matter, he couldn't see any reason to refuse. He'd been raised to see his power as a gift to be used for good. If he could solve a murder with it, he would. If he could reassure a ghost with it, he would. And if he could use it to help a spirit cross to the other side—or even just make him feel better—he should. So he would, at least until the guy made him regret it.

HOPE

Robyn's laptop was in her apartment, which was one place she definitely couldn't go. But Hope was fine with that . . . because Robyn really didn't need to see how easily they could get past a police stakeout.

She'd already seemed suspicious about how Karl had found her. Good thing her scent trail had been recent enough for him to follow or Karl would have needed to return at night and change into a wolf. And if she'd accidentally seen that it would take some real explaining.

At least she hadn't questioned the lies about a witness hearing Portia arguing about a photo and a picture.

Now Hope was off on another chaos-promising mission, one she could enjoy guilt-free. She'd planned to stay at the motel while Karl retrieved the laptop, but Robyn had argued that Karl needed backup. Hope suspected she wanted to be alone, so she went with Karl, which would have been her choice anyway.

A break-in was always good for a chaos snack. Karl wouldn't let her accompany him on a real theft. But one for a legitimate cause was fair game, though this time, there wasn't any actual breaking in to be done. Robyn had given them the keys.

Night had fallen, making it easy to avoid the two cops in the unmarked car. A quick trip alongside the neighboring building, climb the dividing wall, sprint to the back door and break in. There weren't any more cops inside. For a professional thief, it didn't get much easier than that.

Still, the danger had Hope's pulse racing and the steady strum of low-level chaos kept it going. Any adventure with Karl was worthwhile, not only for the chaos vibes he gave off, but for the thrill of getting into trouble together, feeding off one another's excitement.

They made it into the apartment without incident. There was no sign that the police had searched the place yet.

Karl scouted the apartment, hunting for any sign of a nonofficial search by someone looking for Robyn or that photograph. Hope could see the computer through the kitchen doorway, on the dining table, but instead of just grabbing it she just stood there, looking around.

"Hope?" Karl stuck his head in. "What is it? A vision?"

"Imagine this was my apartment. If I'd been here for months and it looked like this—" She opened cupboards, letting them shut behind her as she circled the room. "What would you think? How long am I in a hotel room before I'm unpacked, drinks and food in the fridge, my stuff all set out . . ."

"Furniture rearranged . . ."

"Robyn's the same way. Worse. Last time she moved, she took a week off to settle in and decorate—and she hardly ever takes vacation time. But she's been here three months and has—" Hope opened a cupboard. "—two plates, two bowls and three glasses. The furniture looks like it came with the apartment."

"Perhaps that only means she doesn't plan to stay in L.A. That's good, isn't it?"

While she would have been disappointed to discover the apartment totally decorated, suggesting a permanent relocation, she would have been happy to see Robyn moving on, making a fresh start. But seeing this, she knew Robyn hadn't come to L.A. to start over. She was here to hide.

It was hard for Karl to see the significance. Hope had visited his old apartment once. He'd filled the closets and the fridge and nothing more. At least in his condo, he'd seemed gung-ho furnishing it—the two of them scouring Philly and making weekend trips into New York. That was a good sign, wasn't it? Proof he planned to stick around?

"Hope?"

Karl lifted the laptop. She stuffed it into the backpack.

"Now we need to grab her backup keys and emergency cash, then some clothes—"

He cut her short with a raised hand as his gaze flew toward the front hall. He grabbed the half-zipped backpack in one hand, her arm in the other, dragging her into the living room as the front door lock clicked.

"I don't think I should be doing this," a heavily accented voice said. "Miz Peltier is a good tenant. A very nice woman."

"I have a warrant." A second man's voice, lower pitched with a drawl.

Karl swung Hope in front of him as he hustled to the patio door. The sliding door was ajar, the curtain pulled across, as if he'd prepped for an escape while scouting earlier.

"I'm just looking for anything that might help me find her. Phone numbers of friends, family. An address book, PDA, laptop . . ."

Karl slid the patio door closed behind them. Hope walked to the far side and looked over the railing.

"Four floors," she whispered. "That's not too bad if we—"

"No." He touched her cheek, so light it sent a shiver through her. "Don't look so disappointed. If he doesn't leave in fifteen minutes, we'll consider a more chaotic solution. In the meantime, just keep quiet." His hands moved to her hips, mouth lowering to her ear. "It's still a rather dangerous situation to be in, police just inside the door, more below."

Hope's shiver turned to a shudder . . . and not from fear. She pressed against him, her lips moving to the V of his collar, his sweat tangy, as delicious as the chaos vibes circling them.

"None of that," he growled. "Dangerous situation, remember?"

"Mmmm."

He shifted, ostensibly nudging her farther from the window, hands tightening around her hips, fingers splaying over her rear. She undid the top button of his shirt and tickled circles with the tip of her tongue.

"Hope . . ."

"You could move away."

"And leave you exposed?"

"Hmm, there's a thought." She arched up to nibble his throat.

He wrapped the hem of her shirt around his fist, as if considering. Then he straightened, his werewolf hearing picking up the voices inside. His thoughts gave nothing away. He'd learned to block them from her. But whatever he was hearing, he didn't like it, the chaos flowing off him coming in short bursts of worry.

Hope struggled to keep still, but the vibes were so exquisite that she couldn't help squirming and shivering. A silent laugh vibrated through him and pulled his attention from the patio door. He made the chaos surge, the waves rocking her.

His chin lifted again, gaze returning to the patio door as he tried to listen.

"I've been thinking," she said, running her fingertips along his throat. "Someone has a birthday coming up, which, I believe coincides with our one-year anniversary. A special celebration is in order. Perhaps a fantasy fulfilled. A cabin in the woods . . ."

His eyes glinted. He shook it off and glanced at the door. "We really should—"

"You're right. We should. In fact, I'm making the reservation as soon as we get home. One deep-woods cabin. One very willing girlfriend at your service all weekend, to fulfill your most uncivilized wolf urges—"

The sound of a voice inside stopped her like a bucket of ice water.

"Shit," she whispered, giving her head a sharp shake as she stepped aside. "Okay, that was stupid. Forget I said anything."

"Not a chance." He rubbed her hip before moving back. "We're going to revisit that one . . . just at a more appropriate time."

She smiled. "Agreed."

FINN

IT LOOKED LIKE FINN couldn't even keep a ghostly partner around. And just when he'd been thinking Trent could be useful . . .

He had enough for a search warrant, so he got that, collected a couple of officers and went to Robyn Peltier's apartment. And that's where Trent seemed to decide police work wasn't for him. On the way to the apartment, he'd been in high spirits, razzing Finn about his poor choice in radio station, making him change it to jazz, then singing along in a pitch-perfect tenor. When they arrived, Trent had driven him nuts, rocking on his heels, eager to get to work while Finn tried to talk to the landlord. He'd told Trent to go on ahead, scope out the apartment.

Ten minutes later, Finn had found him in there, pacing, anxious. He'd said he'd wait outside and disappeared, apparently having forgotten he was supposed to search the places Finn's warrant wouldn't cover.

The warrant allowed them plain-sight search only. Usually Finn could find something—an address book, a Rolodex, a laptop, a PDA, business cards on the fridge, numbers written on the wall. But this place was as sterile as a model suite.

He'd asked the landlord about Peltier's friend from Bane, but the man didn't recognize the description, and said he'd never seen Peltier bring anyone by.

Finn hoped to find Trent outside. Maybe there was something in the apartment—some smell or aura—that bothered ghosts. But Trent was nowhere to be seen. Finn found excuses to linger, talking to the officers staking out the building, but when he did eventually leave, he was, as usual, alone.

COLM

COLM WATCHED THE COUPLE walk out of Robyn Peltier's apartment minutes after he'd seen the cops leave. The place was a regular Grand Central Station, his mom would say.

He backed farther into the cubby by the waste-disposal chute, but they headed the other way, toward the stairs. He continued to watch them through his mind's eye. Their figures were faint against a shimmering background, as if seen at the bottom of a lake through a dirty, glass-bottomed boat.

It was a struggle to keep a fix on them. He'd been light-headed all evening—probably from not eating all day. After last night, his stomach was in a permanent knot, refusing to accept even the thought of food.

He'd killed a man. Shot him in the back. He'd had to, of course, for Adele. She'd been so grateful. And his reward . . . He shivered now, thinking of it.

Besides, the man had been an outsider. The kumpania taught that killing a human for survival was no different than slaughtering a cow for food. But last night, watching the man die, Colm hadn't been so sure.

Still, it was over. He'd done the right thing, and now he had to focus on helping Adele again.

The couple was about halfway down the hall now, moving fast, the man holding a backpack in one hand, his other on the woman's back.

Colm wished he could see the woman's face. She looked pretty. He watched her rear moving under her tight pants and felt himself harden. His gaze moved to the man's hand, so confident, so intimate, her hair cascading over his fingers. Beautiful hair, black curls spilling down her back. Nothing like Adele's short, straight, dirty-blond hair. Guilt surged at the comparison, but it trickled away as he imagined what it would be like to touch the woman's hair, to wrap it around his fingers, to see it hanging down as she rode above—

Fresh guilt slapped the image out of his head. She was human. Unfit. Unclean. Even to entertain the thought was a betrayal—

The woman glanced over her shoulder, as if she'd heard his thoughts. His heart pounded, and her image faded. He concentrated on pulling it back, working so hard that the vision snapped into focus, nearly crystal-clear.

Even with the frown, she was pretty. Brown skin and golden eyes like a cat—

"What's wrong?" The man's voice was soft, but carried down the quiet hall. He stopped, pulling her farther into his protection as he scanned the corridor. "Did you—?" The next words sounded like "sense something?"

The woman shook her head and tore her gaze away. She murmured something too low for Colm to hear and they continued to the stairwell. Colm struggled to hold the vision, but by the time they reached the last flight, the scene blinked out.

Colm had presumed they were part of the investigation. Friends of Robyn Peltier's helping the police to find her.

After seeing their cautious glances, though, he reconsidered. Both had been dressed in dark clothes. They'd taken the stairs, not the elevator like the police. Again he saw that backpack swinging from the man's hand.

Colm hurried after them.

HOPE

We're being followed." Karl said this as casually as he'd remark on the weather.

"Cop?" Hope whispered.

He shook his head.

"Curious neighbor?"

"I don't know. I can only hear and smell him."

"Then how do you know—? Ah. The smell is male and you hear only one set of footsteps. The way he's following suggests he's not a cop. Sneaking after us."

"Very good. So, what should we do?"

Hope knew he wasn't asking her advice. With Karl, she'd always be the student. She was fine with that. She was dating a professional thief almost twice her age—she'd long since stopped worrying about the appropriateness of the relationship.

The question was an opportunity for Hope to build confidence in her ability to make good choices. For the demon, the answer sprang to mind with the weight and surety of a sledgehammer blow. She should turn around and confront their pursuer. She had a gun and the element of surprise. Grab the upper hand, shove it in his face and let the sweet chaos of his reaction rain down.

The moment the demon tossed in its two cents, her conscience reared up with the polar-opposite response. Deny the demon. Don't engage—escape.

After considering both arguments, she told Karl what she thought they should do.

•   •   •

TWO MINUTES LATER, Hope was making her demon very happy as she waltzed into the path of her pursuer.

She didn't have the heart to tell it there was no kick-ass confrontation coming. The demon probably knew that, but was keeping silent, hoping for an emergency change of plans, cheered by the gun hidden in Hope's pocket.

In the supernatural world, using a gun was considered a sign of cowardice. Hope didn't play by those rules. She couldn't afford to. Having the ability to sense danger only protected her so far. All the aikido lessons in the world weren't going to save her against a charging werewolf or armed human killer, both equally likely in her line of work. So she carried a gun. Always.

When they'd neared the end of the wall, she'd done the "Damn it, I forgot something" charade, throwing up her hands and gesturing at the apartment. Karl had nodded and said loudly that he'd bring the car around.

He headed across the road, then circled back on the other side of the wall, where he was now lying in wait.

Whoever was following them was hidden in the bushes along the wall. Hope couldn't see him, but his vibes blared loud as a siren. Fear. Anxiety. Misgivings. She caught the emotions and a jumble of thoughts, too muddled to distinguish whole words. As she drank in the chaos, the demon perked up.

See? He's afraid. No danger here. No need to wait for Karl. The daughter of Lucifer doesn't need a werewolf to protect her. Show him what you can—

Hope gagged the demon and kept walking.

Their pursuer moved with her, the bushes rustling loud enough for Hope to track his progress even without the chaos siren.

See? He's an amateur. Easy prey. Just—

She veered from the wall so she wouldn't make him any more nervous. The demon withdrew, sulking.

As Hope neared a place where a large tree overhung the wall, she caught a vision flash of Karl crouched at the top of the wall, hidden in the tree's shadow, waiting to pounce. The vision was oddly distorted, like looking through old glass, and she stopped short, confused.

The bushes erupted. As Hope wheeled, a figure leapt out, gun raised. She opened her mouth to warn Karl, but chaos blasted off the figure— absolute terror, so strong she reeled back, her shout a strangled squeak.

Karl's dark form was already in midjump. He twisted out of the way, but the figure didn't fire, just lifted the gun, then spun and ran.

Hope recovered in time to see a flash of a boy's face, freckled with red hair, not more than sixteen. The shock of that stunned her just long enough for the boy to streak past.

She tore after him. Karl's footsteps pounded behind them. Hope kept her lead but as quick as she was, the boy was faster. He made it through the propped-open rear exit and slammed it shut before she got there.

Hope yanked on the door handle. Locked. She was fumbling with Robyn's keys when Karl caught her hand.

He whispered, "Let him go," but his vibes screamed a very different message, the wolf gnashing its teeth as its prey escaped.

Karl's gaze moved to the parking lot, reminding her—and himself—of the police stakeout. They couldn't afford to be seen hanging around, much less be caught racing after the boy.

"We scared the crap out of him," she whispered. "He won't be coming back."

Karl nodded. Whether he believed that or not, it got them away from that door. One last lingering look, and they headed for the car.

COLM

COLM HUDDLED UNDER THE STAIRS, shaking so hard he thought he was going to throw up.

He'd been so busy watching the woman he'd forgotten all about the man. It had only been a fluke—or survival instinct—that sent him a vision flash of the man crouched on the wall. He could still see him jumping, his face hard and eyes gleaming, lips pulled back. Even in memory that look made Colm's bladder twitch. In real life, it had made him turn tail and run.

He'd seen the man twist in midflight, yet still hit the ground running. An eight-foot wall and he'd jumped down effortlessly. No hesitation, no bracing for a fall.

He wasn't human. That look on his face hadn't been human.

He remembered the woman in the hall, turning. The man had asked if she'd *sensed* something.

Sensed how? Magic? Was she a witch? The man some kind of half-demon?

But why would supernaturals be in Robyn Peltier's apartment?

Maybe because they were looking for the same thing he was: Robyn Peltier. Or the photograph.

What if that photo wasn't an accident? Irving Nast had tricked Adele into that meeting. Maybe he'd had Portia Kane take the picture to blackmail Adele into working for the Cabal. Before Nast could get the photo, Adele had stolen the cell phone. So now these two supernaturals had to retrieve a copy from Robyn Peltier.

So Portia Kane had been a supernatural secret agent? That sounded crazy. But what if the Cabals knew about the kumpania and what they did for a living? Wouldn't a celebrity supernatural be the perfect lure to draw them out?

The Cabals were devious and endlessly resourceful. They'd created an interracial council, supposedly to protect supernaturals, but if you ran to them, you'd be turned right back over to the Cabals. They set up one of their own Cabal sons—Lucas Cortez—as a so-called crusader, but if you ran to him, again, you'd end up back in the hands of the Cabal. You could never underestimate them, never be too paranoid. That's the lesson the phuri had drilled into Colm's head from birth.

But if Portia Kane had taken the photo for the Cabal, why not just send it to them right away? Why mail it to Robyn Peltier?

As he calmed down, he was ashamed of himself for panicking. That couple weren't supernaturals. So he'd seen a man jump from an eight-foot wall. Big deal. Stuntmen did it all the time. This was L.A.

He was making up elaborate stories to excuse the simple truth that he'd screwed up. How he would have loved to return to Adele, say he'd followed a suspicious couple and found Robyn Peltier. He imagined how she'd react to that, the look in her eyes, the taste of her kiss, her voice murmuring in his ear, "How can I ever repay you?"

He squeezed his eyes shut, forcing the fantasy back. He'd still find Robyn Peltier for Adele. He wouldn't mention the couple to her. No need to expose his cowardice. She'd sent him to retrieve a personal item from the apartment and he would, then he'd use it to find Peltier. His powers might be immature, but surely he could boost them for a reward he wanted badly enough.

Since puberty the elders had been preparing him for his eventual role, teaching him all the skills he'd need as a contributing member of the kumpania. Lock picking had come early. When you first got an assignment, you'd need to steal personal items to make a connection. After that, getting a valuable celebrity shot sometimes meant being someplace you weren't supposed to be. Being able to open locked doors and disarm alarms came in very handy.

As he approached the door, he slid the pick into his hand, then set to work.

There was something not quite right with the locking mechanism. As his frustration mounted, he forgot the second part of any break-in job: keeping a constant watch on his surroundings. He didn't hear the whoosh of the elevator doors until they were closing.

"Can I help you, son?"

A uniformed officer started toward him, shoulders squaring. Colm closed his fingers over the pick and pushed it up his sleeve.

"I was looking for Miss Peltier. She bought some chocolate almonds from me for band."

The officer stopped in front of him. "Band?"

"A band trip. I go to LACHSA." When the officer looked confused, he said, "Los Angeles County High School of the Arts." A school he could claim, no matter what part of the city he was in. "I was going to tell her the almonds will be late."

"You live in the building?"

Colm nodded. "With my mom. Number 304."

The lies came effortlessly. More lessons taught from birth. No matter how innocent the question, lie.

The officer seemed to consider taking him down to 304 and Colm was mentally preparing his excuse and escape plan, but after a moment, the officer asked, "When's the last time you saw Ms. Peltier?"

"Last Tues—no, Wednesday. I was waiting out front for my cab to school."

The officer reached into his pocket and handed Colm a card. "If you see her again, give me a call."

"Is something wrong?"

"We just need to talk to her."

Colm read the card slowly, hoping the officer would walk away. But he just stood there, waiting for Colm to leave. After a moment, he did.

ONCE AGAIN, Colm stood in the first-floor stairwell. He'd tried to remotely watch the officer, so he could sneak back up, but he was so nervous he couldn't concentrate. Even clutching the officer's card didn't help.

There was no way he was getting into that apartment now. He couldn't talk his way out of being caught up there a second time.

He wished he could call Adele, but she'd been summoned into a conference with the phuri. With Portia Kane dead, they'd waste no time assigning her a new subject. They always had several on backup. Everyone needed to pull his weight.

In the meantime, he'd come up with a version of events that put him in a better light. No mysterious couple. Certainly no walking into their trap. And there'd been two—no, maybe four—cops searching the apartment. He'd waited for hours, but they hadn't left. Adele couldn't blame him for that . . . he hoped.

HOPE

H ope called Robyn from the car. Robyn sounded as if she'd been sleeping, groggy, confused. Hope said they had her laptop and some clothes and were going to pick up food before coming back. They'd be there in an hour or so.

Then, with the danger past, Karl wanted to hear details of her plans for a cabin getaway. Hope was happy to oblige . . . in every way.

Afterward, still parked where they'd stopped, she took out the laptop. She didn't like snooping through Robyn's files, but if Portia's killer was the supernatural Hope had sensed in the club, she'd better get a look at this picture before Robyn did.

Proof of their existence was something supernaturals *would* kill for—not only to protect themselves from exposure, but to save their ass from the council, the Cabals and every pissed-off supernatural who'd come gunning for them. But when Hope found the picture it was exactly what Robyn said: a picture of Jasmine Wills in the most god-awful outfit imaginable.

Karl leaned over. "Is she going to a costume party?"

"Even I can tell this is one criminal fashion faux pas. Criminal enough to turn Jasmine into a murderer? Portia takes it and calls Jasmine to gloat. Jasmine knows where she'll be that night. She goes to Bane with a gun, planning to threaten Portia. But if you take a gun to a fight, you'd better be damned sure you can control your temper because all it takes is one tug on the trigger."

"True."

"But if it was Jasmine, Portia would have recognized her. So maybe this isn't why her killer wanted the cell phone. Maybe she only went after Rob because she was a witness. Or maybe she didn't go after her at all. A woman definitely shot Portia, and Rob was sure a guy killed the undercover officer. A partner? Totally unrelated?" Hope rubbed her temples. "Okay, tell me to stop blathering."

"Never. I like your blathering."

She glanced over at him. "Are you okay with this? It seems I'm always dragging you into some mess or another."

"You don't drag. I follow for the entertainment value." He angled the laptop more toward him. "So, we have this photo of a girl in an ugly dress. She's on a sidewalk. In the background, there's a store window. Behind her, we have a couple—"

"Shit. Isn't that—?"

Hope turned the laptop back for a better look. She'd been so blinded by the hideousness of Jasmine's outfit that she hadn't even noticed the two people at the edge of the frame. A middle-aged man in an expensive suit and a girl barely out of her teens, deep in conversation.

"That's a Nast."

Karl frowned, leaning over the armrest for a better look. Hope turned the laptop toward him again and pointed to the man.

"You recognize him?" he asked.

"No, but I recognize the look."

The Nasts ran the largest of the four North American Cabals. Their head office was in L.A. Hope had more contact with the Cortezes, out of Miami, but she'd seen enough photos of the Nasts to recognize one. Sixty-five years ago, they could have served as poster boys for Hitler's Aryan army—tall, broad-shouldered, blond-haired, with bright blue eyes. Handsome in a severe, arrogant way, as if they'd sooner crush you under their Gucci loafers than speak to you—and with most Nasts, you were wise to take that as a warning.

Hope pointed at the photo. "If this guy is a Nast, you can bet this is why Portia Kane was killed for this photo. As for why . . ."

"I doubt that girl beside him is his daughter."

"Given the fact that sorcerers don't have daughters, I'd say it's a sure bet. And she's too young to be his personal assistant. If Portia Kane accidentally snapped a photo of a middle-aged guy with his post-pubescent mistress, that hardly seems worth killing her for. But we're talking about a Cabal. If this photo could damage the reputation of a top exec, he'd want it back. Portia Kane and Robyn would be considered expendable." She opened the mail program. "But all that hinges on this guy being a Nast. If you can drive until I pick up a wireless connection, I should have an answer for us by morning."

HOPE DIDN'T NEED TO WAIT until morning. She sent an e-mail, then called to leave a message at Lucas's office, not wanting to bother him at home so late. But someone answered the office phone.

"Cortez-Winterbourne Investigations. Ridding the world of evil, one demonic entity at a time."

"I hope that's not how you normally handle the office phones, Savannah."

"Absolutely. Weeds out the cranks and telemarketers, let me tell ya."

"What are you doing there so late?"

The line hissed, as if Savannah was getting comfortable. "Working my ass off as always. You know those Cortezes. Work supernaturals into the grave, then bring 'em back and work 'em some more. So I'm here and I just got your e-mail. Now, let me get this straight. You have this photo, everyone who touches it goes on some kind of death list, and now you're sending it to me. I've seen this in a movie, you know."

"That was a video."

"Close enough."

Karl glanced over, brows arching.

"Savannah," Hope mouthed.

He rolled his eyes. He didn't have much patience for the nineteen-year-old witch. Hope liked her well enough, but it seemed she had a soft spot for cocky, overconfident supernaturals.

"Okay, so I'm opening this photo and if I die, I am so going to haunt your ass. Let's see. It's—" Savannah let out a shriek. "Holy fucking mother of God. What is that thing?"

"You like?"

"I think I'm blind now. That's the curse, isn't it? Look at the picture and— Wait, isn't that Jasmine something-or-other? One of those Paris-lites?"

"You read the tabloids, Savannah? Say it isn't so."

"Are you kidding? I'm the ward of two well-educated, cultured individuals. I read the *New Yorker, Harper's* and sometimes *National Geographic,* but only for the half-naked guys. I do, however, indulge in *True News* on occasion, to enjoy the journalistic stylings of their intrepid paranormal reporter. Call me crazy, but I think that girl knows of what she speaks."

"You think?"

"I do. So why would you be sending Paige and Lucas a photo of what's-her-name, other than to scar our retinas— Holy shit. Portia Kane. Paige said your friend went to L.A. to do PR work for some celebutante. It's Portia Kane, isn't it? And now she's dead and . . . Hey, is this a case? 'Cause if it is, I've got the weekend off, and I could—"

"It's not a council case. About the photo, it's actually the people in the background I'm interested in. There's a young woman and—"

"Uncle Josef! No, wait, that's Cousin Irving. I always get them confused. God, I haven't seen ol' Irving since . . . well, since the last Nast family reunion they didn't invite me to."

While it was true that sorcerers don't father girls, that didn't apply when they had a child with a witch, who only had daughters. So Thomas Nast's granddaughter was being raised by the son of his bitter rival, the Cortez Cabal CEO, the same son who'd devoted his life to fighting Cabal injustice, until recently when he began dividing his time between that and reluctantly helping prop up his father's sagging empire. And yes, that was all just as complicated as it sounded.

But for Thomas Nast and most of his clan, one thing *wasn't* complicated. Savannah was not his dead son's daughter. No Cabal sorcerer would ever sleep with a witch. Well, except Lucas and . . . yes, it was complicated. Anyone who saw Savannah, though, with her distinctive big blue eyes, knew exactly who her daddy had been.

"So it's a Nast?"

"Yep, and I'm ninety percent sure it's Irving. That would be my dad's cousin, so my second-cousin or first cousin once removed or whatever. We should have a dossier on him. If you need more, I can put you in touch with Sean to answer any questions. Discreetly, of course. I wouldn't want to get him in trouble."

"We'll try to leave your brother out of it. Now, as for that dossier . . ."

"It's on the way . . ." Keys clicked in the background. ". . . now."

THE MAN IN THE PICTURE was definitely Irving Nast—it matched the one in his dossier down to a small mole by the corner of his eye. As for the rest of the dossier, it was . . . interesting.

Cabals are run by a central sorcerer family. If you are a member of that family, you're guaranteed an office on the executive level. In the case of Irving, that family connection seemed to be the *only* reason he got that office. He was VP of some division Hope had never heard of, in charge of a very small department.

According to the dossier, Irving didn't even warrant a bodyguard. Being the CEO's nephew and not getting a guard told the supernatural world you were so low on the totem pole you weren't worth kidnapping—you weren't privy to any secret intelligence and they wouldn't bother ransoming you back.

One reason a family member might rank so low was simple lack of ambition—you were content to coast along on your name, like Lucas's brother Carlos. But it looked as if Irving dreamed of more. The dossier included a string of "independent ventures," where Irving had tried to get innovative and prove his worth . . . and instead had a run-in with Lucas or the council.

"He's a screw-up," Hope said as she finished reading aloud to Karl. "If this photo is Irving and his very young mistress, it might explain what happened. He's already on thin ice with the Cabal, so he came up with a plan to get the photo back."

"And fucked up royally."

"Yep. On the plus side, though, not rating a bodyguard means it would be easy to interrogate him, if it came to that."

Karl checked his watch. "He should be sleeping. We could—"

"I said 'if it came to that.' Kidnapping and questioning a Nast VP would get me into the kind of trouble even I don't enjoy. So don't tempt me." When he opened his mouth, she went on, "And don't say that you aren't bound by council rules. You're bound by Pack rules, as much as you like to pretend otherwise. Relations are strained enough between the Pack and the Cabals already. Jeremy doesn't need that kind of grief."

Hope navigated to MapQuest. "If we don't find leads by tomorrow night, we'll reconsider. In the meantime, I have a home address. It might be wise to swing by, get the lay of the land."

"And if he happens to be out for a late jog or walking his dog, he might be inclined to chat."

She smiled. "Exactly."

IRVING NAST WAS NOT OUT WALKING his dog or running. He was, as far as they could tell, inside with his family—a wife and two preteen sons according to his dossier. Even Karl wouldn't suggest a home invasion when children were involved.

They circled the block, then parked a street over and walked back, playing strolling couple again as they got a closer look at the property and made a note of the vehicles and license plates, anything that might later help them nab Irving if a "chat" was required.

ON THE WAY BACK, they finally picked up dinner for Robyn. As Hope returned to the car, she nearly bumped into Karl, walking around from the building rear.

"They have a bathroom inside, you know," she said as he took the take-out bags.

He only gave her a look, the thought that he would ever piss behind a building clearly not warranting comment.

"What did you see?" she said.

He waved it off, but she could feel the fading chaos vibes still flowing from him.

"Karl?"

"I thought I was being watched. He ducked behind the building. I followed."

"And?" Hope prompted.

"Apparently, *he* didn't find the restaurant facilities to his liking."

"Ah. See, I was partly right. My psychic skills are improving. Someone *was* taking a leak back there."

He opened her door and waved her in, shaking his head.

ROBYN

Robyn lay on her side, staring at Hope's hair fanning over her pillow. It had been that hair, twelve years ago, that made her decide she would not like Hope Adams.

By that point, Robyn and her classmates had pretty much decided they weren't going to like any of the girls they'd been teamed up with for the fund-raiser. After all, they were private school brats, rich little snobs. The popular clique times ten.

Robyn and her friends didn't envy those girls their manicured nails and platinum credit cards. Perish the thought. No, they *pitied* them. Those poor privileged girls, destined for a life stuck in a fifties time warp, as pampered and petted housewives who would one day be chugging back Cosmos at the golf club, whining about their husband's fling with the nanny, while Robyn and her classmates worked in board rooms and surgeries, changing the world.

And Hope Adams? The moment Robyn had been assigned to her as a partner, she'd known who'd be doing all the work—and it wasn't the pretty girl with the flawless skin and long black curls.

That had been Robyn's first lesson in stereotypes. While Hope could play debutante with the best of them, she was happiest in blue jeans, kicking back with friends or chasing down one of her weird tales, not giving a rat's ass what anyone thought of her.

Now Hope was here, sound asleep beside her, exhausted after finding Robyn, nursing her out of her shock, then racing off trying to solve two murders, which Robyn was suspected of committing. And what had Robyn done? Sat on her ass in a hotel room, scarfing down brownie bites and watching TV, like the pampered princess she'd once thought Hope.

When Hope called to say they had the laptop, what had Robyn done? Asked whether her apartment was still under guard? Whether the police had searched it? Whether Hope had looked at the photo yet? Nope. Total disinterest in the situation.

That had to end. She'd had twenty-four hours to recover from the shock, wallow in self-pity and clear her head. Time to start helping herself.

A key turned in the door lock. Robyn went still. Hope rolled onto her back and pushed up onto her elbows. The second bed was empty. Robyn shut her eyes as the door creaked open.

"Is everything okay?" Hope whispered.

"It took a while to find an open drugstore," Karl said.

A rattle, like pills in a bottle.

"Ah, thank you," Hope said. "You're a saint."

"Credits. Rackin' 'em up."

Hope's soft laugh. Pills clicked again, Karl shaking them into Hope's hand. A gulp of water. The mattress moved as Hope lay down again. A soft voice, too low to make out. Robyn cracked open her eyes to see Karl bending over Hope, whispering. She nodded and murmured, "Good," then pulled the covers up.

Karl stood there, watching Hope. His expression made Robyn ache. She knew they were being careful around her. No embraces or kisses. No words of affection. Sleeping in separate beds. It didn't matter. What hurt most were the little things that she'd always taken for granted with Damon, the touches, the looks that said "I love you" better than any words.

At Damon's memorial, her sister, Joy, had sat with her, holding her hand, saying, "He loved you, Rob. He really loved you." Now, as she watched Karl looking down at Hope, the envy and the yearning cut deep, and she understood what her sister had felt all those years, watching her and Damon, yearning for something Joy had never found.

Robyn should call her sister. It had been weeks since they'd spoken. Her family respected her need for privacy and trusted Robyn to climb back onto her feet, because that's the kind of person she was. She'd failed them, retreating deeper into her hole, no longer even looking for a way out. If they ever found out, they'd blame themselves for giving her that space.

Well, no more. It was time to fight.

FINN

FINN'S PHONE RANG at 3:45 a.m. He answered on the second ring.

It was Luis Madoz, one of the detectives helping on the Kane murder. Another officer had picked up a guy trying to fence a diamond bracelet to an undercover officer. The officer ran it and discovered it was registered. The owner? Portia Kane.

When they'd brought the guy in, Madoz had noticed he was wearing shoes with a distinctive tread that seemed to match a partial print found in Kane's blood.

"I've sent it to the lab for a definite answer, but it sure as hell looked like it to me. And the guy still has a stamp on his hand from Bane Thursday night. Thought you might want to come down."

WHEN FINN ARRIVED, he found himself looking for Trent. He wasn't really hoping to see him, but he wouldn't have been disappointed if he did.

Madoz updated him as they walked through the station. They'd lifted a single set of prints from the gun, but until they had Robyn Peltier, they couldn't test for a match. Her record was spotless—not so much as a traffic ticket.

The dress they'd found at Judd Archer's—matching the one Peltier had been seen wearing—was being tested for gunshot residue. If it came back positive, great. Otherwise, it didn't prove anything. The residue wouldn't necessarily transfer onto a dress with short sleeves.

As for the gun itself, the serial number had been filed off, but poorly, and the techs still hoped to lift something. The missing serial number suggested premeditated murder or, at the very least, someone who carried a gun presuming he might need to use it.

ΠEIL EARLEY WAS A JUΠHIE college kid, a type that, in Finn's opinion, wasn't nearly uncommon enough.

Finn had gone to college himself—Oklahoma State—and it had been a struggle. Not the work itself. He was no genius, but he showed up and did the work, and most times that was all it took to succeed at anything in life. The tough part had been paying for it. His family couldn't afford college, and where he came from, credit wasn't an option. You paid your way up front. Paying for tuition himself meant he sure as hell showed up for every class and got his last nickel's worth. Drinking and shooting up and clubbing your way through college? Made no sense to him.

Maybe in ten years, these kids would look back and regret it. Or maybe they'd look back and yearn for those carefree days. One thing this particular kid *would* regret was being at Bane that night, heading for the bathroom, hearing a hysterical server telling her colleague that there was a dead girl back there who looked like Portia Kane.

Earley hadn't been too stoned to see an opportunity. He'd snuck back, cell phone in hand, ready to take pictures of the dead celebutante. Then came regret number two—that he'd invested his money in drugs instead of a better cell phone. The pictures had been too dark—Finn could barely make out the shape of a person let alone identify it as Kane.

As Earley had been looking for a light switch, he'd heard people coming and saw, glittering on Kane's wrist, the second opportunity to profit from her misfortune. Having no idea how to sell a diamond bracelet, he'd gone to the only criminal contact he knew. His dealer was another college boy who knew zip about fencing jewels, but had offered to ask around for a cut. So Neil Earley had ended up in an alley, offering the bracelet to an undercover cop.

Finn would make sure someone followed up on the kid's story and charge him with theft—maybe that would make him appreciate college more—but he had little doubt Earley was telling the truth. That meant he needed a suspect, and Robyn Peltier had regained her spot as the person he most needed to question.

"We've got her family," Madoz said as they grabbed coffee.

"They're in Philly. Parents still married, still residing in the same house where Peltier grew up. He's an engineer. She's a nurse. No criminal records for either."

"Shit," said a voice behind Finn. "You'd better get the SWAT team up there, pronto. I'm sure they're harboring their dangerous fugitive daughter, got the place rigged up like Waco."

Finn looked over to see Trent sitting on a desk two rows away.

"Good thing I came back," Trent continued. "Because, man, if you were any farther afield, you'd be standing in the parking lot."

"If she's innocent, why'd she run?"

"I . . . don't know," Madoz said, eyeing him as if this was a pop quiz. "Do you think she is?"

"Sorry. I was thinking out loud."

Madoz tried to look as if this didn't bother him and failed miserably.

"She ran because she's scared," Trent said. "She's never had any trouble with the law and all of a sudden she's caught over the body of her dead client. She panicked. Now she's trying to figure out how to fix it, and splashing her photo across the papers isn't going to help."

"Finn?" Madoz said as Finn listened to Trent.

"Sorry, you were saying about the parents . . . ?"

Madoz hesitated, making sure Finn's attention wasn't going to wander before answering. "I've persuaded a couple of Philly detectives to stop by and talk to the parents, save us the trip. Is there anything specific you want?"

"Ask if they know Robyn's friends. I'm specifically interested in a young woman who might be in L.A. right now. Probably Indo American. Could be a journalist. Maybe high society."

"Sounds like a gossip columnist."

"Just tell them to take down information on any friend who could pass for Indo American."

Trent sighed. "You are so far out in left field, you're—"

"Can you hold on a sec?" Finn asked Madoz. "Be right back."

"Rule one," Finn murmured when he and Trent were in the empty hall. "Don't talk to me with others around."

"Hey, you don't have to answer."

"Rule two, if you're going to take off, warn me."

"I didn't take off. I tried to get your attention when you left that apartment, and you couldn't see me. Then I lost you, so I hung around the apartment, seeing if I could find anything you missed before coming to the station to wait."

Finn had a good sense for when people were telling the truth and when they weren't, and one glance at Trent told him the split was about fifty-fifty.

Trent hurried on before Finn could call him on it. "While I was at the apartment, though, I saw something. There was a kid trying to break into Robyn's apartment after you left."

Finn stopped walking. "Break in?"

"With lock picks, no less. One of your guys spotted him, but he hid those picks and spun a story so fast your officer let him go."

"I'll follow up on that."

"Good, because this woman you seem so set on—"

"Trent?"

"Yes?"

"Did you see me interviewing a kid a few minutes ago?"

"The dumb-ass college boy? Sure, but—"

"He's being processed. Go keep an eye on him."

"But—"

"Go."

FINN WALKED BACK into the detective room and found Madoz at his desk.

"Do you have the paperwork on Robyn Peltier's husband?"

"Right here." Madoz thumbed through his stack. "I don't see a connection. Just a random act of stupidity. Classic case of why it might not be wise to let Joe—or, in this case, Jane—Citizen carry a gun."

"What happened?"

"Woman was mugged by gangbangers. Gets herself a gun. Few months later, she's on the highway at night, blows a tire. Guy pulls over to help. She sees a black guy coming at her car with a tire iron and shoots him."

"Black guy . . ."

"With a tire iron. Like maybe so he can change your tire, you dumb bitch?" He handed Finn the file. "The guy was a junior high teacher coming home from a conference. Wearing a dress shirt and slacks. Driving a Honda. Clearly a badass carjacker."

Madoz kept talking, but Finn didn't hear him. He opened the file. There, on the top, was a picture of Robyn Peltier's dead husband: twenty-nine-year-old Damon Trent Peltier.

• • •

THIRTY MINUTES LATER, Madoz had left and Finn was at his desk working when his ghostly partner returned.

"How long do you want me to sit on this—" "Trent" saw the open file on Finn's desk, and the photo in it. "Shit."

Finn didn't look up. "Is there something you want to tell me, *Damon?*"

"Shit." Damon slouched into the nearest chair. "I'm sorry."

"What? That I figured it out?" Finn turned his chair to face him. "Did you really think I wouldn't?"

"No, I was just hoping it'd take a little longer."

"Like long enough for you to plant false leads and throw me off your wife's trail?"

"What? No. Absolutely not. I knew you'd figure it out soon, but before you did, I wanted to prove I could be useful—give you real leads. Like that one with the kid. That's totally legit. I can give you his description, the description of the officer he spoke to, hell, I can probably recite their conversation if you'd like." He walked over and sat on Finn's desk. "I'm here to help you find the truth, which I already know—that my wife had nothing to do with this. I don't need to throw you off her trail."

"Just try to sway me off pursuing her as a suspect."

"I—" He stopped. "Okay, that was stupid. Understandable, but stupid, and it won't help my cause or Bobby's."

"Bobby?"

"Robyn. Sorry. From here on, I will try to keep my opinions to myself and if I slip, you can tell me to shut up. And if I don't help you, if I mislead you or I'm a nuisance, you can tell me to get lost and I will. I just . . ." He shifted on the desk. "I need to help her, Finn. She's—"

Finn held up a hand. "For the next twenty-four hours, we'll see how it goes. Then you can tell me your story. For now—"

"Just shut up, do what I'm told and try to dig my way out of this hole."

Finn nodded.

ROBYN

Robyn awoke to the smell of breakfast sausage. Caught between sleeping and waking, she lifted her head with Damon's name on her lips; hot breakfasts had been his specialty. One bleary look around the motel room reminded her where she was.

Fighting the impulse to lie back down and pull up the covers, she tracked the smell to take-out boxes on the dinette, pushed aside to clear a spot for Hope's laptop. Hope sat with her back to Robyn as she read the screen. There was no sign of Karl. The bedside clock said it was past nine. So much for her resolution to jump into the investigation first thing in the morning.

Hope was so engrossed in her reading that she didn't hear Robyn approach. The file on the laptop display looked like records with dates and blocks of text. But before Robyn could get close enough to read it, Hope glanced up.

Hope closed the file window and stood. "Karl grabbed breakfast. It should still be warm."

"He's out already?"

Hope handed Robyn a coffee. "Just walking around the block, getting a feel for the neighborhood and stretching his legs."

A rap at the door.

"And there he is."

Hope checked the peephole before opening the locks. Karl greeted Robyn, then set his take-out coffee on the nightstand.

Hope's gaze followed him. "Everything okay?"

He nodded. "There's a convenience store around the corner and some restaurants a block over." He took a sheaf of pamphlets from his pocket. "I picked up take-out menus from the ones that were open." He turned to Robyn. "They all deliver. While I'm sure you're tired of being cooped up in here, you should stick to delivery for lunch. Keep the doors locked and only open them if you're expecting an order."

She glanced at Hope, who was dumping her leftover coffee in the bathroom sink. "You're heading out?"

"Just for a few hours," Hope said. "We'll be back after lunch."

"I'd like to go with you. Help out."

"You're safer here," Karl said, taking out his keys.

"I—"

"Hope and I need to attract as little attention as possible. It's better if you stay here."

She hadn't thought of that. "Then what can I do here?"

Hope and Karl exchanged a look.

"I want to do *something*."

"We have Internet access," Hope said. "There are a few things you could look up."

Scraps to make her feel useful. "Whatever will help. Just tell me—"

Hope's cell rang and she snatched it from the table, as if grateful for the interruption.

"Lucas, hey," she answered. A pause. "Yep, I got it last night. Thank Savannah for me. It's a match."

A string of uh-huhs. Hope grabbed her notepad and started jotting things down. Robyn tried to see it from where she sat, but Hope's writing was an illegible scribbled shorthand. She always joked it was so no rival could steal her notes, but Robyn knew she'd always written that way, her brain speeding ahead, pen scrambling to keep up. Like everything else in Hope's life, function came before form.

Karl seemed to be able to read it, though, murmuring questions for Hope to ask. Robyn had been able to read Damon's scrawl, too.

"Is that like a scheduled surrender?" Hope was saying.

Hope must be talking to her lawyer friend. Or wasn't it Karl's friend? It didn't matter. Damon's friends had been Robyn's, too. Or so she'd thought, until she'd been uninvited from a New Year's party two weeks before she left Philly.

She shook her head, scattering the memories.

"I'll call you later, then," Hope was saying. "I really do appreciate this."

Pause.

"Yes." Her gaze shot to Karl. "He's right here."

Her fingertips caressed the desktop, face averted as she listened. Then she handed the phone to Karl, gaze following as he took it outside.

"Did you say something about a scheduled surrender?" Robyn asked.

It took Hope a moment to answer. "That would buy us more time, but it won't work in a murder case. He's setting up a short-term scheduled surrender, if we don't find something by six."

Her gaze tripped to the window, as if trying to see Karl's silhouette through the drawn drapes.

"So we have—" Robyn checked her watch. "—just over eight hours. Show me what I can do."

HOPE

Karl had driven three blocks in silence before Hope spoke.

"I wish you wouldn't do that."

He made a noise in his throat, as if waiting to hear which infraction she was referring to before committing himself to a response.

"Sneaking around asking Lucas for updates on Jaz. It would be easier if you'd just give him your number, you know."

"I wasn't sneaking. I could hardly discuss it in front of Robyn—"

"And what was your excuse the last time? Or the time before that? Did you honestly expect me to think Lucas is just calling to chat?"

Another block of silence.

Karl cleared his throat. "About Jasper—"

"Is he dead?"

"No."

"Escaped?"

"No."

"In imminent danger of escaping?"

"No."

"Then I don't care."

She turned to the window, nails biting her palms. Did Karl really think she'd want to know how Jaz was doing? Did he think she'd care?

Last year, after their disastrous first attempt to shift from friends to lovers, she'd tried taking the rebound remedy. If there was one word to describe Jasper Haig, it was fun. He bounced through life with enthusiasm, and he'd pursued Hope with gusto, not caring how big a fool he made of himself. In short, Jaz was everything Karl was not—and exactly what she'd needed . . . or so it seemed at the time.

Jaz was currently incarcerated in a maximum-security Cortez Cabal prison, his execution stayed only while they studied his rare supernatural powers.

Hope knew Karl's main concern was for her safety. Like any good villain, Jaz had vowed to come for her when he escaped, convinced that she was still the girl for him.

And as hard as Karl worked to control his wolf side, there were two instincts that were as strong in him as in any werewolf Hope knew. One was the instinct to protect. As the only person Karl cared about enough to protect, she bore the full brunt of that.

The second was the territorial instinct. The feminist in Hope might be horrified at the thought, but she knew she was Karl's territory. To the wolf, she was his as much as he was hers, to be protected and defended against all comers.

Karl tried to be smooth about it, made jokes about his jealous streak, but when a man looked Hope's way, she saw his hackles rise. The first time he'd seen Jaz, she'd been drunk, straddling his lap and making out with him, as close to having sex as you could get with your clothes on.

Karl couldn't forget that.

It didn't matter that she'd come back to Karl, that she'd chosen him before she'd found out Jaz was a killer. It didn't matter that since his return, she hadn't looked at another man. The human in Karl knew he had no cause for jealousy, but the wolf couldn't forget that somewhere, out there, he had a rival plotting to take his mate.

"I'm sorry," Karl said finally.

They were at a stoplight. She looked over, meeting his eyes, searching for chaos vibes before tearing her gaze away. As tempting as it was, she shouldn't use her powers to read him and gauge his sincerity. Trust him or don't. No shortcuts allowed.

"I do check with Lucas periodically," he said. "His father is supposed to provide me with updates, but I don't trust Benicio to be prompt or truthful if it's not in the Cabal's best interests."

"Did you think I'd disagree?"

"I didn't think you needed the constant reminders that Jasper is still out there."

The light changed and he drove another half-block before adding, "And I don't want you to think I'm obsessing about him."

"Are you?"

"I think about him as little as possible, but I'll rest easier when the writ of execution is carried out."

"Agreed. Make a left at the next street." When he did, she went on. "What's the other thing you're keeping from me?"

Again his gaze shunted her way, trying to figure out which infraction was now the topic of discussion.

Hope sighed. "Are there really so many? Honesty, Karl. It's a good thing."

A twist of a smile. "Perhaps. But in my case, complete and full disclosure of everything I've done in the past would *not* be a good thing. If you're referring to recent events I haven't disclosed, though, there's only one, and it isn't a secret, just a subject I wasn't ready to bring up."

"Until you take care of him?"

He shot her a reproachful look. "Do you think I wouldn't warn you of a potential threat?"

"Another werewolf in L.A. isn't a threat to me—"

"Yes, it is." His tone was firm, almost sharp. "I know you think otherwise, but I'd appreciate it if you humored me on this." Another turn and he concentrated on it more than necessary, struggling to find a lighter tone. "What gave me away? A stray thought last night when I came back?"

"I don't need my powers to read you, Karl. I'll admit, I didn't notice anything wrong last night. I was too busy going along with the drugstore excuse for Robyn—which, by the way, was clever. Sorry I didn't get it right away."

"She didn't notice."

"So you smelled another werewolf last night, then went out this morning scouting. That's when I caught on, from your expression when you came back. Is he near?"

Karl shook his head. "If he was, I'd have moved us. I caught his scent last night, but it was in the air and I couldn't find it on the ground to track. I didn't have any better luck this morning. I suspect I miscalculated the wind and he was farther away than I thought."

"Do you want to go after him now?"

"No. We have work to do. I'll look for him tonight."

ADELE

Never trust a boy to do a woman's job, Adele thought as she marched toward Robyn Peltier's apartment door.

Colm was sweet and useful, but he could be as thick as a board. Not stupid, just inexperienced. When his plan to steal a personal item failed, he was stumped. His only backup plan was to try again tonight. She couldn't wait that long.

When she told him what she planned to do, he'd freaked out. It was crazy, dangerous. Colm didn't understand that to get what you wanted in life, you had to make bold moves.

It wasn't his fault. They'd been raised to hide, not make waves. They were one of the most powerful supernatural races and what did they use those powers for? Pandering to the cult of celebrity. It was humiliating.

She still smarted from last night's meeting with the phuri. Portia Kane had been Adele's first assignment, and she'd done a damned good job, earning her keep and contributing extra to the kumpania coffers. Remarkable for what should have been a training exercise. Even Neala had been grudgingly impressed.

So how did they reward her? By giving her a true celebrity as her next target?

"You've done such a fine job with Portia, Adele, that we'd like you to continue that with Jasmine Wills."

Jasmine Wills? She could have spit in Neala's face. Was she going to spend her life chasing spoiled, empty-headed twits?

If it hadn't been for that photo, she'd be free of the group by now. It didn't matter. She still planned to be free, hopefully before she had to produce results on this new assignment. The others might have better jobs, but they had no hope of freedom. They were too indoctrinated in the kumpania's culture of fear to ever leave the kumpania—they'd certainly never have the nerve or the brains to think of actually going to a Cabal and getting a job on their own terms.

For most in the kumpania, that indoctrination began almost from birth. As toddlers, kumpania clairvoyants underwent "the lessons," which instilled a terror of the Cabals so deeply embedded that they'd need only to glimpse a face on the street to start sweating. Instinct would take over and they'd flee or fight, doing whatever it took to escape. By the time Adele got the lessons, though, she'd been six—four years older than kumpania children. They'd given her a healthy fear and respect for the Cabals, but not the gut-level terror the others felt.

"Perhaps we should not be doing this," the super said, huffing as he hurried to keep up with her.

She fixed him with a wide-eyed look and affected a honeyed accent. "Oh, I don't want to get you in any trouble. If you'd like those officers to escort me, I completely understand. But they said it was okay. I don't think they wanted to be disturbed while they ate their lunch . . ."

"I guess if they said it was all right . . ."

"Or you can call Portia's momma. She's awfully upset right now, but I'm sure it wouldn't be too much of an imposition . . ."

His eyes rounded, hands lifting. "No, no. That poor woman. She has been through so much."

"She'll be so grateful to you for helping us out like this."

The portly little man blushed as he unlocked the apartment door. He paused before swinging it open. "Miz Peltier's things should not be disturbed. She is a very nice lady."

Adele touched his shoulder. "I know exactly what it looks like. Poor Portia wore it the last time I saw her, at the breakfast after our cousin's wedding." Adele sighed. "She looked so pretty. That's how I'll always remember her. Miss Peltier was real sweet to dry-clean it for her, but Portia's momma is worried that with all this nasty business, she might not get it back."

The super ushered Adele inside. She'd hoped he'd wait at the door, but the nasty little man kept right on her heels, twittering away about her family's tragedy while making damned sure she didn't mess up his precious tenant's apartment.

She opened the closet.

"Are you sure you know—?" he began.

"Course I do. It's right here."

She grabbed a silk blouse that Portia Kane wouldn't be caught dead in, but looked expensive enough to pass muster with the super. As he bustled her out, Adele looked wistfully at the clothes hamper. Dirty clothing always worked better. But he wasn't going to give her any opportunity to snatch something. She could only hope Robyn was, like her, too frugal to send her blouses to the cleaners after every wearing.

ADELE HAD BEEN IN HER BEDROOM, clutching Robyn's silk shirt and staring at her photo for an hour, and all she knew was that Robyn was in a motel room.

Fucking lot of good that did. She didn't need the gift of clairvoyance to tell her that's where Robyn would be.

She watched the shimmering vision, trying to find a clue to *which* motel. Robyn sat at a computer, posture perfect, blond hair pulled back in a sleek, gleaming ponytail. Even on the run, her clothing screamed young urban professional. It made Adele want to shred the silk blouse with her nails.

It didn't help that she was trying to concentrate while listening to Lily and Hugh having sex in the next bedroom. Adele had grown up planning to marry Hugh. He was five years older than her and she'd been adopted by the kumpania for breeding, so naturally they'd pair her off with the only unmarried male close to her age. The fact that he was big and broad-shouldered and, in the right light, reminded her of a young Hugh Jackman only added fire to her fantasies. As for Lily, she was no competition. A silly ditz who had yet to successfully complete an assignment. Apparently, the kumpania disagreed.

Even after Lily and Hugh married, Adele hadn't given up hope. Kumpania law said that couples had a year to breed. Then they moved to "stage two," and if that ended with no pregnancy, the fault would be presumed to be the woman's. Lily would become a drone, and Hugh would be married off to the next available girl, which would be Adele.

For the last year, Adele had been feeding Lily birth control pills in her morning coffee. Ironic, then, that Adele herself should become pregnant. But when she did, she'd looked at her options and decided, as fine as Hugh was, there was a better life out there for her. Yet she'd kept giving Lily the pills. It never hurt to have a backup plan. The downside, though, was that the longer it took Lily to get pregnant, the harder they tried and the more Adele had to listen to it.

That soundtrack made watching Robyn at the computer all the more frustrating. What the hell was she doing? Her client was dead. She was wanted by the police and there she was, calmly working like it was any other day.

After another fifteen minutes, Adele stood, the vision evaporating. Enough of this bullshit. It was time to take a shortcut.

ON SATURDAYS, sandwiched between their two busiest nights of the week, most of the others slept. There would be activity only in the main building, where the drones worked.

Drones was Adele's word for them. When Neala once overheard her using it, she'd been sentenced to the worst punishment inflicted on kumpania youth: a month caring for the seers.

The drones were those whose clairvoyance never developed enough to take their place as full-fledged members. So they'd been given the menial jobs that kept the community running—cooking, cleaning and caring for the children.

The chores with children were most popular, especially with the women, probably because drones were sterilized—the surgery performed by a human doctor who, like his father before him, was paid very well to service the kumpania and ask no questions.

A drone's offspring were certain to have powers even weaker than their parents' and there were only so many menial tasks to go around. Just last year, when the phuri finally agreed that twelve-year-old Suzanne would never be a true clairvoyant, the leader—their bulibasha, Niko—had declared there wasn't enough work for seven drones. So fifty-four-year-old Lizette, showing signs of rheumatoid arthritis, had quietly passed in her sleep. Everyone knew what had happened. No one complained. It was in the best interests of the kumpania.

Adele snuck out back to the tool shed. She moved aside the barrel in the corner, found the keyhole in the floor and inserted the stolen key. The trapdoor sprang open, steps below disappearing into the darkness.

She turned on her flashlight and started down, closing the hatch behind her. At the bottom, she inserted a second key, then pressed the buttons on the ancient code lock. The lock disengaged, and she opened the inner door and headed down the tunnel.

Inside was the bomb shelter. Or that's what the kumpania had called it in the fifties when they'd taken advantage of nuclear hysteria to hire a group of workmen who thought nothing of building a fully operational shelter under the old farm.

The hum of the generator was the first thing Adele heard. A few more steps and the raucous shouts and musical sound effects of a cartoon seeped through the next door. Tom and Jerry, Adele guessed. That was Thom's favorite.

When she opened the final door, it was still almost dark. They kept the lights low to save generator fuel. The seers didn't complain. They'd never known anything brighter, and would scream in pain if they stepped into the sunlight. Or Thom and Melvin would. For the third, Martha, the world was eternally dark.

Martha's crib lay just inside the door. She reminded Adele of the grubs she'd sometimes turned up doing garden work, white and wriggling, blind and limbless. Martha didn't wriggle much—only when her diaper was dirty and starting to chafe, and she'd twist and mewl, the loudest sound she could make, her white face thrashing back and forth, smooth pits where her eyes should have been. If she got agitated enough, she'd dislodge her feeding tube. When Adele had been sentenced to her month caring for the seers, she'd learned to check Martha regularly or she'd have an extra week tacked on if someone needed to reinsert the tube.

Inbreeding made stronger clairvoyants, but every now and then, a seer was born—a very powerful, deformed clairvoyant. To the kumpania, they were revered as gifts from the gods . . . just not a gift they cared to be blessed with too often. A seer required constant medical care, and the kumpania didn't need more than two or three good ones. Seers were like dishwashing machines, Niko had explained. Having a couple lightened the kumpania's workload immensely. More than that would be an unnecessary expense.

Martha's albinism was one known condition with seers. As for her missing limbs and eyes, Martha's mother had blamed the drugs she'd been taking for morning sickness, their effect made worse by a genetic predisposition to mutations. Or so Niko had told Adele when he brought her down here. She didn't care about the reason for Martha's condition. All that interested Adele was that this slug was the most powerful clairvoyant in the kumpania.

Unlike the other two seers, Martha's brain was unaffected by her condition. Adele had thought about that—what it would be like to spend your life in a crib, sightless, limbless, unable to communicate except through visions.

She'd mentioned that to her kirvi, Lizette—the drone who raised Adele after her mother sold her to the kumpania. Lizette had held Adele and rocked her and comforted her, talking about pity and empathy and the unknowable will of the gods. Adele had listened, and thought Lizette a fool. She didn't feel anything for Martha. No more than she felt for Lizette, smothered in her sleep when she outlived her usefulness.

Her only interest in Martha was in how she might access the powers of that trapped mind, but that secret belonged to the phuri. That was how they guarded themselves against ambitious younger members. Only they could use the seers.

Or so they thought.

She glanced at Melvin, sitting in one recliner, his vacant eyes fixed on the flickering colors of the cartoon. Veggie Boy, she called him, though not in front of anyone. Niko said Melvin was severely mentally retarded. And he wasn't a boy, but a man in his thirties. He looked like a child, though, with his hairless plump body, and his round, smooth, wide-eyed face.

Other than the hairlessness, the brain damage was his only birth defect, but it also made him the weakest of the seers. Adele had heard the phuri debate Melvin's ongoing care, whether he was enough of an asset to warrant keeping alive. But his father was Niko, and while they were supposed to abandon and disavow their blood relations to the seers and drones, as long as Niko lived, so would Melvin.

" 'Dele . . ."

Adele turned to Thom, who watched her with a sloppy smile, his blue eyes glowing with doglike devotion. Just like his brother.

Thom was a year older than Colm, who knew nothing of his sibling. Colm was supposed to have been introduced to the seers at thirteen, but Neala had convinced Niko that under the circumstances, he should wait a few more years. He needed more maturity to prepare for the shock. He was too sensitive, Neala said, blaming his father's genes. Rhys had been a durjardo—an outsider like Adele—who'd introduced fresh blood into the kumpania. It hadn't worked with Thom, but at least they'd gotten a seer out of it.

When Colm and Thom met, there would be no way for Neala to hide who Thom was. His features were so like his brother's, he could be his reflection . . . viewed through a funhouse mirror.

Thom had an oversized head, bulging and misshapen. His chair was specially fitted with a contoured headrest to support it. Unlike the other two seers, Thom could leave his seat, though he needed the help of a walker, as his legs were shrunken and twisted.

He was what Lizette had called "slow." But he wasn't nearly as bad as Veggie Boy and could communicate, though he usually chose not to. The phuri had high hopes for Thom. At sixteen, he was already a more powerful clairvoyant than Niko. In a few years, he might even surpass Martha.

Being able to communicate through speech made him already more useful than Martha. There was no real secret to using his powers. If he granted a clairvoyant access, they could use him. But getting that permission was harder than it might seem.

Here was where Thom and Colm differed. Colm tripped over his feet trying to help others. Thom was mule-stubborn, and when pushed where he didn't want to go, he'd throw a tantrum, locking down his powers, refusing access to everyone.

Fortunately for Adele, though, she'd discovered that Colm and Thom shared something else in common, though it was probably less related to genetics than to teenage hormones. The moment she stepped into view, Thom's sweatpants tented.

She walked over and bent to rub him through the fabric. He made a noise in his throat, like the rough purr of a cat, again reminding her of his brother.

"How are you today, sweetie?" she asked. "Miss me?"

He arched his hips in answer and reached for her shirt front, balling it in his fist and lifting.

She laughed and slapped his hand away. "Not yet."

The purr hardened to a snarl, Thom's eyes narrowing.

"Oh, all right," she said. "Just a little."

She slid her hand into his pants and stroked him. He closed his eyes, that rough purr returning. After a minute, she dropped her fingers to his balls and fondled them.

"Please, sweetie? I really need your help."

One blue eye opened, his lips curving in a smug smile. Thom might be slow, but he had an animal cunning and an ego his little brother lacked. She had to deal fairly with him and let him know how special he was, how much she needed his help and how grateful she'd be for it.

In the beginning, she'd tried to toy with him, as she did Colm. It didn't work. When she'd realized she'd need to follow through, she'd been repulsed by the thought, only her ambition propelling her through those first few times. But she'd gotten used to him, to the point where, if she was being honest, she didn't mind at all.

She'd been well rewarded. It was Thom who'd made her training assignment with Portia Kane such a success. Whenever she'd been unable to get a lock on Portia, she would come to Thom and he'd show her where she was. While Lily struggled with her first assignment, Adele had shot past her, impressing the phuri. Everyone agreed that Adele was the most powerful clairvoyant they'd had in years. Fat lot of good it did her—still destined to wed a boy five years her junior, still given the lousiest—if most profitable—assignments . . .

Yet again it was Thom who saved her. He had, albeit inadvertently, provided her with the treasure that would buy her way out of the kumpania. Now he'd help her safeguard that dream by finding Robyn Peltier.

She settled onto Thom's lap and handed him Robyn's shirt and photo. He held them a moment, then let out a derisive snort.

"Oh, it's too easy for you, is it? I'm sooo sorry. Next time I'll bring you a tough one." She reached down to squeeze his cock. "You're just too good, sweetie. You know that, don't you?"

He didn't answer. He rarely did. She rubbed him, listening to him purr. When she tried to stop, he held her hand in place, making a warning noise deep in his throat. She only laughed and complied for another minute. One final squeeze, then she wrapped her arms around his neck, leaning toward his ear.

"Can I see, sweetie? Please?"

A grunt. Adele closed her eyes and concentrated. After a couple of minutes, the darkness cleared. This was the true gift of the seers. They could not only see better and farther, but project those visions to other clairvoyants.

Again, Adele saw Robyn Peltier. Still at that damned computer.

"Show me more," she whispered. "Help me find her."

With an ease that made Adele ache with envy, Thom pulled his mental eye back and panned the room.

"Slow down," she said, as she took it all in, making mental notes. Then, "Okay, take me outside."

They passed through the door into a parking lot. Adele guided him to the front of the office, noting the name and address.

"That was exactly what I needed," she murmured, lips to his ear. "You're too good, you know that?"

A hoarse chuckle. He knew it very well. And he knew what was coming.

She stood and pulled off her shirt.

ROBYN

When Robyn saw a shadow pass the drawn motel drapes, her first thought, supported by her growling stomach, was "Good. Lunch. Finally." Then she remembered she hadn't ordered any yet.

She'd meant to. She'd picked a meal from the menu, then decided she wasn't quite hungry enough and wanted to check a few more things first.

Hope had set her on the task of researching rumors about Jasmine Wills, anything that might support the theory that she had a grudge against Portia, and that the photo had pushed her over the edge to murder.

Robyn had started with tabloid and gossip column archives. Finding nothing new, she'd moved to message boards and blogs, and that's where she'd become mired in the hate and vitriol posters directed at Portia—a woman they'd never met. She'd been pulled off track, bogged down again, lunch plans forgotten as her hopes of finding helpful rumors were squashed by the sheer number of blatant lies and slander.

Finally she'd stalled on a "Shoot Portia Kane" Web game. She'd been surprised it hadn't been removed in light of the tragedy. Then she'd realized it had been created *after* Portia was killed.

How could someone make such a game? How could people play it? If Robyn wanted a suspect to replace her, she could just post on Craigslist. People would line up, eager to snatch the glory of killing a young woman whose only crime had been to unabashedly enjoy the wealth and social position she'd been born into.

She was still staring at that game when she noticed the figure approach the curtained window. For at least ten seconds the figure stood there, then moved toward the door. Robyn waited for it to appear at the window on the other side of the door. It didn't.

Should she stay where she was? Or run into the bathroom?

When no knock came, she rose, gripping the back of the chair to support herself as she caught her breath. Okay, she was being silly now. A man outside her door? Could it be the one who was sharing her room? Yet even as she tried to convince herself it was Karl, she had only to recall the slender shadow to know it hadn't been.

She took three steps toward the peephole, then stopped, remembering a crime show she'd watched with Damon, where someone looked out his peephole and got his face blasted off with a shotgun.

The figure passed to the other side. Then his shadow started to shrink as he walked away.

Robyn hurried to the peephole. Her view was distorted, but she could tell he had red hair and looked young. She remembered what Hope had said about seeing a red-haired young man at her apartment. Now she flashed back to another figure. Judd's killer. Male, young, a slight build, below-average height . . .

She checked back out the peephole. The man was walking toward the road.

Robyn darted to the nightstand and picked up the phone. Her finger flew to the pad to dial Hope's cell. But what would she say? If Karl drove really, really fast they might catch a glimpse of the guy before he got away?

She'd wanted to play an active role in the investigation, hadn't she? She put down the phone, and quickly changed back into Judd's sweats.

FINN

AFTER SQUASHING THE JUNKIE-COLLEGE-KID LEAD, Finn's day had continued its pattern of failure.

There had indeed been a boy at Robyn Peltier's door. Confirming that hadn't been simple. First, Finn had to be careful explaining how he *knew* there'd been a boy there. He'd claimed it was an anonymous tip from a neighbor who'd taken his card.

The officer admitted to questioning the kid, but he hadn't bothered getting a name because the story checked out and the kid lived in the building. Well, no, he hadn't confirmed that . . . He'd been going to, then an elderly resident had cornered him and started complaining about crime rates and you know how that goes . . .

Finn asked the officers currently on stakeout duty to follow up. Twenty minutes later, one called back to report that there were no kids in apartment 304. The super didn't recognize the description and he swore he knew every boy in his building, because you had to keep an eye on kids that age . . .

So Finn had one teenage boy, nicely dressed, well mannered and well spoken, skilled in lying and picking locks. An odd combination. What did it have to do with his case? An unrelated crime of opportunity? Stealing Portia Kane memorabilia to sell on eBay?

Next came what seemed a bit of luck. The lab had managed to raise the serial number on that gun. It was registered to a private citizen—an eighty-six-year-old great grandmother, who'd reported it stolen two months ago. The gun had likely passed through several hands before killing Kane, the silencer added by one of them. Someone would follow up, but Finn suspected another dead end.

The Philly police had also struck out with Peltier's parents. They were outraged that their daughter was wanted for questioning in a murder. These folks also knew the law. They refused a search without a warrant, and they phoned their lawyer. Though they didn't have the right to insist she be present for questioning, they stalled until she arrived.

Regarding their daughter, they hadn't spoken to her in four days. The police were welcome to review their home and cell phone records. They also provided her address in L.A., her home and cell number, though they must have known the L.A. cops already had all this— trying to look helpful while not revealing anything that was.

As for the friend Finn was seeking, their daughter was twenty-eight years old. They no longer monitored her friends and didn't know most of them. One detective had taken advantage of a bathroom break to scout the main rooms. In the living room, he'd found a hanging photo of two teenage girls. One matched the description Finn had been given. The other was Robyn Peltier.

When confronted, Peltier's mother claimed it was a friend from Robyn's teen years and she couldn't recall the girl's name. The father, though, blew up at the intrusion, ended the questioning and sent the detectives on their way.

They were lying about the friend.

Finn knew there was an easy way to get his answer. He had a source who was certain to know exactly who Robyn Peltier's friend was. But that source had slipped away the moment Finn got on the phone with the Philly detectives.

Finn still hadn't decided what to do about Damon. The cop in him said to cut the guy loose. No matter what special skills Damon could bring to the investigation, the husband of the main suspect was not partner material. But Finn couldn't help thinking that it wasn't a coincidence that he'd gotten this case, the one detective who could speak to the dead.

Finn believed in God. His mother would have nailed his hide to the back shed if he hadn't. In his family, faith was never a question. What was faith in God if not the belief that the soul existed beyond this life, which his family knew with certainty to be true?

There were those who thought such powers came from the devil. His family dismissed that nonsense the way philosophers scoffed at those who saw an eclipse as a sign the world was being devoured by dragons. God granted some people the skills to become doctors to help the living. God had given their family the power to help the dead. It wasn't always conducive to a peaceful life, but no worse than a family doctor, called out on an emergency at 3 a.m.

Since moving to Los Angeles, though, Finn had stopped attending church. He didn't much see the point. Where he came from, the church was the heart of the community. Here, if there was a community, he hadn't found it. Not one he fit into, anyway.

And, Finn had to admit, his faith wasn't what it used to be—he'd seen too much here, spent too many nights sitting up alone wondering what he was doing so far from home, whether it was making any difference, why he'd given himself over to this empty life if he wasn't sure it *did* make a difference . . .

And when he had been questioning that faith, Damon showed up. The first ghost who'd ever come back, let alone stuck around. And he needed Finn's help. Maybe it was coincidence, but Finn couldn't bring himself to tell Damon to get lost. And when he had a way to test him—demand to know the name of his wife's friend—he couldn't bring himself to do that either. Trust didn't come from forcing a man's hand. Damon had to earn it and, if he didn't, Finn had to let him go.

TWO HOURS LATER, Finn was outside Peltier's apartment door. The super was supposed to follow him up, but had been waylaid by a tenant.

"What are you hoping to find?" Damon kept his voice neutral, but Finn could tell it was a struggle. He wanted to tell Finn he was wasting his time, that he should be looking for real suspects.

"I need to find *her*," Finn said. "That's the easiest way to clear her—"

A door clicked down the hall. A woman stepped out. Noticing Finn, she glanced behind him, as if trying to see who he'd been talking to. Finn returned his cell phone to his pocket. She nodded and smiled as she passed.

"Smart move," Damon said. "You're getting better at this."

The elevator doors opened and off stepped the super, with an irate tenant in tow.

"That drain isn't going to fix itself," the bearded man bellowed.

"I will fix it. But first I need to let this policeman into an apartment."

The tenant peered at Finn, nose wrinkling as if he'd caught a whiff of sulfur water. He wheeled on the super, who was unlocking the door. "You'd better not be letting anyone into our apartments without a warrant—"

Finn held up the warrant. The man snatched it.

"An investigation into the death of that Portia Kane?" he said, voice rising. "She was murdered, wasn't she?" He jabbed a bony finger at the super. "If there's been a murder, you'd damned well better tell us."

Finn plucked the warrant from his fingers, pushed open the door and sidestepped through. The super's hand shot up, telling Finn to wait.

"I know my way around." Finn pushed past the super's outstretched hand. "You take care of this."

He slid in before the super could stop him. Damon walked to the window and looked out. Finn started to search. The voices in the hall faded, presumably as the super gave in and went to check the drain.

"I don't know where she is," Damon said after a minute, still looking out the window. "I know that's what you're wondering and I wish I did know, because you're right. She needs to come forward and get this cleared up."

Finn nodded and resumed searching. When he went into the bedroom, he knew something had changed. The closet door was open—it had been closed when he'd been here—every door and drawer shut, bed made, not an item out of place. He checked it out, but couldn't see anything.

He returned to the living room and found Damon still standing at the window.

Finn cleared his throat. "This morning you were going to tell me your story. How you came back."

"I never left." Damon turned around. "After I died, I was standing on the road, looking down at my body, thinking *'Ah, shit, so much for being home in an hour.'* That's what you think, you know. Not *'Holy crap, my life is over.'* Anyway, there I am, thinking of her, and then there's this . . ."

"Light?"

"Sorry. No light. Just a . . . pull. Like when you're deep asleep on a Monday morning and the alarm goes off and you can just barely hear it. I guess I wasn't ready. So I hit the cosmic snooze button."

"So that's it? You want to stay, you stay?"

"It's a little more complicated. I dug in my heels, though. I needed to stay a little while, make sure Bobby was okay."

"Bobby?"

"Robyn. That's what I called her, because—" He shook his head. "Anyway, I stayed to make sure she was okay, only she wasn't."

Damon was quiet a moment before continuing. "The thing about Robyn? She's always in control. Day before our wedding, the bakery calls to say they're overbooked. So what's she do? First she demands a refund and negotiates a free cake for my parents' thirtieth anniversary. Then she calmly reschedules her manicure so she'll have time to bake our wedding cake." His smile faded as fast as it came. "Point is, whatever you throw at her, she can handle it. But this? This was too much. Too sudden. Too senseless. When she couldn't make sense of it, she just . . . shut down."

"So you've been following her. What did you see that night? At Bane?"

"I haven't seen Bobby since she got to L.A. It sounded like a great plan, sticking around, making sure she was okay, but it didn't take long to see some serious flaws in the logic. What if she's not okay? What the hell can I do about it? I can't talk to her, can't touch her. I can only watch her suffer."

He addressed the window again. "Whatever grand power let me stay also ran out of patience. When Bobby came to L.A., I lost her. Eventually I found out she'd taken a job with Portia Kane and, when I got over the shock of that, I figured finding Bobby would be simple—Portia Kane isn't exactly a recluse. But whenever I get close to her, something blocks me. If they can't make me cross over, they're going to take away my reason for staying."

"That doesn't seem to be working out too well."

A flash of white teeth. "Yeah, I'm stubborn. I know Bobby will get better; I just need to see it. So I—"

The super hurried in, breathing hard. "So sorry. He is always complaining. Not like Miz Peltier."

"I think I'm done here. Just one question. The bedroom closet door. It wasn't open when I came through here last night."

"Oh, yes, that was the girl. Miz Kane's cousin."

"Cousin?"

The super explained that Portia Kane's cousin had come by earlier to pick up a shirt Peltier had dry-cleaned for Kane.

"She talked to the other officers. They said it was okay."

The officers hadn't mentioned it to Finn when he'd stopped by their car. An oversight? He doubted it.

"So what did she take?"

"A blouse. A very nice blouse."

"From this closet?"

The super nodded.

"Was it in a wrapper from the cleaners?"

"No. Miz Peltier must have taken it off."

Finn could believe Portia Kane would make her PR rep pick up her dry cleaning. And he could believe Kane's family would send someone to retrieve it after her death, worried their daughter's employee might "forget" to return a valuable item. But for Peltier to put it into her closet with her own clothing after removing the dry-cleaning wrapper?

Finn took out his notebook. "Could I get a description of Ms. Kane's cousin?"

The super looked alarmed. "She asked the officers. They said it was okay. And she was a very nice girl—"

"I'm sure she was and I'm sure she did speak to them. But I need to make a record of it, and you probably got a better look at her than they did."

He jotted down the information. Why would anyone lie to get into Peltier's apartment? If Peltier was holed up with a friend, Finn could imagine that friend sneaking in to get her some clothing. But a single shirt? Or was it something about the shirt? He tried to recall what witnesses said Peltier had been wearing that night. A dress, the one found at Judd Archer's.

He told the super he'd check with the officers and get their details, and ask them not to let anyone else in without an escort. The super got the message: don't open this apartment door again.

FINN'S "PERSONS OF INTEREST" LIST for the Portia Kane case was starting to look like a roster of ghosts. Phantoms, at least.

As he suspected, no young woman had asked the stakeout officers for access, so he had one more nameless description to add to his list, along with Peltier's Indo American friend, her boyfriend and the red-haired teenage boy. Not to mention the most elusive ghost of all—Peltier herself.

Next the team met for another update so Finn could report to brass. When the meeting finished, Finn gathered his papers and headed for the coffee room. It was more of a closet than a room, barely big enough for the tiny table with the coffeemaker. Someone had made good use of the space, though, covering the walls in the safety posters the department was required to post.

He laid the pages on the table, facedown, and reached for a Styrofoam cup. Beside the stack, the ancient drip machine hissed. The quarter-filled pot was so stained it looked as if they'd misread the "auto-stop" feature as "auto-clean," and hadn't so much as rinsed it since buying it.

Finn lifted the pot and swirled the contents.

"Please tell me you aren't going to drink that," Damon said.

Finn sniffed the opening, judging the degree of burning by both the smell and the quantity of floating flakes. He filled his cup halfway.

"Oh, man. Please. There's got to be a coffee shop around."

"Block away. Two bucks a cup." He added creamer. Sniffed. Added more. "Got two hits for Peltier's friend."

Damon stopped eyeing the coffee cup and went very still.

"The one she was at Bane with Thursday night," Finn continued. "I called a buddy at the *Times*. He came up with two journalists matching the description." Finn picked up his pages and showed the top one to Damon. "One's a photojournalist with the *Times*. The other's a copyeditor at *La Opinión*."

Finn waited. It took almost a minute.

"Neither of those is the woman you're looking for," Damon said finally. "Her name is Hope Adams. She's a reporter with *True News*."

ROBYN

Like any couple, Damon and Robyn each had interests the other hadn't shared. Damon loved detective shows; Robyn couldn't see the attraction, but had watched them with him anyway. If someone had asked her whether she'd learned anything from them, she would have laughed and said she barely paid any attention, usually using the time to mentally plan her week's schedule. In the last couple of days, though, she discovered that even if she hadn't been actively watching, obviously she'd learned something.

Today's lesson? Stalking 101.

For three blocks she'd been following the man who'd stopped at her motel door and she'd come to a matching number of conclusions.

One, he wasn't red haired. What she'd seen through the distorted image in the peephole had been a dark red baseball cap.

Two, he wasn't from around here. The fact that he'd walked four blocks in car-obsessed L.A. suggested it. His constant stopping and looking around, as if getting his bearings, confirmed it.

Three, if he was a private investigator, he wasn't very good at his job. Despite all his looking around, he never once glanced backward to see whether anyone was following him. He just strolled along, confident and unhurried.

Robyn *did* look over her shoulder. Repeatedly. She could be following the guy who'd killed Judd and planned to do the same to her. Shut her up permanently.

She bit back a giggle. There was a classic bad movie line. As silly as it sounded, though, to dismiss the idea would be sillier still. She'd seen two people die and even if common sense told her this was more likely a private investigator than an assassin, she wasn't taking any chances.

So she wasn't doing anything as stupid as following this guy down an alley. But there weren't any alleys here. The motel was in some part of L.A.'s endless suburban sprawl. Which part, she didn't know, and blasted herself for not paying better attention yesterday when Karl had driven her in. Around here, though, it was difficult to be on the edge of anything for long and, as Karl had said, it had taken only a short walk before she found herself in a warren of strip malls, three-story walk-ups and offices. A neighborhood in serious need of a planner.

As a place to follow someone, though, it was perfect. She could dart from hiding place to hiding place, keeping her target in sight while never leaving populated areas. It got even easier when the young man bought himself a snack at an ice cream stand and settled in at one of the umbrella tables out front.

He didn't seem to be in any rush to report that he'd found her. She hadn't even seen him pull out a cell phone. Did that mean he wasn't working for anyone else? Or that he wasn't looking for her at all? Maybe he'd been meeting someone at the motel, arrived early and headed out to pass the time.

That was one problem with having watched all those mysteries: she saw too many possibilities. One thing was for certain. The guy looked like he'd be here awhile, having bought a massive banana split and soda. That meant, as much fun as she was having playing detective, it was time to notify Hope and Karl.

As she headed for a pay phone across the lot, she passed a convenience store advertising prepaid cells. Robyn fingered the emergency money Hope had brought from her apartment. Over two hundred. Should she pick up one of those for later? A cheap, untraceable phone?

Untraceable phone? For what? Her new career as a PI?

But as she continued on, watching her target through dark sunglasses, safely disguised in her oversized sweats and baseball cap, she couldn't deny her pulse was pounding, and that her quickening breath didn't come from walking faster.

Maybe it was exhilaration. Maybe it was plain old fear. But she felt something, and that was more than she'd done in months. She imagined what Damon would say.

See, Bobby, that's all you needed—to become a fugitive, a murder suspect and a possible assassination target.

A snorted laugh made an elderly woman warily glance her way.

Robyn reached the phone, put in her money, dialed the number and pulled the cord as far as it would reach, so she could keep an eye on her target without looking too suspicious.

Robyn Peltier, supersleuth. All she needed was the decoder ring.

Hope's phone rang twice before she answered with a tentative hello.

"It's Robyn."

A relieved laugh. "Thank God. I saw a pay phone number and thought the local cranks with alien abduction stories had tracked me down already. It usually takes them—" She stopped. "Why are you calling from a pay phone? What's wrong?"

"Nothing. Well, nothing I can't handle." Oh yeah, one hour on the job and she was bragging already. "There was a guy hanging around our motel room—"

"What?" The alarm in Hope's voice rose. "Did he knock? Try to break in?"

"No, no, he just skulked around." Skulked? She was picking up a new vocabulary, too. "At first I thought it might be the kid you saw last night." Smooth. She thought it was a harmless kid, no need to mention Judd's killer . . . "So I wanted to see where he went."

"You followed him?"

"Carefully."

Ooh, you sound ticked off, Bobby. How dare she question your skulking competence.

She shushed Damon's voice and hurried on assuring Hope that she'd been very careful, staying in public, populated areas.

"Don't worry," she said. "I remember my stranger danger classes." There was a lightness in her voice she hadn't felt in a long time.

As if surprised by Robyn's tone, Hope gave a soft laugh. "Okay, then. Remember, though, just because he hasn't given any sign that he knows you're following him doesn't mean he doesn't."

"I doubt this guy is that good. He keeps looking around, but hasn't so much as glanced over his shoulder."

A pause. "Not once?"

"Never. I bet it hasn't even occurred to him that I could be following. A total amateur. But I promise if he decides to stroll into any abandoned warehouses, I won't follow."

Another small laugh, but this one tight. "This guy, can you describe him?"

"Well, let me tell you, he looks like one dangerous dude." Had she really said dude? "He's maybe five nine, early twenties, skinny, though he's not going to stay that way if he keeps scarfing down mega banana splits."

"What?"

"Banana split. That's what he's eating right now. A totally dangerous guy. He broke off pacing outside my door to go grab some ice cream."

A moment of silence. "Did you notice whether he drove to the motel?"

"I didn't see him until he got to the door. But I doubt it. He just walked four blocks for this ice cream. Maybe we have a PI who lost his driver's license."

Hope didn't answer. Karl said something in the background, too low for Robyn to hear.

"I know," Hope said, voice distant, as if she'd pulled the phone from her mouth. She came back to Robyn. "Stay there, okay?"

"That's what I planned. Like I said, no long walks into abandoned buildings."

"No, seriously. Stay right where you are. If he leaves, abandoned building or not, don't follow him. Don't go back to the motel. Stay put. Do you have an address?"

She gave Hope the name of the nearest store and the street number.

"We'll find it. Now, stay right there."

"In this phone booth?" Robyn tried to sound light, but could hear the edge in her voice.

"No, find . . ."

A murmur from Karl.

"Are you sure?" Hope's voice was muffled, as if covering the receiver. Karl said something else. Then Hope returned. "Karl says if you're comfortable watching him, keep doing that. Just don't—"

"Follow him anywhere. Got it."

"We'll be there in fifteen minutes."

ROBYN

Maybe it was the ice-water splash of Hope's concern, making Robyn feel foolish for her PI fantasies, but the stakeout quickly lost its appeal. She watched the young man eat and drink and eat and drink . . .

Every now and then he'd break the routine to lift his head, not looking around, just tilting his face up, as if checking the weather. Then, while he was scraping the bottom of the banana boat, he stopped, spoon raised. He scanned one way, then the other, chin lifted. It looked like he was . . . sniffing. As if he'd picked up a strange smell and was trying to locate the source.

Robyn took a deep breath and caught the faint whiff of garbage. If he was downwind of that, she didn't blame him for perking up. Probably glad he'd finished eating first.

The young man's lips curved, not in a moue of distaste, but what looked like a smile.

He started to rise, stopped midway and glanced in her direction. For a moment, she swore he was looking straight at her as she pretended to read a real estate flyer. Her heart thudded. Hope had been right. He *had* known—

His gaze swung away and he pushed up from the umbrella table. One last look in her direction, then he set out at a quick stride, heading around the ice cream stand.

He'd known she'd been following him. But how?

The answer was there, a few feet away, her dim reflection in a store window. At some point on the way there, he'd glanced at a window or shiny surface and seen her behind him.

See, Bobby, a true detective doesn't need to look over his shoulder.

That's what Hope had meant, that if he was a professional, he wouldn't be gawking back to check for a tail. At least Robyn could save some face now by not doing something truly stupid, like following to see what had caught his attention.

Ah, you're catching on.

It had been a clever move, pretending he'd seen or heard something, piquing her interest, then hurrying away from the populated area.

Since she was sure he'd made her, there was no reason to hide in the shadows. She folded the flyer under her arm, walked to the ice cream stand, ordered a small vanilla shake, then found a table near where he'd been sitting.

She imagined his surprise when he came back and found his target sitting right out in the open. Then what would he do?

Well, for starters, he could call the police and report seeing a wanted fugitive enjoying a milkshake.

The first sip blasted her stomach and she shivered. In the excitement of playing PI, she'd forgotten her own predicament.

Maybe that's where he was right now—making that call. She was scrambling up when she heard, "There you are."

Hope was weaving through the tables, curls escaping her ponytail, breathing hard, as if she'd run from wherever they'd parked. Robyn glanced past her.

"Where's Karl?"

"He took off after the guy. That was him, right? Red ball cap? Leather jacket?"

"Karl's going after him? I—I don't think it's the kid you guys saw yesterday. After he left, I started wondering if it could have been Judd's killer. That was a young man about his size. You should call Karl. Warn him."

"Karl's careful. He used to do security, remember?"

Robyn had a hard time picturing Karl in a rent-a-cop uniform. No, not a *hard* time—an impossible one. Either he'd done it a very long time ago, or Hope meant a different kind of security, like designing or managing systems. Neither was going to help him in a face-off with a killer.

Maybe Robyn wasn't the only one enjoying this too much, getting overconfident, taking risks . . .

"We'll wait here and let Karl handle it." Hope started moving toward the ice cream stand. "If he needs me, he'll call." She reversed direction, backtracking to the table and setting down her notebook, cell phone on it. "Can I get you anything else?"

Robyn said no. While Hope got in line Robyn glanced at the notepad. She'd love to see what was inside. Maybe if she nudged that phone off, the breeze would blow it open . . .

She shook her head. Like she could read Hope's notes anyway.

"So did you find anything?" she asked when Hope returned with a Coke.

"We're making progress."

"Do I get a hint?"

Hope laughed. "Sorry. I don't mean to keep it a secret. It's just that we're pursuing all these bits here and there, trying to make sense of it all, not knowing what's important. Right now we're still working on identifying the couple in the photo. We've got the man figured out. The girl is tougher."

"Who's the guy?"

"He's—" Hope's head jerked up. Her face went taut. Robyn looked around, seeing nothing out of the ordinary.

"What's wrong?"

"It's Karl. He— You were right. I shouldn't have let him go after that guy." She was already getting to her feet. "Wait here. I'm going to—"

"Go after him?" Robyn rose. "Hope, you can't—"

"I'll be right back. I just need to make sure he's okay." She stepped away from the table, her gaze glued to some distant spot to the east.

"Um, Hope? Cell phone?"

"Oh, right." She snatched her phone and notepad from the table and started jogging away.

"I didn't mean—"

Hope was already out of earshot.

"I meant, why not *use* your cell phone," Robyn muttered. "To *call* him."

She shook her head. Anyone else and she'd have wondered what the hell had just happened, but Hope . . . Hope was different. She hesitated to say that Hope lived in her own world, because that would make her problems sound worse than they were.

She hesitated even saying problems. Robyn thought of Hope's . . . issues more as eccentricities, like people who talked to themselves. The only lingering aftereffect of that teen breakdown was that every now and then, Robyn had the feeling Hope wasn't really there, that she'd slipped off someplace else. Her gaze would empty and she wouldn't hear what anyone said. Or, like now, she'd leap from "Oh, Karl can take care of himself" to "Oh, my God, I have to help him!"

But Robyn wasn't going to sit back and let her friend tear after a potential killer.

As she stood, she noticed a piece of paper on the ground. She picked it up. A printout of the photo Portia had taken. She pocketed it and took off.

ROBYN WAS NOT AN ATHLETE. Had she dared take a fitness test, she suspected she'd score below average for her age, which was as good a reason as any never to subject herself to one.

When the wives of Damon's friends had urged her to join their softball team, she'd demurred until she felt like a snob and a poor sport. So she'd gone out for three games . . . and they'd discovered what a poor sport she really was, and quickly found a replacement.

"Oh, I'm sure you'd be good," they'd said before seeing her play. "Look how skinny you are."

She was not skinny, as she'd pointed out to Damon that night. She was average size. He'd pointed out that, in comparison to some of the other women on the team, she was indeed skinny, but that was beside the point. Just because she wasn't overweight didn't mean she was in good shape, a truth brought home once again as she huffed and puffed running after Hope.

By the time Robyn had made it around the ice cream stand, Hope was disappearing behind a strip mall. Then she'd zipped into an adjoining three-story walk-up lot, then behind that building . . .

Robyn slowed to catch her breath as she watched Hope's ponytail bob in the distance.

How the hell did Hope know where she was going? She hadn't stopped once to look around.

Robyn groaned and kicked it into high gear before she lost her friend completely. She made it around the next building as Hope was cutting through yet another parking lot.

Between the two parcels of land was a chain-link fence. Robyn ran toward it, expecting to see an opening when she drew closer. There wasn't one. The only way around was where the fence ended over a hundred feet away. Hope couldn't possibly have run that far so quickly.

The only option was . . . Robyn looked up at the six-foot fence.

No way.

Exactly how much of this sort of thing did a tabloid reporter do? Obviously Hope led a lot more adventurous life than Robyn had imagined. She felt a pang of something like envy.

As she jogged to the fence, she thought of how much Damon would have enjoyed this. But surprisingly, how Damon would have reacted hadn't been the first thing that popped into her head but, rather, that jab of envy, the fleeting thought that *she* wouldn't mind leading a more adventurous life.

Was that progress?

She paused at the foot of the fence, looking down to the distant end, then up. Hope was long gone. Time for Robyn to take a chance. Do something unexpected.

She grabbed the fence and started to climb.

Soon she was praying that the office behind her was empty and no one was watching her. At one point she was sure going around—even walking—would have been faster, but it was too late, and when she finally did touch down, the surge of adrenaline gave her a much-needed energy boost and she raced off in the direction she'd last seen Hope.

That surge didn't take her far. It couldn't. She ran around the next building and saw an empty parking lot. Beside it was an industrial complex, an interconnected maze of offices, quiet and vacant.

As she walked to the curb, a security car rolled past. The driver looked at her, but only nodded. Apparently, even in sweats, a ball cap and shades, she still didn't fit anyone's image of a thief, much less a fugitive.

Robyn headed into the complex, walking purposefully, a solitary worker putting in weekend hours. The lanes ahead snaked around the buildings and she followed them, looking and listening as she walked. Finally she heard the murmur of a man's voice. She darted to the nearest cover—a shadowy overhang. With her back to the wall, she crept along it until she reached the end and peered around.

Hope and Karl stood twenty feet away on a strip of grass between two buildings. The other man was nowhere to be seen. Hope had her back to Robyn, Karl gripping her upper arms, leaning over her. His voice was a soothing murmur, as if trying to calm her.

Even from where Robyn stood, she could tell Hope was shaking. Karl's grasp seemed to be the only thing keeping her from collapsing. After a moment, he straightened, eyes narrowing as he looked around. His lips parted, then a flash of annoyance as he swiped at his lip. Droplets of red splattered on white siding. Her gaze slid along the wall, seeing more crimson spots. Blood.

Karl shifted position into the light more. Blood oozed from his lip, more smeared across his face. His white shirt was dappled red.

Robyn looked from Hope, shaking with fear, to Karl, covered in blood.

Oh God, what had she done? She should never have let them get involved. It didn't matter that they hadn't asked permission. She let them get involved.

She squared her shoulders, ready to march over there and say "no more." She was going to the police. They couldn't stop her.

She lifted one foot, replayed her speech and realized how it would sound—as if she *wanted* them to stop her. And when they did, she could tell herself she'd tried—if not very hard—to do the right thing.

Doing the right thing meant *doing* it, not talking about it.

Robyn backed away from the corner.

HOPE

Karl rubbed Hope's forearms as she shivered, caught up in the chaos still swirling around her brain.

"Ride it out," he said. "Stop fighting it."

"I have to get back to Robyn."

"You can't let her see you like this."

"I know," she said through gritted teeth. "That's why I'm trying—"

"—to fight it. And that's why I'm telling you not to. Robyn's in a public place, surrounded by people. Look after yourself first." He bent to her ear. "Enjoy it."

He was right, but that didn't make the advice any easier to take. She wanted to be able to say "sorry, bad timing," and move on.

Karl straightened, still rubbing her forearms as he looked around. "Any sign of him?"

He opened his mouth to answer, then scowled and swiped at the blood dripping from his lip, drops spattering the wall beside them. The blow that split his lip was what had brought Hope running. She'd been talking to Robyn and seen the younger werewolf's fist connecting with Karl's jaw, blood spraying, Karl reeling back.

The vision came without any spark of pleasure, more like the blast of a warning alarm, shutting down common sense and sending her flying to his rescue even when she knew he didn't need it. She could only imagine what Robyn thought. Probably still sitting there, shaking her head.

Hope had followed that chaos burst to find Karl alone on this strip of land where he'd fought the werewolf, cursing as he'd tried to clean his bloodied face with a scrap of tissue, his fury and frustration like a beacon guiding her in.

Earlier, as they'd driven past the ice cream stand, it had taken him only one whiff to confirm his fear—that the werewolf he'd smelled earlier had tracked him back to the motel room. Karl had set out in pursuit while Hope went to watch over Robyn. He'd caught up with the other man—Grant Gilchrist, a younger werewolf he'd bumped into a few years before.

The blow to Karl's mouth had knocked him off balance just long enough for Gilchrist to take off. Karl had been about to follow when a security car had turned the corner. By the time Karl could cross, Gilchrist was running through a busy supermarket parking lot where, with his white shirt covered in blood, Karl couldn't follow. The last thing he'd seen was Gilchrist getting into a cab.

So Karl had retreated to clean up. The blood on his shirt and the wall came from Gilchrist. Karl's only injury was the split lip, which bothered him no more than a broken nail. Still, Hope pulled out napkins from the ice cream stand and wiped his injury for a better look, which he withstood with an exaggerated patience that said he really didn't mind being fussed over.

"That's the best I can do." She balled up the napkin. "And it's still not good enough for you to walk around in public. I'll run back to Robyn, make sure she's okay, then grab a shirt at one of the stores. It won't be up to your standards . . ."

"I'll make an exception."

She nodded and jogged off. She didn't look back, but knew he was there, watching over her for as long as he could.

ADELE

Adele stood in the empty motel room and eyed Robyn's laptop as if it was a coiled snake ready to strike.

"What were you doing?" she whispered. "Checking your e-mail? Your stock portfolio? Your horoscope? Or something I should know about?"

Adele wasn't a computer whiz. She could use one for e-mail, banking, uploading her photos . . . A tool limited to what it could do for her, her interest extending no further.

The green light said it was turned on. The screen was dark, though, presumably to save power. Could she turn it back on without a password? If she tried, was there a way for Robyn to know she'd been on her computer?

Adele spent another minute eyeing the beast. There were other things she could search in Robyn's motel room. She hadn't done more than take a cursory look around, her attention snagged by the laptop, its promise making her heart race.

Bold moves, she reminded herself. She had to make the bold moves. Something on this computer had fascinated a fugitive, which was surely more important than anything she'd uncover rifling through drawers.

She touched the keyboard with a gloved finger. The screen lit up, colored lights flashing, and Adele stumbled back. But it wasn't an alarm. Just a Web page advertising computer games.

She stared at it. Computer games? That's what Robyn had been doing?

While Adele could believe Robyn Peltier would calmly play a game, confident that her name would be cleared any moment, she wasn't about to walk away without a more thorough check.

She clicked the browser's back button and was taken to a site about celebrities. This page seemed to be about Portia Kane. She read a few badly spelled messages—she might be homeschooled, but she was a lot better educated than most of these people, she reflected with satisfaction. Most of the messages seemed to be badmouthing Portia, though, so maybe they weren't as dumb as they seemed.

She flipped through more sites Robyn had visited. Some were on Portia, others on Jasmine Wills, and all nothing more than mockery and rumors, people regurgitating and debating what they'd learned from that most unimpeachable news source—the tabloids.

Why was Robyn visiting sites about Portia and Jasmine?

Had she been checking whether there were any final rumors she needed to deal with before moving on to her next PR project? Compiling a final list of news agencies to contact later, and do her final duties, giving the tabloids something nice to say about the dearly departed, suggesting the best photos to use . . .

Photos . . .

Adele minimized the browser and popped open Robyn's e-mail. And there it was, still in her in-box, an e-mail sent from her cell phone to her computer with that damning photo attached.

The message had been read, but didn't look as if it had been forwarded. So Portia had sent the photo to Robyn's cell and Robyn had forwarded it to her e-mail, where she could compile a message for her tabloid contacts. But she'd never gotten that far.

Adele let out a long, shuddering sigh of relief and pressed her hands to her stomach.

We're safe.

Their future wasn't entirely secured yet. There was still a lot to do, including one task regarding the photo: getting it off Robyn's cell phone. There was a good chance she'd already deleted it, and hadn't sent it anywhere except her laptop, but there was still that second picture—the one of Adele in the alley.

She needed that cell phone. Preferably without killing Robyn. Not that she minded the killing, but it complicated things unnecessarily. A simple theft should finish this. And if Robyn had forwarded the second photo, Adele might need her alive to question and figure out what she'd done with it and how to proceed. But she'd worry about that when the time came.

Adele deleted the e-mail.

Would that be enough or should she take the laptop? No. With all that had happened Robyn had probably forgotten the photo. If her laptop vanished, though, she'd know someone had broken in and that something on it had been valuable, probably linked to Portia's death—

A rap at the door.

"Housekeeping!"

Adele shot to her feet. "I'm—"

The rattle of a key in the lock drowned her out. She wheeled toward the bathroom, but the door swung open and an old woman with a nut-brown face and a shock of white hair peered in.

"Is okay? Clean now?"

Adele checked her watch, ready to make some excuse.

"You say after three," the woman said. "Okay now?"

It was 2:45. The woman's timekeeping was as lousy as her English. But the bigger a deal Adele made of it, the more likely the woman was to remember her, maybe report it to her boss.

"Sure," Adele said. "Now's good."

She cast one longing look around the room, wishing she'd searched it before getting sucked in by that damned computer. Other than a trash can overflowing with take-out cartons, the room was as neat as a pin. Even the beds were made. There was no way she could start hunting now and mess things up with the cleaner watching, and the longer she stayed, the more of an impression she'd make.

"I'll just . . . head out," she said as the woman wheeled her cart in. "Let you work in peace."

Adele got as far as the neighboring room when the door clicked open behind her.

"Miss? Miss?"

Adele turned, her lips smiling, legs tensing, ready to bolt. "Yes?"

"Phone ringing."

"Oh, that's okay. They can leave a message."

She waited until the door had almost closed, then darted back and caught it before it locked. "On second thought, I'd better get that."

She walked slowly to the silent phone, giving the person time to finish his message. When the light flashed, she picked up the receiver and retrieved the message. As she listened, her smile grew.

When she hung up, the light continued to flash, message delivery incomplete. That was fine. She'd heard what she needed to know. Better if there was no sign someone had already listened to the message.

HOPE

When Hope reached the rear of the ice cream stand, she slowed her jog to a more respectable fast walk. Her gaze was already on the horizon, scouring the strip malls for stores selling shirts. If the same store sold moist towelettes for Karl to clean up, all the better. She just needed—

Hope stopped. While her gaze was focused beyond the ice cream stand umbrella tables, something about those tables pulled her attention back. Before she left, six of the eight had been occupied. Now, only two were, and Robyn was at neither.

Their two cups were still at their table. At the ice cream stand a single patron waited—a round-faced teenage girl.

No cause for panic. Robyn might have needed to use the bathroom or decided to grab a magazine.

Hope called Karl. He answered on the first ring.

"Small delay." She walked toward their table. "Rob stepped away. Looks like she'll be back in a sec. She left her drink—" She stopped, staring down at Robyn's cup.

"Hope?"

"Her milkshake melted."

"What?"

"She was drinking a milkshake and it doesn't look as if she touched it since I left. It's melted, with a puddle of condensation under it." Hope shook her head. "Probably because she wasn't that interested in it in the first place. Just buying an excuse to sit down. Sorry, I'll stop worrying."

"Do you see a place to buy a shirt?"

"Not from here, but I'll go across the road and take a better look."

"Just grab anything. I'm going to start heading that way."

"You think something happened?"

"No, but I think you'll feel better buying my shirt rather than sitting around waiting."

HOPE BOUGHT KARL A SHIRT and pack of wipes and hurried across the road. An elderly man was clearing their table, shaking his head at the nearly full cups.

"Excuse me," she said. "That's my— My friend was sitting there."

"Not now," he said, wiping the table.

"You work here, right?"

That made him glance up, watery blue eyes meeting hers. "No, I just like clearing tables. A good hobby for an old—"

"Has this one been vacant long?"

"Long enough." He shuffled off.

One last look for Robyn, then Hope strode around the ice cream stand and broke into a jog.

HOPE HANDED KARL A T-SHIRT advertising Coors Light and a box of baby diaper wipes. He didn't comment, just shucked his shirt, wiped himself down and pulled on the new one as she trashed the old shirt and the bloodied cloths.

By the time they arrived back at the tables, they were almost full again. There was still no sign of Robyn. Hope's racing heart hit full gallop. Robyn shouldn't be gone this long. Something had happened.

"He didn't circle back," Karl said as they wove through the tables. She glanced at him.

"Gilchrist. He didn't come back."

That *was* what she'd been worried about, that while they were recuperating in the office complex, the werewolf had returned and lured Robyn away. Whether he'd connected Robyn with Karl, Hope didn't know, but if he did, he might return for her as a way to get at Karl.

"You were sitting here?" he asked, pausing by the table, now occupied by a couple and two young children.

When Hope nodded, he said to the couple, "Excuse me. My wife was here earlier and she dropped her keys. May I take a look under your table?"

The couple backed their chairs out. Karl crouched and checked one side, then the other. A word of thanks, and he put his fingers on Hope's elbow, guiding her toward the stand.

"Two trails for Robyn, both leading this way," he said under his breath. "One coming, one going, I presume."

When people walk, they shed skin cells and hair, which fall to the ground and lay a scent trail. Hope had researched it, looking up how search-and-rescue dogs track so she'd understand what Karl could and could not do. He wasn't comfortable with questions about what he considered one of the more undignified aspects of being a werewolf.

Canines tracked two ways. One was by air scent, which led straight to a person if he was still around. The other was ground scent, which told where someone had been. What ground scent couldn't tell Karl, though, was which of two recent trails was fresher.

As they drew close to the ice cream stand, he paused. From Karl's expression, Hope knew the trails had grown fainter, meaning he'd veered off course. Short of sniffing the ground, though, it was difficult to find exactly where they'd diverged.

She looked up at the menu board and absently reached into her pocket. She pulled out her change, letting it fall, clinking on the pavement and rolling away.

"Oh, of all the stupid—" she began.

"I've got it."

He knelt, sniffing nearer the ground as he gathered her scattered coins. When he rose, he bent to hand them to her and said, "One goes to the left, through the parking lot. The other heads right, around the back of the stand."

"The second is the way Gilchrist went earlier," she said. "And the way I went."

"Then that's where we'll go."

ONCE PAST THE STRIP MALLS, Robyn's trail became easier for Karl to follow, partly because he could stoop and sniff and partly because they'd figured out where she'd been going—following Hope. When Hope had run to see Karl, she'd checked for a tail a few times, but had been too anxious to do a decent job. If Robyn had stayed a reasonable distance away, Hope would never have noticed.

Robyn's trail ended at the corner of a building. Looking around it, Hope saw the spot where she'd waited out her chaos rush with Karl.

"She saw me," Hope said. "Dammit. What did she think? I must have looked—"

"She didn't see your face, not from this angle. You had your back to her. What she saw was me . . . and a lot of blood."

"Shit! She must have panicked and—" Hope shook her head. "No, not Robyn. She doesn't rattle that easily."

Karl said nothing, but his expression disagreed. The old Robyn would have seen blood and marched over to help. But she hadn't been herself since Damon's death. After witnessing two murders, had seeing Karl covered in blood been too much?

Or had something caught her attention? Lured her away?

Karl followed her trail. This time, it didn't cling to the shadows. She'd made a beeline for the road, crossed to a gas station and headed into a phone booth.

"It ends here," Karl said, crouched in the lot.

"She called a cab."

"That would be my guess."

"So she sees you bleeding, finds the nearest phone booth and calls a cab . . . Where? Back to the motel?"

Hope checked her cell. No missed calls. Maybe Robyn had run out of change and decided to call from the motel.

She hoped so. Otherwise, she had no idea where her friend had gone.

WHEN THEY ARRIVED AT THE MOTEL, Hope leapt from the car while Karl was still parking it. A cleaning woman near their motel room shrank back behind her cart, then relaxed as Hope pulled out her key, as if the cleaner had thought she was racing over to demand extra towels.

Hope opened the door. Their room was empty.

She remembered the cleaning woman. Had she been in here? Hope had told her to come after three, so she could get Robyn out first.

"Excuse me!" she called as she hurried back outside.

The cleaning woman's shoulders tightened, but she didn't turn, as if praying Hope wasn't hailing her.

Hope jogged up beside her. "The room looks great. I just wanted to give you this."

Hope passed her a five. She looked at it, still in Hope's outstretched hand, her sunken eyes wary.

"Really, thanks," Hope said. "I appreciate you coming later for us."

The woman took the money.

"Oh, and before you go. Did you see another woman in my room? My friend was supposed to meet us there."

"Friend . . . ?" She shook her head. "English no good."

Hope switched to Spanish and repeated the question as best she could, though her Spanish was probably worse than the woman's English. Karl came up behind and took over. His international jobs meant he had a working knowledge of about a half-dozen languages.

Karl translated on the fly. There had been someone in their room when the cleaner arrived. A young woman with shoulder-length blond hair, who'd left right after the cleaner arrived. She'd seen her get into a cab a few minutes later.

Hope thanked her. As the woman pushed her cart away, Hope checked her watch. It was 3:15. "Fifteen minutes to clean our room? I think I overtipped." They headed back toward their door. "But I guess that means I can relax. Wherever Rob went, she won't expect the cleaning to be done for a while, so I'll take advantage of the wait and make a few calls."

As Karl opened the door, Hope noticed the light on the bedside phone blinking. "Oh, we have a message. Let's hope it's Robyn."

It was. And she *was* calling to explain where she'd gone. But it wasn't "to the corner for a coffee."

ROBYN

Robyn's resolve took her within a hundred yards of the police station, then sputtered out. She'd spent the last twenty minutes in a coffee shop, steeling herself for the next step while savoring a vanilla latte like it was her last meal. Maybe, if she was feeling particularly adventurous, she'd follow it with that monstrous slice of Irish cream cheesecake taunting her from the display.

You're a wild woman, Bobby.

She smiled, felt the first prickle of tears and blinked them back. Damon wouldn't want her feeling sorry for herself. He'd expect her to have that cheesecake, fortify herself with sugar and caffeine, and march over to that police station. Well, minus the cheesecake part, but he'd get a kick out of that.

The bell over the café door tinkled and she glanced over. She had looked every time it rang, expecting to see Karl, mysteriously tracking her down again.

By now Hope would have listened to her message and, while Robyn hoped she'd accepted her decision, she knew better. Hope would try to find Robyn to change her mind. She'd expect her to go to the nearest police precinct, so Robyn had made sure not to choose that one or the one where Detective Findlay worked.

The two new arrivals walked in and her heart thudded as she saw their police uniforms. The fear only lasted a moment. Earlier a couple of officers had come in and looked right at her. They hadn't pulled their guns. Hadn't phoned for backup. Hadn't even given her a second glance. Just ordered their coffees and left.

When these two had their coffees, the younger one noticed her, then looked again, his pale brows knitting. His partner bumped into him, jostling his arm, coffee bubbling over the lid. The young officer cursed and grabbed a napkin, and they continued on their way, exchanging jibes.

The younger officer didn't look back, her face already forgotten. It would probably resurface later, when he saw her picture somewhere and the lightbulb went off. By then, she'd already be in custody.

She went up and ordered her cheesecake. While the server was getting it, Robyn pulled out what she thought was money, and it turned out to be the printout of the photo.

The cheesecake arrived and Robyn returned to her table, photo still between her fingers. She smoothed it, then stared at it as she ate.

The young woman behind Jasmine looked familiar. She hadn't noticed it when Hope first showed her the picture. In truth, she hadn't really looked at the girl at all. Hope thought the man was the important one, and the girl was just a poor kid seduced by some bigwig. Another victim in this ugly mess.

It didn't help that the girl wasn't exactly memorable. Average height. Thin, even skinny. Plain-faced. Straight, dishwater-blond hair. Robyn hated that term—*dishwater blond*. Even worse than dirty blond. She preferred dark blond. But for this girl, Robyn hated to admit, dishwater blond was most accurate. A dull, common color on a dull, common-looking girl.

And it was that description that jolted her memory so fast her fork fell, clattering against the plate, a chunk of cheesecake bouncing off. Robyn *had* seen this girl before.

When Robyn had started working for Portia, her first self-assigned task had been repairing her client's image problem with the media. She would start by identifying those members of the paparazzi who took the most damaging photos of Portia. Then she'd train Portia how to be on the lookout for them. Presumably, once they realized they weren't going to get a juicy photo, they'd go in search of less media-savvy targets, leaving only those paparazzi who didn't mind selling photos of Portia helping in soup kitchens or attending charity events.

A lofty goal. And it proved how little Robyn had understood her new job. While there were tabloid photos Portia would rather not see, soup kitchen photos didn't make tongues wag. As Oscar Wilde once said, the only thing worse than being talked about is *not* being talked about. For the celebutante on the rise, rumor and innuendo were the helium that kept her fragile balloon afloat.

Understanding none of this, Robyn had doggedly pursued her course. She'd scoured back issues of the tabloids, digging up the worst pictures and noting the photographer. One name topped the list. Adele Morrissey.

Adele seemed to be able to find Portia anywhere, in any disguise, snapping pictures of her cuddling with a male stripper while all the other paparazzi waited at the charity function Portia was scheduled to attend. Unable to find identifying information on Adele, Robyn had asked Portia to point out the woman. Portia had laughed. She could barely remember the names of her house staff. She certainly wasn't going to learn those of the paparazzi.

Undaunted, Robyn soon discovered why Adele Morrissey was able to snap photos, anywhere, anytime, undetected. Apparently the woman was a ghost. She didn't exist in any records, and no one in the business seemed to know who she was.

Everyone presumed it was a pseudonym. Some speculated it was one of the more notorious paparazzi, using the fake name to shelter income from a bookie or third wife. Others were convinced it was a plant on Portia Kane's own staff.

Eventually, Robyn gave up her hunt for Adele Morrissey. Even if she did manage to force Adele to cease and desist, she might actually be fired for ending Portia's best source of exposure.

Still, Robyn would find herself scanning the crowds around Portia, ticking off the names of the photographers she knew, hoping to narrow it down and identify Adele, if only to satisfy her own curiosity.

Finally, Robyn thought she'd solved this particular mystery. Portia had been still dating Brock Masters, who'd wanted her to stop seeing other guys. When an old flame returned from a year in Paris, Portia wanted to see him. Purely platonic—she really had been crazy about Brock. So she'd had Robyn arrange a secret lunch at an obscure diner near San Clemente.

Portia had insisted Robyn accompany her. She'd said she wanted to go over her schedule, but Robyn knew she just wanted company on the hour-long drive. Once there, Robyn sat across the restaurant, eating alone. Then she'd seen another, younger woman also eating alone.

It'd been a total fluke that Robyn noticed her at all. The girl had been reading a medical thriller by an author Robyn's brother liked. Robyn always made a point of grabbing the author's latest hardcover for the cash-strapped med student, so she'd noted it in her PDA and continued eating.

Later, when a photo of Portia eating with her ex appeared in *True*

News, credited to Adele Morrissey, Robyn made no connection to the girl reading in the diner. But then, at a movie premiere, she'd seen the same young woman in the crowd.

Robyn had pointed her out to Portia, suggesting that might be Adele. Portia had laughed so hard she'd nearly choked.

"Does that *look* like an Adele to you?" she'd said as the girl bounced on her tiptoes, watching the limos arrive. "Anyone named Adele has got to be, what, fifty? That's more of a Beth. No, Bethany. Mousy little Bethany."

"But she was at the diner—"

"Well, she must have followed me, then. It's just another pathetic groupie, studying what I wear, what I eat, how I walk, hoping to copy it and be like me. As if."

It still bothered Robyn. But no photo by Adele Morrissey appeared after the movie premiere, and even if Robyn found Portia's argument about Adele's name facetious, she had to admit that this girl, barely out of her teens, was too young to be a top-notch paparazzo.

And Portia was right about one other thing—the girl *was* mousy, with dark blond hair cut in no particular style, clothing that didn't really suit her coloring or her figure, and eyes that dipped away whenever they were in danger of meeting someone else's. Now, seeing this photo and thinking the same thing, Robyn realized her mistake. She *had* seen Adele Morrissey. And now she was seeing her again.

Adele had obviously been following Portia, probably dining in the same restaurant, camera hidden, waiting for Portia to do something or meet someone inappropriate. And the man with her? Maybe a tabloid bigwig, hoping for an exclusive contract with the talented Ms. Morrissey. That was ballsy, having lunch while "on the job" tailing Portia. Or maybe it was brilliant—what better way to prove to a prospective client or investor that she could get so close to her target and not be made as a paparazzo?

So Adele and this guy had been leaving the restaurant shortly after Portia. They'd been passing Jasmine Wills—maybe accidentally, maybe intentionally—and Portia, in the car, snapped a picture.

And then . . .

That's the case-breaking question, isn't it, Bobby? What happened next?

Robyn closed her eyes and pictured that dark hall at Bane. She heard a moan. Then footsteps. Light footfalls. A slender figure with light hair . . . one that could pass for Adele Morrissey.

Did Adele see Portia snap the photo and freak out because *she* was supposed to be the one behind the camera? That was crazy. No one would kill for that.

Robyn thought of her scrapbook, filled with stories of senseless death, ones that made you shake your head and say: "That's crazy. No one would kill for that." But they had.

Still, there had to be more to it, a motivation she was missing.

Motive is secondary, Bobby. Follow the clues. Find the who and the how, then worry about the why.

She stood and moved to the window, looking outside for a pay phone. This time, she was out of luck. She walked to the counter instead and asked to use their phone. She called information first, and got the office number for *True News*. Being a Saturday, there was only one person in the small office. Fortunately, it was an editor.

"Hello," Robyn said. "This is Monica Douglas. I represent Jasmine Wills."

The editor obviously recognized the name, and asked how Jasmine was doing, in light of the recent tragedy. Robyn could picture him, pen poised, straining for a juicy sound bite on Jasmine's reaction to Portia's murder. Robyn gave the standard line about what a tragedy it was and how devastated her client was.

"I'm calling about Adele Morrissey," she said. "I believe she sells photos to you."

"Adele, yes. Of course. Excellent photographer. And another person who will feel Portia's death, no doubt. She was Adele's favorite subject."

"That's actually why I'm calling. Jasmine is something of a fan of Ms. Morrissey."

"Oh?"

Robyn laughed. "Well, she did get Portia a lot of page space, if not exactly the sort I'd endorse . . ."

"Yes, of course."

"With poor Portia gone, Jasmine thought Ms. Morrissey might be interested in a new subject, particularly a more willing subject."

"Ah, I see."

"Jasmine insists I set up a meeting with Ms. Morrissey as soon as possible, but I'm having a horrible time tracking down contact information."

The editor chuckled. "Yes, she's elusive, our Adele."

"I was hoping you could help." She paused. "Jasmine would be very grateful."

In other words, they'd owe him a hot exclusive.

A moment's silence, then the editor cleared his throat. "I'd love to, but when I say 'elusive,' I'm not exaggerating. We don't have contact information for Ms. Morrissey. She calls us when she has a photo and we wire the payment. I've never even met her."

"Oh, that is unfortunate. I'd really hoped—"

"But I'm sure she'll call in soon. I could relay a message then, asking her to contact you."

"Would you? That would be wonderful. Have her call my office." She gave the number on the café phone.

She signed off and hung up. It had been worth a shot. And if the editor wasn't being entirely honest, Robyn was sure his weird-tales reporter could dig up the information. Once Hope knew she was looking for a paparazzo who sold to *True News*—

Robyn's finger froze on the keys. She flashed back to that office complex, Hope shaking with fear, Karl covered with blood.

It didn't matter that Robyn knew who the girl in the photo was. Their investigation was over, and she sure as hell wasn't tossing Hope another lead, then traipsing off to the safety of a police station.

She stuffed two dollars into the tip mug, and thanked the server for letting her use the phone before heading back to her table.

This Adele Morrissey lead wasn't going to anyone except Detective Findlay. She'd show him the photo and say she recognized the young woman as Portia's paparazzo stalker. If this detective was as good as Judd had claimed, he'd run with it. No one ever needed to know that Hope and Karl had been involved.

Robyn took one last mouthful of cheesecake, washed it down with a swig of latte, then strode to the door.

ADELE

Adele closed her eyes as she fingered the silk shirt folded inside her jacket pocket. She caught a vision of Robyn Peltier sitting in a café across the road, as she had been the last two times Adele checked. The first time, Adele had been in a cab, racing toward the nearest police station when she'd seen Robyn at the table. She'd spotted the café name on a napkin, and had realized Robyn was miles away, near a different station.

Now pretending to read, she sat on a bench between the café and the police station where she presumed Robyn would head when she got around to it.

Adele had no idea why Robyn would pick this particular station. She must have known someone there and hoped for special treatment. As for why she'd stopped in a café first, maybe she was waiting for advice from that cop friend. And in the meantime, she might as well kick back and enjoy a coffee and some cheesecake—

Adele stopped. By the gods where had that cheesecake come from? How long did Robyn plan to camp out there? Adele slumped, the book nearly sliding from her fingers.

She closed her eyes and found the vision again. Robyn was digging into the cheesecake as she folded a piece of paper. Adele bet it was a surrender speech. Someone as perfect as Robyn Peltier couldn't even turn herself in without rehearsing.

Adele released the vision and turned the book page.

The situation wasn't ideal—a busy street on a weekend afternoon,

cop shop within shouting distance—but she had a plan. She'd intercept Robyn and ask to use her cell phone. It hadn't worked with
Portia, but Robyn wouldn't want to raise a fuss so close to the station
because if she brought a cop running, she'd lose any brownie points to
be gained by turning herself in.

If anything went wrong, well . . . Adele patted the bulge under her
jacket.

Adele glanced at her watch. How much longer was she going to
stay in there? Adele touched the shirt again, focused and found
Robyn. She was on her feet, finally, at the counter, shoving bills into a
mug labeled Tips.

Okay, Robyn, you've done your duty. Now move your ass . . .

Robyn returned to the table and, still standing, sliced off a chunk
of cheesecake, then lifted it to her mouth.

By the gods! Was she thinking of all those starving kids in Africa
who didn't get enough cheesecake? Pack it up and send it to them!

The vision clouded, and for a moment, Adele saw one of Robyn
Peltier in an alley, sprawled on the ground, blood pooling around her.
She smiled. Too bad clairvoyance didn't grant the gift of prophecy, because she'd love to see that image in person—a fitting payback for the
crap Robyn had put Adele through.

The café door opened. Out stepped Robyn Peltier. Good. If only
she didn't decide she needed a damned pedicure on the way.

Robyn didn't seem inclined to stop for anything. She came out that
door and strode, purposefully . . . in the opposite direction.

Robyn stopped at the light and waited for the signal, even as jay-
walkers jostled past her, taking advantage of the gaps in traffic. When
the light changed, she crossed, chin lifted, posture perfect, walking
like she was on her way to an important business meeting, elegant and
poised even in ill-fitting sweats and a baseball cap.

Adele stopped grating her teeth and pictured Robyn in prison garb
instead. Cheered, she got into position behind a trio of teenage boys
who looked like they weren't going anywhere for a while. Robyn
drew closer, closer . . .

Adele stepped into her path. Robyn pulled up short, her eyes going
to Adele and widening, as if shocked to see someone there.

"Can I borrow your phone, ma'am?" Adele gave a sheepish smile
and waved her cell. "Mine's dead and I really need to tell my dad
where to pick me up."

Robyn kept staring.

"Ma'am?"

Robyn's lips parted and she said a single word swallowed by a laugh from the teen boys. It sounded like "cell."

"Right, I need to borrow a cell phone. Can I use yours? I swear it's not a long-distance call."

Robyn stared at Adele as if she was a beggar asking for her last buck. Adele glanced down at Robyn's side. No purse to snatch. Damn, the phone must be in her pocket.

Adele stepped closer. "Please. I *really* need to call my dad."

She reached down and pulled her jacket open. Robyn inhaled sharply as she spotted the gun.

"Your cell phone?" Adele met her gaze.

Robyn's hand slammed into Adele's chest, knocking her into the boys. She smacked into one and he shoved her back. She stumbled, recovered and wheeled to see Robyn disappearing down the alley.

In that moment, as she tore after her, she saw Robyn's lips move again, heard that single word and knew what it had been.

Adele.

FINN

IN TWENTY MINUTES, Finn would meet Robyn Peltier's elusive friend, and he wasn't looking forward to it.

At first, she'd seemed surprised by his call, but that quickly passed, as if he'd caught her off guard and once she considered it, wasn't so surprised after all. She'd agreed to come to the station right away and talk to him. And, yes, she'd bring her boyfriend—he was with her already.

So it wasn't the prospect of a hostile interview making his stomach sour. He could chalk it up to the coffee. He hadn't meant to drink all of it, but the more he sipped, the more disgusted Damon got, until the ghost finally went his way, leaving Finn alone to research his upcoming interview without his input.

It was the research that made him dread the interview. Hope Adams wasn't a celebrity-chasing tabloid reporter. He should have guessed that when he discovered she was on a transfer from *True News*'s Philadelphia headquarters—a city not known for its glitterati.

Adams chased another kind of target, one just as entertaining and just as elusive—supernatural encounters. As a guy who could *be* one of her targets, the idea made him mildly uncomfortable. But only mildly . . . at first.

The more he dug into Adams's career, the more that feeling grew.

She'd been at her job since graduating from college. She couldn't expect to start out on the staff of the *Philadelphia Inquirer*, but to be in the same job now suggested there was a reason she'd been twenty-three before she graduated.

So Adams could be written off as a hack. Or, considering her background, more like that college druggie he'd interviewed—a rich kid slacking her way through life.

That had settled his worries . . . until he read a half-dozen of Adams's articles. Her writing was on par with big-paper journalists and, unlike most of them, she was entertaining. On the surface, her pieces were breezy and fun, the language uncomplicated and informal, yet beneath that, she'd obviously done her research.

She took her job seriously, but not earnestly. If readers didn't believe in the paranormal, they could interpret that light tone as "we both know there's no such thing as vampires, but sit back and let me tell you a good story." If they did believe, though, there was nothing condescending. She never talked down to her readers, and she treated her sources and witnesses with respect. If you knew, like Finn, that the paranormal wasn't pure fiction, then you could come away with the sense that, maybe, just maybe, she believed, too.

By the last article, Finn was as nervous as a corrupt politician about to meet a journalist specializing in exposés. He knew he was overreacting. Adams was here to *be* interviewed. He had nothing to worry about . . . unless she'd done her research on him as well, and learned of his reputation.

He was reading an article about a haunted inn in Vermont when he got a call. Someone had recovered Robyn Peltier's cell phone from a pawn shop earlier. It had now been processed for prints, and those prints matched a set on the gun.

Right now, Finn was more interested in getting a look at Robyn's cell phone, which the techs said came with a personal organizer. Contact names, schedule, notes . . . there had to be something of interest there.

He'd made it as far as the hall when Jane peeked from the front.

"Finn? That *True News* reporter is here to see you. Hope Adams?"

He waved for Jane to send her back.

"Hope Adams?" a detective said behind him, looking up from his work. "I talked to her a couple of years ago. I was investigating a kidnapping. She was investigating it, too . . . as a possible alien abduction."

A wave of laughter from the room.

"Hey," someone called. "What's she want with you, Finn? A feature?"

More laughter. Finn shut the door to the detectives' room as Jane rounded the corner, followed by a couple. Finn introduced himself, then quickly got them into an interview room.

• • •

FINN DIDN'T GET PAST the preliminary questions before realizing he didn't need to worry. Adams was no ruthless reporter. Maybe it was just the circumstances—her concern for her friend overriding her journalistic instincts—but Finn couldn't imagine *ruthless* was ever a term applied to Hope Adams.

Living in L.A., Finn had learned not to be dazzled by a pretty girl. Adams had an easy, offhand beauty that asked you—politely, he suspected—to pay it no heed. So he didn't. He tried, too, not to let her size make an impression. She was small and fine-boned, with an air of fragility. There wasn't any fragility in her manner, though. She was steady and articulate, answering every question concisely and completely. Cooperative without tripping over herself to prove it. In short, the perfect witness.

The boyfriend—Karl Marsten—was another matter. His good looks came with the polished sheen and casual arrogance Finn was more accustomed to in L.A. Without so much as a word, he made it clear that he considered this interview a waste of his afternoon. Finn could deal with that. It was the hard edge underlying the casual arrogance that got under his skin.

Again, it was all in the body language. Marsten took the chair directly across from Finn. While Adams talked, Marsten leaned slightly forward, like a lawyer getting between the detective and his client, his cold stare telling Finn he'd damned well better watch his step or this interview was over.

When he'd first taken that chair and fixed Finn with that stare, Finn had inwardly groaned. He'd seen this before. The guy who "protected his woman" by not letting her get a word in edgewise. But Marsten simply stood guard, never interrupting. Even when Finn fished outside the boundaries, he only got a warning look from Marsten, as if he knew Adams could handle it. And she did, deftly avoiding anything that smacked of speculation.

While they were talking, Damon slipped in. He said nothing, just stood off to the side, listening. Adams finished relaying her account of the night Portia Kane died, then came the big question: "When's the last time you spoke to Robyn?"

Adams's gaze shifted to Marsten, and Finn knew that night at Bane hadn't been her last contact with Robyn Peltier. The lies were about to begin.

"An hour and a half ago."

Finn blinked and repeated the question, sure he'd misheard.

She checked her watch. "Ninety-five minutes. I'd looked at the time just before I got her message, because I was wondering how long the maid had been cleaning our room." She paused. "I suppose that's what you meant—when's the last time we had contact. I didn't speak to her, though. She just left a message where we'd been staying, saying she was on her way here."

"Here?"

"To the police station. To turn . . ." Adams let the sentence trail off, her eyes meeting his. "She *is* here, right? That's why you called. We were at Bane together, so she gave our names to back up her story . . ." Seeing his expression, her hands tightened on the chair arm. She twisted to Marsten, but he was already leaning toward her, his fingers on her forearm, murmuring under his breath. When he turned on Finn, his voice wasn't nearly as gentle.

"Robyn was turning herself in. If she's not at *this* station, I'd suggest you start making calls."

Finn looked at Damon, who uncrossed his arms and straightened, worry darkening his eyes.

Finn excused himself and stepped out.

HE RETURNED TEN MINUTES LATER to a quiet room. Too quiet, as if they'd heard him coming and stopped talking. He glanced at Damon, but he was lost in his thoughts.

"Ms. Peltier hasn't turned herself in to any precinct or any officer," Finn said as he sat. "That may have been her intention, but when it came to doing it . . ." He shrugged. "It wouldn't be easy."

"I guess not," Adams's admission came slowly, her lashes lowered. "If we're done here, Detective . . ." She started to rise.

"I have a few more questions."

As she sat, Marsten glanced at his watch. "Is it really necessary for us both to be here?"

If Marsten hadn't noticed anything at the nightclub, then there was nothing he could tell Finn that Adams couldn't, and there might be a few things she'd say without her boyfriend around. So he sent Marsten on his way. As he was leaving, though, Finn discreetly gestured for Damon to follow.

"When's the last time you saw Robyn?"

"I last *saw* her Thursday night, when we left Bane."

"And spoke to her?"

"Earlier this afternoon. She called from a pay phone to let me know she was okay and ask for advice. I wanted to meet, but she didn't want to get me involved. When I insisted, she hung up. We went back to our hotel, and that's when we got the message."

"And before that? Had you spoken to her since Thursday?"

Adams shook her head. "I tried calling her cell Friday morning, after I saw the paper. Some guy answered. I think he'd found the phone. Anyway, that freaked me out, so I phoned her apartment and left a message. She didn't return it. It's probably still on the machine."

"And then?"

"I went into the office for an hour, just doing paperwork. I usually spend Fridays writing from my place, but I wanted to stop by, in case she tried calling me there. I kept hoping she would. But she didn't until this afternoon."

FINN WALKED HOPE ADAMS to the front desk and thanked her for her time. As he watched her leave, he saw Damon on the front steps. So much for following Marsten.

"Lost him?"

Damon turned, startled. "Ah-ha. Now you're the one sneaking up on me. Payback's a bitch, huh?" His words were light, but no humor reached his eyes.

"I thought I asked you to follow him," Finn said under his breath.

"I did. He went outside."

"I meant follow him wherever—"

"I *did*."

He pointed. Finn followed his finger to see Marsten striding over to meet Adams, thirty feet from the precinct steps.

"That's as far as he went," Damon continued. "He made three phone calls. For the first two, no one must have answered because he seemed to be leaving a message. I got as close as I could, but with the noise out here, I didn't hear much. He's one guy who lowers his voice on a cell, instead of raising it, and while I'd normally appreciate such consideration, it really didn't help for eavesdropping."

Finn watched Adams and Marsten. His hand rested on her back, rubbing it. Reassuring her again, as he had in the interview room.

"You said he made a third call?" Finn prompted.

"Someone answered and they talked for a few minutes. It sounded like business. If you'd like me to speculate on what kind of business . . ."

"Go for it," Finn said, still watching the distant couple.

"My guess is he called his lawyer. There was some definite legalese going on. As for what, I can probably speculate on that, too . . ."

Finn motioned for him to get on with it.

"I don't know Karl that well. He'd only been dating Hope for a few months before I got shot, and I could tell he was never going to be hanging out on my couch, chugging beer, watching the game. But I got a decent feel for the guy. He acts smooth, but he's hard as nails. Guys like Karl know their rights and they don't give an inch, innocent or not. He'd contact his lawyer to find out what his obligation is, and he'll give you that much, no more. Anything remotely approaching harassment? You'll be talking to his lawyer. And if he thinks you're harassing her—" He nodded to Adams. "Watch out. That's not a guy you want to cross."

Marsten had straightened and was scanning the street, as if looking for a taxi. He glanced toward the steps. Their eyes met. Adams turned, following his gaze. She said something. Marsten shook his head and responded.

"What did they talk about earlier?" Finn asked.

"Hmm?"

"When I left the room to make those calls. What did they say?"

"Nothing."

He turned to Damon. "She just found out Robyn hadn't turned herself in. They had to say—"

"Zip. They aren't stupid, Finn. They knew that room was wired for sound. When you left, Karl told her not to worry, he was sure it was a mistake. She leaned over and said something. He nodded. End of conversation. And what she said, I'm sure, is 'Watch it, that detective could be listening.' "

Adams and Marsten were walking away now, ignoring passing taxis, presumably heading to a parked car.

"So do you think your wife lost her nerve?" Finn asked. "Couldn't turn herself in?"

He blinked his worry away, then said, softly, "No."

"Neither do they."

Finn headed down the steps.

"Where are you going?" Damon called.

"Wherever they are."

HOPE

A necromancer?" Karl said as they got into the car.

"That's what I was trying to say in the interview room, when I said we shouldn't talk. I'm sure there was a microphone, but I also think Detective Findlay had another kind of listening device. A ghost."

"So he's a necromancer."

She nodded. "I caught the warning vision when we met Findlay in the hall, but it was so weak it took me a while to figure out his type. Even then, because it was weak, I thought it was someone else in the building. I picked up mild chaos vibes when I got in the room, and I caught a few snippets of his thoughts, enough to tell me *what* was bothering him. Me. My job."

"A reporter."

"A paranormal investigative reporter."

"Ah." Karl pulled from the parking lot.

"The third and final clue? He kept glancing toward the door."

"I noticed that. I thought he was expecting a partner to join us."

"So did I. But he was looking a little too long, like he was watching or listening. I've spent enough time with Jaime Vegas to recognize that look—a necromancer with a ghost in the room. Like when Eve's around—Jaime can't help looking her way, listening to her. She's better at hiding it than he is, though."

"So we have a necromancer homicide detective assigned to Portia Kane's murder? A murder involving the Nast Cabal?"

"I agree. When there's a Cabal involved, there's no such thing as coincidence."

"Your mind-reading skills are improving."

"No, just my Karl-reading skills."

He checked the mirrors. "So what else am I thinking?"

"That Detective Findlay is a plant. A legitimate homicide detective, but on the Cabal payroll. When the call came in, the Cabal pulled strings, and he got the case. That means we need to find Robyn, and if she hasn't turned herself in yet, stop her before she does." She stopped. "Shit. He has our names. Our real names."

"Not much we could have done about that. He found yours and I wasn't taking any chances with an alias. My record is clean—"

"I mean, if he reports our names to the Nasts, and they run them against their database, we're going to pop up. So I need to warn the council. Right now, though, my main concern is Robyn. Between placing that call and getting to the station, something happened."

"It's probably just a mix-up. But we'll make sure of that, obviously. I placed a few calls while I was waiting for you—one to the motel and one to our hotel, in case she did back out and went there." Another mirror check. "I also called Lucas, and he's going to contact all the precincts, as Robyn's legal representative, claiming she wanted to turn herself in alone and was supposed to phone him once she had. He'll say he hasn't heard from her, so he's calling around, seeing whether she went to the wrong one."

"Good idea. Especially if Detective Findlay is on the Cabal payroll. He probably never made those calls." She stopped. "Or maybe he already knows where Rob is."

"Because he has her? I don't think so. We've picked up a tail."

"Detective Findlay?"

"So I would presume."

"Let's lose him, then start looking for Robyn."

FINN

FINN LOST ADAMS AND MARSTEN. He'd followed them to their hotel, waited, waited some more, then flashed his badge to the desk, and gotten a room number. He'd sent Damon up. He returned to say they weren't there.

Finn had been tempted to go up himself and verify this. But Damon was right: it wouldn't take more than a toe over the line for Marsten to scream harassment. If they were in their room, they obviously weren't meeting up with Peltier, which is why he'd followed them. If they'd snuck out again, then he'd lost them.

BACK AT THE STATION, they looked at Peltier's cell phone. Her schedule was entirely business-related. Remembering that barren apartment, Finn wasn't surprised.

Robyn Peltier seemed to be all business these days. Finn knew what that was like. He'd been in L.A. six years and still didn't have what anyone would call a social life. He'd come here to start a new job, then built his life around it. Even the last woman he'd dated was a paramedic, and she'd asked *him* out. He wasn't ashamed of this. It was just that kind of job. If you wanted, you could make it your life. He had.

So Peltier's schedule revealed nothing. Same with her contact list. Every L.A. number had a business connection, neatly typed, no shorthand or code. Those that looked like friends and family were non-California area codes, most from Pennsylvania.

Hope Adams's cell phone number was there, and matched three entries on the log of calls received, all made Friday morning. Exactly as she'd said.

Before that, the last call Peltier received had been Thursday from Portia. Around midnight she'd placed the call to 911. Nothing after that until Adams the next morning. The next outgoing calls were long, four of them on Friday morning.

"I'll bet they're from the guy who found the phone," Damon said. "Calling everyone he knew out-of-state, getting a little added value before pawning it."

Finn suspected he was right.

"There should be a notes section." Damon settled onto the desk. "Bobby always keeps notes. I'd check the text message log, but you won't find much. She doesn't like texting."

There were notes, but all business, like the schedule. And she'd only used text messaging to reply to messages from Kane. He skimmed those. Some were business. Others more ambiguous, Kane wanting Peltier's opinion about this or that, like she was asking an older sister. Peltier's responses were diplomatic but personable, gently guiding Kane to make better choices.

The final text message, sent Thursday afternoon, read "Wait til tabs see this!!!" and had a photo attached. Finn opened it, but with the tiny screen, he could only make out a woman in a dress.

"Mail it to yourself," Damon said.

"Hmmm?"

"Forward it to your e-mail account and open it on your computer. That's what Robyn did." He pointed at the screen. "See that symbol? It means she forwarded it."

Finn nodded and did that, his thick fingers clumsy on the keys. How the hell did kids these days do this? They must all have the dexterity of spider monkeys—

Had he really just thought "kids these days"? He sounded like one of the old men in his apartment building who were always stopping him to complain about the college girls on the fourth floor. Some days it was hard to remember he was only thirty-four, especially when he hung around someone like Damon, so easy with a laugh, quick on his feet, full of . . .

Full of life? A cruel slip of the tongue. Dead at twenty-nine—the same age Finn had been when he'd come to L.A., when he'd felt like he was just starting his life, leaving home and heading out to the big city. What if, on that trip, he'd seen someone pulled to the side of the road? He would have stopped, like Damon. That was how he'd been raised. What might a woman like Damon's killer have thought, seeing a guy Finn's size bearing down on her on a dark, empty road?

"It should be there now."

"What?"

Damon pointed at the computer. "The file should have arrived by now."

"Right."

He spoke too loudly both times and the other detectives in the room—Vanderveer and Scala—looked over, then shared an eye roll.

"You okay, Finn?" called Vanderveer, a burly detective approaching retirement, his pitch-black hair screaming dye job.

"Yeah. Just trying to open a photo Portia Kane sent Robyn Peltier. Computers aren't my thing."

"The Kane murder?" Scala was around Finn's age, recently transferred from vice at the insistence of his third wife.

Both detectives rose from their desks. Neither was any more computer literate than Finn, but his task sounded more interesting than the paperwork they'd been trudging through.

"Holy Mother of God," Vanderveer said as Finn opened the photo. "Is that one of those altered pictures or did that girl's parents actually let her out of the house dressed like that?"

"That girl does what she wants, when she wants," Scala said. "And she can do it at my place anytime."

"You know her?" Finn asked.

"I wish. I'd give my right nut to enjoy what that girl's got."

Vanderveer shook his head. "Well, you can see it all in that picture."

"I meant her more liquid assets." He rubbed his fingers together. "She's rich?"

"Wouldn't know it from that outfit. I've seen twenty-dollar whores with better fashion sense. But that's Jasmine Wills, your vic's frenemy."

"Her what?"

"They pretend to be friends but really they can't stand each other. Frenemy, get it?"

"No," Vanderveer said. "We don't. But *we* don't read the tabs."

"You just chat with their reporters, huh, Finn? So how'd that go? Did that *True News* chick promise you an exclusive? Hell, if she'd promise *me* an exclusive, I'd put on fangs and go bite a neck. Preferably hers. She was one sweet little—"

Vanderveer waved the younger detective to silence. "So what's Portia Kane doing with that picture?"

"She wanted her PR rep to send it to the tabloids."

"Seems the tabs are right—that frenemy thing had slid into full-blown enemy." Scala slapped Finn on the shoulder. "Well, the good news is we just solved your case. Jasmine Wills killed Kane to keep that photo out of the papers. I know I would." He started back to his desk, then stopped. "Oh, could you pass a copy my way? For safe-keeping?"

"Sounds nuts, but maybe what started as a simple catfight turned lethal," Damon said as Vanderveer returned to his paperwork. "If people carry guns, it becomes too easy to use them. I know all about that."

Before Finn could respond, the phone rang.

"Detective Findlay?" a man's voice said. "This is, uh, Officer Alec Weston. My, uh, sergeant wanted me to, call you. I'm sure it's nothing, but he, uh, insisted . . ."

A recent recruit. Finn could tell by the hesitation. Still new enough to view the homicide squad the way freshmen did the senior class. Finn encouraged him with an "um-hmm."

"I think I might have, uh, seen that woman you're looking for. From the Kane case. Robyn Peltier."

Finn's gaze shot to Damon. "You saw—"

"I'm probably wrong," Weston hurried on. "But my sergeant insisted I call."

"Where'd you see her?"

"Well, that's the thing that doesn't make sense, sir. She was in the coffee shop across from our station."

ROBYN

"Miss? You wanted out here?"

"J-just a sec," Robyn said.

She stared at the police station steps. Another precinct, ten miles from the last, chosen at random from a phone book when she stopped to catch her breath, certain she'd finally lost Adele.

As it turned out, she'd only temporarily misplaced her. When Robyn tried to hail a cab, she'd seen Adele step from a side street. She'd changed course then, taking another route into a busier commercial area, cutting through such a crowd she even stopped saying "excuse me" as she shouldered her way past people.

She'd lost Adele then. She was certain of it. There'd been no sign of her for two blocks. Then, seeing people pouring from a matinee, she'd merged with the crowd and jumped into one of the cabs waiting at the curb.

It was then, after she'd given the police station address to the cabbie, that she'd finally relaxed, resting her cheek against the cool window and closing her eyes as her heart slowed.

Adele Morrissey, at the police station, asking to use her cell phone. The cell phone with the photo Hope thought was responsible for Portia's murder. A photo of Adele Morrissey.

How had Adele found her at the station, when no one knew she'd been going to that one? Impossible . . . and therefore the first sign of Robyn's mental collapse. The second had been Adele Morrissey, paparazzo, chasing her with a gun. Both, however, paled in comparison to this—absolute proof that she had gone mad.

After losing Adele in the crowd, after watching for anyone following the cab, after sending the poor driver on a roundabout route, who was standing there on the steps of the police station even before she got there?

Adele Morrissey.

Robyn squeezed her eyes shut and prayed she'd open them to see only a young blond woman who resembled Adele Morrissey by a trick of the light and a panicked mind.

A bang on the window sent Robyn jumping, bills falling from her fingers. There stood Adele, reaching for the handle.

Robyn smacked the lock shut and dropped two twenties over the seat. "Drive. Please, just drive."

He looked at her in the mirror. Then his gaze lifted to the rearview mirror as Adele circled behind the car.

"Please. She's got a gun. Drive!"

He spun from the curb.

WHILE THE CABBIE had been quite willing to take her away from the armed girl yanking on his car door, his sympathy meter expired after a couple of blocks. He pulled to the curb with, "You get out now," and jabbed his finger at the sidewalk, to which Robyn had responded by reaching over the seat and taking back one of the twenties.

"Crazy bitch," were his parting words as she closed the door.

There had to be a logical explanation for what had happened. She hadn't imagined Adele—the cabbie had seen her, too.

Obviously Adele had been following Robyn to get that photo. She'd killed Portia for her phone. Then she'd discovered Portia had sent the picture to Robyn . . . and Robyn took another photo of her near the murder scene. So she'd followed Robyn to Judd's house. As for how she'd found Robyn today, obviously it had something to do with that young man who'd hurt Karl. A partner, maybe Judd's killer.

As for how *he'd* found Robyn, she wasn't dwelling on that, no more than she'd dwelled on how Karl found her the day before. It happened.

Adele and her partner must have seen Robyn get into the cab and Adele followed her. After the incident at the first police station, Adele figured out that Robyn was trying to turn herself in. Once she'd realized which precinct Robyn was heading to, she'd gotten there first to stop Robyn from surrendering while she still had that cell phone.

Problem was, Robyn didn't have the phone. Otherwise, she'd have tossed it to Adele, gotten to the police safely and told her story. Somehow she doubted telling Adele she'd lost the phone would solve the problem.

As for why Adele was willing to kill for a photo, Damon would say that motive wasn't important. The important thing now was to get the hell away from her.

YOU'RE PRETTY DAMNED PLEASED *with yourself, aren't you, Bobby?*

Robyn hadn't heard Damon's voice since she'd seen Adele at the first police station. Now she'd finally relaxed enough to imagine what he would have said.

She *was* pleased with herself. She'd called for a cab, requesting pickup a block over. She'd ordered the taxi to a cluster of hotels where she used to visit Portia for lunch. When it had dropped her off at one, she'd gone inside and taken the walkway to a second hotel. Out the lobby doors, into a new cab and off again.

Now she was walking toward music and the hum of voices. Some sort of street concert, she presumed. Where there's a concert, there are police. If Adele wasn't going to let her get to a police station, she'd find another way to turn herself in.

But, as people always said, there was never a cop around when you needed one. The concert turned out to be a small street festival on a road lined with shops boasting free hearing tests, Alaskan cruises and the lowest pharmacy dispensing fees in town. The music she'd heard? A live polka band. A seniors' fair, with a shocking lack of police presence.

Seemed she'd need to hail another cab. It was a good thing she was turning herself in because, at this rate, she'd run out of cash. L.A. cabs were not cheap.

Her chances of getting one on this street were nil. It was blocked off for the festival. So she set out in search of the nearest busy road or pay phone, and walked two blocks, finding neither. Then, as she glanced down a quiet side street, she laughed. There was an LAPD bike patrol officer stopped in front of a parked car as he drank from a water bottle. Another bike was propped against the mailbox behind him. Twenty feet away a second officer was walking into a restaurant.

Apparently she'd just needed to stop looking for a cop and they'd be everywhere.

She took a deep breath, then strode toward the drinking cop, his helmet swaying on the bike handles. He was in his thirties, light haired, with ears that would favor a longer haircut.

"Officer?"

He capped his bottle.

Robyn waited until she was close enough to speak without shouting, and said, "I'm Robyn Peltier."

His thick lips pursed. He pulled off his sunglasses, but his eyes remained as blank as the dark lenses. Great. Even with an introduction she couldn't get recognized.

"Detective Findlay is looking for me," she said as she stopped in front of him. "He wants to talk to me about Portia Kane's murder."

With *that* name, recognition hit. He glanced past her, as if looking for his partner, one hand sneaking toward his gun belt.

"Can you take me to Detective Findlay? Or call a car?" A weak smile. "I guess that bike isn't built for two. I know this isn't the best way to turn myself in but . . . it's a long story."

His hand moved away from the gun, taking his radio instead. He lifted it to his lips, then motioned for her to wait, as if she might wander off. Again he glanced behind her, still hoping for his partner. She thought of suggesting he handcuff her to the signpost, but from his expression, he might take her up on it.

He made the call. On reflex, Robyn glanced away to give him privacy, feigning great interest in the nearest closed store. The officer asked for Detective Findlay, giving the precinct, explaining that he had—

A blow hit Robyn in the shoulder, knocking her off balance. She recovered, twisting to see the officer standing there, mouth open, her shock reflected back in his face. Why had he hit her? His hand rose to his chest and she followed it to see a dark stain spreading across his breast. His eyes met hers, then his knees gave way.

As Robyn reached to catch him, a figure stepped from behind a parked car, gun rising. Adele Morrissey.

Robyn dove as the gun went off. An awkward drop, more of a fall, and she hit the pavement hard, skidding hands out, skin peeling from her palms, pain disappearing under a burst of agony from her shoulder. She saw blood spreading across her sweatshirt. Shot. Oh God, she'd been shot. That's what she'd felt, the bullet passing through the officer and hitting her.

Another explosion of pain, this one in her side. She rolled as Adele slammed her foot into Robyn's ribs again. Robyn tried to jump up. Then she saw the gun, pointed at her head.

"All you had to do was give me your cell phone, Robyn," Adele said, her voice as high and light as a child's. "How tough was—?"

Robyn grabbed Adele's pant leg and yanked. As Adele staggered back, Robyn flew to her feet, her shoulder flaring again, the pain excruciating. Adele regained her footing, gun going up—

Robyn slammed her fist into Adele's arm. Not much of a hit, but the movement startled Adele. She released the gun and it fell, skidding across the pavement.

Robyn started to run for the gun, but Adele was closer. She looked around, hoping to see the other officer. No sign of him. Seeing the alley Adele must have come out from, she raced toward it.

FINN

FINN WAS A BLOCK FROM WESTON'S STATION when he got a call from the dispatcher at yet another precinct. One of their bike patrol officers had been phoning in wanting to speak to him, then the line had disconnected and the officer's partner had returned from a bathroom break to find him dead on the pavement, shot in the back.

AN OFFICER KILLED in the line of duty meant every available tech was there gathering evidence as a dozen officers scoured the neighborhood. Having the shooting happen at sundown in a commercial area only added chaos to the mix, as citizens gathered to gawk.

Finn flashed his badge to a gray-faced rookie with distant eyes, too busy reconsidering his career choice to watch where Finn went, much less direct him to anyone in charge. The person Finn was looking for wasn't anyone the rookie could have led him to anyway.

As he picked his way through, he took in the wider scene. Hell of a place to shoot a cop. A commercial street in a neighborhood of adult-only condos and retirement villages. In the distance . . . was that polka music?

His gaze skimmed the uniformed officers and came to rest on one, sitting on the curb, ramrod straight, staring at the corpse being zipped into a body bag.

Finn walked over and sat beside him. The officer—stocky, thirty-ish, light brown hair—didn't even glance his way.

"I'm sorry," Finn said.

He looked at Finn, head tilted, lips pursed.

"I'm sorry."

"You're talking . . . to me?"

"Yeah."

"You mean you can see—" He leapt to his feet and took three steps toward the crowd of officers surrounding the body bag. "Gord! Hey, Gord!"

Finn rose and walked over. "He can't hear you."

"So I'm . . ."

"Yeah."

Silence fell. Would Finn ever figure out the right thing to say under the circumstances? The instructors at his academy had said the worst part of police work was breaking news of a death to loved ones. That's only because they'd never had to do this.

Finn cleared his throat. "I'm John Findlay. You'd phoned—"

The ghost slowly turned.

"But that's not why I'm here," Finn hurried on. "I want to find who shot you, and anything you can tell me about what happened here will help."

The ghost gave an odd snort of a laugh, then rubbed his mouth. "Sure."

"Can we go . . . ?" Finn motioned to a place outside the tape.

The ghost nodded, eyes still dancing with what seemed like genuine amusement.

"You're Officer Kendall?" Finn said as they walked.

"Lee. You can call me Lee." Kendall shook his head. "Man, I hope I remember all this when I wake up."

"Hmm?"

"I'm out on patrol. Gord takes off for a piss. And who walks up while I'm rehydrating? One of the most wanted suspects in L.A. Turning herself in to me. On my bike. I call it in and, bam, I get shot. Who shows up then? The same detective I'd been calling, who just happens to be able to see ghosts."

Kendall stopped by a storefront. "It's Gord's fault, you know. This morning he was going on about the Kane murder, saying people like that are just asking to get popped. That poor PR chick just got sick of all the bullshit Kane put her through. So after listening to him all day, what do I dream? This."

Finn nodded. What else could he do? Spend his few precious minutes with the ghost convincing him he was dead? Maybe not the most ethical choice, but Finn had a job to do.

"So Peltier approached you . . ."

Kendall sighed.

"Please. Before you wake up."

"Fine. Okay. So she came from there—" He pointed to one end of the street. "The street festival."

"Street festival?"

"Golden Years Jamboree or whatever. An excuse to sell crap to old people. Not that she was anywhere near old enough—she's younger than me. That's dreams for you, huh? They never make sense."

"I guess not. Can you tell me what she looked like?"

His description matched Robyn Peltier right down to the white and navy sweatsuit the other officer had seen her wearing earlier. Then Kendall told him what she'd said.

"She was having trouble turning herself in?" Finn repeated.

"Hey, it's not supposed to make sense, remember? So I made the call. And then . . ." Kendall glanced at his chest, as if expecting to see a bullet hole. "Bam."

"She shot you?"

His lips pursed. He had big lips, thick and bowed, as if they got pursed a lot and had permanently reformed.

"No, I don't . . . Let me think. I'm on the radio, asking for you and she moved . . . back. She staggered backward."

"Away from you?"

"Then I felt the shot." He pursed his lips again. "Or maybe I felt the shot before that. Hard to say. It's all a little blurry."

"But she stumbled around the time you were shot?"

"She fell back, looking at me like I'd smacked her and . . . and there was blood on her shoulder." He blinked. "She must have been shot, too."

Finn glanced across the scene at Damon, busy examining the crime scene. Finn had told him to stay away if he found the ghost—it was too much to explain otherwise.

Kendall continued, "The bullet must have gone right through me and into her. Huh." He pondered this a moment, calmly, as if piecing together a random crime.

"Then what?"

More pondering and pursing. "I'm not sure. Everything went black, then I was standing over my body."

"Was Peltier around?"

"Nope. It was just me until Gord came running over."

ADELE

Adele hadn't meant to kill the cop. She just hadn't seen any way to avoid it.

It was Robyn's fault. Apparently she decided being a fugitive made her a movie action heroine. Running through alleys, hiding in the shadows, giving Adele the slip, then kicking and punching her before tearing off again.

Adele rubbed her knee. That was going to bruise. The joint complained with every step, setting her teeth on edge. Robyn was just lucky she hadn't hit Adele in the stomach. If she'd hurt the baby . . .

Adele wasn't sure how to finish the threat. She already had to kill Robyn. She put her face together with her name.

Not that the name would get her far. Adele Morrissey was a business, not a person. It was a corporation owned by another corporation, ultimately held by the kumpania, but behind so many layers that no layperson would connect them. Adele couldn't even remember her real name.

Still, the cops might make the connection, if they tried hard enough, and they would, now that two of their own were dead.

If things spiraled further out of control, Irving Nast would come to Adele's rescue. She and her baby were too valuable to lose over a few dead bodies. If it came to that, though, she'd be indebted to them. Better to handle it herself.

She checked her watch. She'd missed dinner. Niko would not be happy. The communal Saturday dinner was a must—a chance to discuss the busy night to come and reallocate resources if needed. Damn Robyn Peltier. Adele needed to wrap this up before she got into serious trouble.

She reached into her pocket and touched the silk shirt. A few days more and the link would be so strong she wouldn't need the prop— she could just visualize Robyn and see her, as she'd been able to do with Portia. It would never get that far, though. Robyn would die tonight, then Adele would call Irving Nast and continue negotiations.

She closed her eyes.

Oh, look, there she was, coming out of yet another store. What did you buy this time, Robyn? She'd already picked up a clean shirt and bandages and water to clean her wound. When Robyn retreated to a bathroom stall to fix herself up, Adele would have had her best shot to kill her . . . if Neala hadn't picked that exact moment to return the message Adele had left for Colm. Neala had phoned back to say Colm could not help her practice tracking Jasmine Wills. He had a lesson with Niko and, really, if Adele was going to learn to track Jasmine, didn't she need to be doing it by herself?

Bitch.

Adele could have really used Colm. After she finally got off the phone and fixed on Robyn, she'd seen her in a bathroom stall, dressing her wound. Which would have been perfect, had there been any way to identify the bathroom. The last time Adele saw Robyn, she'd been on a street filled with eateries, any one of which could have housed the stall she saw Robyn using.

Robyn's wound hadn't seemed too debilitating. Still, Adele had hoped it was slow-acting, that the bullet would work its way toward some vital artery and, any moment now, Robyn would keel over dead.

The whole situation was ridiculous. Robyn Peltier might be older than Adele, but she was light-years behind in world experience. A sheltered upper-middle-class girl, recently moved to L.A., didn't know the city, probably never set foot in an alley for fear of stepping in something icky. Now she gets shot in the shoulder and what does she do? Fights back and runs. Field dresses the wound in a bathroom.

Stores were closing now. Restaurants would follow. All that running would start taking its toll and Robyn would begin to grow tired, to wear down, and then . . .

Adele smiled.

ROBYN

Running about like a chicken with its head cut off. That's what Robyn had been doing since Adele shot the bike officer.

She'd had a few patches of lucidity. Holding a newspaper to hide the blood, she'd bought a shirt and first-aid supplies, then she'd found a bathroom to change and fix up her shoulder. She'd also bought a cell phone using most of her remaining money. She'd intended to use it to get help. But she hadn't turned the phone on yet, much less made a call.

Every time Robyn got her head on straight, Adele would pop up, like an ax-wielding killer in one of those movies she hated. Now she was living her own version. How did the woman keep finding her? In the bathroom Robyn had even removed and shaken all her clothing, looking for a transmitter.

She'd given up trying to lose Adele, and her game plan now was to stay in populated places while she figured out what to do. But her exhausted brain couldn't contemplate any one-step long-term strategy.

She kept hoping Adele would give up. Go home, get some sleep, try again the next day . . . giving Robyn a chance to rest and regroup. Yet Adele was as tireless and relentless as any of those cinematic monsters.

As the stores closed and streets emptied, Robyn knew she had to find a place to sit and get her wits back. A club or movie was guaranteed to be full of people, but dark, too, and Adele wouldn't hesitate to shoot her there.

She hailed yet another cab.

"Where to?" the driver asked as she climbed in.

She wanted to say "any place that's busy," but she had enough experience with cab drivers thinking she was nuts.

"I'm in L.A. on business," she said. "I'm looking for something fun, but not a club. Something outdoors would be great." She thought of the street festival earlier. "Maybe a festival?"

She braced for a gruff brush-off, but the cabbie smiled. "You like carnivals? There's a spring fair over in Wilshire Park. A couple of schools are putting it on as a fund-raiser. My girls were talking about heading over there tonight."

A spring fair. Lots of lights. Lots of people. "Perfect."

ROBYN STOOD A DOZEN FEET from the admission booth, where two teen girls chatted and giggled. Beyond the temporary fence there was a midway. Even before she'd gotten out of the car she'd heard it—the shrieks of fake fear, the shouts of the barkers, the boom of music over blown speakers.

She bought a pay-one-price bracelet, then stepped inside. Fairs could never be too loud, too cheesy or too garish for Robyn. One time, for their anniversary, Damon had found this tiny—

Okay, enough of that. This was no time for skipping down memory lane. She had to stop running like that decapitated fowl and act like a woman with her head fully attached.

So she got cotton candy, telling herself it was necessary cover for playing a happy fairgoer—and, if held in front of her face, excellent cover for a fugitive. Then she staked out the perfect place to sit—a bench backed against a refreshment trailer. At one end sat a woman her age, holding a sleeping toddler. And, for the first time in months, Robyn could look at that and not feel a pang of loss.

There, surrounded by lights and people, yet obscured by shadow and cotton candy, Robyn finally relaxed a little. She scoured the path for the now familiar head of dark blond hair.

Are you out there, Adele? Go ahead, pop out and say "boo." Bobby's not going anywhere.

She plucked off a tuft of spun sugar, let it melt in her mouth, then turned on her cell phone and dialed.

"Hope? It's Robyn."

"Oh thank God. Are you all right?"

The words rushed out on a sigh that stabbed Robyn with guilt. She should have called sooner. And what? Told Hope she was being pursued by a crazy girl with a gun?

"I'm fine," Robyn said, which was, for the moment, true.

"Where are you? What's that noise?"

"I'm safe. I'm just having some trouble turning myself in."

"I totally understand that. I don't think I'd have the guts to even *try* to do it without support—moral and legal. So here's what we'll do—"

"That's not it. I—" Two kids went by, screaming about wanting to ride the Avalanche before leaving. Robyn waited for them to pass.

"Rob? Are you still there? What's that racket?"

"Busy place. I do want to turn myself in. I tried. I can't. It's the girl from the photograph. Adele Morrissey."

"Adele? How'd you—?"

"I know her. She used to take pictures of Portia. She's a paparazzo."

"What?"

"A paparazzo. And a fucking psychopath, apparently."

The woman beside her looked over sharply. Even Hope had gone silent in shock at her language. Robyn mouthed an apology to the woman and inched down the bench, lowering her voice.

"She was at the police station."

"Adele? From the photo?"

"Right. She intercepted me. She wanted my cell phone. She had a gun, so I ran. She chased me. I grabbed another cab, went to another police station and she was there, waiting for me on the steps. She got there before I did."

"Okay, so—"

"I can't lose her, Hope. No matter what I do, where I go, she finds me. Finally, I found a police officer—a bike patrolman. She—she shot him." The air seemed to thin at the memory and Robyn had to inhale and exhale to catch her breath before continuing. "She shot him from behind. Killed him. I got a bullet through my shoulder."

"She shot you?"

"I'm fine. But she's still following me, and the minute I give her a chance, she's going to kill me, for a cell phone I don't even *have*."

"Okay, then, we aren't going to give her that chance, are we?" Hope's voice was calm.

"She can find me, Hope. *Anywhere*. I've lost her over and over, and no matter where I go, as soon as I think I'm safe, she pops up—"

"Are you someplace safe now? Where you can wait?"

"Yes, but—"

"Then tell me where you are and we'll come and get you."

"You aren't listening, Hope. She'll kill you. She'll kill Karl. She'll kill anyone who gets between me and her."

"We'll handle it. Just tell me—"

Robyn hung up. Seconds later, an unfamiliar ring made her jump. Her phone.

She flicked it off and back on, then dialed 411, called the station and asked for Detective Findlay. She offered to leave her number, but when the woman heard who it was, she had her stay on the line.

"John Findlay," a voice said a couple of minutes later.

"Detective Findlay? It's Robyn Peltier. You've been looking for me."

"Are you okay?"

That wasn't what she expected and she hesitated a moment before saying, "I'm fine. I'm at a spring fair in . . ." She wasn't sure of the exact neighborhood, only remembering that the cabbie said it was the Wilshire Park district, so she told him that.

"Fair?"

"It's a long story. I've been trying to turn myself in but—"

"You've been having trouble."

She paused. How'd he know that?

"I'll be right there," he continued. "Stay in a public area. I'll phone when I arrive. Give me . . . twenty minutes."

"Okay."

"How's your shoulder? Do you need medical attention?"

"My . . . ?"

The bike officer. He must have lived. He'd told Findlay about her being shot and said she'd had trouble surrendering.

"I'll need it looked at, but—"

"Hang up the phone," said a voice beside her.

Robyn twisted, expecting to see the woman with the sleeping child. Instead, sitting at the other end of the bench was Adele Morrissey.

"Hello?" Adele said. "Do you speak English, Robyn? Hang up the phone."

She did, still dazed. "What do you want?"

"Duh. The same thing I've wanted for two days. We call it a cell phone. Let's see if you can do something bright for a change and hand it over before you kill more people."

"I haven't killed—"

"Of course you have. That cop friend you ran to Thursday night? That bike cop a few hours ago? Boohoo, poor me, I need a man to protect me. See what happens? You make me kill them and I'm tired of it. I have better things to do, you know."

Robyn searched Adele's eyes for some sign she was trying to be funny. There was none.

"You want my phone?" Robyn lifted the cell and waggled it. "*This* phone?"

Adele glowered like a child having candy waved in front of her face.

Robyn whipped her arm so fast a man ducked as if narrowly avoiding being hit.

"You—" Adele began.

"Better run," Robyn said. "You can't trust folks these days. If someone gets it before you . . ."

Adele glared at her, then jumped up and disappeared into the crowd to find the phone.

Robyn waited until Adele was out of sight, then slid the cell phone from her sleeve and sneaked off the other way.

ROBYN

Robyn looked out over the multicolored haze of the fairgrounds as her Ferris wheel car climbed. Was Detective Findlay on his way? If he did come, what would he do? Quietly search for her? Or commandeer the PA system, sending Adele into a murderous panic?

She dismissed the last thought by focusing on a lighter one. Tomorrow's headline: "Double Murder Suspect Apprehended on Ferris Wheel." She tried to laugh, but the sound came out shaky, whisked away on the updraft as the car descended, the swaying setting her wounded shoulder afire.

When her car dipped to the bottom, she saw Adele in the crowd by the ride's exit gate. Robyn couldn't summon even a spark of surprise. She was beyond thinking she could outwit Adele. To get through this, she had to believe the unbelievable—that this young woman could find her wherever she went. Accept it and work around it.

So when the car descended the next time, Robyn pretended to search the crowd for Adele, as if she hadn't seen her. As it rose again, she used the cell phone and called a cab. The dispatcher said a car would be at the front gates in twenty minutes. Robyn checked her watch, calculating. She took a deep breath of chill night air. She'd been playing cat and mouse with a psychotic killer for six hours. She could survive another twenty minutes.

Robyn erased all calls from the log. If she had to hand this phone over to Adele, she wasn't taking the chance of her going after Hope when she realized she'd been duped.

Once in the cab, she'd go to the nearest police station. If Adele somehow managed to get there first, Robyn would continue on, from station to station, until she found one where the driver could drop her off right at the door. Then she'd make a run for it.

As plans went, this one sucked, as Damon would say. But it would have to do.

The Ferris wheel was unloading now. Robyn leaned over the side, making a show of searching the crowd. She'd already seen Adele slip behind a burly man at the exit.

Finally Robyn's car reached the platform. She let the operator help her out, and started toward the exit. A few steps from it, she stopped, checking her pockets, then shaking her head. She walked to the bank of cubbies where riders stashed backpacks and stuffed bears. She pretended to root around in the last cube, then darted to a nearby gap in the fencing. The attendant at the gate let out only a halfhearted "hey" as she squeezed through.

Sixteen minutes left.

Robyn didn't run—too obvious—just walked quickly, scouring the attractions for one that would whisk her out of Adele's reach for a few minutes. But the lines were now swollen with laughing, jostling teens who scared away anyone over twenty. Robyn would stick out like a sore thumb among them. What she needed was—

A profanity-laced outburst exploded behind her, and she glanced back to see Adele bowling through a knot of teens, her gaze fixed on Robyn, shouldering aside anyone who got in her path.

Okay, Bobby, browsing time is over. Pick something and hustle your ass in there.

Robyn skirted one large group. Then she saw the answer, shimmering and winking under blinding floodlights. A house of mirrors.

She jogged over, startling the dozing attendant. Clearly not one of the more popular attractions at the fair tonight. All the better. Robyn flashed her wristband, climbed the steps and dashed into the maze.

She snaked down the first few corridors, feeling her way, paying little heed to her surroundings until, deciding she was in deep enough, she slowed.

Think you can find me anywhere, Adele? Try this.

She leaned against the cool glass wall, smiling as she caught her breath. Beyond the trailer, the lights of the fair flashed, distorted bubbles of color.

Uh, Bobby . . . You shouldn't be able to see that. Not through mirrors.

She told herself it was an illusion, that the lights were actually inside the trailer, reflecting off the mirrors. Then she saw the distorted shape of a man carrying a child on his shoulders, the little one's white shirt glowing.

A house of mirrors? No, she was in a house of glass.

Don't panic, Bobby. You're the only one in there, right? If you can't see the faces of people outside, Adele can't see yours from out there.

But that didn't matter with Adele. She could find Robyn anywhere.

The trailer steps creaked. A figure appeared at the distant entrance. Robyn wheeled and stumbled the other way. Three strides, and she smacked into a pane of glass. Both hands shot out, feeling her way, finding glass in front and to either side, and then she understood the idea of a glass maze. You could see the exit sign, but couldn't get to it, banging around like a bird caught in a sunroom.

She kept feeling. Glass in front and beside, trapped—

Bobby? Relax. You're just caught in a dead end.

She turned and saw the other figure moving through the corridors. She could make out only a light-colored shirt and dark pants, a description that could fit half the people at the fair.

Take a deep breath . . . then get the hell out of there, Bobby.

Robyn headed back the way she'd come, sweeping the sides and front, taking any turn that would bring her closer to that exit sign. The other person—she refused to think of it as Adele—kept moving, too, getting closer, then farther away as she navigated the maze.

Finally, Robyn saw the exit sign right ahead, above the glass, so close she could jump—

She smacked into the wall.

She frantically ran her hands around all three sides. The exit was *right there.* She could see the steps, the faces of passersby, just one pane of glass separating them.

She turned around. The other figure was closer now, no more than ten feet and a few glass panes away. A woman with dark blond hair and a yellow shirt. Just like—

Don't think, Bobby. Just keep moving.

But moving meant getting closer to Adele. She kept picturing the gun and her knees locked. Finally she closed her eyes and, feeling her way, took one step, then another. The junction that led to the exit couldn't be far. She'd just taken a wrong turn.

Only she hadn't. There hadn't been another route all along that back corridor. Finally she reached the end, turned, and turned again, each move bringing her closer to that searching figure.

Just keep going. If she made it to the entrance, that was good enough. Ignore Adele. It was a public place—

At a smack against the glass, Robyn jumped and even as she turned, the memory of Adele at the taxi window resurfaced and she knew—

There she was, right on the other side, her face twisted by the warped glass, pulled into something monstrous, all eyes and gaping mouth. Even through the distortion, Robyn could see her hate and felt a twinge of outrage. What had she done to deserve this girl's hatred?

She's nuts, Bobby. She doesn't need a reason. Just run—

Adele pulled out her gun.

Robyn sidestepped, unable to tear her gaze away from the weapon.

It's on the other side of the glass, Bobby. She's trying to spook you. Don't let her. Just get out of there.

Another slow step sideways. Robyn slid her hand into her pocket and took out the cell phone, then motioned throwing it over the wall. Adele nodded and lowered the gun.

Robyn reached as high as she could and dropped the phone over the wall. She didn't wait to see whether Adele caught it. She was turning to run when, out of the corner of her eye, she saw Adele let the phone hit the floor, her hands rising, the gun swinging up.

Robyn dove. The bullet sliced through the glass and whizzed past her.

Holy shit. Holy shit!

Robyn scrambled up and ran, hands out, veering when she felt glass. She heard another crack behind her. Another bullet.

Wasn't anyone out there? Couldn't they hear it? Adele had a silencer on the gun, but it made a noise. An unmistakable noise, along with breaking glass. With the racket from the carnival, though, no one noticed. Robyn could scream as loud as she wanted and she'd only be mistaken for a girl on the Zipper next door.

The glass in front of her cracked into a spider web, bullet hole in the center. Robyn spun, wildly feeling for another passage, found one and took it, leading her toward the rear of the trailer.

A distorted, painted clown leered from the back wall. Something about the image wasn't right, the costume off-kilter, as if someone had put up a painted panel wrong, leaving a black line through it. Then she realized the line was the night sky, the painting masking a door, the distortion meaning it was cracked open.

She barreled toward it, hands out, expecting another glass wall, ready to smash through it. But her luck held and in three steps she was at the door, stumbling forward in her eagerness, hands hitting hard. The door flew open under her weight and she staggered, about to fall face-first off the steps when a figure caught her and slammed the door behind her.

She opened her mouth to shriek. A hand clamped over her mouth. The figure yanked her around, one hand at her waist, the other around her neck, pulling her back against him.

"Shhh," a man's voice said. "You're okay."

She struggled to turn around, managing to catch a glimpse of dark hair before he grabbed her shoulders, propelling her down the steps and into the shadows behind the trailer. Then he pulled her against him again, his hand ready to clamp over her mouth, waiting until she gave him cause.

Adele's footsteps sounded across the trailer floor.

"Karl?" Robyn whispered.

"Shhh, yes. You're okay."

"How—?" She'd been about to ask how he found her, then remembered the phone call and Hope overhearing the background noise.

He leaned into her ear. "Count of three?" He pointed to a narrow dark strip behind the row of trailers.

He started counting. On three, she ran, with Karl behind her. She tried to glance back once, but he gave her a shove, hissing for her to keep going.

Finally they reached an exit marked Staff Only manned by a pimply teen. Still pushing her forward, Karl grabbed the gate.

The kid lowered his magazine. "Hey, are you—?"

"Staff."

Karl prodded her through. Again, she tried to slow, to talk, to turn and look at him, but he shoved her, even less gently this time, with a gruff "move."

Now she could see why the fair had been crammed into one end of the park. The other was hilly and wooded. When she squinted, she could make out a sign telling cyclists to stay off the footpath. That was where Karl took her, onto that path and into the woods.

They'd gone about fifteen feet when his steps slowed to a walk.

"This looks like a good place," he said. "Suitably nondescript. She won't find you here."

The voice, no longer distorted by whispering, was not Karl's.

Robyn turned. Behind her stood the young man she'd followed that afternoon. The one who'd attacked Karl.

FINN

IF THIS PARTNERSHIP WAS GOING TO WORK OUT, Finn needed to be a lot more careful what he let Damon overhear.

After Officer Kendall's body was removed, Damon had circled behind Finn, trying to eavesdrop, and he'd gotten into earshot at the worst possible moment.

"So . . . a shoulder shot," Damon said—again—as Finn drove toward the fairgrounds.

"It's one of the safest places to be shot. The bullet usually passes through—"

"You said that. But this *usually* part. What if it doesn't pass through? Is it only safe if it does? Can something go wrong?"

"It's usually nonfatal—" Finn caught the qualifier even before seeing Damon's wince. "It's nonfatal."

Damon leaned over to check the speedometer, clearly no happier with what he saw there than he'd been with Finn's answer.

"She said she was okay," Finn said.

"Bobby would say that if she'd been run over by a truck and could still crawl from the scene. Did she sound—?" He broke off with a disgusted snort. "You wouldn't know."

He meant Finn didn't know Peltier, but Finn didn't imagine that clip of annoyance in Damon's words. His wife had been shot and Finn was moseying along, having deemed her life unworthy of sirens and an ambulance.

Explaining why he was proceeding cautiously would mean telling

Damon what Peltier said, that her shooter was still hot on her trail. Whoever was following Peltier had already proven himself ready to kill her and anyone who got in his way. So Finn wasn't about to tear in there with a full squad car escort. He'd called his lieutenant, who'd coordinated it from there. A backup team would cover exits discreetly while Finn searched inside for Peltier.

Had Finn made the right call? He hoped so. Peltier had sounded calm and rational on the phone and, from everything Damon had said, this was normal—she wasn't in shock. Finn trusted she could keep herself safe, whether it took him ten minutes to get there or fifteen.

And if he was worried about why the line disconnected? And who'd been that voice in the background? More things Damon didn't need to know.

"Promise me you'll get her to a hospital?" Damon said.

"That would be standard procedure."

Damon watched the light pass, then looked back at Finn. "She might argue. She'll want medical attention—she doesn't take risks like that—but she'll downplay the injury and try to get the interview over with first. That's how she prioritizes."

"I'll tell her we can conduct the interview at the hospital."

"Good. Efficient. She'll like that."

Damon turned back to the window. Finn thought about what it must be like for him, wandering alone in limbo for six months. Then, when he did find someone who could hear him, he had to talk about his wife without really talking *about* her, to a stranger who didn't know her, whose only interest in her was as a subject in a case.

It was different where Finn had come from. There, you were part of the community. You knew Bobby Miller was having a tough time with his parents' divorce and it would be enough to give him a stern lecture and make him pay for the broken window. Just like you knew that Ray Thomas, bawling in the drunk tank, might very well be telling the truth when he said he was sorry, but if you let him get away with it, next time the Sooners lost a game, he'd take it out on his wife's face again.

Then Finn came to Los Angeles.

To survive here, Finn had to squelch that part of himself and emulate Joe Friday. Just the facts, ma'am.

Now, riding with Damon, Finn realized how much he hated this, how much happier he'd been back on that small-town force. It wasn't in his nature to be cold and clinical, and it was gnawing away at him like frostbite. But there was little need for his gift back home, where more than one homicide a year would be a crime wave. If Finn was going to make proper use of his abilities he had to stay in L.A. and dream of the day he'd be back home, driving his squad car, asking his passenger "so how's your wife?" and knowing the answer mattered.

"Flashing lights ahead," Damon said. "Either that's the mother of all accidents or we've got ourselves a carnival."

Finn followed his gaze to colored lights twinkling beyond the next block.

"Something tells me I'm about to do a disappearing act." Damon's fingers silently drummed the armrest. "If I do, when you find her, don't tell—" He inhaled sharply.

"Don't tell her about you."

"Yeah."

Finn turned at a hand-drawn parking sign.

"It wouldn't be right," Damon said finally. "She'll have a lot on her mind and that would just freak her out."

"I need her to trust me—and telling her I see ghosts, even yours, isn't going to help."

A tight laugh. "Yeah."

"Later, though, we could . . . figure something out."

Damon nodded. After a few seconds of silence he said, "Sure. If it works out. That would be good."

FIVE MINUTES LATER, Finn was flashing his badge at the ticket girl and stepping inside the fairgrounds. The backup team hadn't arrived, but Damon was still at his side.

"Maybe whatever power decided to let you help me is going to let you see her," Finn said.

"Or maybe it means she isn't here." Damon shook his head. "Damn, I'm a regular ray of sunshine tonight, aren't I?"

But as they walked to the midway, Damon's mood did grow sunnier. The bounce returned to his step. He started singing along to a song playing at the rides. His gaze scoured the crowd, hope sparking in his eyes every time he caught sight of a blond head.

"So where are you supposed to meet her?" Damon asked.

"Here."

"I meant *where* here."

"She didn't specify."

Damon stopped walking. Finn slowed, waiting for him to catch up. He didn't.

"Either you think I'm a complete idiot or you're hoping I'm too worried to think straight. This is my wife we're talking about, Finn. She'd never hang up without giving you a meeting place, complete with a description, the nearest entrance and optimal parking. Hell, the fact she didn't offer to send MapQuest directions to your cell phone already told me she's worse off than she's letting on."

Finn had resumed walking, scanning faces. "We got disconnected."

"What?" Damon strode up beside him.

"I was having trouble hearing her, then we were disconnected. I thought I heard a woman in the background. Maybe Adams. I couldn't make out what she said."

A passing boy turned to stare up at Finn. "Who's that man talking—?"

His mother shushed him, then tugged him closer, arm going around him as she cast a nervous glance at Finn, stopping well short of making eye contact. At a place like this, people talking to themselves wouldn't be that uncommon. Still, he should be more careful or he'd find himself explaining the situation to security.

"Did she call back?" Damon asked.

Finn shook his head.

"Did you call her?"

He nodded.

"And?" Damon prompted.

"Her phone's turned off."

"When's the last time you tried?"

Finn motioned for Damon to keep looking as he took out his cell. This time, he didn't get the message that the customer was "unavailable." It just rang and rang.

"So?" Damon said when Finn hung up.

"Nothing."

Damon nodded, presuming that meant the phone was still turned off. Finn started to pocket it.

"Shouldn't you keep that out?" Damon said. "You can use it when you're talking to me instead of scaring the kiddies."

Finn wasn't comfortable with the subterfuge—which explained why he kept forgetting to do it—but it had to be better than talking to himself in public.

Still scouring the crowds, they passed a row of games.

"Hey," Damon said. "Ring toss. I remember Bobby . . ."

He let the sentence fade.

The cell phone rang. He checked the caller ID.

"It's her," he said.

He retreated into a quieter spot between two booths, then answered. For a moment, he heard only the noise of the fair through the phone, a tinny stereo to the commotion around him.

"Hello?" she said, her voice tentative, as if he'd called her.

"Robyn?"

"Yes. You called?"

"It's Detective Findlay. I'm at the fair. Where are you?"

A longer pause now. Damon had climbed onto a game booth and was scanning the crowd.

"Robyn?" Finn said.

"Sorry, I . . ." Another pause. Then, "He's here, Detective. I'm—" a sharp breath. "I—I'm just so scared. I thought I was safe, calling you, and then he was right there, coming for me, so I had to hang up and run, and then I tried phoning back but my phone wasn't working and—"

"Slow down, Robyn."

Hearing that, Damon glanced over.

"He's here, Detective. He's here, somewhere, and I can't see him and I—"

"Slow down, Robyn. Who's there? Who's following you?"

Damon jumped off the counter, the alarm in his eyes tempered by confusion.

"I-I need to get out of here, Detective. I can't stay. He'll find me and then he'll kill me. I know he will. Just like he killed that poor cop and—"

"Robyn, I need you to take a deep breath and calm down."

Damon stepped close enough to listen in.

Finn continued, "The man who's following you. He's the one who shot Officer Kendall?"

"Right. And the other one, Portia's bodyguard. I went to his house—"

"Judd Archer."

"Right."

"Are you sure it's the same man?"

"Of course I'm sure. He was right there. On that street and at

Judd's house. He's tall with dark hair and a scar under his eye. I'm not sure if it's the left or right eye. Left, I think. He's wearing a green jacket. He's here somewhere, at the fair. I can't stay. I have to get out of here. Will you find him for me? Stop him?"

"I'll do my best."

The line went dead.

"That—" Damon began.

"—wasn't Robyn. I know."

ROBYN

Robyn turned to run from the man. She knew it was futile—he was close enough to grab her. But he didn't. She was so surprised that she stumbled, twisting to look back at him.

He stood there. Smiling. "Ten. Nine. Eight."

Robyn ran.

The forest couldn't be that big. The path had to lead to the other side. Unless it just looped around to where it started . . .

"Ready or not . . ."

Robyn dove into the brush. She hit the ground, skidding through the undergrowth, shoulder flaring, a branch scraping her cheek a mere inch from her eye. She scrambled in deeper, every move making the brush crackle and snap like gunfire.

She dropped, turned toward the path and stretched out on her stomach. The vegetation sprang back up, cradling her. Flat on the ground, she watched the man's pale face bobbing along the path. It stopped directly parallel to where she lay.

He turned and crossed his arms. His sigh wafted through the quiet forest. "Oh, come on. If you're going to play, you have to do better than that. I can smell you. I can see in the dark. What the hell did Marsten teach you about werewolves?"

Robyn choked back a laugh. Did he really say werewolves? *He* was going to have to do better than that if he wanted to scare her.

He couldn't see her. He'd just approximated where the noise had come from.

"Are you going to make me come in there after you, blondie?"

Like to see you try, Mr. Werewolf.

He took a step into the forest. Then another, and another, saunter-ing along as easily as if he was still on the path, ducking branches she couldn't even see, heading straight for her.

Her shirt.

She'd tried to buy one as dark as possible, but it had white stripes. Against the darkness, she must stand out like a zebra on a dimly lit plain.

She tensed, but held still, hoping she was wrong, that he was still guessing—

He stopped four feet away, his face turning to hers, teeth flashing against the night.

She leapt to her feet and barreled through the undergrowth, glanc-ing over her shoulder to see him still sauntering, unhindered by the brush, not even bothering to run.

She was veering to circle back to the path when she caught the flash of reflective tape on a tree and ran for it. The path. Thank God. She rammed through the last patch of brush. Vines grabbed her feet, but she yanked free and hit the path at a run.

Just find the end. This wasn't the Amazon jungle.

Footsteps pounded on the path behind her. Now he was running.

Just keep going. Keep—

Robyn tripped over a root and sprawled face-first to the dirt, hands flying out, her skinned palms and injured shoulder screaming.

Ignore it. Get up and—

A hand grabbed her foot and yanked. Her face slammed into the dirt. With a bone-wrenching jerk, he flipped her onto her back.

"Not bad, blondie. Not bad at all. Wanna have another go? I fig-ure we have—" He checked his watch. "At least ten minutes before the cavalry arrives. Marsten's good at following a scent, but he'll hate sniffing the ground to do it. Grass stains are a bitch to get out of Armani. Or so I hear."

He was casual and relaxed, still smiling. Sweat dripped into Robyn's eyes. He wasn't even breathing heavy. Just a pleasant jog through the woods. She couldn't escape him, no more than she could Adele.

Ah, but you did escape Adele, Bobby. Look around. She's long gone.

Sure, that was because she was still back at the fair, sipping a soda while her thug partner beat the crap out of Robyn.

She hadn't escaped. She'd run straight into a trap.

"Well, are you getting up? I'm going to give you another chance."

"Sure, like Lucy gives Charlie Brown another chance to kick the football."

He threw back his head, laughing. "Sharp one, aren't you? I'm glad to see you still have some spunk. Now let's see you use it. Of course, I don't plan to let you get away, but you don't really have much choice, do you? How about I give you to the count of twenty this time?"

Robyn rose slowly, brushing herself off as she looked around, getting her bearings. The man eased back, relaxing.

"Come on now," he said. "We're on a schedule here."

"Before I do—"

She wheeled, as if to bolt. The man lunged at her. She spun and kicked, aiming for his crotch. She saw her foot flying, on target. At the last second, he grabbed her ankle, so fast she saw only a blur. He whipped her off her feet and threw her. She hit the ground and lay there, gasping, her brain struggling to comprehend why she was on her back and how she got there.

The man stood at least ten feet away. He'd *thrown* her. Grabbed her by the leg and thrown her like a doll. She stared at him, his slight build, his wiry arms.

He was barely bigger than she was. How the hell had she mistaken him for Karl? Forget that. How the hell had he thrown her ten feet?

"That was good," he said, advancing. "A double fake-out. Of course, I wouldn't be nearly as impressed if you'd succeeded with that kick." He smiled, teeth flashing. "In fact, I'd say if you had managed it, you'd have been in for a double-dose of pain."

Wheezing, she pushed up onto her elbows and inched back. The man strolled over and planted a foot on her chest. When she rose, tentatively, he kicked her injured shoulder, bringing tears to her eyes.

And still he smiled.

"So, what are you?" he asked. He said something that sounded like "bitch," then continued, "Because if you are, I'd say you need some serious practice with your spellbook. If you cast one, I didn't even notice."

Witch? Had he said witch?

"Maybe half-demon, like your friend?" he continued. "Mmm, now there's a cutie. Nothing against you, blondie, but I like them more exotic."

Was he talking about Hope?

"And from what I hear, she's definitely exotic. Some rare kind of demon, isn't she? The kind that likes trouble." A low, growling laugh. "*Really* likes trouble, the way I hear it. No wonder Marsten hooked up with her."

Marsten? Robyn struggled to remember Karl's last name. It *was* Marsten, wasn't it? What the hell was going on?

She squeezed her eyes shut. Forget it. If this was Adele's partner, he was probably just as crazy as she was. Demons and witches and werewolves. Insane.

The man's next words were cut off by his cell phone.

He checked the display. "Ah, the boss. Now keep your mouth shut, blondie, okay? Or else . . ." He put his foot on her shoulder, making her gasp. Then he answered with a "Hey."

A moment's pause.

"Not so well. Got a bit of a problem. I was following Marsten and his girlfriend, and they led me to the blonde. Adele was chasing her with a gun. I rescued her, which I figured was what you'd want, but I couldn't do it without making contact. She's not nearly as grateful as she should be."

He listened.

"That's what I figured. I was going to bring her to you, but Marsten's hot on my trail. We've been dodging them, but they're gaining. I can hear him coming right now."

Robyn heard only the wind sighing through the trees.

"I'm just saying, this might not go down the way you were hoping. I have a feeling, as hard as I try to avoid it, fur is gonna fly." His grin belied the regret in his voice. "Marsten's a cold-blooded bastard. Negotiations with a guy like that usually end with corpses. Just so you know."

A pause.

"All right then. I'll do my best—"

Robyn grabbed his foot and heaved. When the man staggered back, off balance, she leapt up, wrenching his leg. He toppled over backward, phone falling.

Robyn ran.

Curses rang out behind her. This time, she was sure the word he used *wasn't* witch.

She ran full out, adrenaline pumping so hard that if her lungs were complaining, she didn't feel it. She kept her head down, watching the moonlit path for obstacles this time.

The path had to end soon. It had to—

And there it was. The end. A barricade across the path with a white sign so big she could read it in the dark. "Soil erosion. Path closed. We apologize for the inconvenience."

She let out a huffing laugh. They had no idea how damned inconvenient it was. Screw soil erosion. She was going through.

She vaulted over the barrier. Amazing what adrenaline could do.

She ran another dozen paces, then pulled up short on the edge of a ten-foot drop-off.

Uh, I do believe that's the soil erosion, Bobby.

She considered jumping, but couldn't see the bottom in the dark and would probably impale herself on a retaining rod.

There had to be a way around. She ran into the bushes and found herself in a veritable jungle, so thick she'd need a machete to chop her way through. The running footsteps sounded again.

She flailed about until she found a clear path. Once she got in deeper, she could take advantage of the thick woods to hide—

A figure loomed in her path. She let out a shriek. He lunged and grabbed her, his hand slapping over her mouth, his other arm swinging her off her feet, carrying her, kicking and writhing before setting her down in a clearing, still gagged, with one hand pressing the top of her head.

"Get down. Hope?"

Another pair of hands tugged her shirt. "I've got her. Rob, get down."

Robyn recognized the voices but after the last time, she didn't trust herself. She followed the hand over her mouth and saw Karl.

"Down," he said.

Hope grabbed her arm and pulled her to her knees.

"Come out, come out, wherever you are," the man's voice sang out. Brush rustled, then stopped. "What's that I smell? The big bad wolf took the bait?"

Karl swung toward them. "Get her out of here," he said to Hope.

Hope didn't move. Robyn looked over to see her staring into the forest, her eyes gleaming, unseeing, her face blank.

"Hope," Karl snapped.

"She's scared," Robyn snapped back. "I'll get her out. Which way—?"

"Hope," Karl said, getting her attention. "Control it."

"Sorry. I'm fine." Hope shivered.

"Asshole," Robyn muttered.

Karl's gaze swung her way, as if he'd heard. She imagined Damon's chuckle. *I don't think he expects insults after rescuing you, Bobby.*

"Come on." Hope tugged her arm.

Robyn glanced at Karl, who'd turned away, dismissing them as he scanned the forest.

"He'll be fine," Hope said. "We need to go."

Um, Bobby, if the dude wants to play he-man, that's his problem. Get the hell out of there.

Robyn unlocked her knees and let Hope lead her through the undergrowth. After a few steps, Hope slowed, her chin lifting, that same blank look crossing her face. Robyn took her elbow, but Hope yelled "Karl!" grabbed Robyn and yanked her back.

"Damn, she's good," said a voice in front of them.

Robyn froze and squinted into the darkness. It was another moment before the man stepped out of the trees, right in their path. Clutching a gun, Hope stood between Robyn and the man.

Where the hell did Hope get a gun?

"Guess I can't sneak up on you, can I, demon-girl? So how does that work? You catch a vision, right?" He lifted his foot, easing forward. "You see me coming."

"Stop," Hope said.

"Have you got silver in that gun? Because if you don't—"

"I don't need silver bull—" Hope glanced over at Robyn, then back at the man. "Just stop."

Karl stood a dozen feet behind Robyn. He seemed to be measuring the distance between himself and the man, gauging whether he could get to the guy before he pounced on Hope. His jaw tightened, as if he didn't like the answer.

"Hope?" Karl said. "Back up toward me."

Hope didn't move. Robyn couldn't see why she had to—she was holding a gun on an unarmed man.

"Hope?" Karl's voice sharpened to a razor edge.

Robyn shot a glare at him.

"I don't think she wants your help, old man," the other guy said. "She's having too much fun. You like a little danger, don't you, babe? Gets your motor revving."

Hope's eyes were glittering again. Sweat sparkled across her cheeks and forehead. She breathed fast through her mouth. Not fear, Robyn realized. Excitement.

"Got a real lust for trouble, don't you, babe? How hot are you right now? I bet you're so wet—"

Karl snarled, an inhuman sound that sent Robyn spinning to look at him. He strained forward, face twisted with rage.

"Karl." It was Hope's turn to snap a sharp warning.

Robyn tensed for Karl's reaction, but he only murmured, "I know, I know," then rolled back on his heels. "Just back up. I'll be okay if you back up."

"Am I making you nervous, old man? Why? Just because I could break her neck before she fired that gun? Don't worry, babe. Killing you isn't what I have in mind. How about a deal? You come along with me. See how much more fun you could have with someone your own age. We'll leave the old dog with blondie. She's more his speed."

"Do you want him, Karl?" Hope asked.

"Yes, please." Karl's words were a growl.

"Robyn, step back. I've got you covered, Karl."

The younger man just stood there, smirking, like a wolf listening to the foolish little rabbits plotting to overthrow him.

"Be careful," Robyn said. "He's fast and he's a lot stronger than he looks."

That made the man laugh. "Really? Fancy that. What the hell are you teaching these girls about werewolves, Marsten?"

Hope's gaze shunted to Robyn.

"Or maybe at your age 'strong' is relative, huh, old man?"

"Karl?" Hope said.

"I'm right behind—"

The man lunged. Hope did the same—diving off to the side as she fired. The bullet caught the man in the side and he spun. Before he could recover, Karl tackled him and the two men went down.

"Robyn!" Hope scrambled up, gun trained on the fighting men. "Get back to the path."

The man wriggled out from under Karl. He sprang to his feet. Karl twisted out of the way. He grabbed the man on the rebound and threw him.

The man sailed through the air and crashed into the undergrowth fifteen feet away.

Robyn stared.

He threw him. Just picked him up and hurled him, like the guy did to me.

"Robyn!" Hope yelled. "The path."

Robyn couldn't move. As the man wobbled to his feet, Karl glanced over, blood streaming from his lip. He swiped at it.

"Hope? Get her out of here."

Hope looked from Karl to Robyn, clearly reluctant to leave him.

"N-no," Robyn said. "I-I'm okay. I'll—"

The man ran at Karl. They hit with a smack that echoed through the trees. Karl's fist connected with the man's jaw with an even louder *thwack*. The man howled in rage. His face— His face changed. Rippling. Contorting.

Robyn was wrenched backward, almost off her feet. She looked to see Hope clutching her arm, dragging her.

"Come on."

"No, Karl needs—"

"He doesn't need us."

When Robyn resisted, Hope heaved hard enough to make her stumble.

"He can't concentrate with us here."

One more backward glance at the fighting men, then Robyn let Hope lead her back to the path.

FINN

FINN TRIED PELTIER'S CELL NUMBER again and, again, got the message that the customer was unavailable, meaning it was turned off . . .

The plan had seemed straightforward enough. The woman who'd returned his call was almost certainly the person who'd killed Portia Kane and two officers, and Finn had her here, within a block radius. Sure, it was a block swarming with people, but the crowds were starting to thin and with Damon's ear for music, they'd used the background music to pinpoint where the woman had made the call. Of course she wasn't there when they arrived, but she couldn't have gone far.

Finn knew she wouldn't have left the fair, despite what she'd claimed—that was just for his benefit, making him think "Robyn" was safely out of danger while he hunted for the scarred killer. She was here, and she was staying until she found Peltier.

So he just had to find her. He'd notified the backup team, now in place. But no one had the faintest idea what this woman looked like. Though her voice had sounded young, Finn knew better than to prejudge and had said only that she sounded under fifty. As defining factors went, that didn't help. In twenty minutes, he'd seen one woman over fifty.

He'd told Damon to pay attention to women who seemed to be searching for someone. But as the clock ticked past midnight and families cleared out, half the women seemed to be hunting for a spouse or a child.

Their best hope was that Damon would find his wife, and *that* would help them find the woman. But there was no sign of her either.

Finally, at Damon's prodding, Finn had called the cell phone while the ghost climbed onto a trailer to search the crowds for a woman answering.

Great idea. Or it would be, if she hadn't turned off the phone. Finn had tried three more times since, to no avail. She wasn't stupid; she didn't want him phoning back for more details or, worse, insisting she meet up with him.

"If Bobby's here, she's hiding," Damon said as he hopped from his latest perch. "Which is smart, and what I'd expect, but it doesn't help us worth shit. I want her safe, but she'd be safer if we caught this bitch."

Finn grunted and kept surveying the crowd. Even if he heard her voice, he still might not recognize her, but he couldn't stop looking and listening. She was here, a cop killer, and this might be his best chance to catch her.

"We'll keep looking," he said.

Damon looked relieved, as if he'd expected Finn to declare the mission impossible and call it off. If this woman killed Peltier, she and Damon could be reunited in death, and maybe a lesser man would want that, but Finn could tell it hadn't entered Damon's mind. His life ended early; he'd never wish the same on the woman he loved.

"Wherever Bobby is, she'll eventually pop out for a look around."

THEY SEARCHED FOR FIFTEEN MINUTES MORE. Finn called the cell phone twice, with no answer. As they rounded a corn dog stand, Finn reached for Damon's arm. Two teens turned to gawk at the guy clawing the air.

"You really need to stop doing that," Damon said. "What's up?"

"That girl over there."

Finn started to point, then stopped himself and turned the gesture into an awkward chin-scratch while jerking his thumb toward his target, getting more stares than he had by pointing.

"Man, we need to work on your subtle communication skills," Damon said. "You mean the girl in the cowboy hat? Yeah, it's damned ugly."

Finn lifted his cell phone, pretending to talk into it. "To my left, outside the fence. Light hair, yellow T-shirt . . ."

Damon squinted at the girl, then strode over, through people, through the fence, stood in front of her and yelled back, "This girl?"

Finn nodded. The girl—woman, he supposed he should say—was

on the other side of the fence, walking toward the fair, coming out of a field beyond. Her strides were short and choppy, as if she didn't really want to be heading in this direction, but had no choice. Her scowl seconded that.

Damon strode back. "She doesn't look like the type to try sneaking in without paying, but if you want to alert security . . ."

"Do you recognize her?"

Damon looked back at the girl, now marching along the fence line. "Should I?"

"From the photo. The one on Robyn's phone."

"Uh, no, Finn. Sure, they're both blond and about the same age, but that is *not* the girl in the dress—"

"I meant the one behind her. In the photo."

"There was a girl behind the one in the dress?"

"A couple. An older man and her." He jerked his chin toward the girl, still marching, still scowling, still searching for a way back in.

"Shit. Guess I'm not quite the sleuth I thought I was. I honestly never noticed anyone else. But if you think that's her . . ."

He didn't think; he knew.

"And you think it can't be a coincidence she's here," Damon continued.

Again, Finn *knew* it. "Look where she is. You said yourself she doesn't look like the sort to sneak in. And if she *is,* she's picked a hell of a spot. Everyone can see her. Besides, she's wearing an admission band."

"Wearing . . . ? Damn. Missed that, too. I'm striking out tonight. What's she doing, then?"

"Or who is she looking for?"

Damon didn't seem to hear Finn, having already figured it out and started moving toward her, cutting through the crowds the way only a ghost could.

She was maybe twenty, average height and skinny with dark blond hair cut to her shoulders. With her mousy hair, long face and sallow complexion, she was the sort of girl you expected to see at a state college, walking alone, avoiding eye contact, books clutched to her chest.

She wasn't avoiding eye contact now. Her mouth was set in a hard line. As she found a gap where she could squeeze through the fence, she shot the onlookers a scowl that dared them to comment. At least a dozen people watched her, not one saying a word, all presuming if she was doing it so openly, she was allowed to.

Finn placed a call to dispatch, giving the girl's description and requesting immediate backup. "Immediate," though, wasn't going to be fast enough.

He intercepted her. "Miss?"

That glower swung up at him. He saw a flicker of something blander, as if she was trying to force a more polite expression for him. After a moment, she gave up.

"Yes?"

Finn flashed his badge, too quick for her to read it, hoping for a reaction without pushing her to panic. But her expression didn't change.

"Security? Fine, I'm not supposed to come in there. But I've paid, see?" She waved her wrist.

"This isn't about whether you've paid—" He held up his badge. She made no move to read it, her gaze already moving on, scanning the crowd.

"I'm Detective Findlay. I believe we spoke earlier on Robyn Peltier's phone."

Her head swung around fast enough to cause whiplash, and what little color she had in her cheeks drained.

She bolted, but Finn was ready, lunging and catching her arm.

"Hey," a voice slurred. "You can't do that." A kid, not old enough to drink, lurched toward them, eyes glazed as he waved at Finn's badge. "I got a cell phone, you know. Let go of her or you'll be starring on YouTube, asshole."

Finn kept his grip on the girl's arm, deftly steering out of the drunk kid's way, while keeping him in sight.

"Miss, I need to ask you—"

Someone whacked him between the shoulder blades. His grip relaxed just as she yanked. She slid free and dove into the crowd now surrounding them, cell phones out.

Finn went after her, shouldering his way through the mob. He kept looking for his backup. No sign of it. He called his lieutenant, updating him as quickly as possible, then getting off the phone. The girl was running now. Everyone got out of her way. Not everyone got out of his, a few intentionally stepping into his path, making him veer around them.

"Finn! I got her!" Damon's voice rose above the din. "She's heading toward the kiddie section. I think there's an exit there."

Following Damon's voice, Finn rounded a corner. The people there, not having witnessed the altercation, saw only a big man bearing down on them . . . and stepped aside. Ahead he could see the girl's yellow shirt flashing through the darkness.

Damon continued shouting, keeping him on track, as they headed into the children's area. It was all but empty and that's where she made her mistake. Finn might be big, but he was in top condition—and she wasn't. As the gap between them closed, she kept glancing over her shoulder, slowing herself down all the more, but unable to stop checking.

Finn broke into an all-out sprint. The girl weaved toward a quartet of retirees enjoying cotton candy under a tree, away from the fair hubbub. Alarm flashed over their faces as they spotted a man chasing a young woman. Finn waved his badge, and they fell back to give him room. The girl swerved straight for one of the women.

"Finn!" Damon shouted. "She's got—"

Finn saw the woman backpedal, frantically trying to move aside. Then the confusion in her face turned to horror. Her husband pitched toward her, hands out, as if to shove her from the girl's path. But he was too far away. The girl was bearing down on her, a gun in her outstretched hand. The woman screamed. The gun fired. The woman tottered back, eyes wide with disbelief. Then the girl gave the woman a shove, knocking her down like a bowling pin.

Shot her, shoved her out of the way and kept going.

Finn skidded beside the woman as her husband dove for her.

"Finn!" Damon shouted. "No! That's what she wants. They've got it. Keep going."

Finn sent a silent apology to the woman . . . and raced past her, shouting back for them to call 911.

He could see the girl's yellow shirt ahead, but he had to slow, calling his backup. And though he didn't stop moving, didn't stop watching that yellow shirt, by the time he reached the midway, she had too much of a head start. She disappeared into the first large mob. He caught a glimpse of her once on the other side, but by the time he made it through the crowd, she was gone.

THE BACKUP TEAM HAD SHUT DOWN all exits and was patrolling the perimeter. They were still searching the park, but in his gut, Finn knew she'd gotten away. He'd seen how easy it had been for her to sneak into the park. She wouldn't have bothered with the exit. She'd have found another way out, dodged patrols and escaped. And she'd have done it right away, knowing she'd bought a limited amount of time with her distraction.

She had shot that woman to slow Finn down. Of all the senseless reasons you could have for killing someone, there was none as cold as that.

She could have knocked the woman off her feet. Could have fired the gun in the air. Could have winged her shoulder. But she hadn't. She'd looked a stranger in the face and killed her.

And now Finn stood near the crowd surrounding the fallen woman, and while everyone else's attention was on the paramedics working frantically to revive her, his was on two people sitting apart on the curb. Damon and the woman's ghost.

Damon held the woman's hands, leaning in close and talking to her as she nodded numbly, her gaze fixed on the crowd around her body. Finn stayed where he was. There was nothing the woman could add that would help him solve her murder, and there was nothing Finn could add that would comfort her more than Damon already was.

Gradually, the woman's shock seemed to thaw. She added words to her nods. Then she made eye contact with Damon while she spoke to him. Finally she twisted to face him. He said something, and she nodded and replied. He helped her to her feet and, still holding one of her hands, led her to the edge of the crowd.

Damon stopped there, releasing her hand. She took his back, squeezing it and saying something. Then, leaving him on the edge, she walked to where her husband knelt beside her body, tears streaming down his face. She stood behind him and touched the top of his head, stroking it even as her fingers passed through. Her husband stopped. He lifted his head. She smiled and bent, murmuring, hand still resting on his head.

Then she was gone.

ROBYN

Robyn followed Hope onto the path. They'd emerged near the barricade. Hope looked around, then jammed the gun into the back of her jeans like an action-movie chick.

"Which shoulder was it?" Hope asked.

"What?"

Hope waved for her to sit on the barrier. "Which shoulder were you shot in?" When Robyn paused, Hope prodded her until she was sitting, then said, "Take off your shirt," as she pulled what looked like a first-aid kit from her pocket.

"Karl . . ."

Hope glanced toward the forest, then blinked, erasing a flash of worry. "He'll be fine. Let's get that shoulder cleaned up before we go."

Robyn shed the shirt and Hope set to work, as competent as any field medic.

I don't know her. I don't know her at all.

She shivered.

"Cold?"

Hope took off her denim jacket and started pulling it around Robyn's bare shoulders. Then her face lifted, eyes closing. A soft gasp. When she opened her eyes, Robyn saw the same gleam from before, now fading into a glow of rapture.

"It's over," she whispered. "He's okay."

"Hope?"

She jumped, startled, then busied herself tugging the jacket on

Robyn. "I don't hear them fighting anymore, and I think Karl called out. Once he gets here, we need to leave—"

"What happened?" Robyn's throat was dry, her whisper like the rustling of dry leaves.

"Hmm?"

"Back there. In the forest. The man."

"My guess is that he's the partner of that girl who shot you. Luckily she seems to be relying on him to bring you in and staying clear. One less problem for us to deal with."

"He's not working with her."

A tight laugh. "That would be awfully coincidental, you having *two* people hunting you for unrelated reasons. I'm sure he's—"

"He's not. He took a call. He was talking about her—Adele—about getting me away from her."

"Oh?" Hope's head shot up. "What did—?" She stopped. "You saw a man at Judd Archer's house, right? I bet that was him. Her *former* partner, now pursuing his own agenda."

"And, according to what he said on the phone, pursuing Karl."

It took a moment for Hope to find the proper expression of surprise. "I guess we'll have to figure it all out later. For now—"

She looked up, then quickly plastered on a fresh bandage before hurrying to the forest's edge. Robyn heard and saw nothing, but a moment later, Karl appeared. He and Hope stayed there, a dozen feet away, murmuring in voices too low for Robyn to make out.

Hope checked Karl's lip, then fingered a bloodied rip in his shirt. He bent over her, talking, Hope nodding.

Then Karl brushed hair back from her face, leaning to say something more intimate. The other Karl—the one in the forest, the one who'd pushed them aside—was gone.

"I'll walk you two back to the car first," Karl said as they approached Robyn.

Hope shook her head. "We'll be fine. You finish here, then meet up with us." She looked at Robyn. "Karl has to clean up."

"Get rid of the body," Robyn said.

Hope let out a chirp. A laugh? Or a choke of surprise? "Damon really did subject you to too many crime shows, didn't he? I meant Karl needs to clean *himself* up." She waved at his bloodied shirt and split lip. "He can't go traipsing around in public like that."

Robyn gave him a look. Hope met it without flinching. Robyn continued to stare, trying to make Hope look away, give another nervous laugh. When she did neither, Robyn strode toward the forest. She got to the edge. Then Karl's hand fell on her shoulder.

"You're going to the car," he said.

There was no menace in his voice. No room for questions either. She looked back at him, lifting her chin to meet his eyes.

"Yes," he said. Nothing more. It could have meant "yes, you're going to the car" or "yes, I will stop you from taking another step." But she knew it didn't. It meant "yes, you're right." That was all she needed. She backed onto the path and followed Hope.

IT TOOK NO MORE THAN FIVE MINUTES to walk from the forest. As Robyn saw the woods opening up, the field ahead, she slowed, certain the edge couldn't be so close. When she'd been running she'd told herself repeatedly how small the woods had to be, but with everything that had happened in there, it felt like those trees should go on forever, that they'd been miles from civilization.

And here, just ahead, was civilization, as garish as it got. The fair. The music still boomed. The kids still screamed. The lights still colored the night sky. The air smelled, not of fear and blood and dirt, but of corn dogs and cotton candy.

Robyn rubbed her arms and blinked. They'd been gone less than an hour, but she'd somehow expected to walk out and find the fair packed up, the field a desolate wasteland of half-filled Coke cups and unwanted prizes. She felt like Lucy, stepping from the wardrobe to see that despite everything she'd seen in Narnia, the everyday world had continued, oblivious.

"Where's the car?" she finally asked. Her first words since leaving Karl.

Hope didn't break *her* silence—only pointed at the fair, then headed deeper into the field, leaving Robyn squinting to see why she wasn't taking the direct route along the fence. When she asked, Hope just shook her head.

"Hope?"

Her friend stopped. It was a moment before she turned. The moon had slid behind wisps of cloud, leaving Hope's face shadowed, her expression unreadable. It was another moment before she spoke.

"You said Adele can find you anywhere."

Robyn nodded.

"I'm making sure she doesn't."

Hope resumed walking. Robyn trudged behind her, the late-night dew soaking her shoes. Exhaustion slumped her shoulders, the injured one aching. The adrenaline rush from earlier was long gone. Like a midafternoon caffeine-and-sugar-crash, all she wanted to do was follow Hope, let her worry about Adele and find them someplace safe to hide, and to hell with the questions, the whys and hows. But those questions buzzed in her brain like bees, stinging her every time she tried to ignore them.

How did taking this route protect her from Adele? The field was empty—all Adele had to do was glance out when the moon reappeared and she'd see them.

She remembered when they'd first entered the forest, the man saying it was "suitably nondescript" and would keep Adele from finding them.

"She can see me, can't she? She's . . . like one of those psychics the police use to find people." Even as Robyn heard the words, she couldn't believe she was saying them, and worse, saying them as if she believed them.

"Adele sees me," she pressed on. "She sees what's around me and that's how she tracks me down. If there aren't any hints in the landscape—"

"—then she can't find you."

There, Hope had admitted it.

They traveled another twenty feet before Hope stopped. "Going to the car might not be the wisest idea. Something tells me Adele wouldn't hesitate to turn the parking lot into the O.K. Corral." She took the gun from her waistband. "We'll wait for Karl to come. He'll find us."

Of course he would. He always did. An unnatural ability to find them anyplace they left a trail. Like a tracking dog. She shivered and looked over at Hope. She was scanning the field. At a glance, Robyn could see there was no one around, but Hope kept looking, slowly turning. Robyn leaned toward her to say something. Hope's eyes were closed.

"Hope?"

She lifted a finger, telling her to wait. After a few seconds, Hope flinched and went rigid. Her eyes flew open, gaze swinging to something white in the grass a dozen feet away.

Robyn walked closer and saw a small, white cross with a faded plastic wreath. "Someone must have died here."

"Yes." Firm, as if Hope knew that for sure.

Robyn rubbed the goose bumps from her arms, started to sit, then felt the cold, wet grass and changed her mind. Arms wrapped around her chest, she looked at the forest.

"What happened back there?"

"I don't know. You said that guy seemed to know Adele and know she was after you, but he definitely wasn't planning to rescue you, at least not in the sense of letting you walk away—"

"That's not what I meant."

The wail of an ambulance filled the silence. They both turned to follow the sound. It seemed to be heading for the fair, but with all the flashing lights, it was impossible to tell. After a moment, Robyn wasn't even sure it was an ambulance at all, not just the sirens on a ride.

When it stopped, Robyn waited. Still Hope didn't respond.

"That's not what I meant," Robyn repeated.

Hope nodded. And said nothing. At least thirty seconds passed before she looked over.

"What *did* you mean?" she asked.

Robyn blanched under that look—a hard challenge that dared her to elaborate and maybe warned her not to, told her she was better off letting it go. Robyn knew it *would* be better to forget. Chalk it up to exhaustion and strain. Hope was offering her an easy way out. A safe way out. But nothing in Robyn's nature would let her take it.

"Tonight I saw my best friend pull a gun I never knew she had, and know how to use it. A man threw me like a rag doll, then I watched another man do the same to him. I heard a man talk about demons and witches and werewolves like I knew what he meant, like he was discussing something as undeniable as the trees around us. And I know that man is now lying in the woods, beaten to death by a guy I thought wouldn't know how to throw a punch."

"Did you see a body?"

"No, but—"

"Yes, Karl beat the crap out of him. That's all. Now he's checking his ID to see why he was following you, then he's getting himself clean enough to walk out here. Yes, Karl knows how to fight. That story I told you about him being in security? A lie. Any security Karl did was from the wrong side of the law. That's all in the past, but he has a reputation and he has enemies and he knows that at any time he might need to protect himself, so he keeps in shape. As for the talk of werewolves and demons and witches? Someone is off his meds."

In the world of public relations, there are two kinds of spin. One is the totally plausible alternative explanation, like "Yes, my client was arrested for DUI, but the reports show she was barely over the limit so she must have picked up the wrong drink at the party." The bigger and more convoluted the problem, the harder it is to find a perfect excuse. In that case, publicists have to settle for the second type, the kind that says "I know it's far-fetched, but work with me on this one, okay?" like explaining that yes, your client blew double the legal limit, smashed into a Victoria's Secret window, stripped to her underwear and posed for pictures, but she must have picked up the wrong drink and it reacted badly with her cold medication.

Hope's explanation fell squarely under type two.

"I want to know the truth," Robyn said.

"Do you?"

"Yes, I do." The bite in her words hid the undertone of hurt. "I'm your friend. Of course I want to know—"

"Then, as a friend, I'd suggest you spend a little more time thinking about it. Decide whether you really want to know more. As a friend, I'd suggest maybe you don't."

HOPE

Robyn didn't ask any more questions after that. She didn't get a chance.

First Hope had to deal with the problem of getting Karl, unnoticed, through the stream of exiting fairgoers. He'd taken the T-shirt from the mutt—Gilchrist—and put it on backward to hide the blood on the front, then topped it with his jacket. To anyone drawing near, the skintight shirt riding up his abs clearly wasn't his. It might not have looked out of place on any of the strutting teens surrounding them, but when worn by an impeccably groomed guy Karl's age, it was noticeable. It didn't help that every time he so much as twitched his lips, the split reopened, trickling blood. Hope had Karl and Robyn wait in the shadow of a closed convenience store as she retrieved the car.

Once in the car, Hope put Robyn in the middle of the backseat, away from the windows, and instructed her to close her eyes for the trip. She had no idea whether the closed eyes would help keep Adele from Robyn, but it couldn't hurt. Earlier they'd picked out a hotel where they could get to a side door without passing a sign. It was about fifteen miles away, but it took almost an hour, as Karl traveled through residential areas, avoiding business districts and *their* signs.

When they finally reached the hotel, Karl parked at an unmarked side door. Hope checked them into a suite and let them in the exit. They bustled Robyn upstairs, Hope scouting ahead to cover signs. Then Robyn waited inside the doorway as Karl and Hope drew the blinds and emptied the room of every pen and comment card that bore the hotel's name.

Once Robyn came in, it was time for a more professional evaluation of her shoulder. Karl called his Alpha, Jeremy, the Pack's medical expert. The bullet had passed through with no serious damage. Jeremy said it should be seen by a doctor, but if the wound was properly dressed and checked, she'd be fine for a few days.

Robyn was ready to turn in. Somewhere between the fairgrounds, the endless trip and the furtive dash into the hotel room and the re-redressing of her wound, she'd apparently decided that Hope was right—the truth wasn't something she needed to hear.

They checked the bedroom one last time. Then Hope waited by the door and made sure Robyn was settled before returning to Karl on the sofa.

"On to patient two. Time to take it off for me."

The joke fell as flat as her smile. Karl had said little since meeting up with them in the field, and the low strum of worry flowing from him made her stomach twist. She'd hoped it was only concern over what Robyn had seen and heard, but even now, he stayed quiet, shucking his shirt, those vibes still pulsing.

"I gave her a reasonable story," Hope said. "Not perfect—nothing was going to cover all that. If she wants an explanation bad enough, she'll take that one, but we should discuss how we'll handle it if she doesn't."

It took a moment for him to nod. She couldn't tell if he'd been considering his answer or if he hadn't heard a word she'd said.

She continued to wait, hoping he'd pick up the conversation, make suggestions, but from his expression she knew he wasn't thinking of Robyn.

Hope brought over the first-aid kit. Other than that reopened split lip, he had only the gash on his chest that had ripped his shirt. She pulled a splinter from it. It looked as if he'd caught it on a broken branch. The rest of his injuries were bruises. Fighting in human form avoided fang and claw damage, but from the welt on his chest she suspected his ribs were bruised, maybe even cracked.

When she touched the welt, he didn't flinch, only blinked as if wondering what she was doing. "Those are fine," he murmured. "I just need to clean that cut."

He rose. Hope tapped his shoulder, telling him to stay sitting and she'd do it. He hesitated again, as if confused, before another nod and another murmur, this one unintelligible.

As she returned with a wet cloth, she said, "Robyn says that Gilchrist knew who Adele was, which suggests he didn't just happen onto your trail today."

"Hmm."

"We'll need to get the details from her tomorrow."

"Yes."

Hope cleaned and bandaged the wound, and still he sat there, as if in a trance, moving only when she asked him to shift positions, speaking only when prompted. And even though he kept his thoughts cloaked, the sharp pulses of his worry gradually dissolved into a steady flow of despair.

"It all worked out tonight," she said finally. "However tense it got, Robyn's fine, I'm fine, you've only got a few bruises and none of us need to worry about Gilchrist again."

Karl nodded.

"He never even laid a finger on me," she continued. "I felt him coming before he could sneak up on us. I got my gun out, got Robyn behind me . . ."

He nodded.

"And when he did pounce, I did the right thing—diving out of the way—but I still managed to fire off a round. I think I nicked him."

"You did."

"I'll admit, I did have a momentary blip there, when the chaos surged, but I didn't completely freeze up. I *am* learning, Karl."

"I know."

"Well, then, no harm, no foul, right?" Her laugh squeaked, and she stood there, fingers trembling around the first-aid kit, knowing she hadn't said the right thing. Damn it, why hadn't she said the right thing? Why didn't she *know* the right thing?

"The problem," he said after a moment, "wasn't you. It was me."

"But he wasn't after you. This has something to do with that clairvoyant girl, and if you weren't helping me with Robyn, he would never have found you."

"Never?"

"Probably not. And so what if he did? You handled it. *We* handled it. If you hadn't been there, he still would have grabbed Robyn—"

"Would he?"

"Prob—" She stopped herself. "Yes. Yes, he would have, and I would have had to shoot the son of a bitch and dig the shallow grave."

He shook his head. "He was only interested in Robyn as a means to an end. That end was getting you, and he targeted you because of me."

"Oh, sure." That squeak-laugh again. "Thanks a helluva lot, Karl. I'll have you know I'm quite capable of attracting assholes on my own."

The lines around his mouth only deepened. "In the forest, you weren't overwhelmed by chaos from Gilchrist; you were overwhelmed by chaos from me. Fear, rage. I couldn't control it. Even knowing it was endangering you, I couldn't—"

He rose, walked to the window and stood there, looking out as if oblivious to the closed blinds. "Jeremy is always very cautious about who knows he's involved with Jaime. She's not a werewolf, and being with one puts her in danger. I told myself that didn't apply to us. You can defend yourself a hell of a lot better than Jaime Vegas. And I'm not the Alpha. I'm barely even a Pack member. There would be nothing for another werewolf to gain by hurting you, except to force me into a fight. And if they want a fight, they don't need to go after you. I never turn down a challenge."

"Exactly, so—"

"I've spent my life building a reputation, not caring how many enemies I made because having that reputation makes my life easier. If those enemies want revenge, they know where to find me. There's no other way to hurt me. Now there is."

"I'm careful, Karl. You know I am. If you need me to take more precautions, I will. More self-defense classes, more shooting lessons, maybe training on another weapon, like a knife. Or carry mace or pepper spray."

God, how pathetic did she sound? The words kept coming, each one underscored with a whine of please, please, please. *Please don't leave me, Karl. I'll do whatever you want.*

"You could bite me." Hope heard the words, the softest whisper, as if she barely dared give them voice, and she couldn't believe she *was* giving them voice, that someone else hadn't crept up behind her and spoken them.

Karl didn't move. Just stood there, back to her. He hadn't heard. Thank God, he hadn't heard. Then, slowly, he turned. The look on his face, the horror . . .

"No." The word was a strangled whisper as he stepped toward her. "Never, Hope. I would never—"

She reeled back out of his reach, her cheeks blazing.

"I-I-I—" She rubbed her throat as if she could push the words out. "I'm sorry."

She fled, stumbling, into the bathroom as he called after her. She locked the door and leaned against it. Burning tears of shame blurred

the room. The doorknob turned one way, then the other. A pause.
Then a rap.

"Hope?"

"I-I'm having a bath."

Which was, quite possibly, the lamest excuse she could think of.

"Let me come in—"

"What I said, I didn't mean it. I'm wiped out and I'm worried
about Robyn and I'm stressing over what she heard tonight, and I
just— I need a bath."

Hope could sense him at the door, but he didn't answer. She had to
follow through, but the tub looked an impossibly long distance away.
She staggered to it and turned on the tap. *Hear that? I really am having a bath.*

She undressed and lowered herself into the tub without waiting for
it to finish filling. Her words pounded against her skull.

You could bite me.

She couldn't believe she'd said that. Worse, even now, shaking and
crying in shame, she wasn't sure she hadn't meant it.

Bile washed over her tongue.

In movies, she'd heard romantic heroines declare they couldn't live
without their man, and she wanted to tell them to grow a backbone.
But she needed Karl. Without him . . .

She couldn't bring herself to say she'd die without him, but in the
last few years, there'd been times when she'd seen the abyss yawn before
her, the chaos hunger grow from a craving to an all-encompassing
I-must-have-it need, the demon whispering new ways to feed the
hunger. She'd stared into that abyss and she'd known what she could
become, and that if she ever became that, she would sooner die.

But she'd always had Karl to pull her back. To support her and
teach her to deal with that darkness, to accept and control her demon
the way he did the wolf. To tell her she'd be okay, she was doing fine,
he was there and they'd handle whatever came.

Even if Karl walked away now, he wouldn't abandon her. He
wouldn't stop pulling her back from the edge, being her friend. Just
not her lover. She could live without that part of the relationship—she
just didn't want to.

But everything Karl did—buying a condo in Philly, switching his
territory to Pennsylvania, following her to L.A.—told her that he was
committed to this relationship and he wasn't going anywhere. Even
tonight, she knew he'd only been trying to figure out what he needed
to change so she'd be safe *with* him around.

So why was she constantly worrying? Needing proof he planned to stay? Reminding herself that he might not stay and she needed to be prepared for that?

Because she wasn't prepared for it. What terrified her was not Karl leaving, but her fear of Karl leaving. She needed him so badly that she'd risk her life becoming a werewolf to keep him.

What kind of person did that make her? Not one she wanted to be.

"You're shivering."

Karl had picked the lock and come in without her realizing it. Now he was beside the tub, sitting on his haunches, his back against the door, hands folded on his knees.

He straightened. "Watch your feet. I'm going to add more hot water."

He bent at the taps, touched the water, then jerked his hand back. "It's ice cold, Hope."

She mumbled something about it cooling off too fast. Better than admitting that she was so out of it she'd sat in a tub of cold water without noticing.

Karl pulled the drain and Hope watched the water drop, the *chug-chug* of it echoing in the silent room. When it was two-thirds empty, he replaced the stopper, then nudged her feet farther from the faucet before turning on the hot.

Once it was refilled, he returned to his spot by the door without a word.

"I didn't mean it," she said after a moment.

"I hope not."

Hope's cheeks flamed. "I'm tired, Karl. Absolutely wiped out, and I just started babbling. I feel like an idiot for saying it. I don't want that at all. I was just . . . babbling."

He moved to sit on the side of the tub, where she had to look at him.

"You know it's not what *I* want, don't you?" he said. "That when I joke about the mating instinct and dragging you off to a cabin in the woods, I mean *you*. As you are. I don't mean—"

"I know."

Hope fixed her gaze on her toes bobbing over the water. He turned her face toward him, fingers resting on her chin.

"I mean it. That's not what I want. Consciously, subconsciously, unconsciously . . . I'm not fighting any temptation to turn you into a werewolf."

When she nodded, gaze down, he lifted her chin.

"You know that, don't you?"

Hope had never thought she was in danger of Karl biting her without her permission, as Clay had done to Elena, or that he'd ever find a way to do it "accidentally." But maybe she did worry a little that he'd prefer it. Werewolves weren't like other supernaturals. Like wolves, they preferred the company of their own kind.

"No," he said, as if reading her thoughts, his gaze locked with her, challenging her to read his vibes for any sign that he was lying. When he was satisfied she believed him, he pulled a washcloth off the rack and picked up a bar of soap.

"I'm not going anywhere, Hope," he said as he unwrapped the soap. "Tonight, I was just furious with myself for being too cavalier about the threat Gilchrist posed. Even before today I've downplayed the threat of you being attacked. I didn't want to admit that being with me might not be safe. I was thinking about how to resolve the problem, Hope, not how to run away from it. I need to make sure you understand the threat, and I need to teach you how to deal with it—how to fight a werewolf. That's all."

She'd known that. But she'd still flipped out. And the more she flipped out, the more her reaction—not his—terrified her.

He dipped the cloth into the water, squeezed it, lathered it up and wiped the back of her neck. "You picked up some dirt in the forest."

She bent her head forward, letting him wash. He moved down her back, moving in slow circles, the rough cloth sloughing away the night. Her eyes started to close.

He leaned her back against the tub, setting her head on the edge, then washed her shoulders. "I know I left you once."

She opened her mouth, wanting to say it didn't matter, it was forgotten. But it wasn't.

"I know I hurt you."

Again, she wanted to argue. But she couldn't.

"I know I said I won't leave again, but I also know that's not enough, and that the only way you're going to trust that I won't leave is if I don't."

He slid the cloth over her arms. "If this ends, Hope, it won't be me that ends it. I think you know that."

She twisted in the tub, rising, put her arms around his neck and kissed him. He scooped her up, dripping water, and carried her into the other room.

ROBYN

Robyn had been standing at the hotel bedroom door for ten minutes, her fingers on the handle as she listened for sounds from the other side.

Last night, she'd been too tired to ask questions and had used that as an excuse to herself for not asking. But, her first thought on waking had been *I have to know.*

She'd showered, dressed, made the bed and was now stalled at the door to the main room, where Hope and Karl were sleeping.

She counted to three. Then to five. Then told herself, on the count of ten, she absolutely would—

Goddamn it, just open it!

She knocked. It took a moment before she heard Hope's sleepy "come in." She cracked open the door. Hope was alone on the sofa bed, sitting up, blinking at the empty space beside her.

Robyn pointed at the closed bathroom door, light shining under it. "I think he's in there."

Hope nodded. She looked at Robyn, then her gaze dipped away. Karl came out of the bathroom. Hope murmured something, then slipped in behind him. The door closed.

Robyn looked at that door, wondering what was up with Hope this morning. A rough night, she supposed. After their ordeal, she couldn't blame her.

"Good morning, Robyn," Karl said.

She managed a response. He crossed to the desk and picked up the room service menu. Robyn stayed where she'd stopped, watching him leaf through it.

She thought of what the other man had said Karl was, and even if she couldn't bring herself to form the word, she couldn't stop thinking about it. Couldn't stop hearing his snarl from last night. Couldn't stop seeing the pulsing rage in his face. Couldn't forget the other man's face, pulsing with something else, contorting, changing . . .

"That fair last night, it didn't have a freak show, did it?" Karl asked, still reading the menu.

"What?"

"Freaks. The Bearded Lady. The Three-legged Man. The Lobster Boy. Pay a dollar to see the freak?"

"Um, no, I didn't see . . ."

"But you've seen exhibits like that before. Hope says you like fairs, particularly small, out-of-the-way ones where the questionable qualities of a freak show might be more acceptable."

"Sure . . ."

He glanced up. "Have you ever paid your dollar?"

"No, never. I—"

"When you see the signs, though, do you ever consider what it would be like to be the person inside that tent? On display? With everyone staring, satisfying their morbid curiosity, wondering how you live, how awful it would be to be you . . ."

"I . . ." She stopped, realizing what he was getting at. "I'm sorry. I didn't mean to . . . gawk."

"Personally? I don't care." He set the menu back on the desk. "But Hope does. She's already uncomfortable. Having her friend gaping at her like she's on display . . ."

Was that why Hope ducked into the bathroom? Robyn didn't think she'd been gaping, but she must have been looking at her differently, thinking, wondering . . .

"I want to know," Robyn said.

"Hmm." He plucked his jacket from a chair back. "Room service is apparently not one of this hotel's strengths. Tell Hope I went out to find a more suitable breakfast."

She stepped in his path. "I mean it, Karl. I want to know what's going on. Everything."

"We'll discuss it over breakfast. Don't jump on Hope about it the moment she gets out of the bathroom."

"I wouldn't."

His lips parted, but he settled for a nod, a curt good-bye, and was gone.

HOPE CAME OUT SHORTLY after Karl left. Robyn tried to avoid awkwardness by making small talk, asking about Hope's mother's plans for her big May Day charity ball, which only made it obvious there were a million things she was *avoiding* talking about.

Hope squirmed under those questions as much as if Robyn had gaped at her. She'd promised Karl she wouldn't ask more, but *not* asking felt even stranger. It was like sitting with one of those freaks, discussing the most mundane subjects imaginable, pretending you didn't notice you were talking to a woman with a beard.

"We need to talk about what happened last night," Hope said finally.

"Oh, I— No, that's okay. I—"

"I mean about the guy who grabbed you, what he said about Adele and Karl."

"Oh, right." Robyn kicked herself for not thinking of this safe-but-pertinent topic. She seized on the diversion and was still explaining when Karl arrived.

He set up breakfast, waving them aside when they stood to help, asking questions when Robyn finished her explanation. Then Hope and Karl exchanged a look, one that Robyn had come to know well and now understood: "We'll discuss it later, when she's not around."

"Did Robyn tell you what she wants?" Karl asked as they dished up breakfast plates.

"I was warned not to bring it up," Robyn said.

Hope followed her look. "Karl . . ."

He only shrugged, unapologetic, and bit into his croissant.

"I told Karl I want to know," Robyn said.

"Know . . . ?"

Robyn gave her a look—it was like leaning around the proverbial pachyderm in the room to ask, "what elephant?"

"Everything," she said.

Hope and Karl exchanged another look.

"Let's start with what's important right now," Hope said. "This Adele Morrissey . . ."

"She's psychic."

Hope paused, as if fighting the temptation to leave it at that, then said, "We call them clairvoyants."

"So she sees the future?"

"No, just the present. It's remote-viewing. Have you ever heard of that?"

Robyn shook her head.

"They used to do it at spiritualist shows, back in Victorian times. The spiritualist would sit behind a screen or in a back room and would describe things in the audience."

"I didn't know that," Karl murmured.

Hope flashed him a smile, as if grateful for the diversion. "That's because you're not *True News*'s weird-tales girl. This stuff is my life, remember?"

Robyn hadn't even thought of that, Hope's unusual specialty. There was more to it than a job, obviously.

"Most of that remote-viewing was fake, of course," Hope said, relaxing now, in her element. "Real clairvoyants are extremely rare. It's passed down through generations in varying degrees, so even if you have the blood, you may not be able to remotely view. But those who have the power can see farther than past a screen or into an adjoining room. They focus on a person, using a picture or personal effect."

"Like a psychic."

Hope nodded. "All that stuff has to originally come from somewhere, right? By using that object and focusing, Adele can see you. I have no idea how big a window she gets—like I said, true clairvoyants are rare, so we don't know a lot about them. She'd use that view, though, to pick up clues about your surroundings—a street sign, a landmark . . ."

"A napkin with a café name on it," Robyn said, remembering the day before.

"Exactly. You said she's a photographer, that she took pictures of Portia for the tabloids. I guess that's how she used her talents."

Clairvoyant paparazzi, able to find their targets anywhere, watch and wait for that moment when they were most likely to do something tabloid-worthy, slip in, snag the shot and leave, while their colleagues chased and hounded and prayed they'd get lucky.

Robyn considered herself a rational person. Too rational, some said. The summer she'd been fourteen, she'd followed a friend to a camp for the arts. At the end of the two weeks, her creative writing instructor told her, as gently as possible, that not all people were cut out to be novelists and if she enjoyed writing, she might want to consider nonfiction instead. In other words, Robyn didn't have an imaginative cell in her body. She'd come to accept that.

But now, faced with the existence of people with real psychic abilities, even her too-rational brain was satisfied that this *did* make sense, given the evidence. Was it that preposterous, when there were branches of science devoted to studying such phenomena? As Hope said, the stories about ESP and remote-viewing had to come from somewhere. As long as they were talking about people seeing the present, not the future, then yes, Robyn could accept it.

"So Adele is part of this . . . group," Robyn said. "This community, of people with . . . extraordinary powers."

"We have some idea who Adele may have aligned herself with and, yes, it's an organization, but for now, the important part is that we know what she is. We'll be able to deal with her."

"But the larger group, community, whatever, the one made up of everyone with paranormal powers . . ."

"I wouldn't exactly call it a community."

"You know what I mean."

Hope sipped her coffee.

Robyn waited a moment for Hope to answer. When she didn't, she said, "So we have clairvoyants and . . ."

Hope added another cream. Stirred. Sipped.

"Clairvoyants and . . ." Robyn prompted.

Hope set her cup down and leaned back. "What else do you need to know?"

"I said I want to know—"

"Need," Karl said.

She looked from one to the other. Both met her gaze, expressions blank.

"So you won't tell me," she said finally.

"Won't, shouldn't, can't . . ." Hope said. "Anything you *need* to know, though, I'll—"

"Oh, this is silly." Robyn slumped into the chair, arms crossed. She felt childish doing it, but at least she managed to avoid pouting. "I'm not exactly asking for national security secrets."

"Aren't you?" Karl said. "Perhaps not national security, but certainly very valid security concerns for a group of people."

"Why? So what if the world suddenly discovered people who could remote-view?"

"Have you ever heard of the Inquisition?" Karl asked.

"Now that *is* silly. Yes, people were afraid of witchcraft in the Middle Ages. They also thought dragons inhabited the edge of the world. Are you honestly going to tell me that if people today knew about clairvoyants, they'd hunt them down and burn them at the stake?"

"Perhaps not."

"There's no *perhaps* about it, Karl. This isn't the Middle Ages—"

"What if you read a headline announcing the discovery of a mutant gene found in a very small group. This gene forces them to murder one person each year to stay alive, and to feed off people the rest of the year, like parasites. Would you say *vive la différence*? Live and let live?"

"Well, no, but whatever those people are—"

"Vampires?"

Robyn blanched. She didn't mean to, but she couldn't help it.

"But if there are . . . vampires, they aren't people," she said.

"I wouldn't try telling them that," Hope murmured.

Robyn looked at her. Were they serious? Or were they only giving the most outrageous example they could? She straightened and met Karl's gaze.

"Fine, I wouldn't approve of vampires. But that's not—"

"Let's take another example then. A slightly larger group. People with no biological imperative to kill, but with a strong—sometimes overwhelming—instinct to do it. An instinct to see man not as a conscious being, but as just another threat and food source. Many resist the urge, some successfully. Some don't bother to try. Should we exterminate them all? Just to be safe?"

Werewolves. He had to be talking about werewolves. And if what she suspected was true, it wasn't an imaginary example.

"No," she said. "You don't execute people because they *might* kill."

"Noble, but would everyone agree with you? After all, we're talking about a very small group. Perhaps thirty in North America. Wouldn't it just be easier to round them up and kill them, eliminate the contamination, just to be safe?"

She opened her mouth, but Karl continued. "Of course, not every supernatural is a predator. The majority are not, and wouldn't pose an obvious threat."

"Exactly my point, so—"

"Someone like a clairvoyant or medium or witch would be perfectly acceptable, as long as you don't pull religion into it?"

"Religion?"

Hope answered. "They're all considered, at least by Christianity, to be in league with the devil."

"Oh, that's—"

"Silly? Tell that to every other group that's been persecuted because there's something in the Bible that could be interpreted to mean God disapproves of them. If you had, say, demon blood, how quick would you be to announce it?"

Robyn considered that . . . and didn't care for the answer.

"And let's return to the original example," Hope went on. "Clairvoyants. Would you want people to know you could see what they were doing, anytime, anywhere? What would your friends think of that? Your husband or lover? Knowing you could spy on them?"

Robyn couldn't hold Hope's gaze. Yes, she had a point. But Robyn wasn't asking her to tell the world. Just her.

Damn it, Hope, she thought, *I'm your friend.*

"Yes," Hope said softly. "You are my friend."

Robyn looked up sharply. Had she spoken aloud? She looked into Hope's eyes, and knew she hadn't. And she shivered. God, she didn't want to, but she couldn't help it.

"Is *that* something you'd want to announce to your friends?" Hope said. "Is that something you really wanted to know about me?"

Robyn opened her mouth, but couldn't form words.

"I didn't think so."

ROBYN QUICKLY REALIZED how foolish she'd sounded saying "tell me everything." Hope gave her only what she needed to know, with no mention of werewolves or demons or witches, keeping it all in the simplest terms possible. But even so, before long Robyn was totally lost.

Apparently the guy in the photo *was* an executive with a corporation . . . a corporation that employed people like Adele and Karl and Hope, and was known in their circles as the supernatural corporate Mafia. As for what that meant, how such a company operated, why no one ever noticed? Robyn didn't ask. The concept of a "supernatural corporate Mafia" masquerading as a regular business was enough for her to assimilate.

Hope was certain that what this Irving guy wanted was Adele. Apparently, being a rare race, clairvoyants were very valuable. As employees, Robyn presumed, though by this point, if Hope said he'd wanted Adele for a ritual sacrifice, she wouldn't have blinked.

"What all this has to do with the photo, and why Adele wants it back, I don't know. It would make sense if *Irving* was behind Portia's death. If he was trying to hire Adele, he wouldn't want the photo splashed over the tabloids, where a rival could track her down and make a better offer."

"He'd kill for that?"

"Sure." Hope said it with absolute conviction, as if it was no more in question than whether a rival *would* make Adele a better offer.

That would mean this guy knew Portia told Robyn to send the picture to the tabs. Maybe he'd been tapping Portia's phone. Or maybe Adele had used her powers and seen Portia type the message. It didn't matter. Adele had killed Portia and was after Robyn, and that was what counted.

Hope and Karl also suspected that this supernatural corporation was involved in the murder investigation, through Detective Findlay.

"He's a supernatural," Hope explained. "One of my powers is that I can detect other supernaturals. I picked it up with Findlay. I confirmed that the Nasts do have employees on the police force. Homicide would be one of the key positions. It's another way to survive unnoticed, heading off exposure threats and squelching the stories."

"Like you do with *True News*," Robyn said. "So how did *I* get mixed up in all this? I seem to be the only person involved who's norm—not supernatural."

"It happens. Most of the population has no supernatural powers and we don't live in communes and caves. Imagine what would have happened if Karl hadn't been here to find you Friday. What would you have done?"

Robyn thought about it. "Eventually turned myself in. Then, I guess Detective Findlay would have taken over and I'd have found myself framed for murder. That is, if Adele didn't get to me outside the station."

"And if either of those things happened, would you have had any suspicions that Adele wasn't just a crazy woman? Or Detective Findlay wasn't just another cop doing his job?"

"No." She paused. "So I guess I should thank you guys for being here."

"You might not want to be too quick with that. Wait until after you hear our plan for getting you out of this."

ADELE

"Ah, Adele, there you are."

Adele glanced up the stairs to a stocky figure with a ring of steel-gray hair, tucking in his shirt. Niko, the kumpania's bulibasha.

"Are you just getting in?" Niko lifted his arm, as if to check his watch, but his wrist was bare.

"Yes, I just got home."

He beamed an avuncular smile as she stopped beside him. "I guess Jasmine Wills had quite a night."

"I don't know. I kept losing her." Adele rubbed the back of her neck, wincing. She didn't need to fake that. She *had* spent all night looking for someone. Just not Jasmine. "I didn't get a single picture. I'm sorry."

"Don't be, kiddo. Can't expect results the first night."

He rumpled her hair, as if she was still five. Of course, when she was five, there'd been very little hair-rumpling from Niko. Even now, his touch made her flinch, remembering the beatings—those cold, methodical beatings as she'd lain naked on the cot in the main house basement, strap lashing down again and again until she was sobbing so hard she could barely draw breath to gasp her apologies, to promise she'd stop asking for her mother, stop crying for her, stop trying to run away.

Finally the beating would end. Niko would tell her she was a good girl, his breath coming fast, as if the exertion of the strapping was just coming upon him and he'd stroke her hair, her shoulder, her thigh until he'd abruptly leave the room. A few minutes later, she'd hear his footsteps on the stairs, leaving her alone in the cold, black basement until morning, when Lizette would come with fresh-baked lemon loaf and tell Adele she had to stop being so selfish, so naughty, wishing for a mother who'd abandoned her when the kumpania was happy to take her in, even if she was a durjardo—an outsider clairvoyant.

Once Adele's rebellion stopped, so did the beatings, as if she was a wild horse that had been broken. From then on, all she got from Niko was rumpled hair and avuncular smiles and, occasionally, a wistful look, as if he wished she'd show a little spark again, so he could take her back to that basement room and strap it out of her.

Now his hand rested on her shoulder as he talked to her. She didn't know about what, and faked a yawn, stifling it and saying, "Sorry, sir. It's really been a long night. What was that?"

"I said you might find getting photographs of Jasmine Wills easier than you think. Seems she's a fan of yours."

"Fan?"

"Her publicist called *True News*. With Portia dead, Jasmine is very interested in your—" He flashed a smile of too-bright veneers. "—creative talents. Now, you can't meet with her; that wouldn't be in the kumpania's best interests."

"No, of course not."

"And what's not in the kumpania's best interests . . ."

". . . is not in my best interests."

The rote response came automatically, and earned her another smile. "That's my girl. I left the publicist's number in your room. You may want to call her, see if you can get Jasmine's schedule. It would be a nice shortcut. Save you from long nights chasing her."

"Thank you, sir. I appreciate that."

Niko's chest puffed, as if he'd arranged the whole thing. Adele thanked him again—with Niko, there was no such thing as too much gratitude.

As Adele passed Lily's door on the way to her bedroom, she glanced in and saw the young woman sitting on the edge of her bed, smoothing her rumpled skirt, her eyes red, her underwear a white ball at her feet.

Adele glanced back at Niko's balding head as it disappeared down the stairs. Then she looked at Lily's nightstand, where his watch lay.

She smiled.

For a moment, she enjoyed the scene, then she erased the smile— or most of it—and leaned against the doorway. "I guess the phuri finally decided Hugh wasn't up to performing his husbandly duties."

Lily looked up and swiped her eyes with the back of her hand. "They gave him longer than they had to, and we're grateful for their consideration, but it's my obligation to provide the kumpania with children and I'm happy for the chance."

Puling idiot. Even now she didn't have the guts to complain. Adele would have preferred sobbing rage, but her quiet tears were enough. By the end of her fertile period, she *would* be sobbing, curled up on the bed, with cold compresses between her legs. The thought cheered Adele, if only for a moment.

"I'm all right," Lily said, misinterpreting Adele's reason for lingering. "But thank you for stopping in. You're a good sister, Adele."

Sister, my ass. If Adele had a sister, she'd be a lot brighter than this twit, who'd thanked Adele for bringing her coffee every morning, never noticing the bitter aftertaste of birth control pills. At the last meeting, when Niko had declared they might need to take the next step to impregnate Lily, Adele had watched the men's faces as they struggled to console Hugh, to act as if resigned to an unpleasant task. For the next year, the kumpania would monitor Lily's cycles and, when her time came, she'd be confined to her room for three days, while the men streamed upstairs to take their turn.

Adele excused herself and backed into the hall. As she turned, she saw Lily's cousin, Bernard, top the stairs, his corpulent frame quivering from the exertion, the crotch of his pants already straining with anticipation. Ah, duty.

"She's waiting for you," Adele said, as he lumbered past her into the room.

ADELE'S GOOD MOOD lasted only until she closed her bedroom door and caught a glimpse of herself in her full-length mirror. Thoughts of Lily's impregnation made her consider her own predicament. She pulled her shirt tight and turned to survey every angle. Nothing. She lifted the shirt. Her stomach still looked flat.

Though the book said she shouldn't show for another month at least, it also mentioned that "small" women might show earlier. Adele didn't consider herself "small," but if that was a euphemism for skinny, then yes, she was thin.

Kumpania living didn't allow the level of privacy she'd need to conceal a pregnancy under oversized shirts. She had to be gone before she was showing.

If she didn't find those photos soon, she might need a backup plan—someone she could point to as the father. Someone in the kumpania. Otherwise, they'd presume she'd been sleeping with an outsider, and the kumpania would kill her for that, as surely as if they saw that photo.

She sat on her bed and considered her options. Her initial plan, if things went poorly with the Nasts, had been to seduce Niko while she negotiated with another Cabal. It would be hard for the phuri to punish her if their leader had chosen to bless her with a child. But now that idea might, ironically, have been thwarted by the unexpected success of her earlier scheme to get Hugh. If Niko got to enjoy Lily, he might not be as easy to seduce.

Her second choice was riskier. Seducing Colm would be easy enough, but Neala wouldn't like it. Still, Adele reminded herself, she had no intention of being around long enough to need this backup plan. She just needed to launch it so that if things went wrong, Colm could say, with conviction, that he was the father.

As she stood, she saw a message pad page on her nightstand. The phone number for Jasmine Wills's publicist. Adele was about to shove it into her drawer. She hoped to be gone before she ever had to produce a photo of Jasmine. But the note bothered her. It was too . . . convenient.

She dialed the number on her cell phone. After the fourth ring, a harried voice answered with what sounded like "café au lait." Adele paused, letting the woman say it again, the words plucking at a memory. Not "café au lait," but "Café Olé." Adele had stared at that sign for an hour yesterday, its play on words another source of annoyance as she'd waited for Robyn Peltier to finally exit the coffee shop.

Adele crumpled the note. She told herself it didn't matter, she'd already suspected that Robyn knew who she was, but that lead was a dead end anyway. Or was it? Her message had gotten to Adele's home, left with the kumpania leader himself. She could just as easily have told Niko everything. As Adele stared at the paper ball, she realized that's what this was: a warning.

See, I can get to you. I can expose you. I can kill you.

Adele pitched from her bed, her breath coming hot and fast. So Robyn fancied herself a player, did she?

Food and sleep would have to wait. Time to kill two birds. With two brothers.

FINN

"MS. ADAMS? It's Detective Findlay. Could you please call me back as soon as you get this message?"

Finn rattled off the number, then went to put the cell phone in his pocket, thought better of it and set it on his desk, on the remote chance that Hope Adams called back.

The detective room was empty. At ten on a Sunday morning, it often was. Anyone working was out on the street. Which is where he should be, and where he would be, as soon as he could haul himself to his feet again.

He'd called Hope Adams three times since last night, leaving three messages. He'd started with the simple *call me back*. Then he'd moved to the mysterious *there's been a change in the case I need to discuss with you*. Finally, urgent: *I have reason to believe Robyn Peltier is in danger*. No response.

At 8 a.m., he'd called *True News,* getting a sleepy editor who'd been there all night and offered to leave a message on Adams's cell phone—the same number Finn already had. At eight-thirty, he'd even borrowed another detective's cell phone, hoping the unfamiliar number might entice her to answer.

"Still nothing?" Damon said as he returned from eavesdropping on conversations pertaining to last night and the case.

Finn shook his head.

"I hope she's okay."

Finn tried to look concerned. He had no doubt Hope Adams was okay. Just ignoring him, listening to each message and rolling her eyes. *If that detective thinks I'm dumb enough to help him put my friend in jail, he can think again.*

He knew Robyn Peltier wasn't responsible for the deaths and he was quite certain he'd met the young woman who was, but he couldn't leave that on voice mail or it could come back to haunt him in court.

Last night he'd rounded up a few witnesses who'd said they got a good look at the girl who'd killed Margie Damascus—the victim.

"We've got three similar sketches, Finn," his lieutenant had said. "And none of them could possibly be your girl in the photo." He'd laid a hand on Finn's shoulder, his fingers damp enough to leave a stain. "It's a common phenomenon. You saw the photograph. You were working through its significance as you followed Peltier to the fair. You saw this young woman acting suspiciously, and the three events merged into one—the girl on the phone was the girl in the photo, who was this girl at the fair." Lieutenant Balough had squeezed his shoulder. "I didn't get a degree in psychology for nothing. The mind is an amazing thing. Sometimes, though, it takes a few shortcuts."

To his credit, Balough had put a rush on the ballistic. But the technician had taken one look at the recovered bullet, which had slammed into a stone monument after passing through Margie Damascus, and doubted he could make a viable comparison.

Finn pulled up the photo on his computer and studied it.

"So she's walking with an older guy." Damon moved behind Finn's shoulder. "Looks like he has money."

Finn glanced back at him.

"That suit." Damon pointed. "Top drawer."

Finn wouldn't know, but he could tell that the suit fit the man better than his own fit him, so he supposed that was a good sign it was expensive.

"Top-drawer suit means a top-drawer executive," Damon continued. "I bet he'd be a lot easier to identify than the girl."

Finn agreed.

COLM

COLM FOLDED HIS HANDS behind his head and watched the morning sun dance across his bedroom wall. The breeze from the open window tickled his chest. He reached out and laid a hand on Adele's bare thigh. She murmured something and snuggled into his side.

The house was silent, everyone off doing Sunday chores. A good thing, because he would have hated to be stuck out in the back woods where he and Adele usually met. She deserved better than to lose her virginity rolling around in the dirt.

That's where they'd started—in the forest. She'd found him working in the vegetable garden. He'd caught her watching, and she'd said she liked to watch him work, his shirt off, sweaty and dirty . . .

They'd gone into the forest then. He'd left his shirt off. Maybe that had helped.

She'd pushed him against a tree and wrapped herself around him, kissing him so hard *he'd* been hard in seconds. She hadn't pulled back, hadn't slowed him down like she usually did.

They'd been going into the woods for almost a year now and he could usually get his hands up her shirt, but only twice under her pants, sliding his fingers into her, so hot and wet . . . He'd spent a lot of time in the shower with those memories, but they didn't compare to the third, just a few days ago, when he'd shot that undercover cop for her. She'd forgiven him for losing Robyn Peltier, saying they'd find her and he'd been so brave, so strong, protecting her. She'd leaned against him, nuzzling him, breasts rubbing his chest. Then unbuttoned his fly, her hand sliding inside, stroking him, tentative at first, saying she hoped she was doing it right. When he'd assured her she was, her confidence had sprung back, stroking him, her grip so firm and hard that he'd . . .

But she'd said that was okay. It proved how much he loved her, how much he wanted her.

He only hoped he hadn't taken advantage of her. She'd been so excited, the way she'd clung to him, kissed him, the heat of her mouth, her skin, her wetness, her soft moans urging him on, whimpering if he slowed down, pressing against him, wriggling on his fingers, whispering, "We shouldn't, Colm. You're too young. We should wait. Oh, God, Colm, don't stop. Please, don't stop."

He'd been gentle. He had been there when the men in the kumpania had coached Hugh before his wedding night, telling him it wouldn't be easy the first time, that he might hurt Lily a little. So Colm knew he had to be careful, but Adele had been so excited that when he'd hesitated before that first thrust, she'd pulled him in, arching up to meet him, letting out only the smallest cry and if it had been pain, she seemed to have forgotten about it quickly enough. So he'd done well, and he was proud of himself. He—

The smallest sniffle stopped him midthought. Adele still lay on her side, her back pressed against him. She was quiet, asleep it seemed.

Another sniff. He scrambled up as she sat, wiping her eyes.

"You're crying," he said.

"No, I just—"

"Did I hurt you? Gods, Adele, if I did, I'm so sorry. I tried to be gentle—"

"You were." She smiled through her tears. "You were perfect, Colm. It didn't hurt at all." The smile twisted. "Well, maybe just a little, at first, but it was worth it. That's not why I'm crying."

"You regret it. You wanted to wait and now—"

She took his hands and pulled him to sit beside her. "Never," she said fiercely. "I love you. I don't care if this isn't right, if you're too young. I can't wait anymore. I love you so much. If I can't be your wife yet, I want to be your lover. If that's okay . . ."

"S-sure."

She kissed him, still clasping his hands. Then she lowered her gaze and a fresh tear slid down her pale cheek. He freed one hand and wiped it away, then leaned down, trying to meet her eyes.

"What's wrong, Adele?"

She shook her head.

"Please tell me."

She nibbled her lower lip, then lifted reddened eyes to his. "I understand why you didn't want to help me last night."

"What?"

"With Robyn Peltier. I needed your help catching her, so I called and left that message—" She shook her head. "It doesn't matter. You're right. This is my problem."

"I never said that. If you left a message, I didn't get it."

She looked away. "That's okay, Colm. You don't need to lie—"

"Lie?" His voice cracked as he got to his feet. "I'd never lie to you, Adele."

She reached for him, but he sidestepped her grasp.

"That's not fair, Adele. I've never lied. Not to you."

"I'm sorry."

He looked away, but let her catch his hand, pulling him back to her.

"I'm sorry. I just thought—" She squeezed his hand. "I wouldn't blame you. I've gotten you into this mess enough already."

"You didn't get me into anything. I offered. You were in trouble and it wasn't your fault. I was happy to help, and I would have been happy to help last night if I got the message."

"Your mother must have forgotten to tell you."

His mother took the message? That explained it then. She hadn't forgotten, but Colm was happy to let Adele think that, and shield her from the truth—that his mother hated her. She'd been trying to discourage friendship between them for years. Then, last fall, when she'd caught them kissing behind the communal building, she'd exploded and gone to Niko. Colm had crept after her and listened.

His mother had wanted Niko to cancel Colm and Adele's betrothal. She'd said it wasn't right, a nineteen-year-old girl making out with a fourteen-year-old boy, and that only proved what she'd suspected for years—that there was something not quite right about Adele, something sneaky, manipulative, *wrong*.

Niko had laughed it off. She was just having trouble seeing her baby grow up and let another woman into his life. After that, his mother had worked on Colm directly, trying to convince him Adele couldn't be trusted.

Colm loved his mother. His father had left the kumpania when he was two, but he'd never felt the lack. His mother had made sure of that. He knew that she was just looking out for him, but he wasn't a child anymore and he wished she'd see that and let him lead his own life.

As angry as he was, though, he trusted his mother would come around, and he wasn't going to say anything to turn Adele against her, so he nodded and said, "Yeah, she must have forgotten. But if you still need my help . . ."

Adele chewed her lip again, hands clasped, gaze down.

"Adele, I'm here for you. Just tell me what you need."

She did.

HOPE

Hope sat at a diner window, watching the front door of another restaurant across the road. Robyn was inside, having lunch and waiting for Adele Morrissey. They'd considered having her sit at the window, but given that Adele had no compunctions about shooting people in broad daylight, it seemed unwise to tempt her.

Robyn had a new prepaid cell and a panic button. Karl had miraculously produced the button last night, saying he'd like Hope to start carrying it. With that, she knew that even before last night he hadn't been underestimating the danger she faced.

Karl must have taken the button and receiver last year, when he'd had Benicio Cortez supply it for a job they'd been working. He'd kept it all this time, even bringing it to Los Angeles, where she'd expected to do nothing more dangerous than her regular job. In other words, he'd been waiting for the excuse to pull it out and say, "I think you should carry this."

He shouldn't need an excuse. But he wasn't wrong to think he did, at least not if he expected her to give in without a fight.

If it made him feel better, she'd start carrying it. Time for her to grow up and realize no matter how hard she trained, there would be some situations she couldn't handle alone.

For now, though, Robyn had the panic button and she'd taken it without question, accepting that this was not something she could handle on her own. So now Hope sat at a diner table, cell phone out in case Robyn called, panic button receiver on her lap. Karl was outside, scouting the perimeter while making a phone call. When he returned, Hope asked, "What did Jeremy say?"

"He's going to give it some thought."

She picked a bacon bit from her uneaten salad, hearing her mother sigh about table manners. "You told Jeremy that she suspects what you are, but we haven't confirmed it, right?"

"Yes."

"I know Pack Law says any human who learns the truth has to be—"

"That's not going to happen, Hope. Jeremy wouldn't consider that unless Robyn did something stupid."

"Like stealing tissue samples from you and selling them on eBay?"

"Which we both know would never enter her mind. She's nothing if not trustworthy."

The knot in Hope's stomach eased. The Law had always seemed reasonable. The Pack was very careful. Even if someone spotted them as wolves, they'd mistake them for very large dogs, so the chance of anyone accidentally discovering their secret was next to none. So if the Pack had to very, very rarely kill a person to protect themselves and, by extension, the supernatural world, it was a small price to pay. But if that "threat" was her friend, a reasonable rule suddenly became barbaric.

"Do you think I'd let them do that?" Karl asked after a moment.

"It's Pack Law."

"The Law can go to hell, and if Jeremy ordered me to do it, I'd tell him he could follow."

She wasn't sure she liked that answer much better. The Pack was supposed to be a werewolf's first loyalty. After a lifetime as a lone wolf, Karl had trouble with that, and it worried her.

He caught her gaze, misreading her lowered eyes. "I wouldn't do that to you, Hope."

She picked another bacon bit from under a salad leaf.

"As I said, though, it isn't an issue. Jeremy understands the circumstances and that it wasn't anyone's fault, including Robyn's. Moreover, if we avoid answering questions, it'll only make her more curious. He suggested we don't hold things back—just slow her down, giving her time to take it in and decide whether she really wants to spend her life seeing new threats in every dark alley and wooded path."

Hope's cell phone rang. She checked the display. "Lucas."

Karl took it. Earlier he'd asked Paige to look up a number from Grant Gilchrist's cell phone, which he'd taken last night. Robyn said someone had called Gilchrist and it sounded like the other person had set him on her trail. They'd tried calling the number—the only one in the call list—to find it disconnected.

"Prepaid cell phones," he said as he hung up. "Both Gilchrist's cell and the number he called."

Hope looked out at the street. "We've had her in there almost ninety minutes. Much longer and if Adele does show up, she might realize it's a trap. Time to move on."

HOW DO YOU CATCH SOMEONE who is watching your every move? Let her watch.

If Adele wanted Robyn, then they'd give her Robyn. Maybe she'd realized it was a trap. Or maybe after that long night, she was sleeping. They were counting on the latter. They moved Robyn to location two: a big-box bookstore that encouraged browsing, where she wouldn't look out of place.

As for the chance that a concerned citizen would recognize her from Friday's paper, she'd been wandering around L.A. for three days, and no one seemed to notice. It was a big anonymous city. Robyn was young, blond and attractive. Los Angeles was full of younger, blonder and more attractive women.

Their new choice came with an even better surveillance location— a coffee shop on the second floor, overlooking the first, where Robyn sat. They'd been there just long enough to buy coffees when Karl said, "We're being followed."

When Hope looked up, he shook his head and touched the side of his nose, meaning he'd smelled someone, not seen him.

"Someone from the diner?" she asked.

"No, from when I was circling the block. I noticed it then because the scent seemed vaguely familiar. Now I've picked it up again, so it's not likely a coincidence."

"You said it seemed familiar . . ."

He nodded. "I'm still trying to figure out from where. It's nobody I know—likely just a scent I've crossed."

In other words, someone may have been following them for a while. Not a werewolf, though—Karl would have mentioned that. Hope put out her own feelers, presuming anyone following them would be a supernatural, but she didn't detect anything.

"I don't think he's up here," Karl said. "I just caught a note of scent. I'm going to scout downstairs."

He left and she continued watching, her attention divided between the front doors and Robyn, who'd settled in with a history book, seated beside a sign announcing an author signing and giving the store branch name.

There was no sign of Adele. Earlier, when Robyn mentioned that Adele provided photos for *True News,* Hope had contacted her editor. It turned out they *did* have a phone number for Adele. Paige was running it now, but tracking its origins was turning out to be an ordeal. Whoever Adele was, she'd covered her tracks well.

Hope's cell phone vibrated against the table. Probably Detective Findlay. He'd left five messages. The last one mentioned a death at the fair. She'd paid attention only long enough to hear that the victim wasn't Gilchrist or Adele but an elderly lady. He hadn't given any other details, telling her to look it up in the morning paper.

A threat. Hope understood that as clearly as if he'd said: "Here's another one I can pin on your friend." He'd known Robyn had been at the fair last night. In fact, she wouldn't put it past the Nast Cabal to manufacture another murder, just to hammer Robyn's coffin shut.

But when she checked the caller ID, it wasn't the detective.

"Behind you there's a hall," Karl said when she answered. "Down it you'll find bathrooms and a handicap elevator. Take that elevator to the first floor. Then head right, along the wall, into the children's section. He's in the stacks there. See if you can pick up any vibes."

"Got it." She stood. "What does he look like?"

"No idea. I can smell him, but I don't dare get close enough for a look. From where I am, if I step out, he'll see me."

"It's a man, then?"

Karl confirmed that. Hope found the elevator where he said it would be. She presumed he wanted her to take it so if their pursuer was watching her, he'd think she'd just gone to the bathroom.

At the far side of the children's section, she thumbed through a Disney book. The vision came quickly, blurred at first, like viewing it through a greasy lens. She saw . . . someone standing at a bookshelf?

Damn it. A chaos vision. She shook her head sharply to clear it, startling a preteen girl reading beside her. It was like shaking a snow globe, though—the image obscured for only a moment, then settled back. Someone at a bookshelf. What kind of chaos event was that? She barely had time to wonder before the picture flipped like a slide show, moving to a man walking past a bank of tables. He was just as blurred as the woman, but she recognized him by his stride. Karl.

The image flipped again. The woman. She could make out a long ponytail of black curls falling over a denim jacket. Hope groaned. Really, she should be able to recognize herself a little faster than that, even if she didn't often see her back angle. The picture returned to Karl, now leafing through a book on a table.

Why was Hope seeing *them*?

She remembered that night at Bane, catching blurred and disjointed images of Portia Kane and other club-goers. She'd told Karl later she was certain it was the "signature" vision for a supernatural, but had no idea what kind.

Clairvoyants.

Instead of a static signature image, Hope briefly saw what *they* were seeing with their powers.

The image switched to a third. Another woman, this one with light hair, sitting beside a sign. Robyn.

Hope spun so fast she dropped her book and startled the girl beside her again. She murmured an apology as she hurried past. Her fingers were already hitting her cell phone speed dial, her gaze scanning the aisle, straining to see around the end before she reached it. She got there just as Karl answered.

She stopped abruptly, closing her eyes to vision-check before leaning out.

"Hope?" he said when she didn't speak.

"Just a sec," she whispered.

When no vision came, she peered around the shelves. Robyn still sat where they'd left her, no sign of Adele nearby.

"She's here," she said. "Adele."

"Where?"

"I have no idea. I just caught a—" She glanced around, making sure no one was listening in. "—a vision."

"Okay, I'm coming around the—"

"I see you."

He was across the store, near the row of cashiers. Robyn was twenty feet away, close enough that he could get to her in a sprint. They held their positions, looking, listening, smelling, sensing.

"No sign," he said.

"Same here."

"Head toward the front doors. I'll cover you. I'll circle around

Robyn and see if I can flush Adele out. If she comes your way, let her leave. We want—"

"To get her outside. I know."

Hope stepped from her hiding spot, phone still at her ear as she scouted for Adele. As she cut across to the front doors, she picked up the vibes again, telling her a supernatural was close. Then the vision sparked again, the same flipping of scenes, from her to Karl to Robyn.

She slowed and looked around. To her left, a young Latina pushed a stroller. To her right, a knot of girls whispered about a boy she couldn't see. Just ahead, an elderly man perused the True Crime display. Beside him, another man talked to an employee.

Lots of people. None could pass for Adele Morrissey.

She took another three steps. The vision returned, looping through again, strong as ever.

"Hope?" Karl said.

It took her a moment to respond, having forgotten she was still on the phone.

"Just . . . sensing," she said.

"I can see you."

"Anyone else?"

"Not Adele, but perhaps that's not who you're sensing. Robyn did say she thought Adele might have a male partner, the one she saw at the undercover officer's house. And the person following us was definitely male, likely supernatural . . ."

Another clairvoyant? They were one of the rarest races, but clairvoyance *was* hereditary.

The vibes told her whoever she'd detected was very close. But the only men she could see were the elderly one and the one talking to the clerk. Not to downplay the ability of the elderly, but this guy, despite his interest in crime, was clearly getting his thrills vicariously. He had to be eighty, and leaned on a walker, and while she knew that would make a great disguise, she could pick up mild chaos vibes from chronic pain and depression, and that couldn't be faked.

The guy talking to the store clerk was rapt in his conversation, paying no attention to his surroundings, open to attack. All no-no's in the evil-spy handbook.

But because he was the only apparent possibility for those clairvoyant vibes, Hope took a closer look. He was midthirties, slightly under average height.

He looked like a high school gym teacher. Maybe it was his

outfit—jeans, a rugby shirt and ball cap, a team jacket on his arm. Maybe it was his build, his shirt sleeves pushed up to show lean athletic muscular forearms. The clerk seemed to think he was good-looking, ignoring the toe-tapping customer awaiting her turn.

Could he be Adele's partner? Maybe her lover? He was almost twice her age, but Hope knew that didn't mean anything.

"There's a guy here," she whispered into the phone. "Ball cap, dark green shirt . . ."

"I see him."

"Does he look familiar?"

Karl paused. "No, but I see someone behind him who does."

Before she could ask "Who?" a figure stepped from behind a display.

"Is that who I think it is?" Karl asked.

It was.

HOPE

From their separate spots in the bookstore, Hope and Karl watched Adele's partner. It was the redheaded teenage boy from Robyn's apartment. He crept around the displays near the front door, like a shoplifter waiting to make a break for it. After a moment, he slipped farther into the store, sticking to the wall.

Hope headed for the aisle beside his. After a moment, the clairvoyant vision came again, this time flipping between Robyn and random faces. The boy was right on the other side of the shelf, with no one else around, meaning the vibes had to be coming from him.

Robyn had said the figure in Judd Archer's house sounded young. This kid, though, was younger than any of them had imagined. Hope caught a peek of him around a display. If he was old enough to drive, she'd be surprised.

It wasn't just that he didn't look dangerous, with his freckles and red hair and smooth cheeks. When they'd seen him at Robyn's apartment he'd run away, spooked at the first sign of trouble. Even now, his every move, his very bearing screamed that he didn't want to be there. Chaos vibes pulsed from him. Anxiety, fear, confusion. Not a single tremor of anger or hate.

So Hope followed him now with care, knowing he'd seen her Friday night and one glimpse would have him bolting like a rabbit. As she followed, she kept her eyes and sensors on the lookout for the real threat—Adele. If Hope had been picking up a clairvoyant in the store before the boy arrived, it must have been Adele, meaning she was likely still here.

When Hope peeked through a display, she saw the boy straining, his face red with exertion. She recognized that expression as surely as if she was looking in a mirror. He was trying to catch a vision—in his case, a clairvoyant one.

He seemed to be struggling to get a fix. When he finally did spot Robyn, it was with his eyes. Then he ducked behind a shelf, his thoughts a chaotic jumble of indecision. She picked up enough to know his task—get Robyn out of the store.

Hope moved to the aisle beside Robyn. She bounced on her toes, as if the shelf between them wasn't six inches taller than her.

She'd wanted to warn Robyn that the boy was here and Adele likely nearby. But Robyn was nervous enough and if they added this strain, she might tip him off. Yet it soon became clear Robyn was in no immediate danger, because the boy had no immediate hope of completing his assignment.

Flushing Robyn outside must have sounded easy, but now he'd stalled. And wherever Adele was, she wasn't helping.

Hope called Karl and whispered what was going on, then said, "Adele must still be here somewhere. *And* the guy who was following us. As for how he's involved—maybe he's with Irving or—" She shook her head. "It doesn't matter. Point is, we need to take him into consideration, too."

"Leave them to me. You watch the boy."

"I don't think he's going anywhere. We may need to flush *him* out. Get him on the run, track him down and question him."

"Good idea."

They hammered out a plan. Then she called Robyn and relayed it to her.

HOPE TURNED A RASPBERRY CHOCOLATE BAR OVER, as if looking for a price tag. She watched Robyn through the mirrored display as she passed a table of remaindered books. Behind her, the boy peeked from a shelving unit, then slid out to follow.

Hope counted to ten and turned. The boy was so intent on Robyn that he didn't see Hope until Robyn stopped beside her. Even then, he only hesitated, foot lifted, head cocked, frowning as if she looked familiar but . . . The memory clicked.

He mouthed a silent "oh." His lips didn't follow up with "shit," but his thoughts did. He moved his raised foot backward and he looked around for Karl. He wouldn't see him—Karl was still hunting for Adele and the mystery man—but the boy's anxiety vibes edged toward panic and his hand inched toward his pocket. Hope had a good idea what was in that pocket, and looked quickly at Robyn, as if she hadn't noticed him.

"Ready to go?" Hope said.

The boy continued through on his backward step, still looking around, but his hand staying outside his pocket, the panic vibes ebbing.

Good. Now if he'd just turn and walk away . . . Get out of the store, then Karl could follow his trail.

The boy took another slow step backward and smacked into the old man with the walker. It wasn't a hard collision. But the old man was unsteady enough, making his way to the cashier with his prize— a massive hardcover—and that nudge was enough to knock him off balance. The big book hit the floor with a *thwack* that made everyone within earshot jump.

The boy froze. Except for his hand, which darted into that pocket.

"Well?" the old man barked. "Are you going to pick that up for me or not? Bad enough you can't watch where you're going. Don't just stand there . . ."

He continued to harangue the boy, but Hope couldn't hear him, her attention riveted to that pocket, as the chaos swirled about, as rich and smooth as the best chocolate.

The boy stared at the book, as if praying it would float back into the man's hand. Finally, hand still in his pocket, he bent, stiff-legged, scooping up the book as he mumbled apologies.

As he straightened, a figure stepped from behind a rack, his gaze down, fixed on the book in his hand. It was the gym teacher who'd been talking to the clerk. He noticed the crowd and looked up. He saw the old man still grumbling, and he started to veer out of his way. But then he saw who the old man was chewing out. And he stopped dead.

The chaos vibes surged. Confusion and disbelief and something sharper and stronger, too muddled for Hope to make out. Then the vibes smoothed away as the man's eyes lit up. He said something. A single word. It was too far for Hope to make it out, but the boy wheeled.

The man said it again and moved forward, absently setting his book on a shelf as he passed. The boy stumbled back. He hit the remaindered book table. His free hand windmilled, his other hand flew from his pocket, pulling the gun with it, the weapon sailing into the air and hitting the floor, the clatter swallowed by a clerk's scream.

Everyone stopped. All eyes went to the gun, and that scream echoed through the store like the wail of a siren.

Then, as people realized what was happening, the chaos tsunami hit. Hope reeled under it. Her eyes rolled back, the chaos bliss blinding her. She caught only still shots. The boy, staring at the gun. The man, staring at the boy. The customers, scrambling back in slow motion. A security guard, inching forward, hand going to his holster.

Another wave, so strong Hope's knees buckled. Robyn grasped her arm. Hope pushed her off and grabbed the chocolate display rack. Focus! Damn it, focus! She blinked, jaw clenched.

When Hope could see again, her gaze swung to the security guard. He wasn't much older than the boy, and no less terrified.

Hope tried to move, to do something, anything, but the demon fought to keep her still, smelling disaster and warning her not to interfere, not to get involved, it wasn't safe, just sit back and drink it in, prepare for the chaos feast to come.

Hope grasped the display tighter and pushed off, propelling herself forward. Robyn caught her arm again, whispering for her to let it play out. But Robyn couldn't hear the thoughts pinging through the air; she couldn't feel the fear and confusion. To her, letting it play out meant letting the guard take the boy down quietly and call the police. Only that wasn't going to happen.

Hope pushed past her, but she could tell she wasn't going to make it in time. The guard was only a few steps from the boy. He had his gun raised now, ready. The boy saw that, then glanced at his own weapon on the floor.

"No, no, no," Hope whispered. "Just leave it there. Don't do anything stupid."

She knew the boy and the guard wouldn't listen even if they could hear her. All they could see was that gun on the floor, and all she could see was tragedy pulsing there between them.

The gym teacher broke from his trance, staggering back as if just now realizing he stood between the two young men. As he backed away, he looked over his shoulder, gaze fixing on a carousel of bookmarks. Then he redirected his "stagger" that way, grabbing the carousel as if for support. He wrenched and it toppled into the guard's path.

At the last second, the guard saw the falling carousel and veered out of the way. The boy cast one last glance at the gun, then ran for the doors.

The gym teacher fumbled with the bookmark carousel, as if trying to right it, but only making it worse, blocking the guard so he couldn't follow the boy. The guard finally extricated himself.

The old man waved toward the doors. "He went—"

"The gun," Hope said, pointing. "It's still there."

The guard looked from the gun to the doors. A manager crept over, slinking around the shelves as if trying to assess the situation without getting involved.

"You can't leave the gun there," Hope said. "There are kids in the store."

The manager stepped out then. "She's right. I'll call the police. He didn't steal anything, did he?"

"I don't think so, but—"

"Good. Let the police handle it then. Just get that thing out of here."

Hope backed away, waving for Robyn to head toward the doors before anyone stopped them for a statement. As they escaped, Hope looked for the gym teacher. He was gone.

FINN

FINN HAD PASSED THE PHOTO of Jasmine Wills all around the station before finding a detective visiting from another precinct who thought the man in the background resembled a guy he'd interviewed as a witness a few years back.

"But my guy died before the case came to trial," the detective said. "Arrogant son of a bitch. Wouldn't give me the time of day, so I was looking forward to putting him on the stand, just to screw up his week. Guy was some head honcho for the Nast Corporation. You heard of it? I hadn't. One of those companies that doesn't seem to produce anything except other companies. My guy's name was Chris, I think. Your guy looks like he could be his brother. I'd pay a visit to the company tomorrow, flash the photo around. From what I heard, the whole damned family works there."

Finn looked up the case. It was almost seven years old. A carjacking. The witness had seen the whole thing, but didn't bother to call the police. Unfortunately for him, a civic-minded passerby had been busy writing down the license numbers of all the not-so-conscientious people who drove off. Kristof Nast. Now deceased, as Finn verified.

Now Finn was trolling the Nast Corporation Web site, searching in vain for photos of the executives while Damon continued roaming the department, eavesdropping. Madoz arrived, looking for an update. Finn gave it to him, then showed him the photo.

"That's Irving Nast," he said without hesitation.

"Are you sure?"

"Yep. Works for the Nast Corporation. Vice president of something or other. He's the CEO's nephew. I had a case a couple of years ago, one of their employees was killed in a hit-and-run. The widow had this nutty conspiracy theory. Claimed the company did it."

"Orchestrated a hit-and-run?"

Madoz laughed. "Yeah. Apparently the guy quit his job the week before. Definitely a hanging offense." He shook his head. "Total bullshit, but I had to follow through. I think the widow was hoping they'd pay her to shut up. Anyway, my liaison with the firm was Irving Nast. Nice enough guy. Confused as hell about the whole thing, but cooperated fully. Wish they were all that easy."

"Did you have a home number for him?"

"I think so. Let me grab the file."

FINN CALLED Irving Nast's home number and got his wife. That made things tricky. Nast had cooperated with Madoz, but he might be less inclined to do so when the matter involved a potential indiscretion with a very young woman. Without admitting why he was calling, Finn was able to get Nast's wife to tell him where he was—at the office for a few hours—but couldn't persuade her to part with a cell phone number. So a drop-by visit was in order.

As Finn drove to the Nast head office, Damon's fingers drummed against his leg. He had been like that since the shooting, disappearing into his thoughts, sometimes so much that he faded, once vanishing completely for a few minutes before surging back with a fresh spurt of energy.

The woman's death had bothered him, Finn knew, but more than that, watching her husband's shock and grief had reminded him of Robyn. Last night, Damon said he expected he'd be kept away if Finn found Robyn. But Finn knew he'd hoped that being allowed into the fair meant the barrier had been lifted. He'd expected to see her. Now that disappointment kept pulling him under.

Damon balled his fist and shook it. When he rested his hand on the door handle, though, it took only a minute before he started drumming again. His fingers made no sound, and the unnaturalness of it made Finn turn the radio up another notch. It didn't help. He could still feel the weight of Damon's mood.

"How'd you two meet?" he asked finally.

He had to say it twice before Damon responded, "Huh?"

"You and Robyn. How did you meet?"

Damon's eyes lit up, but the smile was hesitant as he studied Finn, judging whether he was just being polite.

"Did you go to college together?" Finn asked.

Damon shook his head. "She was a friend of my younger sister."

"So your sister introduced . . ."

"Not exactly." Damon's hand moved to his lap, fingers still now. "We met at her wedding—my sister's, that is. Her fiancé was this hot-shot stockbroker, liked to throw his money around, so he insisted on a huge wedding. Robyn was more of an acquaintance than a friend, but she made the guest list. They had this wedding planner who was big on forced mingling. You know, putting guests at a table where they don't know anyone? Bobby got the seat next to me. Everyone else was from the groom's side—coworkers and friends."

"So you talked to her, made her feel welcome."

"Bobby didn't need help mingling. She's quiet—compared to me—but she's great at making small talk. Gotta be, in her job. These girls we were sitting with, though? They only knew two kinds of small talk. Gossip and snark. Now, if you want to engage in a serious conversation about the propriety of the groom's stepmother wearing a leather miniskirt to the wedding, Bobby's your girl. But sniping and backbiting? No. That was the first thing that got my attention—the way she handled it. Most people would have joined in just to be included. Bobby tried, very politely, to steer the conversation in more constructive directions. When that failed, she backed out."

"And talked to you."

Damon's smile burst into a grin. "By that point, I was the one do-ing the initiating. I asked about her job, she asked about mine. Few things kill a girl's interest faster than 'I'm a junior high math teacher,' and I came this close to mentioning my band gig instead. But I could tell that wouldn't fly with Bobby. So I told the truth, and she was cool with it. Interested even. We got talking so much, I didn't notice when dessert was served, which, for me, is a miracle."

He paused, as if watching the movie in his head, one he'd replayed so many times he could mouth along with the words.

"And that was it then," Finn said. "You asked her out."

"Wasn't quite that easy. We were both seeing other people. For me, that other relationship was over before the meal was. Robyn had to be convinced, and that wasn't easy when she wouldn't even have coffee with me while she was involved with another guy."

Finn liked that. It supported the picture he was forming of Robyn Peltier as someone principled and honest, someone he could work with and help . . . if only he got the chance.

"You ever read *The Godfather*?" Damon asked.

It took a moment for Finn to slide back from his thoughts. "Seen the movie."

Damon's eyes rolled up in thought. "Not sure if it's in the movie. I read the book when I was young. There's this part where Michael Corleone meets his first fiancée, in Sicily, and this old guy says Michael was hit by the thunderbolt. I remember rolling my eyes at that. Really schmaltzy, like something from a bad romance novel. But the night my sister got married, I understood what it meant. Sounds corny as hell, but it's true. You can meet someone and, bam, it's like being hit by a thunderbolt."

"Love at first sight."

"Mmm, I guess so. But that always sounds so . . . passive. It's not like that at all. It wakes you up with a jolt and you know your life is never going to be the same. Say what you will about fate and that metaphysical shit, but I don't think our meeting was a coincidence, us sitting together, alone, our significant others unable to attend. Me and Bobby, it just . . . works, you know? We have something." He paused. "*Had* something." Another pause, then Damon looked out the window. After a moment, his fingers returned to the armrest, silently drumming.

COLM

COLM HAD TO WARN ADELE.

He took out the cell phone she'd given him, the one she'd taken from Robyn. She'd set up a speed-dial number to her cell phone. He called it . . . and got a message saying she was unavailable.

He tried twice more. She must have accidentally turned it off. He had to get to their meeting place. He ran behind the bookstore, his chest so tight that each breath seemed to lodge in his throat.

What had happened in there?

Adele had made it sound so simple. Get Robyn Peltier out and Adele would take it from there.

But she hadn't said *how* to get Robyn out. Maybe she thought it was so simple he didn't need instructions. But it hadn't been simple at all.

He'd hesitated and, in that hesitation, he'd betrayed Adele.

The kumpania taught that the gods punished mortals for laziness, for letting fate lead the way, for failing to take decisive action in shaping their own destiny. Adele knew how to please the gods. She'd never hesitated to take the most difficult steps to protect herself and the kumpania. A strong, shining example, like his mother. Colm was weak, indecisive and afraid, like his father.

His mother never said anything negative about his father, but Colm had heard the rumors. His father had been a durjardo, like Adele, an outside clairvoyant welcomed into the kumpania. Unlike Adele, though, he'd failed to assimilate and in the end, he'd abandoned his family, and for that he'd died. Killed by the gods. Given a chance at the best possible life for a clairvoyant, he had turned his back on it.

Now Colm saw himself failing, like his father. He'd followed Robyn Peltier . . . and walked straight into a trap. He'd never told Adele about that couple at the apartment. He'd seen the man's supernatural powers. He'd suspected the woman's powers. But he'd refused to consider the implications. He'd run away.

Adele had thought Robyn was an unwitting pawn. She'd been wrong. Robyn was part of the plan to capture Adele for the Nast Cabal. If there had been any doubt, any sense he might be overreacting, it had been erased when he'd seen the man in the ball cap.

Colm knew him. He had no idea how or from where, but one look at the man's face and recognition had hit like a fist to his stomach. With that recognition came the feeling that seeing him was bad, horribly and impossibly bad. That meant the man had to be from the Cabal.

Like every kumpania child, Colm had undergone "the lessons." He couldn't remember much about them, but sometimes he'd have nightmares and wake gasping and shaking, remembering snippets of a basement room and Niko's voice and photographs being flashed on a screen and jolts of indescribable pain. Seeing that man, and feeling that dread, Colm knew he must have seen him in those photographs—pictures of people who worked for the Cabal.

The man had said Colm's name. Not once, but twice. And Colm had seen his future—locked in a Cabal cell, forced to use his clairvoyant powers until he fell into madness, consumed by his visions.

The accidental dropping of his gun had seemed almost a stroke of good luck. As the security guard bore down on him, gun at the ready, Colm had seen his escape route—the final release every kumpania child was taught to take if he was ever cornered by a Cabal. All he had to do was reach for the fallen gun and the guard would free him.

But the Cabal man hadn't been about to let that happen. And when he distracted the guard, giving Colm a chance to escape, he'd taken it.

He hurried around the rear corner. No sign of Adele. That was okay—she'd be hidden ahead, trusting he had everything under control.

He slowed, thinking of how he could slant the events to favor him without downplaying the danger. When he had his story ready, he picked up his pace and looked behind the bin where Adele was sup-posed to wait.

She wasn't there.

Disappointment and dread prickled under his skin, and he stamped his feet, shaking it off. He had to focus. So she wasn't here. Big deal. He'd been gone a long time and she must have set out to see what was wrong.

But why not just call him?

Her cell phone must be broken, which is why he couldn't get through. Or maybe his was. If it came from Robyn and Robyn was with the Cabal, then he shouldn't be using it at all. Maybe Robyn had planted a trace in it. That would explain how they'd known he was in the bookstore.

He took out the cell phone and pitched it against the wall. It didn't break, but made a satisfying crack. He kicked it under a bin. Then he strode back around the building to find Adele.

COLM CLIMBED THE FENCE behind the store, dropped to the other side and huddled there, knees clasped to his chest, his back to the fence, gaze darting side to side, knowing he wouldn't see anyone, but looking anyway.

He'd circled the store and weaved through the parking lot looking for her, one eye always fixed on the store doors. There was a police car in the lot, meaning officers were inside. When they'd come out, he'd hid between two minivans, then balled up his nerve and tailed a group of kids his age into the store. Adele hadn't been in there either.

He'd found a pay phone and tried her cell, but got that same "un-available" message. He'd even tried catching a vision of her. He knew he couldn't—clairvoyant powers didn't work on one another—but he'd hoped their connection, their love, might help him past that bar-rier. It hadn't.

He couldn't find her. And he couldn't find any of the others—Robyn, the pretty Indian girl, her boyfriend or the ball-cap-wearing man. That could only mean one thing: they'd taken Adele.

That's why they hadn't chased him. He was just a boy, coming into his powers. Adele was a trained clairvoyant, her powers proven. She was their only target.

The incident in the store had been staged. Robyn led him to the pretty girl, making him realize something was wrong, making him worry. Then the man called his name, sending the worry into full panic, distracting him while the girl's superhuman boyfriend snatched Adele outside.

He had to call the kumpania.

But what if he was wrong? What if Adele was looking for him? And if Niko learned she'd been targeted by a Cabal and had said nothing, leaving the entire kumpania exposed . . .

Colm rubbed his hands against his jeans to clear the images from his head. Niko wouldn't kill Adele, no matter what kumpania law said. He'd give her another chance. He had to. Colm couldn't bear to think—

He rubbed harder, the rough seam scraping his palms, skin burning from the friction.

Why hadn't she told Niko from the start? By not admitting it, she'd only made the situation worse and now he was stuck making decisions he should never have to make.

He clenched and unclenched his hands, exhaling slowly. He'd make one more round of the parking lot and store, and then he'd call his mother. If Adele didn't like that, too bad. Saving her from the Cabal was all that mattered.

He hefted himself up onto the wooden fence, a simple sound barrier that wobbled under his weight. He made it to the top when a slender, light-haired woman rounded the bookstore back corner.

Adele's name sprang to his lips. Then the woman stepped from the shadow, shading her eyes to look up at him on the fence, and he saw it was Robyn Peltier.

He twisted to scramble back down.

"Wait!" she called. "We need to talk to you."

He leapt from the fence. One knee buckled as he landed, and he fell on all fours. A shadow passed over him. He looked up to see the man from the apartment vaulting the fence.

Colm tried to bolt, but the man landed in his path. His eyes met Colm's and something shamefully like a whimper bubbled in the boy's throat. The man lifted his chin. A slight tilt of the head, raising his nose, nostrils flaring . . . and Colm knew what was standing in front of him. A werewolf.

Colm's insides liquefied and a few drops trickled down his leg. The werewolf's nostrils flared again, as if he could smell Colm's humiliation.

The man lifted a finger, a subtle "wait" to someone. Colm noticed the pretty girl from the apartment on the fence. The man kept his gaze locked with Colm's.

"We're not going to hurt you," he said. "We just need to talk."

Colm's gaze shunted to the side, looking and praying for Adele.

"She's gone," said the girl from her fence-top post. "We just want to talk. We can go someplace that you'll feel safe, someplace public—"

Colm bolted. He knew it was useless. The man was a werewolf— he could lunge and break Colm's neck before he made it five feet. When he didn't, he glanced back to see the man still standing where he'd left him.

As Colm turned, he saw why. A middle-aged man stood in the medical building lot, his key fob extended, now stopped to watch what was unfolding at the fence line.

Colm checked over his shoulder one more time, then broke into a full out run for the building. The man in the parking lot watched Colm, his key fob still in hand, other reaching toward his car door. When Colm reached the building door, the man nodded, as if he'd done his duty, seen the boy to safety. He opened his car door.

Colm reached for the building door. If it was locked, he'd run to the man in the car, make up some story. If it opened, that meant there were more people inside and he could hide there.

He pulled the door. It swung open. He ran through.

FINN

IN POLICE COLLEGE, one of Finn's instructors claimed the greatest impediment to justice was prejudice. The ability to assess a situation free from those shackles was the greatest gift an officer could possess. And any officer who thought he could achieve that absolute lack of prejudice was deluded.

The human brain is designed to make connections. It looks for similarities and patterns, and when it finds them, it is happy. A cop can't help that initial flood of associations and, yes, prejudices. But he can recognize them for what they are and reassess based on facts.

Standing on the sidewalk, looking up at Nast corporate headquarters and instantly disliking it, Finn was aware that this was a conclusion based on stereotyping.

The building annoyed him, plain and simple . . . maybe because the building itself was not plain or simple. The block was full of historical landmarks, stately and dignified. In their midst, the Nast building looked like a Euro-chic runway model swanning through a room of refined dowagers, contempt in every glance she cast on her elderly neighbors.

Finn guessed that one of these grand old dames had been felled by a wrecking ball to make way for this soaring postmodern blot. Could he overcome that prejudice?

He doubted it.

Though it was Sunday, the lobby lights blazed. When he pulled a door open, it made a sucking sound, as if the vestibule was vacuum sealed. Past the second set of doors, a young man sat behind a stainless steel desk that bore an uncanny resemblance to a morgue gurney. His trim build and suit suggested he was more reception than security, but Finn suspected that was for appearance's sake.

Finn reached for the interior door. Locked. The young man looked up sharply, as if Finn had set off an alarm. There was a whoosh as the door behind him closed tight.

He couldn't help thinking of those movies where a guy walks into a tiny room that seals behind him and slowly fills with poisonous gas. The faintly metallic smell of the cold air blowing down on him didn't help. Nor did the guy at the desk, who watched him, blank-faced as a cyborg.

Finn turned to say something to Damon . . . and saw him still outside on the sidewalk. He discreetly gestured for Damon to walk in. Damon not-so-discreetly gestured that he couldn't.

Finn opened the outer door, abashedly relieved to see that it *would* open. Damon walked up to the opening and bounced back. He put his hand out and his palm flattened and whitened, as if pressing against glass.

"Huh," Finn said. "Maybe you're a vampire now. You need to be invited."

"A joke? I'm impressed. We'll need to work on your delivery, though. Right now . . ." Damon rapped his knuckles against the invisible barrier. "Small problem."

"Is this what happens when Robyn's around?"

Damon's eyes lit with hope, then it faded. "Nah. With Robyn, I get relocated, like a raccoon wandering into the city. I'll look for another way in."

When Finn stepped back into the vestibule, the guard was still watching him, face still impassive, as if he saw guys leaning out the door talking to themselves all the time. On the Sunday shift, he probably did.

The guard made no move to come to the door or turn on the intercom and ask Finn's business. Even when Finn buzzed, the man continued to sit there.

As Finn raised a hand to buzz again, the man finally pressed a button. A speaker overhead clicked.

"Nast Corporation. How may I help you?"

Finn held his badge to the glass. "Detective John Findlay, LAPD."

For almost twenty seconds, the man sat there, as if waiting for a better explanation. Finally, he pressed another button and the door opened.

As Finn approached the desk, the young man sat robot straight, his eyes gray ball bearings fixed on Finn's forehead.

"I'm looking for this man." Finn lifted a cropped version of the photo, without the girl. "I've been told it's Irving Nast."

The guard's gaze flickered across the image. "I couldn't say, sir. The photo quality appears degraded."

"Let's pretend it is Mr. Nast, then. I need to speak to him. His wife said he was in the office this morning."

"Mr. Nast has left for the day."

"Could you check that? Call his office for me?"

Those ball bearings bored holes over Finn's eyebrows. The young man waved at the computer display embedded in his desktop. "Our security system monitors all access. Mr. Nast used his code to exit the rear doors at 11:23 and did not reuse it to enter."

"All right. Then I'll take his cell phone number."

"I'm not at liberty to divulge that information."

"This is a matter of some delicacy," Finn said, in the same measured tone. "I'm sure Mr. Nast would prefer I didn't call on him at home. Why don't *you* call him and ask if you can give me the number. Or call and hand me the phone."

"Mr. Nast has left for the day. I don't expect him to return. It's Sunday."

"Which is why I'm asking for his number."

The guard checked his display screen. "Oh, I'm sorry. Mr. Nast is unavailable this weekend."

"Has he left town?"

The young man's lips pressed together for—yes, Finn counted—eight seconds. "I'm not privy to the personal plans of our employees, sir. Mr. Irving Nast has indicated he is unavailable this weekend and if a situation requiring executive attention arises, it should be directed to another vice president. Would you like me to do that for you?"

At the sound of footsteps, Finn looked to see a man striding from the elevators. He was midtwenties, tall and slender, carrying a briefcase and wearing a navy-striped crewneck and dark jeans. Finn pegged him as a fresh MBA. Part of that expensive education should have taught him that as important as it was to put in overtime, corporate success was just as dependent on image, and the casual look and blond ponytail wasn't going to score him any points with upper management, even on a Sunday.

"Sir?"

Finn looked back at the guard.

"Would you like me to contact an alternate executive?"

"I don't think that would help with my investigation and I'd hate to waste anyone's time. It's very important that I speak to Irving Nast himself, and I can't wait for tomorrow, not on a case that involves four murders, including the deaths of two LAPD officers."

"I'm quite certain Mr. Nast would know nothing about that."

"I'm sure you're right." Finn sucked the sarcasm from his words. "I still need to speak to him."

"Let me contact Josef Nast for you. He's our CFO. Perhaps he can—"

"I don't think you understand. The CFO—"

"—will really not want to be bothered on a Sunday," said the young ponytailed man from behind Finn. "My uncle Josef is at church, as I'm sure your schedule shows, Mark."

The clerk jerked up, like a soldier snapping to attention. In the consternation that crossed his face, Finn saw the first proof that the man was indeed flesh and blood.

"Mr. Nast, sir," the guard said.

Finn took a closer look at the young man, seeing his face full-on, the resemblance to the photo now clear in the coloring and the brilliant blue eyes, though his build and features were thinner. That would explain how he got away with the ponytail.

The young man extended his hand. "Sean Nast."

"Mr. Nast is our COO," the guard said with a note of sourness that blamed Finn for making him look bad in front of a VIP.

Finn shook his hand and introduced himself.

"You wanted to speak to . . . ?" Nast prompted.

"Irving Nast."

"Ah, you just missed him." Nast checked his watch. "Irving won't be home yet and I suspect if I call his cell, he won't answer." A wry smile. "I spent the morning pestering him with questions on a project and he was eager to be off. Why don't we go up to my office and I'll call his house in a few minutes, explain the situation and get him back here for you? He'll likely prefer not to have the police come to his home."

COLM

COLM LEANED OVER the stairwell railing, watching the second-floor door, ready to fly up the stairs if it opened. After a moment of listening, he closed his eyes and concentrated. The werewolf's image popped open like a computer window. Colm smiled.

Colm took this as a sign he was back in the gods' favor. He'd tried fixing on the Indian girl or Robyn or the man in the ball cap. But that was pushing his luck.

He watched the werewolf move through a room on the second floor, dropping to his knees by an adjoining door, trying to determine whether Colm had passed through it. The man straightened, brushing off his pant legs with a swipe of annoyance. Colm hadn't made the trail easy, setting a winding path that slowed him down.

If there were any other people in the building, Colm hadn't found them. That was okay. As long as he could see the werewolf, he could outwit him and escape. Or that was the mantra he repeated to keep the terror at bay.

The Cabals claimed they didn't hire werewolves, but the kumpania said that was a lie. Of course Cabal employees wanted to believe it. A werewolf made an ideal assassin, a hunting machine, and now the Cabal had set one on his—

He squeezed his eyes shut. A werewolf might be a cold killer, but they were stupid beasts—everyone knew that. He just needed to keep evading the monster until he could find a phone, call his mother and get help.

The next time Colm checked for a vision, though, he couldn't get a lock, and panic congealed in the pit of his stomach as he clenched the railing, straining to hear—

The werewolf's image popped into his head, so clear he could see the crease lines around his mouth. He was in a hall. Which one? Colm couldn't pick up any clues.

The vision vanished. Colm struggled to recapture it.

"I know you're up there." The man's low voice echoed through the empty stairwell.

Colm jumped and backed against the wall.

"You're above me," the werewolf said in that same calm voice. "You're standing just below the third-floor doorway."

How—? Oh, scent. A dog couldn't just track by a trail on the ground; it could smell you. The werewolf could smell him up here, smell his fear, the piss dried on his legs, the sweat streaking—

He swallowed, shoulder blades rubbing the wall, desperately trying to get farther from that railing, from the werewolf. He glanced up at the door. Only three steps away. Three seemingly endless steps.

Colm shut his eyes, not trying for a vision now, concentrating solely on sound. He hadn't heard any footsteps or shoes squeaking on the steps. Maybe the werewolf didn't know for certain that Colm was here. Maybe he was guessing.

"Have you heard of the interracial council?" the man continued. "They help supernaturals in trouble. My—the woman you saw with me, she works for them. We're here to help you."

Werewolves were as stupid as everyone said. Or maybe he thought Colm was the stupid one, especially if he expected him to buy that old lie about the council.

"If you don't know of the council, perhaps you've heard of Lucas Cortez?"

The man's voice remained steady, volume unchanged, meaning he hadn't moved. The moment he did, Colm was up those three steps and through the door.

"Lucas Cortez is famous for fighting the Cabals. If you're in trouble with the Nasts, Lucas can help."

This guy just didn't know when to quit. If one lie didn't work, spew another.

"I can phone him right now," the werewolf went on. "You can talk to him. Or you can talk to his wife, Paige Winterbourne, one of the council leaders. Just tell me who you'll trust and we'll get in touch with them."

The only people Colm trusted were the kumpania.

"Tell me what I can do to make you feel safe. I only want to talk to you."

A movement flickered on the stairs below. Then the top of the werewolf's dark head appeared. Colm blinked, certain it was a vision caught at a weird angle. He should have heard him climbing, heard his voice getting louder.

The man looked up, eyes meeting Colm's. Colm scrambled up the steps, his feet barely catching the edges, shoes skidding, the stairs seeming to move under him like an escalator, those three steps to the landing an impossible distance.

"There's no place to go," the man called, his words barely piercing the pounding of blood in Colm's ears.

He finally hit the landing. As he dove for the door, the handle turned. He spun before seeing who was on the other side, stumbling to the stairs and tearing up the next flight, his feet remembering how to climb now. He glanced at the fourth-floor door, but didn't need to be clairvoyant to guess that if he opened it, someone would be waiting on the other side.

As he raced to the next floor, he glanced over the railing. The werewolf was still two flights down, taking his time. Why not? He could get Colm anytime he wanted. He was a werewolf; Colm was a skinny fifteen-year-old clairvoyant.

The werewolf was still climbing, still not rushing, letting the distance between them grow. He reminded Colm of the kumpania barn cats—overfed beasts slipped scraps by the kitchen staff, they didn't need to catch mice to survive, so they toyed with them, getting close, falling back, batting them around until they finally tired of the game and chomped through their little necks.

Colm missed the next step and fell, palms smacking the concrete, shins striking the step edge, the pain so sharp it blinded him, and he started crawling up on all fours, feeling his way. When his vision cleared, the pain shifted to his wrist, and he glanced down to see the odd angle, a protruding knob of bone that wasn't right. He'd broken his wrist as a child and the doctor warned him it could happen again. Not now, please not—

"You need to slow down," the werewolf called up. "You're going to hurt yourself."

He hit the fifth-floor landing, ignored the door and ran up the next flight. Just keep going.

There wasn't much farther he *could* go. This flight was the last. He lurched for the door. He tripped, his hands flying out, hitting the door. The pain that jolted down his arm was excruciating.

With his good hand, he twisted the knob, but it didn't budge. He yanked on it. Yanked and yanked and—

It was obviously locked. He needed to slow down and do something about it.

There was a deadbolt, but it was on his side, to keep people from breaking in. The lock on the knob was a simple one. He pulled out his fake ID card, pushed it into the jamb, wriggled it and . . .

The door opened.

Colm pulled open the door and flew through, then reeled back, blinded by the sun.

He was on the roof.

He spun, blinking hard, praying this was a vision that would disappear, leaving him with a cool dark hall and a red exit sign to safety. It didn't happen.

There had to be a fire escape. He jogged the perimeter. Nothing. The door stayed shut. If the werewolf had followed, he should be up here by now.

Colm's cheeks ballooned as he puffed, calming down. Where he'd exited there was a closet-size "room." He could get behind it and hide, then—

Stop planning and move. Act, don't think.

He circled wide to his goal. He needed to get downwind— No, upwind. Or was it downwind?

Stop thinking! Just—

The door swung open.

Colm twisted out of the way.

"Wait!"

A woman's voice. He glanced over to see the Indian girl standing by the open door, her hands up, genuine fear on her face. Fear that he'd jump off the roof and her boss would punish her for losing a clairvoyant slave.

"It's okay." She took a measured step toward him. "It's just me, okay? I only want to talk to you."

They kept saying that, as if by repeating it enough, they'd eventually hit the right note of conviction.

She took another step from the door, her hands still raised. Then she stopped. "I'm going to stay right here, okay? I'll keep my hands up. You can see I'm not armed. Now, I know you're scared . . ."

He bristled at that, shoulders squaring.

"You're nervous," she amended. "Concerned about your friend, Adele. She's okay."

So they did have her.

"I mean— We— She got away. Yes, we were following her. But she drove off, so we came back to talk to you."

Couldn't these people open their mouths without lying?

"She parked at the McDonald's a block south of the bookstore plaza, right? In the side lot, near the patio tables. We followed her trail that far, but she was already . . ." She trailed off, eyes studying his. "Look, I know you don't believe me. I don't blame you. You don't know me and you're sca—worried. But people have died. Maybe Adele has a good reason. I'm sure she thinks she does and I'm not saying she doesn't. But we need to stop it or we risk exposing all of us. You understand that, right?"

Oh, he understood. Understood that she'd talk and talk until she wore him down. Brainwashed him, like the rest of the Cabal slaves. Like she'd been brainwashed.

"We're not—" She stopped herself and eased back. "My name is Hope Adams. I work for the interracial council. Do you know what that is?"

He glanced around. If he could lure her away from that door before the werewolf found them . . .

"Do you want to talk downstairs? Or maybe at that McDonald's?" She took a step and he tensed, but she was moving sideways, away from the door. She squinted over her shoulder. "I think the cops are gone. They didn't stay very long."

She craned to see over the edge, but it was too far, so she took another step. Then another. Moving away from the door . . . He sent up a silent thank-you to the gods.

"I need to be sure," he said.

She started, as if surprised to hear him speak.

He cleared his throat, lowering his pitch a notch, hoping it made him sound older, more confident. "I'll go downstairs, but I need to be sure the cops are gone. Do you see any?"

"Hold on."

She headed for the edge. He counted her steps. At five, he'd run. Two, three . . .

He squeezed his eyes shut, bracing himself to bolt for the door. An image flashed. The werewolf. Leaning against that exit door, hand on the knob, face tense with strain as he listened.

Colm backpedaled. The girl wheeled, hands flying up again.

"It's okay," she said. "I was just checking . . ."

He saw her lips keep moving, but the sound didn't penetrate. He was trapped. Well and truly trapped, and a fool for thinking otherwise. A coward, desperately trying to avoid the unavoidable.

He glanced toward the edge of the roof and he knew what he had to do. What the kumpania would want him to do. What Adele would expect him to do.

Take action. Be a man.

Out of the corner of his eye, he saw the girl's face paling, her eyes going wide, mouth opening in a shout. He wheeled and ran.

He heard her then, a wordless shout, her shoes crackling in the gravel. He saw the edge of the roof, saw it, and threw himself forward.

Then . . . nothing. There was nothing under his feet.

His heart seized, shock ramming into his throat as he realized what he'd done. He twisted, arms flying out, praying he could stop this, that she'd save him. He didn't care if that made him a coward. This wasn't what he really wanted.

He saw a figure flying over the edge after him. Not the girl, but the werewolf. Colm reached out, flailing for the man's outstretched hands. His fingers made contact, skin brushing skin. And then . . .

And then nothing.

HOPE

She knew the boy was going to jump.

Hope saw him look at the edge. She felt his terror. She heard his thoughts. She *knew*.

Everything they'd done so far had only scared him more, and now, hearing that awful, unthinkable thought, what went through her head was *don't move*! So she didn't. And in that hesitation, she'd lost him.

He'd bolted. She'd sprung after him. And Karl, on the other side of the door, heard it happen, heard whatever she screamed, and the door flew open and he barreled through and she'd seen his arm swing up, palm going out, thought he was warning her off. Then she felt the blow, his hand slamming into her solar plexus and the wind flying out of her lungs, her feet sailed out from under her and she hit the roof. Then Robyn was there, pulling her up and Hope scrambled to her feet, gaze shooting to the roof edge, seeing not the boy jumping but Karl.

Karl had lunged to catch the boy, grabbing for him, then realized that he'd gone over the edge. Anything the boy felt at that moment was drowned out by Karl's stunned mental *oh shit*, his fear slamming Hope in the gut, knocking the wind out of her again, an iron spike of chaos power-driving into her skull. And if there was any pleasure to be found in that chaos, she didn't feel it.

The boy fell.

Hope saw Karl's hand brush his, but it was only a brush. He twisted, catching the edge, and then the boy fell, and there was, for a horrible moment she would never purge from her memory, a surge of incredible relief. The boy fell. But Karl did not. That was all that mattered.

Hope dropped to her knees at the edge. She threw up. Heaved and spewed, vomit splattering over the metal ledge, dappling Karl's fingers, gripping the edge.

A sob hiccupped out, the burn of tears, shaking her head so hard she couldn't see.

"Shhh, shhh, shhh," Karl whispered. "I'm fine. I've got it. I've been in this situation before, as you may recall."

He'd shown her memory-visions of a time he'd tried to jump between buildings and missed, a chaos treat that she wasn't sure she could ever enjoy again.

Robyn raced up behind Hope. "Here, he can grab—"

"No!" Hope turned on her, spitting the word. "Don't touch him."

"I'm okay, Robyn," Karl said. "Hope's right. Best not to help. I can do this."

"Quickly," Hope said. "Please."

It took two heaves, the first failed one jolting Hope's heart into her throat, but on the second, his feet swung up and stayed.

Only when he was safe did she remember the boy.

Hope leaned over the edge, but Karl caught her hand as he got up, and said simply, "No," and with that she knew the boy was dead.

"I have to check," she said.

Karl's jaw set, biting back the words. Hope still heard them, carried on a wave of anxiety and frustration.

"Hope's right," Robyn said, stepping forward. "We should check. Call an ambulance if there's any chance."

The look Karl would have liked to give Hope he shot at Robyn instead.

Robyn's confusion swirled around Hope. There was too much going on here, too much subtext Robyn could feel and couldn't understand.

This wasn't about checking on the boy; it was about Hope. She'd been so absorbed by the chaos of Karl jumping that she'd missed the boy's death. Those vibes would come later, in visions and nightmares, the horror and the bliss. She needed to get that over with now.

So they went downstairs. Or they did after cleaning up the vomit and searching the gravel roof for anything they might have dropped. The police might search up here, and that had to take priority.

When they arrived at ground level, there was still no wail of sirens. The boy had jumped at the side of the building, landing between it and a fence, and until someone happened to glance over and see a body on the pavement, he wouldn't be found.

But as they walked out the exit door, a wave of grief hit Hope, and she knew he *had* been found.

She caught Karl's sleeve. "Someone's there."

His chin lifted, nostrils flaring. Then he shook his head. The ping of frustration from him told her he meant the wind was wrong, not that no one was there.

Robyn stepped closer. "The police already?"

"No. I sense— It's someone who knew him."

"Adele," Robyn murmured. "She must have circled back and seen."

"Robyn?" Karl said. "Can you shoot?"

Her expression answered.

"*Will* you, then." Impatience touched his voice. "*Could* you?"

"I don't understand," she said.

Hope did. Adele was in a pseudoalley. The best way to take her down was with people at either end. The one who currently held the gun couldn't be trusted not to float off to chaos candy-land when she got near the body.

"Between the two of us, we'll manage," Hope said.

FINN

IN FINN'S EXPERIENCE, corporate executives fell into two groups: arrogant bastards and smarmy poseurs. There were exceptions, Finn recognized, and Sean Nast seemed to be one. On the elevator ride up to his office, he asked where Finn's precinct was and how long he'd been in homicide, and said he imagined it wasn't an easy job, genuine civility mingled with natural curiosity.

Nast's office was as big as the detective room at the precinct. They were walking in when Finn's cell phone rang. Nast waited with that same politeness, devoid now of unbecoming curiosity, and when Finn said, "I need to answer this," he nodded and crossed the room to give Finn privacy.

It was Madoz. He had some time to spare and offered to help Finn track down Hope Adams, doing a sweep by her office and her hotel. Finn gave him the hotel name, but couldn't recall the room number.

"I've got it somewhere if you need it, but they were pretty good about giving it out. It's under her name. Hope Adams." He must have been louder than he thought, making Nast glance up from his Rolodex. "If you do find her, give me a shout."

When he hung up, Nast was walking around the desk.

"Seems I still have Irving's old cell number. His updated one is on my laptop, which I didn't bring in today. Give me a minute and I'll dig it up. Can I grab you a coffee on my way back?"

"Water, if you have it."

"There's a fridge by my desk. Just grab a bottle and anything else you'd like."

• • •

WHILE NAST WAS GONE, Finn conducted a plain-view search of the office. He didn't suspect the young man of anything—not yet.

There was, as expected, a framed MBA. From Yale, also expected. Less expected was the location—on the same wall as the door, partly hidden by palm fronds. Lieutenant Balough, always quick to put that psychology degree to work, would say the partly hidden MBA showed signs of shame, as if Nast had cheated or bought his way through college. Finn saw it more as modesty, maybe borderline ambivalence.

He took note, too, of the name on the degree. Sean Kristof Nast. Kristof—the Nast who'd tried to slip out of testifying on the hit-and-run. His father?

The subject of family made Finn turn his attention to the photos. He counted nine on the desk and the filing cabinet top. Five featured Nast and a younger man—brother?—and an older one—father?—at various ages and in various combinations, with no sign of a mother.

There were only two women in the other pictures. Girls, Finn amended. One appeared in a group shot with Nast and friends. The other got two pictures, one of her and Nast arm-in-arm, making Finn leap to the "girlfriend" conclusion before noticing she had the same oddly bright blue eyes. In the other, she was alone, on horseback, and younger, maybe fourteen. He was examining that one when Nast returned and caught him looking at it.

"Sister?" he asked.

Nast stopped in midstride before giving a soft yes.

As Nast took shelter behind the big desk, there was a rigidity in his shoulders that hadn't been there earlier, and Finn knew he'd been taken aback, maybe even offended.

"She picked a nice spot to go riding, those mountains and all. Oregon, I bet."

A pause, then a curt, "Yes, Oregon. Now, I have Irving's cell number, so let's give that a try."

He dialed, listened, then shook his head. "Straight to voice mail—Irving? It's Sean. Can you give me a call?" A tight smile. "It's not about the Boulder project, I promise."

The smile loosened only a fraction as he hung up. "Well, there. If he calls back, I'll tell him you want to speak to him. Do you have a card?"

They exchanged business cards, Nast writing Irving's cell number on the back of his before handing it to Finn.

"Maybe you'll have more luck. I'm persona non grata with Irving today, after dragging him away from his family. Which reminds me, he mentioned he was taking them up the coast this afternoon. Visiting the in-laws, I think. So you might have trouble getting together. But he's usually in by eight-thirty. If you'd like an introduction tomorrow, have the desk buzz me."

DAMON WAS WAITING OUTSIDE the front doors. "I circled the whole building. There was one spot, around the back, where I made it two feet through the wall before hitting the invisible one. Weird."

Finn nodded, not really listening.

"Was Irving in?" Damon asked.

Finn shook his head.

"Can you take out your cell phone and actually *talk* to me?"

He gave Damon a play-by-play. "When Nast left that room, something happened. One minute he was Mr. Helpful, the next he couldn't get me out fast enough. I think when I was talking to Madoz, Nast had second thoughts about making the call to Irving in front of me. He did it from the other room and whatever his cousin said made Nast decide he shouldn't be so eager to help."

"So what happened when you tried the number yourself?"

"I haven't."

"Because you know it's fake."

"I'm sure it isn't." Finn rounded the corner.

"So— Hey—" Damon grabbed for Finn's arm, letting out a hiss of frustration when his fingers passed through. "One of these days, I'm going to stop doing that. I was saying, the car is that way."

"I'm not going to the car." Finn backed against the wall. "Hold on while I try the number."

It rang through to voice mail, as he'd thought it would. Sean Nast wouldn't risk giving him a fake. He'd just warn Irving not to answer. Finn left a message and made a note in his pad.

"Are you going to tell me where we're going?" Damon asked as Finn pocketed the notebook.

"I'm backtracking to the front door, now that the guard has seen me leave. You'll cover the rear. If Nast comes out your way, follow—" He stopped, remembering his partner was the Invisible Man. "*You* cover the front; I'll get the back. You see him? Whistle."

ROBYN

Robyn peeled one hand, gummy with sweat, from the gun, flexed it and readjusted her grip.

"You're doing fine," Hope whispered as they edged along the building.

Fine? Robyn didn't even know *what* she was doing. She knew the plan, but she felt like a computer processing ones and zeros with no concept of what it meant, how it fit together in a larger context.

Shot by a psychotic paparazzo? No sweat. Kidnapped by a werewolf? Okay. Best friend turns out to be a demon? Sure. She'd even played bait to catch a killer, and still kept her cool. But when that boy leaped to his death her emotional core had shut down altogether.

She still saw his face, floating before her wherever she looked, his expression frozen at the moment when he'd realized he was falling.

And now she was going to see his body.

Robyn wanted to slap the gun back into Hope's hand and say, "You deal, because I can't."

Hope tugged the back of Robyn's shirt. "I'll do this."

"I'm fine," rose to Robyn's lips. Then she realized Hope must have read her thoughts. "I'll be okay. If you were up to it, Karl wouldn't have given me the gun."

"It's just that— When we get close, I'll see . . . it. The boy's jump. I black out. I only see that."

A replay of his death?

"I'll be okay," Robyn said again, and meant it.

As they neared the corner, Hope took out her phone. Robyn kept her gaze forward, waiting while Hope called Karl to say they were in position.

When she didn't, Robyn glanced back. Hope stood there, phone still in her pocket, her face a copper mask, immobile and gleaming, amber irises stuttering, like Damon's when he'd fall asleep watching TV, eyelids not quite closing. Dreaming. Or seeing a vision.

Robyn reached for her friend's arm, then stopped. You weren't supposed to wake sleepwalkers—would the same logic apply?

"It's her—Adele," Hope said. "Grief. Guilt. God, she feels so guilty. She—" Hope's chin jerked up, ricocheting from the vision. "Sorry, I was . . ." She reached toward the wall, as if to steady herself, then noticed the phone clutched in her hand and stared at it, confused.

"You need to call—" Robyn began.

"Right." She hit the speed-dial button, didn't raise it to her ear. Just let it ring twice, then hung up and said, "I'm going to take a look. If I freeze up, don't worry unless you hear anything. Then just yank me back."

Hope eased past Robyn. She was still a foot from the edge when she went rigid. Then she backed up.

"It's not Adele," Hope said.

"What? You didn't see—"

Hope held up a finger as her phone buzzed, the vibration as loud as a ring. Robyn circled past her, to peek around the corner.

Beside the boy's body crouched the man from the bookstore. The one who'd brought that display carousel crashing down.

THEY WERE IN THE RENTAL CAR, heading . . . Robyn wasn't sure where exactly, and she supposed it wasn't important.

"So you said you recognized his scent?" Hope was saying to Karl in the front seat. "He was the guy following us earlier, right?"

"At the diner and the bookstore, yes. And earlier than that. Remember Friday night, when you were getting takeout . . . ?"

"You thought a guy was watching us and followed him around the back. That's where you knew the scent from. It was him. So he's involved. He clearly knew the boy. The grief and guilt was so—"

Hope's head jerked up.

"Do you sense something?" Robyn leaned farther over the seat.

"No, I hear something."

The *bzz-bzz* of Hope's cell phone vibrating. As Hope struggled to get it from her back pocket, Karl reached over and deftly plucked it out.

"Thanks. I'm sure it's just that detective again. He keeps calling from other numbers, hoping I'll answer if I don't recognize—" She glanced at the display. "Whoops. This one I do recognize."

She answered. "Hey, Lucas. Do you have more on clairvoyants for me?"

Hope's smile dropped. "Who?"

She glanced at Karl. He'd stopped at a light, and was frowning at Hope as if he could hear, which Robyn supposed maybe he could.

"Are you sure?" Hope paused. "No, I understand." Another pause. "Sure, how about . . ." She glanced at her watch. "Tell him half an hour."

Hope hung up. "We need to make a pit stop."

ADELE

Adele watched through the car windows as a stretcher carried Colm's body away.

Colm was dead. Thank the gods.

She put the car into drive and continued past the ambulance and the cruisers lining the road. Two officers glanced at her car as she drove by, then returned to their watch. As long as she didn't stop to gawk, they weren't interested in her.

Driving past hadn't been a step she'd wanted to take. Added risk. But she'd had to know. Adele had been remote-viewing Robyn when she'd run onto the roof and Adele had seen Colm jump.

If he wasn't dead, she prayed that he'd still be there, and she'd get to him first so she could put him out of his misery. Suffocation, she decided—it could be attributed to the fall. She couldn't take him, injured, back to the kumpania or she'd have to explain how he got that way.

On the drive, she'd cursed Colm. She'd trusted him and he'd betrayed her with his incompetence. After all she'd done for him.

But now, seeing that he was dead, she granted his memory a smidgen of grudging respect. He might have screwed up, but he'd realized his mistake and made the right choice, protecting her.

Still, she'd have to explain his death to the kumpania. As she drove, she crafted a few stories, rejecting each as casting too many droplets of blame her way. Before she passed the city limits, she realized the solution—the man at the bookstore.

It didn't matter that it had been thirteen years since she last saw him. His face was imprinted on her brain, invoking a wave of comforting warmth, a flare of icy rage and then, as if in afterthought, a tingle along her spine, the feeling of seeing not a man, but a phantom.

"YOU'RE CERTAIN IT WAS HIM?" Niko asked, forefinger rubbing his chair arm.

They were in the meeting room, usually reserved for the phuri—a wood-paneled library with bookshelves, a bar and leather chairs, the Victorian atmosphere ruined by the hum of computers.

"Yes, I'm certain."

Neala leapt up, her shredded tissue fluttering to the floor. "I won't sit and listen to this. She killed my—"

"Neala . . ." Niko's voice was thick with reproach.

"I didn't kill Colm," Adele said. "He was like a brother to me. More than a brother. My husband-to-be, my future, my—"

"Oh, stuff it," Neala snapped. "Don't play the grieving lover if you can't even squeeze out a few tears, Adele."

"Can't you see I'm in shock? I almost died."

"Colm *did* die. But it's all about you. Nothing else penetrates that nasty little mind—"

"Neala!" Niko said. "That's enough. Adele didn't kill—"

"She was responsible for his death even if she didn't push him off that roof, which I'm still not convinced she didn't—"

"Neala . . ."

"And she now compounds it with this . . . this outrageous lie."

"Neala, I don't think Adele means—"

"She means to torment me, and in tormenting me to serve herself by deflecting attention from what she's done. And she's succeeding, isn't she?"

Niko turned to Adele. "You say you're certain it was him?"

"Is anyone even listening to me?" Neala said. "We know it wasn't him. You know for a fact that it could not have been him. He's *dead*."

"Neala?" Niko said. "I think you should leave now."

Adele watched her carefully. Naturally, hearing he was still alive would come as a shock, but Neala seemed to be overdoing her outrage.

Neala stormed out muttering about fools and phantasms. Not like Neala to abandon a fight . . . Yet she couldn't seem to get away fast enough.

Niko waited until her footfalls faded, then turned to Adele.

"Yes," she said before he could ask again. "It was him."

"And he saw Colm? Recognized him?"

"I believe so."

"Did he see what happened to Colm?"

Adele considered lying and saying yes, but it wasn't just Neala scrutinizing her every twitch and inflection now. Niko didn't want to believe what she was saying—the kumpania had a vested interest in not believing it. Her answers here were more important than those regarding Colm's death.

"I don't know," she admitted.

Niko settled back in his chair, fingers templed. "We have to presume he did. And if he did, he'll be on his way here. We must be ready for him."

HOPE

Karl pulled into an empty day-care parking lot, so they could talk. They left Robyn in the car.

"She's exhausted," Hope said. "We need to find her a motel room while I—"

"Then she can nap in the car while you meet him, and I'll watch over you."

Hope bit back her protest and went quiet, looking out over the play area with its eight-foot fence, security cameras and warning signs. A scary world when your kids needed to play in what looked more like a prison yard than a playground.

Karl thought she needed his eyes at this meeting as much as these parents thought their kids needed to play under a video camera eye. Whether the danger was real or not, the fears and the concerns were.

"All right," she said. "We can push on and keep her sidelined."

Karl's narrowed eyes fixed on the bright red and yellow plastic equipment, as if its cheerfulness offended him. "No, you're right. She needs to stay with us, and to do that, she needs to keep up. I'll drop you off at the meeting place and find a motel. You can take a cab there when you're done."

They stared at the yard, as if watching the ghosts of children at play. A gust shrieked through a crawl tube and Hope shivered. At a warm pressure on her hand, she looked down to see she was holding Karl's and realized she had been the whole time, more clutching than holding, fingers locked tight, thumb rubbing the back of his hand.

"I know you saw it," he said softly. "His death."

She sucked in the bitter air. Like chomping down on ice cubes, her molars aching.

"I could meet with him," he said. "If you aren't up to it, say so."

"As long as my brain's busy, the vision won't come back. You might want your own bed tonight, though. It'll be a rough one."

"Not if you're sleeping soundly enough. I'll make sure of that."

A laugh circled her stomach. It didn't make it out, but the tickle lifted her mood and she looked up at him. "And how are you going to do that?"

His free hand went to her hip, pulling her close enough to shield the wind, his breath thawing her numb earlobe as he sent the rest of her mood scattering with promises that left her trembling.

"I'll find a few chaos memories for you, too," he said. "New ones."

"As long as none of them involve leaps from rooftops."

"I know." His lips brushed her ear as he straightened.

"What you did back there, on the roof, it was very . . ." Hope struggled for a word, but every one—brave, selfless, heroic—would make him cringe.

"Stupid?" he offered.

She leaned against him and laughed. "That, too. But I appreciated it. Just don't ever do it again."

He nodded, which didn't mean he agreed, only that he'd take it under consideration.

WHEN HOPE SAW where the meeting was being held, her anxiety jumped a notch. It was in the midst of a business district, where the only glowing Open sign was on her destination, a little shop called The Scone Witch. It made sandwiches from scones. Scone-wich, get it? She didn't either until she saw the helpful picture below, complete with the kind of wart-ridden hag that made real witches gnash their teeth.

The choice made her nervous because, given the location, it was sure to be empty. While that might seem perfect for a clandestine meeting, "empty" still meant there would be servers or counter help, probably very bored and quite happy to eavesdrop on the weird patrons talking about clairvoyants.

But when Hope drew closer, she realized it wasn't going to be a concern. It was like approaching a barn at feeding time—the cackle of conversation, the neighing of laughter, the honking of voices trying to be heard over the din. She made it inside the door, then was blocked by a guy in unrelieved black with a bad bleach job, flirting with a silver-studded girl.

When a shoulder tap and a loud "excuse me" failed, she was about to "accidentally" knee the back of his kneecap, when the guy stumbled and smacked hard into the wall.

As he glowered around for his assailant, Hope slipped past and followed a wave from a blond young man alone at a side window table.

"You looked like you could use some help," he said.

"Ah, knockback spell. And here I thought I'd developed a new power."

She sat down opposite him. Sean Nast, Savannah's half-brother and grandson of the Nast Cabal CEO. Sean was a couple of years younger than Hope, but with a quiet seriousness that made the age difference easy to forget.

She'd have thought Sean would prefer someplace farther from the head office, but he reasoned it was better here, where if anyone spotted them, he could say he'd invited her for coffee to discuss a business proposition.

Speaking of recruiting valuable supernaturals, Lucas had already filled him in on their theory about Irving trying to hire Adele. Sean confirmed that Cabal lower executives did that all the time, trying to get ahead by finding and cultivating new employees, which Hope knew, having been the subject of just such an independent project once herself.

But it didn't really matter what Irving had been doing with Adele. The problem was that photo, linking him to a cop killer. To squelch that threat, Sean would do what he could to help Hope find Adele.

As for Detective Findlay, Hope had been wrong about his being on the Nast payroll. Nor would he be a Cabal executive's "independent project"—if so, he'd never dare show up at the head office, flashing his badge.

Sean explained how he found Detective Findlay at the office and, on hearing him mention Hope's name in a phone call, he'd excused himself to phone Lucas.

"I planned to call Irving in and play it straight while I figured out what was going on. But when I came back, he was checking out a picture of Savannah. He asked about her, and I started wondering if dropping your name hadn't been an accident. I decided to brush him off and look into it some more."

"So he seemed to recognize Savannah?"

"I probably overreacted and he was making conversation. It just rubbed me wrong." He sipped his latte. "You told Lucas this detective is a necromancer?"

She explained. Sean hadn't known Expiscos could detect other supernaturals. Hearing that, most Cabal executives' eyes would glitter as they pondered the applications. Even Lucas, when he found out, hadn't been able to suppress a pensive moment of consideration. But Sean reacted with mild curiosity, as if it was an interesting but esoteric fact, like discovering sloths slept with their eyes open.

"Findlay could be working for someone else. A gang or a counter-Cabal group . . ." He trailed off, gaze sliding up, as if making mental notes. "I'll check that out. In the meantime, I pulled up our records on clairvoyants in L.A."

"And . . ."

"Current records? None. At least, none who aren't already on the payroll."

"You have two clairvoyants on staff, don't you?"

He nodded. "Granddad brags about that, but it's not as impressive as it sounds. One has severely limited powers and the other is approaching retirement."

She noticed he didn't say "approaching retirement *age*." Cabal clairvoyants rarely survived long enough to collect Social Security checks. "The Cabal must be looking for a replacement, then."

"Even if they had a powerful one at every satellite office they'd still be looking for more. It's an incredibly valuable power. The problem is finding them. With rare half-demons, like an Expisco or Ferratus, sometimes we get lucky and you guys come to us for work. Other times, we stumble on you and the negotiating begins. We'll take no for an answer because we know somewhere out there is another one willing to say yes. We want to entice you into employment. *Voluntary* employment. It's just good business. That never happens with clairvoyants. They're well compensated—come to us and you'll live like a millionaire—but it's selling your soul."

"Or, in this case, your sanity."

He nodded. "Clairvoyants have underground networks for hiding and protecting their members. Even if a family hasn't had a bona fide clairvoyant for generations, they're part of the network, ready to dis-

LIVING WITH THE DEAD · 265

appear if they ever do. They also have the lowest birth rate of all the races. Intentionally, it's presumed."

"Genetic Russian roulette."

"Most choose not to play."

She'd gotten all this from Lucas, but talking obviously relaxed Sean, and a second opinion never hurt.

He continued. "This girl is young and she seems to be voluntarily talking to Irving. As for why, my guess would be simple youthful ignorance. She figures she can make a lot of money and get out. It happens now and then—the misconception, not the getting-out part. My guess is that her family isn't part of the underground network and hasn't properly warned her. She's moved here recently, on her own, hoping to make her fortune."

She studied his face for any sign he was misleading her. But it was open, relaxed, his hands flat on the table. In his element now, not discussing his family or his firm, just having a casual speculative conversation with a fellow supernatural.

"I don't think she's new to L.A., and I don't think she's alone," Hope said.

"With other supernaturals?"

"Other clairvoyants."

That made him blink in genuine surprise, but even after he'd digested it, there was no gleam of discovery. It was like a diver finding a treasure chest and thinking only of the historical significance.

She was sure Sean Nast was good at his job. He had to be—Irving was proof that Cabals didn't promote on genetics alone. But whatever instinct was needed to truly embrace a Cabal family's philosophy, to look at a fellow supernatural and see only an asset, Sean didn't have it.

Still, she didn't mention Adele's paparazzo double life or her teenaged clairvoyant partner. However much Lucas trusted Sean, Hope had learned her lesson often enough. In this world, when you can keep your mouth shut, do it.

They talked a little more, and he promised to dig deeper into the Cabal files. Then she finished her tea and called for a taxi.

FINN

TWENTY MINUTES AFTER FINN LEFT Sean Nast's office, the young man had come out the front door and headed to a sandwich shop. Then they'd watched as Nast did exactly what Finn had expected—he'd met someone. Just not anyone Finn expected.

"You said this was Adams's second work exchange in Los Angeles?"

"Huh?" Damon jerked, blinking, from his thoughts. "Right. She did one a couple of years ago— You think that's how she knows this guy?"

"She clearly knows him." Finn waved at the pair sitting in the window. "And it's gotta be related to what's going on . . . unless the girl I've been trying to contact all day just happens to be messing around with the guy who just blew me off."

"Hope wouldn't screw around on Karl." Damon studied the couple. "It must be connected, but it's not coming together for me."

It wasn't coming together for Finn either.

"How well do you know her?" he asked.

"Hope? Of Bobby's friends, I know her the best. You know how it is. Well, maybe not, but when you marry someone, they bring their friends along. For better or worse. When your wife tells you one of them is coming over, sometimes you suddenly remember library books that need returning. Sometimes you retreat to watch the game or grade papers. And sometimes you say 'cool' and stick around. Hope was one I always stuck around for."

"They're close, I take it."

"Friends since high school. Hope's got her own stuff going on and they might not spend as much time together as they used to, but if you ask Bobby who is her best friend, she'd say Hope. Hope took this work exchange to help Bobby. I'm sure of it. Whatever is happening here, it's all about that. Helping Bobby."

Finn waved for Damon to go inside and eavesdrop on the conversation.

TEN MINUTES LATER, Hope Adams was standing and putting on her jacket. Damon came down the restaurant steps and hurried to Finn.

"So . . ." Finn said.

"I don't know."

"Don't know what?"

Finn gave him a moment before repeating the question. Damon didn't answer, only watched the shop door, eyes following Hope as she appeared on the stoop with Nast. They walked down to the sidewalk, still talking.

"What did they say?" Finn asked.

"I don't know."

"You couldn't hear them?"

"I just . . . I have no idea what they were talking about. It didn't make sense."

"Code?"

"You use code when you don't want to be overheard saying something strange, right? If that's what they were doing, they were totally blowing it, because that was the strangest conversation I've ever heard."

"What did—?"

Finn stopped as a cab pulled to the curb. Nast opened the door for Adams, then closed it behind her.

"Go with her," Finn said.

"Huh?"

"She already gave me the slip once. Get in that cab. I'll follow. If she loses me, find out where she's going, then meet me at the station."

ROBYN

Robyn checked the bedside clock and wondered whether she'd been napping long enough. She felt like she was back in kindergarten, past the age of needing a nap, forced to "rest" before she could zoom back into playtime.

Karl had stepped out to scout the area, leaving Robyn to sleep. Now, though, she was rested and raring to go, and Karl hadn't returned. She suspected he wasn't thinking of her at all, just circling the building, waiting for Hope.

She peeked out from behind the curtain, trying several angles, but seeing only slivers of the parking lot. Karl had told her to stay away from the windows and keep the door chained until he announced himself. But they'd been careful to avoid any landmarks on the way here, and as long as Robyn kept her wits sharp, there was no reason she couldn't peek out, tell Karl she was up and they could go meet Hope.

She did, keeping the chain engaged. But she couldn't see any more than the same slice of parking lot she had from the windows. So she undid the chain, eased open the door and leaned out.

No sign of Karl.

Maybe she should take a walk—

Maybe you should do what you were told, Bobby. Maybe the guy had a reason for telling you to do it.

Right, of course. Even if it was safe, she didn't relish getting caught by Karl.

She retreated into the room, pulling the door shut—

It stopped.

She looked up to see fingers holding it open. Men's fingers, long and smooth, nails perfectly trimmed. She relaxed her grip.

"Sorry, I was just—"

The door swung open. And for the second time in as many days, it wasn't Karl. This time it was the man from the bookstore, the one who'd been crouching by the boy's body.

Bracing the door with his foot, he lifted his hands as if to say "see, I'm not armed." At one time, that might have reassured her. After what she'd seen and heard in the last twenty-four hours, it didn't. In this new world, "armed" had little to do with "dangerous."

She tried to slam the door, quite willing to crush his foot if necessary, but he grabbed the edge again, holding it fast.

"Your bodyguard is at the corner, meeting your friend, who just pulled up in a cab," the man said. "They'll be along in a moment. If you want to scream, I can't stop you, but it won't get them here any faster, and it'll only call attention to us. So why don't we step inside and wait for them?"

Robyn backed up, walked stiffly to a chair and sat, straight-backed, hands in her lap. She felt like a stick figure, barely able to flex even at her elbows and knees.

The man surveyed the room, then took the other chair, positioning it out of sight of the window and out of the line of fire should anyone swing through the door.

When he took off his ball cap, Robyn got her first good look at him. His hair was dark red and his freckles were faint, but the resemblance was clear.

"He was your son," she said.

His reaction told her she was right. Like the resemblance, it was nothing overt. Just a burst of grief dispersed by a blink. Seeing it made her chest hurt, thoughts of Damon crowding her head.

"It seems we have a collision of interests." The man's words were light, but his voice gruff. "I understand why the council got involved. They're trying to help you out of a jam, and they didn't realize it involved a clairvoyant, but now that they do, I'm here to ask you to let me handle this. Clairvoyant concerns are not council concerns."

Whatever this "council" was, it had to be supernatural, and this guy thought she was part of it—or at least a supernatural herself. She could set him straight. But she didn't see the point . . . and did see a few good reasons why it might not be wise to admit she was human.

"That's right," she said. "We didn't realize a clairvoyant was involved. But *I* am involved. *Still* involved. Meaning I'm not about to step away."

His chin dipped in a slow, bobbing nod, and he leaned forward, elbows on his knees.

Earlier, when they'd talked about him, Hope had called him "the gym teacher." Robyn could see it now. He looked like a beloved coach. The one teen girls would ogle in his gym shorts, whispering that he was "kind of cute . . . for his age." Pleasant and unassuming. An impression she couldn't shake even knowing he *wasn't* a gym teacher, wasn't unassuming, probably wasn't all that pleasant.

Robyn glanced at the door. Were Hope and Karl really coming? "You said this isn't council business because it involves clairvoyants. I presume that's what you are?"

"Hmmm."

His gaze stayed fixed on a spot by her feet, as if too wrapped up in thought to answer her question. Thought? No. He was lost in a vision, watching Karl and Hope. She shivered.

No time to get freaked out, Bobby. It's a brave new world. Adjust.

She rubbed the back of her neck. "Do you speak for the clairvoyants, then? Is that what this 'collision of interest' is about? The council is trespassing on your jurisdiction?"

"The concerns of the clairvoyants are very specialized. We don't expect the council to understand."

"You represent them, though? The clairvoyants?"

He straightened, eyes finally focusing. "Your friend is an Expisco, isn't she? I heard that, but I thought it was a mistake. *Hoped* it was. I guess not. Which is going to make this—"

He vaulted from his chair. Robyn didn't have time to do more than shriek before realizing he wasn't jumping at her, but toward the bed, executing the kind of perfect leap only seen in movies. He twisted, hands raised, as Karl barreled from the bathroom, surprising Robyn. She gave yet another shriek followed by a mental promise that next time she was leaping up to defend herself like a proper twenty-first-century heroine.

The front door whammed open. Hope flew through, gun swinging toward the intruder. Robyn did manage not to scream. Not that anyone noticed. As always seemed to happen in such situations, the hostage was quickly forgotten, kidnapper and rescuers facing off, focused only on one another.

"I'm not armed," the man said.

He held his hands up like stop signs, one toward each attacker, his gaze flipping between them, as if trying to figure out which posed the greater threat: the big pissed-off werewolf or the tiny gun-toting half-demon.

"He didn't hurt me," she said. "I let him in and we were talking, waiting for you."

"You're okay?" Hope asked.

"Fine. Let's hear what he has to say."

"We should get you someplace else," Hope said. "You don't need to—"

"I'm good."

And she was. That strange sense of clarity had settled over her now, and she realized it wasn't shock but balance. She could handle this. Werewolves, demons, clairvoyants . . . *A brave new world, Bobby.* Take it in stride.

When Karl checked out the drapes, the man said, "I came alone."

"I didn't see anyone else," Robyn added. "But I didn't get a chance to look either. Like I said, he hasn't been here long. We didn't even get to introductions." She turned to the man. "I'm Robyn."

He paused, as if he'd rather stay anonymous, then said, "Rhys."

"He's a clairvoyant," Robyn told Hope and Karl. "He was the boy's father."

Rhys cut in. "What I want has nothing to do with—" His voice caught. "—with Colm. You're Hope Adams, with the council, am I right?"

Now it was Hope's turn to hesitate.

Rhys didn't wait for confirmation. "I understand you're trying to help your friend here, but as I told her, the council has no place in clairvoyant affairs."

"And as I was telling him," Robyn said, "since this involves me, suspected of a murder committed by a clairvoyant, I'd say I have a vested interest in *not* handing it over."

"We aren't handing anything to anyone," Hope said. "If you're suggesting the council has no business investigating a clairvoyant—"

Rhys lifted a hand. "I didn't say they had no business—"

"You're getting us tangled in semantics," Robyn said. "Let's cut to the chase."

She thought a smile touched Hope's eyes.

Rhys said, "The 'chase' is that you're involved in a situation you know little about and the deeper you get into it, the worse it will become."

"So you want us to back out?" Hope said. "I don't think so."

"I'm suggesting we reach an agreement that allows me to pursue this investigation properly."

"And alone," Robyn said. "Without us."

His lips tightened. He didn't like being forced into a straight answer. Too bad. Robyn had engineered enough snow jobs to recognize one.

"Not entirely alone," he said finally. "With my people."

"Who are?" Hope prompted. "The clairvoyants have no governing body. You say the council doesn't have the right—"

"I didn't say *right*."

"You say they have no *place* investigating clairvoyants, but they've done so in the past. Because clairvoyants, lacking that governing body, don't have anyplace else to go."

"In this case, they do."

Hope nodded. "You. And you are . . . ?"

He said nothing.

"You represent . . . ?"

Still nothing.

"Fine. If you can't present credentials that I can take to the council, then I'm going to keep investigating this—"

"And get another child killed?"

Hope stiffened, gun jerking up, as if she'd been smacked. "I was trying to save him. He jumped—"

"Because you didn't understand the situation."

Karl swung on Rhys, fast enough to make the other man pull back, chair legs squeaking.

"You can leave now." Karl walked toward Rhys. "In case Grant Gilchrist didn't tell you how this works, let me explain. You have the rest of the day to pack and leave the city. If you don't? Come sundown, I hunt you and I kill you."

Rhys held fast as Karl approached, but Robyn was sure he blanched.

"That *was* your boy you set on us last night. Gilchrist?"

"I—"

"He didn't come home last night, did he? I warned him that afternoon. Told him he had until sundown. He didn't listen. Perhaps you'd like to take that as a lesson."

"What happened with Grant was a mistake. My mistake. I under-estimated how much it would mean to him, to his reputation, to take you down. I thought I had him on a tighter leash than I did."

The flash in Karl's eyes said he didn't appreciate the doggie reference. Robyn couldn't blame him.

"What happened to your son—" she began.

"—was not intentional." He looked at Hope. "You had no way to foresee what he'd do, and I'm sure you did try to help him, but my point is that what's happening here goes beyond the simple help the council has given clairvoyants in the past. If you'll back off, I can stop this young woman—"

"Adele Morrissey."

He straightened, a sudden shift to cover his reaction—the one that said he'd hoped they hadn't gotten as far as a name.

"Yes, that's what they call her," Rhys said. "I can handle Adele. She won't bother you again." Robyn noticed he didn't mention getting *her* off L.A.'s Most Wanted list. "What I need is for you to—"

"Back off and let you handle it," Hope said. "A clairvoyant. The father of Adele's partner in crime—"

"Colm was not Adele's—" He took off his ball cap again, holding it on his lap, finger tracing the bill. "I haven't been a part of my son's life for thirteen years. So, no, I don't know what he was doing, and I shouldn't defend him. But I'm going to ask you to give me twenty-four hours to handle the situation."

"To get Adele and anyone else involved out of town, and out of reach of the council."

"I'm not—"

A crack from the bathroom. Robyn leapt up, brain screaming "gun!" But it only took a second to realize that wasn't it at all. A metallic clang, not a bang. Then another.

"Down!" Karl shouted.

A hiss from the bathroom, like a broken pipe. Karl dove for Hope, knocking her to the floor as Rhys plunged from his chair.

"It's okay!" Robyn yelled. "It's not a—"

Karl kicked her feet from under her as the room filled with smoke.

HOPE

Karl knocked Hope to the floor as gas filled the room. She yanked her shirt collar over her mouth, then looked to make sure he was doing the same, but he'd flipped around, grabbing Rhys's legs as the man dove for the floor.

Smoke swirled around them, thick as Maine fog. The men disappeared into it, a leg or arm appearing for a second, then gone with a *crack* and a grunt as they fought. Her eyes stung, watering. She blinked hard and peered into the fog, smacking the floor as she searched for her gun.

"Get Robyn!" Karl shouted, knowing she'd be trying to come to his rescue instead.

"Rob?" Hope yelled.

A cough answered.

"Cover your mouth," Hope called, choking back her own cough as the gas burned her throat. "Close your eyes. I'll find you."

She crawled, hunching along on one hand, the other holding her shirt over her mouth. She closed her eyes—she couldn't see anyway. Chaos eddied through the gas, steady waves tickling over her skin like a lover's touch, making her shiver.

Robyn coughed again, to her left now.

"Stay where you are!" Hope called.

A grunt of pain and a curse from Rhys. Chaos shuddered through Hope, the demon begging her to stop and enjoy it. She gritted her teeth and told the demon this wasn't the time. It ignored her until another *crack,* this one followed by a hissing growl that the demon recognized as Karl in pain. That shut it up.

"Robyn?"

A hacking cough, to the right now.

"Stay put! I can't—"

Booted footfalls clomped into the room. Shadowy figures appeared in the fog. Hope scuttled to the side and flattened up against the bed. The figures passed.

The room had gone quiet now.

Another cough. Robyn must have mistaken the men for cops. But a murder suspect didn't warrant a riot squad takedown. Gas and SWAT teams were the Nast's trademark. Hope knew now who Rhys worked for.

Hope slithered across the floor, toward Robyn. She couldn't be more than a few yards away—the room wasn't that big. The footsteps stopped. Hope did, too, lifting her head to listen.

A dull thump right beside her. A voice, muffled, as if by a gas mask, the words indecipherable. When the response came, Hope was concentrating hard enough to make it out.

"Think so."

A hollow, echoing snort. "Comforting. You gonna . . ." The rest was muddled. The answer was a laugh.

Robyn coughed.

Hope held her breath, but the men kept talking. Then a voice came from the back near the bathroom. "Move it. Mr. Nast wants us on the road pronto. We've got to grab that clairvoyant girl before dark."

"Take his legs and I'll . . ."

Hope didn't catch the rest or the response, but the gist of it was that they were trying to get someone outside. Rhys. The gas would hold the rest of them until they'd moved their comrade to safety.

She waited until they'd gone. Then a cough came, so soft it was more a throat clearing. Hope crawled toward it. A sliver of light filtered through the fog from the drawn curtains, meaning Robyn was next to the front door. Perfect. A few more feet and Hope would be—

Her forehead smacked into the door. Hands caught her, tugging her down with a "shhh."

She reached to pat the hand, tell Robyn she was okay. Her fingers touched a ribbed cuff. Rhys's sports jacket.

Hope spun, fists flying into the fog. One struck home, the impact jolting up her arm. She swung the other in the same direction. It hit with a smack. Then fingers vise-gripped around her wrist hard enough to make her yelp. Rhys wrenched Hope's arm behind her back. Her eyes flooded with fresh tears, salt stinging her burning cheeks. She tried to punch with her free hand, but he slammed her onto the floor, nose hitting hard, pain exploding.

Rhys crouched over her back, pinning her down, arm still jacked up behind her back. When she wriggled, he ratcheted her arm higher, making her gasp.

"Shhh!"

She smashed her foot into his leg. He yanked her arm higher and she bucked until the pain forced her to stillness, panting and blinking back tears.

Rhys yanked Hope to her knees.

"Up," he whispered, with a heave that forced her onto her feet.

She heard fingers sliding along the wall, as if searching for the knob. The door eased open, and a breeze gusted in, pushing the fog back as Rhys propelled her through. The fresh air hit like an icy blast. She gasped. Her throat and lungs and eyes burned. Even her skin felt hot. Her stomach roiled.

Rhys kept pushing her. She smacked into someone. A hard blink and she could make out a short figure in front of her. Another blink brought the face into focus—a preteen girl fixing Hope with a glower before shouldering past, muttering.

Hope glanced behind her. Rhys was blinking hard, eyes streaming. He swiped his jacket sleeve across them and reached into his pocket. Hope threw herself forward. He pulled her back, wrenching her arm up without a beat. A shake of his hand, unfolding his sunglasses, and he put them on.

"Keep walking."

Hope looked around through the glaze of tears. Another gust of wind rattled along the motel front, shaking the screen doors and sending fast-food wrappers swirling about their feet. The sun needled her eyes. Strands of hair whipped her face. One head shake and she knew she had more hair outside her ponytail than in it.

She pictured what she looked like, rumpled and disheveled, eyes streaming as she grimaced against the sun like a kidnap victim pulled from an underground hole. With a guy at her back, wrenching her arm up, she obviously wasn't out for an afternoon stroll. If anyone noticed, they decided not to care.

As her eyes and lungs cleared, her stomach chimed in, wanting its share of attention. Typical. Motion sickness or nerves always set her gut roiling like a teakettle, bubbling over at the slightest provocation. And right now, the tear gas had it feeling provoked.

When she stumbled over a sidewalk crack, her mouth filled with bile. She gagged and forced it down, the taste only making the nausea worse.

"What's wrong?" Rhys said gruffly.

Hope swayed, her free hand clutching her stomach. "The gas. I feel . . ."

"It does that. Just keep going."

"I-I don't think—" She took a deep breath, head tilting back. "Okay. That's better." She took one more step, then doubled over, moaning and gagging.

"Oh God, I'm going to—"

She swung, so fast his slackening grip fell from her arm. He grabbed for her, catching her wrist. And that is when the Aikido lessons paid off, Hope's body instinctively recognizing the hold and reacting without instructions. A wrench, a grab, a flip and he was on the ground with *his* arm now pinned up behind his back.

At that moment, someone decided to notice. A burly middle-aged man lumbered from the parking lot, glaring at Hope from under bushy brows. A woman being forced along a motel sidewalk hadn't been worthy of his attention, but apparently, that same woman pinning a man twice her size was somewhat suspicious.

"He—he attacked me," she said, gulping air between words.

"Hope," Rhys said under his breath. "You don't want to—"

"The—the manager. Get the manager. Please."

Hope lifted her teary, reddened eyes, and the man jogged off toward the front office. She flew off Rhys, gave him one hard kick in the ribs and ran.

A man shouted. Rhys? The burly man? She didn't know and, frankly, didn't care, just hunched down and pummeled the pavement.

As she veered into the lot, she slowed to a jog. A very fast jog, arms pumping, trying to look like an ordinary runner.

She jogged to the edge of the motel lot, just past the boundary fence, then wheeled, running along it. She measured the distance until she'd be at the rear of the motel. Then she turned to the fence, ready to climb.

In front of Hope was an eight-foot-high sheet of solid two-by-fours. Not a finger- or foothold to be seen, and not a chance in hell of jumping up and grabbing the top.

In the past twenty-four hours, she'd scaled two fences, so she'd seen this one and thought *no sweat* without making sure it *could* be scaled without grappling hooks.

The demon growled in her gut. *Get the hell over that fence. Get through it. Smash it down. Karl is over there, in danger.*

Which was all very fine, but unless the demon could conjure up real superpowers for her, she wasn't flying over or through that fence. She kept jogging along, hoping a way over would miraculously appear. A ladder would be good. A rope just fine. Hell, at this point, she'd settle for a strong vine or overhanging branch. She found two knotholes, but even her size-five toes weren't squeezing in them.

Could she get around the back end? If the fence belonged to the motel, it would stretch the full perimeter.

Just get past it, the demon screamed. *Around, over, through. Get Karl!*

Every second she fussed was another second for the Cabal to load him into a van . . . if they hadn't already. She had to go back the way she'd come. She turned . . . and there was Rhys, running full tilt toward her.

FINN

FINN SAT IN THE CAR and watched the building. A cookie-cutter motel—an ugly block of rooms with an office at one end, a cleaning cubby and vending machines in the middle. He imagined a motel salesman back in the fifties, drumming up customers. "You want one of our Model A roadside motels. Model B? Well, actually, we don't have a Model B . . ."

The problem with Model A was parking. The layout presumed you *were* in the fifties, heading down Route 66 on a family road trip and, naturally, you only needed one parking spot, which was conveniently located right outside your room door. If you brought a friend or towed a trailer, you needed to park it in the dirt lot out back, which was quite possibly the worst location for a stakeout. So Finn was stuck in one of the empty spots along the front. Uncomfortably exposed and, worse, unable to see one half of the building, now that a billboard of a minivan had pulled in beside him.

He'd gotten out once to scout, but he wasn't inconspicuous enough to loiter for long, so he was stuck with two hopes. One, that Adams was in the part of the motel he could see. Two, that Damon would get his phantom ass the hell back from wherever he'd gone and *tell* Finn where Adams was.

Making Damon hitchhike in the taxi had been an inspired plan. And like all his inspired plans these last few days, it had played out much better in his mind than in reality. Finn had managed to follow

Adams's cab for a few miles. Then he'd lost it as a transport cut him off. When the transport had passed, the cab was gone. A half-mile later in his rearview mirror he'd seen the cab pull from this motel.

All he had to do then was pull in and wait for Damon to come out and tell him which unit Adams was in. That had been ten minutes ago.

As Finn leaned back in his seat, a man jogged past his car. Anytime Finn saw someone running in L.A. without a jogging suit—hell, sometimes even with one—he paid attention. The guy was nearing forty, clean shaven, wearing a team jacket and a ball cap, heading toward the road, no sign that he was chasing or being chased.

Finn relaxed. Then another man, older and heavyset, ran past, this one along the sidewalk in front of the motel rooms.

"Hey!" the second man yelled. "Hey! Someone stop that guy!"

That got Finn out of the car. He strode to the sidewalk. Ahead of the running man stood a girl, no more than eleven, dressed in a halter top and denim skirt that wouldn't be out of place on a street hooker.

"What's happening here?" Finn said, flashing his badge to the big man, who'd stopped now, doubled over, panting.

"There was a girl . . ."

"That girl?" Finn jerked a thumb at the preteen.

"No, a—" He caught his breath. "Woman. Young woman. She said that guy attacked her. I told the manager to call the cops, but I don't think he's going to."

"Where's the young woman?"

"Took off," the girl said.

"Is he chasing her?"

"Dunno."

"Which way did she go?"

"Dunno."

She scuffed worn sneakers against the pavement. Crossed her arms. Scowled as if she was being asked to do a chore. Finn started walking, taking out his phone to call for backup.

"My dad's right," the girl muttered behind him. "Too many foreigners in this city. Stupid lady smacked right into me. Never even said sorry."

Finn stopped and looked back. "The young woman?"

"Yeah. Mexican or something."

"East Indian, I think," the man said. "Tiny thing, but the way she threw that guy down—"

Finn didn't hear the rest. He was already running down the front sidewalk. A young couple blocked the way. They'd stopped to look at a partially open door.

As Finn passed, the young man plucked his sleeve. "You smell that?"

He caught an odor that made his guts knot, remembering a training seminar where they'd sprayed new LAPD recruits with CS gas.

Wisps of smoke spiraled from the cracked-open door. Inside, someone coughed. He pulled out his gun and eased the door open another inch. The distinct peppery smell of tear gas wafted out, mixed with another smell—whatever caused the smoke, he supposed.

The smoke had almost evaporated, and he could make out a figure on all fours, hacking. A woman. Young. Slender. Dark blond hair in a ponytail. His hand tightened on his gun, the image of Adele Morrissey popping to mind. Then the woman lifted her head and Finn saw the face that had been taunting him for three days.

Robyn Peltier.

A careful look around the empty room, then he holstered his weapon and hurried inside, grabbing her under the arms and lifting her. Once they were past the door, she staggered to the wall and leaned against it. Her head dropped forward as she sputtered and gasped, tears streaming.

Finn called for backup and an ambulance. When he gave his name, Robyn stiffened, head rising, watery reddened eyes meeting his. Then she dropped her head again, racked by a fresh wave of coughing and dry heaves.

"It's Detective Findlay, Robyn," he said when he got off the phone. "You called me last night."

She tried to nod between coughs, face still lowered.

"Paramedics are on their way," he said. "That was tear gas. It's not dangerous, just . . ." He was about to say something suitably neutral, as the department taught, but remembering what it felt like, what came out was: ". . . vile."

Her cough softened into a laugh. "That would about sum it up."

Finn shifted his weight, resisting the urge to take her arm.

He'd spent three days searching for this woman, and now here she was, hacking up her lungs, and all he could think was that she looked . . . small.

He glanced around for the ambulance. "Keep breathing. Do you feel like you're going to be sick?"

She shook her head and went to swipe her sleeve over her eyes.

Finn caught her arm. "Don't rub. You'll only make it worse. We need to get your eyes washed out. Same with your skin. Does it burn?"

"Ice," she croaked.

Good idea. There'd be water in the vending machine, too.

He plucked a bill from his wallet and looked around for someone to run the errand. The tiny crowd had dispersed, which may have had something to do with the stinking fog still seeping from the opened door. He closed it, scanned the lot and found the heavyset man, hanging back as he stared at Robyn.

When Finn waved the man over, he shook his head, still gaping at Robyn with the horror one usually reserves for Ebola victims.

"It's tear gas," Finn called. "It's not—"

The man climbed into his car, shut and locked the door.

"The ice machine's right over . . ." Robyn squinted to see, her eyes still streaming tears. "Over there," she said resolutely, then took an equally resolute step before faltering against the wall.

Finn went to grab her only to realize he still had hold of her arm. He tightened his grip, helping her find her balance.

"Sorry," she said. "Guess I'm a little off."

Now it was his turn to laugh, a rusty rumble. "I'd say you've got a right to be. I'll get the ice and water. Stay here and catch your breath."

Finn jogged to the vending machine. He fed his bill into it while scouring the cubby for something to hold the ice. He bought a water and a Coke, then snatched up an empty chip bag, filled it with ice and put it into his pocket.

The sidewalk was empty.

Finn strode to the spot where he'd left Robyn. He looked around. Even opened the motel room door again. She was gone.

He dropped the bottles. Threw them, if he was being honest, as he started running.

How stupid had that been? He finally catches his fugitive suspect, only to leave her unattended while he trips over himself to get some water, some ice . . . Hell, she could probably use a Coke, to boost her blood sugar.

He reached the side corner to see her race around the back, remarkably agile for someone unable to take two steps a few minutes ago.

She'd played him.

He tore down that side stretch so fast he barely had his gun out before he wheeled around the back corner and—

There stood Robyn Peltier. Holding a gun on him.

HOPE

Hope raced down the fence line, Rhys's feet pounding behind her. She rounded the corner. Still no sign of an opening. Why would there be? The motel wouldn't encourage anyone to cut through its property.

She pressed herself against the boards and waited, her eyes half closed as she tracked the pound of Rhys's shoes. Closer, closer . . .

He came around the corner and she pounced. She caught him in a hold, but this time he was ready and before she could flip him, he countered, throwing her onto her back.

"Hope, you have to listen to me."

Hope hit him with a head strike, grabbing his outstretched arm and slamming her open palm under his chin. He should have flown back. But he recognized the move, countered with a wrist twist and threw her to the ground again, harder this time, wind whooshing from her lungs, head hitting a rock, fireworks of pain and light exploding. He stood over her, his lips moving, some new variation on "Let's talk about this," but the gong ringing in her ears drowned out his words.

The demon wended through her body like an electric eel, sparking and jolting with every twist, battering itself against Hope's insides, fighting to escape. It had escaped before. Once Hope had even seen it in a mirror, a nightmare version of herself, wild with rage. Now it whipped through her, begging to be free.

So Hope set the terms . . . and opened the gate.

She flew at Rhys, martial-arts training forgotten, animal instinct—

demon instinct—taking over, tackling him with everything she had, a dervish of nails and feet and fists. Expecting another scripted martial-arts move, he staggered back. She launched herself at him. They went down.

If any low-flying plane had passed over at that moment, Hope suspected they'd have seen a scene straight out of a Tasmanian devil cartoon as she scrabbled in the dirt with Rhys, a dust cloud enveloping them.

Throughout the fight, she kept control. And it was glorious, the purest adrenaline and chaos rush imaginable. Sweeter even than surrendering to the demon. Sweeter because, for those few minutes, her halves found their whole, demon and conscience in sync. Which was not to say the demon didn't push the boundaries, tossing out suggestions that involved the permanent destruction of body parts—eyes, ears, teeth . . . and parts no guy really deserves to lose. But she controlled the demon and she used it.

It worked fine until Rhys pulled out a whip-thin strap of plastic that Hope didn't even notice until it was fixed around her wrist. She jerked back, thrown off enough for him to take advantage, flipping her onto her stomach and snapping the cuff around her other hand.

She rocked and writhed, trying to kick, but he stayed out of reach. He grabbed her hair and ground her face into the ground. She coughed and spat dirt—and a few obscenities.

He leaned over her. "I want to talk to Hope."

"Who the hell do you think you're—?"

His fist tightened in her hair, jerking her head back. "I want to talk to Hope."

She bucked and flipped fast, the demon power-boosting her strength. Her feet flew up, scissoring around his waist and throwing him to the side with a deftness that left her blinking.

He fell face-first. As he pushed up, Hope pounced, landing on his back, knees digging into his spine as her hands twisted wildly, trying to break the strap cuffs. She felt the tie slide over wet skin, and glanced over her shoulder to see her wrists bloodied.

The surprise of seeing blood was enough to make her pause. When Rhys bucked, she fell back. He shot up and lunged for her. She scrambled to her feet and kicked. When her foot didn't make contact, she swung off balance, shoulder-checking the fence with a crack.

Rhys grabbed her shoulders and whammed her face-first into the fence. A splinter drove into her cheek and the demon screamed, as outraged as if she'd been stabbed. Fresh adrenaline pumped through her and she flailed, writhing and kicking.

Rhys slammed her against the fence hard enough to knock her wind out again, and this time her body said to hell with what the demon wanted, *it* had had enough, and she leaned against the wood, panting, sweat dripping into her open mouth, eyelids fluttering, legs trembling with exhaustion.

"Good," Rhys said. "Now let me talk to Hope."

"What the hell are you? An exorcist?"

A humor-free chuckle. "If I have to be."

He flipped her around to face him, pinned her by the shoulders, then leaned down toward her face.

"I know you can hear me, Hope."

"Of course I can. You're spitting in my face."

He inched back and lifted his chin before continuing. "I know it feels good, letting the demon take over. But I need you to take control. You're getting hurt—"

"Because you keep throwing me around. Hello? I'm *in* control. No head spinning, see? I could manage projectile vomiting, though, if it'd make you feel better."

"So you're back?"

"I never went anywhere. I control her; she doesn't control me."

"Her?"

Hope flashed the image of Karl for the demon. Karl in trouble. It was like being seven again, telling her mom about the riding instructor who liked to caress her rear as he boosted her onto the horse. Like her mom, the demon went wild, protective instinct kicking in full steam. The snarling, teeth-gnashing dervish returned, thrashing until the bite of the handcuff strap knocked her sober.

"There." She flicked her head to toss sweat-sodden hair out of her eyes. "If you'd like a better demonstration, just undo this strap." She flashed her teeth then, a warning smile, pure Karl, another lesson assimilated and never used until now.

Rhys blinked and eased back. "So it can be controlled." His lips moved. It took a moment for her to recognize the expression as a smile. "I was right."

"Yes, apparently—" Hope nailed him in the shin with a satisfying crack. "—you were."

He staggered back, wincing.

"Now cut this strap and walk away or—"

"I'm on your side, Hope."

Another classic fight line. Her laugh came harsh. "Of course, you are. That Cabal SWAT team attack? Total misunderstanding."

"Yes, it was the Cabal. Which means, I had nothing to do with it."

"Because you couldn't possibly be working for the Nasts." She lifted her chin, meeting his eyes. "You set us up. Friday night, when we went by to check out Irving Nast's place, you were there. You followed us, then you set Grant Gilchrist on our trail. You were trying to find Adele for Irving and didn't want us getting to her first."

Hope expected him to say he'd been at Irving's place for the same reason they'd been—scoping it out. An equally plausible excuse. But after a moment, he scooped up his ball cap, pulled it on and said, "Yes, that's how I found you were involved and, yes, I was hired by Irving Nast to find Adele. But I'm not a Cabal employee. I'm an independent contractor."

"A mercenary."

"Not the word I'd choose."

"You don't like it? Well, I don't like being tied up. So how about you let me go and I'll promise never to call you that again."

"Yes, Irving Nast hired me. He thought that was clever—getting one clairvoyant to find another. I was making sure he *didn't* get her. A Cabal rips the soul from a clairvoyant."

"Considering who we're talking about—killer of cops and celebutantes and innocent bystanders—I'm not convinced a little soul ripping isn't in order. And, no, that isn't the demon talking."

"Adele is . . . broken."

"That's one way of putting it."

His gaze flicked away, her flippancy unappreciated.

"You've got me, okay?" she said, toning it down a notch. "I surrender. Now take me to the Nasts."

"You don't believe me."

"I want to go—"

"Marsten's fine, Hope. The Cabal wouldn't touch a Pack werewolf, and unless Grant was wrong, that's what Marsten is, and the Cabal knows it. If they wanted him dead, they'd have shot him. They just tranquilized him, neutralizing the biggest threat first."

"Fine, so take me—"

"I can't do that when I'd be in as much trouble as you. And they don't *want* me going back. Don't you get it? This is a set-up. Do you think letting us escape the front door was an oversight?"

"No, it's proof that you're working for them. They let you go so you could get me out and pretend to have rescued me."

He rocked back on his heels. "What are my vibes telling you? Anything negative there, besides frustration? Anything to suggest I'm lying?"

"As a mercenary—hired gun, hired spy, hired con artist, whatever—you're a professional liar." She met his gaze. "Right?"

He tugged his cap brim, as if adjusting it, a subconscious attempt to pull back under its shadows. A man who preferred the security of anonymity.

"A professional liar can outwit an Expisco," Hope said.

"Not if you were properly trained."

How much *did* he know about Expiscos? This was the second time his words suggested she wasn't the first one he'd met. The demon jumped to attention, straining forward with questions. Hope hauled it in and muzzled it.

"What possible reason would I have to fake-rescue you?" Rhys said. "To lead me to Adele? You have no idea where she is."

"Okay, then. I'm useless. So let me go."

"You aren't useless to *me*. I brought one operative on this mission, and your boyfriend killed him. I need help, and I have a feeling you're going to be a lot more useful on this mission than Grant."

"What mission?"

"You haven't asked why the Cabal let me escape that hotel room. What does Irving want?"

This wasn't the time for a pop quiz. But as Hope squirmed, she could tell she wasn't getting out of these strap cuffs until he let her. "You know where Adele is. Irving has figured out you're not handing her over. He thinks if he swoops down on us and you escape, you'll run off to warn her. Lead him to her. That's why he had one of his men suggest they know where she is."

"*Suggest?*" Rhys laughed. "That was one of the most obvious tricks I've seen. There's a reason Irving hasn't shot through the Cabal ranks."

He took a penknife from his pocket and flicked it open.

"Your hands," he said.

"I'd like to keep them."

"And you aren't going to if you keep yanking at that strap, digging it in deeper." He flipped Hope around and sliced off the cuffs. "Now we need to get that cleaned up. I have a first-aid kit in my car. Then we're going to the kumpania." Seeing her expression, he shook his head. "You don't even know what that is, do you? Remember what I said about being in over your head? The kumpania is where we'll find Adele."

"But that's exactly—"

"—what Irving wants me to do? Yes."

"I'm not helping the girl who—"

"I'm not warning Adele. I'm warning Neala." Again, he saw her confusion. "Colm's mother."

"Your wife."

He shook his head, gazed down as he returned the knife to his pocket. "Not for a very long time. But she saved my life once. I owe her."

"So you're going to warn her about the Cabal."

"And, more immediately, about Adele. Which she already suspected. I just didn't listen. She tried—"

He broke off, shaking his head and prodding her along the fence line.

Hope dug in. "Whatever problem you have, it's *your* problem. Mine is Karl and Robyn. I don't even know where Robyn is—"

"Picked up by the Cabal, I'm sure. You want them back from the Cabal SWAT team, and I want to get to the kumpania without that SWAT team on my tail. The two goals, I think you'll agree, are not mutually exclusive." He took her elbow. "Come on."

FINN

THAT SPRINT ALONG THE MOTEL had burned off Finn's anger, and when he saw Robyn clutching the gun, the first thing he noticed was not the black hole of a barrel, but those slender hands trembling. Robyn struggled to hold her expression immobile, eyes narrowed, in a desperate attempt to hide her terror. It was a look Finn knew well. He'd seen it on too many people at the other end of a gun, fighting to show that they weren't scared, that they *would* pull that trigger, and that made them ten times more dangerous than the most hardened gangbanger. Because at the smallest move, the slightest sound, they fire before their brain could interfere.

"You don't want to do this," he said.

Robyn's laugh wobbled as much as her hands. "Are you going to remind me of the penalty for shooting an officer of the law, Detective? I bet that comes in handy, doesn't it? Your boss sends you after someone like me, and if I stand up to you, you just play the cop card, make me think twice about defending myself."

"My boss?"

"The people you work for."

"I work for the city of—"

"Cut the crap, Detective Findlay. Hope already figured out your game."

"Hope?"

"Ah, so now you're going to pretend you never met her."

"If you mean your friend, Hope Adams—"

"That's the only Hope both of us know. Only you didn't know her as well as you thought. You overlooked that magic power detector of hers."

"Magic power?" He remembered interviewing Adams, remembered being afraid she'd somehow pick up on his secret.

"Are you going to parrot everything I say? I bet that's what they teach you at double-agent school, huh? In case of exposure, whatever your interrogator says, repeat it back?"

"Double-agent—" He stopped himself. "I don't know what—"

"—I'm talking about. Lesson two: deny everything. Now you'll tell me that Hope's wrong, you don't have supernatural powers."

He felt his jaws part. He wouldn't go so far as to say it dropped, but it definitely opened.

"Better yet, gape at me like I've lost my mind."

He shut his mouth.

"Over the last few days," she continued, "I have had very good cause to question my sanity, but if I know one thing right now, it's that I'm not crazy and nothing you can say is going to convince me otherwise. Now, are you going to tell me you don't have supernatural powers?"

He should deny it. He'd been raised to do that until he was married, and then only to tell his wife, warning her the same way he would if his genes carried a disorder.

But Robyn Peltier would see his lie. She'd condemn him for it worse than she'd ever condemn him for the truth. Considering she was a fugitive currently holding a gun on him, her opinion shouldn't matter. But it did. And he knew if he was going to solve this case, and find not only justice but truth, his answer—and her opinion—would be critical.

"No," he said.

"So you *are* going to deny it."

"I mean no, I'm *not* going to deny it."

She took a second to recover, loosening and regripping the gun.

"Can you put that down?" he asked.

"Right now, this gun is the only thing guaranteeing me the truth."

"No." He met her gaze. "It isn't."

She faltered again, her fingers peeling off and finding new holds. Then, slowly, she lowered it to her side.

"You have them, don't you?" she said.

"Who?"

"Hope and Karl."

"I don't have any—"

"Your employer does, then."

"My employer—" Finn exhaled, air whistling through his teeth. "Okay, let's back up. Who do you think I work for?"

"The man in the photograph. The one Portia sent to me, that started this whole thing."

"You mean Irving Nast?" He took out his badge. "This didn't come from a cereal box, Robyn. You can call in the number right now and check. I'm a real detective."

"Of course you are. That's the beauty of it. They get you on the LAPD and anytime a crime involves you people—"

"You people?"

She flushed, as if caught making a racial slur. "Your . . . your sort. People with . . . supernatural powers. Werewolves, demons, clairvoyants, whoever works for the Nasts. If they get into trouble—or cause it—you swoop in and clean up, keep your world a secret."

There was, Finn reflected, a bizarre logic to that . . . once you got past the part about werewolves and demons employed by a nefarious organization posing as a Fortune 500 corporation, which, he admitted, was rather a large roadblock.

"Irving Nast . . . ?" was all he could say.

Robyn crossed her arms, gun dangling from her fingers, fixing him with a sharp look of disapproval. They'd finally gotten past the parroting and denials, and now he was backsliding.

"If I'm working for Irving Nast, why was I at his office a few hours ago?"

Her disapproval slid into disgust. Obviously if he was working for Irving Nast, he'd have reason to meet with him.

"I went to question him on this case," he said. "Instead I met Sean Nast. Does that ring a bell?"

"Should it?"

"Ask Hope. She met him an hour ago—right after I left the Nast offices. You think that's a coincidence?"

She uncrossed her arms.

"Hope did meet with someone, right?" he prodded.

"Yes, a contact."

"Who was Sean Nast, the guy I met, who stonewalled me, shooed me out of his office, then raced off to meet your friend. So I would suggest *I'm* not the one working for the Nasts."

Robyn shook her head, her arms falling to her sides now. "Not Hope. Sean Nast is her contact in that organization. You talked to him, so he called her . . ."

"And I followed her from that meeting to this motel. All of which should mean I don't work for Irving Nast."

It wasn't a bulletproof argument and her look told him so, but she did ease back, thinking.

"You do have some supernatural power, though, right?"

"If you call it that."

"Hope said you're a necromancer."

That was the second time this week he'd heard that word. He didn't like the way it made him feel—uneasy and unbalanced. Like being the star in every school play, coming to L.A. and finding yourself one of a thousand actors who'd starred in every school play.

"I have no idea *what* a necromancer is . . ." Robyn continued.

It took a moment to notice her watching him expectantly.

"It means . . . ghosts," he said. "I see ghosts, communicate with them."

He braced himself for her eyes to light up, for her to say, "You can talk to the dead? My husband passed away six months ago. Can you . . . ?" He'd promised Damon he wouldn't tell her, not yet. But if she gave him that look, if those green eyes lit with hope, if she asked . . .

But it didn't register. Maybe because he'd said "ghosts" not "the dead." Maybe because, right now, Damon was miles from her mind.

"You talk to ghosts," she said, nodding as if assimilating. "Okay, that I can live with. It's a lot easier to believe than some of the others."

"Others?"

"The—" She stopped, studying him. "You really don't work for the Nasts, do you?"

He shook his head.

"You know nothing about the Nasts, do you?"

He shook his head.

"But you do know you're a necromancer."

"If that's what it's called, I guess so. I just know that seeing ghosts runs in my family."

"But the rest of it . . . ? Clairvoyants? Demons? Werewolves?"

"Uh, no."

"Oh, boy."

As silence settled over them, a figure flickered to Finn's right, by the side fence. An arm appeared. Then a leg in midstride. Finally a faint figure shimmered, heading his way. A few paces later, Damon popped into full view.

"Oh, so *now* you can see me. About time. I've been—" Damon turned the corner and saw Robyn, and his face—

Finn looked away, feeling like he had when he'd come home from college early one weekend to walk in on Rick proposing to his girlfriend, his face raw with longing and hope. Finn had known she'd turn him down, and that had made it all the more painful to see, knowing the moment couldn't end in anything except disappointment, as this one would for Damon.

As Finn pretended to look for the ambulance, he scratched the back of his neck, not because it itched, but just to have something to do. Out of the corner of his eye, he saw Damon approach Robyn, slowly, warily, as if expecting her to disappear.

Whatever powers had kept Damon from being near his wife had evidently lifted that ban. Maybe because Finn still needed Damon's help to solve this case, and now he needed Robyn's, too. Or maybe just because it was time to let him see her again.

"Uh, Finn? Why is my wife holding a gun?"

Finn turned. Robyn looked confused, as if she was trying to figure out why he'd turned away.

Damon stood beside her, so close his arm was through her. His brows arched as he gestured to the weapon.

"Bobby . . . pulled a gun on you?"

Finn searched for an excuse. Then Damon smiled, like a man seeing his wife pull a martial-arts move he never realized she knew, proud of her ability to defend herself . . . and touched with sadness that she had to.

Damon leaned into Robyn. "A brave new world, huh, baby?"

"You don't know the half of it," Finn muttered.

"Detective?" Robyn followed his gaze to her side. "Is there . . . a ghost?"

Damon pulled back sharply and shot him a look, reminding Finn that he'd promised not to tell Robyn about him. Damon was right— this was no time to tell her. That would come later. After they got through this and she was safe. For now, Damon would just have to be Finn's anonymous spirit helper.

"She figured out that I see ghosts." He gave Damon a meaningful look. "That's it."

"Detective?" Robyn said.

"Yes, it's a . . . ghost. Can you give us—me—a moment?"

Finn backed to the corner. He was about to turn away, then re-membered the last time he'd left Robyn alone.

"It's okay," Damon said. "I'm watching her."

Which he was. Couldn't take his eyes off her, even as he explained to Finn what had happened, how he'd followed Hope to the motel room, then been blocked at the sidewalk and known Robyn must be inside. He went back only to find Finn's ghost radar on the fritz again. He'd been hammering away at Finn for a while before the motel room door opened, and Hope and a man came out.

"Karl Marsten?" Finn kept his voice low, so Robyn wouldn't overhear.

"No, a red-haired guy in some team jacket."

"I saw him."

Damon told Finn that Adams had been in rough shape. Finn pre-sumed it was from the gas, but he hadn't mentioned that part to Damon, who was already eyeing Robyn like a mother hen with a bedraggled chick. Damon said the man seemed to take Adams against her will, but she'd escaped. He'd been about to run through the side fence, taking a shortcut to follow them. Then he'd seen a van around the back, Karl Marsten in the rear of it.

"He left Adams?"

"Not willingly. He was out cold, being loaded in by two guys dressed like SWAT, and I thought you must have called it in. But they'd cut out the bathroom window and taken him through there, so no one would see, which doesn't sound like the LAPD to me."

"They weren't."

"So we have private citizens in riot gear, kidnapping a guy through a motel room window, and strong-arming a woman out the front door . . . in broad daylight? This case is getting stranger by the minute."

Again, Damon didn't know the half of it, and if Finn stopped to think about it all, he'd get mired in the morass of *his* confusion.

"Where's Adams now?" he asked.

"Over there." Damon pointed to the back fence. "She kicked the crap out of the guy. I know Aikido is supposed to be good self-defense, but man, that was something else. Bobby definitely has to start taking those lessons with her. Way better than a gun."

"So Adams is okay?"

"I think so. When they were going at it, I came back to find you, couldn't, went back and they were done brawling. They seemed to be negotiating." He paused, gaze still fixed on Robyn, and rubbed his thumb over his chin. "I guess I should go check on her. Hope, that is."

Finn tried to think of some way to agree without sounding heartless. They both knew that once Damon left, he might not get this close to Robyn again.

"I'll go." Damon wrenched his gaze away. As he did, he leaned for a better look at the front lot. "An ambulance just pulled in. Is that for Bobby? Is she okay?"

"Just thought I should get her checked. Should be a squad car, too. I'll send that over to help Adams."

Damon hesitated. "Might want to hold off. She's okay and . . ." He rubbed his chin again before looking at Finn. "What I heard at the sandwich shop? Hope and that Nast guy? It was . . ."

"Strange?"

"Yeah. What did Bobby—?"

"Go keep an eye on Adams."

Whatever was going on here, he had a feeling that if the police descended on the situation too quickly, answers would dissipate like smoke signals. As Damon loped off to the fence, Finn collected Robyn and headed around front.

HOPE

A block away, Rhys had parked a nondescript car with local plates. In the car, he efficiently tended Hope's wounds, then managed to pick up the Cabal tail while looking like he was trying to avoid it. Independent operative, hired gun, mercenary . . . whatever Rhys called himself, he was adept at it, which was good because as a clairvoyant, he sucked.

Hope gave him props for admitting it. In the supernatural world, the strength of your powers is like intelligence level for humans. Everyone lets on they have it in spades, if only as untapped potential. Saying your powers are weak is as tough as admitting you're not too bright.

When he tried to check on Karl, he couldn't pick up anything, which suggested Karl was still unconscious. He did get a brief flash of Robyn. She seemed to be sitting on the tailgate of an ambulance. There was a man with her. From the description, it was Detective Findlay.

After talking to Sean, Hope was sure Findlay had nothing to do with the Cabal. The fact that he'd waltzed through their office doors meant he was either one hell of a ballsy necromancer or he didn't know what the Nast Corporation was. But she hadn't had a chance to tell Robyn that. If she was with the paramedics, though, she must have realized that whatever Findlay was, she was safe for now.

For now, Robyn *did* seem safe, and Hope had to leave it at that, because after a brief snapshot of Robyn, Rhys's mental camera screen went blank. Not so much a substandard model, then, as a battery hog, needing plenty of downtime between shots.

They were being tracked by two vehicles—a black car and a van, which were taking turns in the tailing position. Rhys wasn't fooled.

"Are you sure Karl is in that van?" Hope asked.

"Positive."

"But if you can't see him . . ."

"He is. Relax, Hope."

"I'm being sensible, not sensitive. There's no shortage of vehicles at a Cabal. Why not exchange that van for another, take Karl back and get him locked up before he wakes?"

"Because they're *waiting* for him to wake up. Irving isn't particularly bright, but he is resourceful. If I take off on foot and his guys lose me, he has a werewolf."

"For tracking."

"Presumably the original plan was to take you as a hostage and force Karl to help."

"But now you have me, and that works just as well, as motivations go."

A moment of silence, then, "Check out the van behind us. Can you tell me what he's doing wrong?"

One might think a mercenary would jealously guard his knowledge, but Rhys spent the next ten minutes teaching her how to spot, lose and *be* a tail. In part, Hope was sure it was a distraction from thoughts of his son, but she also got the sense he liked to teach. So she shut up and absorbed.

Or she did until, in the distance, she saw the big-box bookstore from earlier.

"Where are we going?" she asked.

"Back to those medical offices where Colm— Where you were earlier."

It was a moment before she managed a cautious, "Why?"

"I need a quiet place to take care of the Cabal team."

"By taking care of them, you mean . . ."

"I have tranquilizer guns in the trunk."

She hoped her sigh of relief wasn't too loud.

He went on. "The problem with stopping to do that is that I need an empty place where, logically, I might go before heading to the kumpania. Irving will be wondering why I grabbed you. Going here will answer his question."

Hope was about to ask how. Then the vision replayed—the boy

running off the edge, twisting, his face— She shivered, the chaos pleasure cut short by a cold snake of dread slinking up her spine.

"Revenge," she whispered.

He didn't seem to catch the chill in her voice. "Right. If they
haven't already woken Karl, they will when I take you inside. He'll tell
them why we're here, and the team will rush in. Your death isn't in
their best interests. They'll try to rescue you, while letting me escape
so they can continue the hunt."

The car slowed to take a corner, heading into the complex behind
the big-box store. Her gaze straight ahead, Hope waited until the car
decelerated, then grabbed the door with one hand, and her seat belt
with the other. The door flew open, her seat belt whirring as she threw
herself against—

Rhys's arm slammed into Hope's chest, catching her square in the
solar plexus, forcing her back in her seat, gasping and sputtering as
the brakes squealed. Rhys lunged across her to yank the door shut
while the car shot up on the curb and bounced down again.

As the car hit a full stop, Hope jerked against his arm, coughing,
eyes watering, like she'd been hit with a fresh dose of tear gas. He
made a sound, one that sounded suspiciously like . . .

He was laughing.

Hope gasped, mouth opening and closing, nothing going in or out.

"Shallow breaths." He withdrew his arm. "It'll come back. And,
no, I'm not going to apologize for hitting you that hard. Never go easy
on allies if you have to take them down. *Especially* allies. You're already fighting the urge not to hurt them. Counteract that and hit them
with everything you've got."

She stared as he talked, calmly twisted in his seat, hand on the
wheel, lecturing her as if they were still cruising along, talking about
how to tail a car. When her fingers edged toward the door, he pressed
the electronic lock.

"I know what you're thinking, Hope. I said I'm going to make the
Cabal believe I want revenge for Colm's death, and you're wondering
if that's exactly what I want, that I'm saying it to throw you off track.
I don't think I have a single operative who would see that far ahead,
and I've *trained* them to always be on the lookout for a trick. I'm
impressed."

She kept staring.

"First-rate survival instincts." He leaned toward her. "Does that
come from having demon blood? Or a professional thief boyfriend?"

She said nothing.

"Either way, I'm impressed. You can never be too paranoid, Hope. That's what I meant about coming down as hard on allies as on enemies. It doesn't matter whether you work for the council, a Cabal or on your own. Never trust that your allies won't turn on you, and never presume your enemies can't be turned to help you."

He checked the rearview mirror. "Good. They've seen us. It'll be obvious something happened, maybe you tried to escape, which will support the story."

He cranked the wheel away from the curb, then accelerated. "It *is* a story, Hope. Yes, I want revenge against the person responsible for my son's death, but that person isn't you. You tried to stop it. In your place, I would have done the same. So it's not you I'm after."

"Adele."

He slowed near the medical center, checking for police before turning into the lot. "Neala—his mother—tried to warn me about Adele. I've been gone since Colm was two. I stayed away. That was the deal." Silence as he circled the lot. "But Neala kept in touch, let me know how he was doing. Then, last year, she called me in a fury. She'd caught Adele and Colm making out."

"How old is Adele?"

"Exactly Neala's point. You get it. I didn't. Maybe as a guy all I could think was that, at his age, I'd have been in heaven if a nineteen-year-old came on to me. Like Neala, I suppose you see the problem. It's fine for a fourteen-year-old to fantasize, but for a young woman to reciprocate . . ."

"Something's wrong."

"Which is what Neala said. I knew it wasn't normal, but the kumpania is very insular. Adele wouldn't have a lot of options for a sexual outlet. Maybe she was immature for nineteen. Maybe Colm was mature for fourteen. I made excuses and chalked up Neala's reaction to a mother's jealousy." He paused a moment, then jackrabbited into a spot, slamming on the brakes hard enough to smack her forward, ribs aching.

"Stay put," he said as he opened the door. "We need to make a good show of this, in case they're already watching."

ROBYN

Robyn sat on the ambulance tailgate as the paramedic checked her eyes. He hadn't looked at her shoulder. He didn't know he needed to.

Robyn had made a deal with Detective Findlay. If he was going to find Adele, he needed her help, and he wasn't getting it by dumping her in a hospital room. So she wouldn't mention the shoulder and he'd pretend not to know about it.

He hadn't liked that, his blue-green eyes cranking up the frosty blue, his square jaw getting squarer. But she was right and, as she pointed out, it was her safety, therefore her decision. He hadn't liked that either, his look saying that, as a murder suspect, she didn't have that right, but he was too polite to say so.

He reminded her of the cops they used to send to her school, parading them as proof that Officer Friendly really was friendly. Robyn wasn't so sure *friendly* was the word she'd use to describe Detective Findlay. Just . . . courteous, which was more than she deserved, after pulling a gun on him and ranting about werewolves and demons.

As Robyn looked around, Detective Findlay ambled back to her. No, *ambled* wasn't the right word either. It implied aimlessness, and Detective Findlay carried a decisive air that forbade anything that vague. But he took his time, like a grizzly bear fixed on a target, in no particular rush but broaching no deviations to his path either, presuming all smaller beasts would get out of his path.

One of the officers did scamper into his path to intercept him. It was a young officer, barely twenty, with an eager smile, big eyes, big feet and a tendency to stumble over them. The detective didn't seem to notice the officer until he was a hairbreadth from smacking into him.

Lost in thought? Or busy listening to his ghost? He had the same distant look Hope got, the one Robyn now knew meant she was seeing a vision. When he saw the young officer, he snapped out of it with that same blinking jolt of surprise.

What was it like to see ghosts? What did they look like? What did they say?

The ghost Detective Findlay had been communicating with seemed to be some kind of spirit guide, helping him by scouting for Hope and Karl. Did Detective Findlay only see that one spirit helper? Or a world of ghosts? If it was ghosts, did that prove life after death? Did that mean Damon was still out there, somewhere, and if he was, could Detective Findlay—

Robyn banished the thought. Hope and Karl were missing. Adele Morrissey was still at large. Making contact with her dead husband sat at the bottom of Robyn's priority list. It had to.

Detective Findlay spoke to the officer, then continued on to Robyn. "You okay?"

The paramedic answered for her, in far more detail than needed, the detective's patient nods belied by his fingertips tapping against his leg.

"If she's okay, I need to get her back to the station."

"Sure," the paramedic said. "We could—"

"I'll take her in my car." He looked at Robyn. "Ms. Peltier?"

That was all he said, his broad face impassive. No meaningful look passed between them, but those tapping fingers told her something was up. He hadn't been so eager to get her into custody until now.

Robyn slid from the tailgate. Detective Findlay dismissed the paramedics, gave final instructions to the officers, who were canvassing the motel guests and staff, then led Robyn to his car.

"We have a fix on Hope," he said as he fastened his seat belt. "She's with the guy from your motel room. Ball cap and sports jacket."

"Rhys. Is she okay?"

"Seems so. She's going with him willingly, as far as . . . my source can tell. We'll follow."

HOPE

When Rhys came around to Hope's door, holding a gun, she put on a very convincing show of resistance. And he taught her another lesson in not giving the ally any quarter, wrenching her arm to the breaking point again and forcing her inside the building, where he pointed out that the gun was filled with tranquilizer darts, and he had a second one for her.

He could have told her this in the car, but she guessed that booster shot of true panic hadn't hurt the act.

"Aim for their legs," he said as they huddled in the stairwell. "Presume they're wearing body armor. I doubt Irving will come in, but he might follow if his men are slow getting back out. If you see him, tranq him. Then use this."

He handed her what looked like a key chain tape measure. When she stared at it, he grabbed the ring and pulled out a fine wire.

"Have you ever garroted anyone?"

She moved her stare to his face.

"I take that as a no."

"You said—" She looked down at her tranquilizer gun.

"That's for the team. We have to kill Irving." His tone made Hope feel like a naive journalism student, shocked at hearing she might have to do something underhanded to get a good story.

"If Irving lives, he'll come after us. All of us." He enunciated as if she wasn't quite as smart as he'd thought. "He wanted Adele—and the glory of her recruitment—for himself. His team is just following orders. He won't have trusted anyone with details. So if he dies, so does the project . . . and his revenge against those who screwed it up."

"But the council— A Nast— Unless my life is in immediate danger—"

"—the council doesn't condone murder. Laudable and just . . . and one reason why the council is not, and never can be, as effective a body as the supernatural world needs. But now is not the time for political lectures. If you let Irving live, he won't show you the same mercy."

When she hesitated, Rhys said, "What would Karl do?"

There was no question. He would eliminate the threat as he had with Gilchrist and that would be the right decision for him. But Karl would be the first to say she wasn't him and she shouldn't try to be.

"I don't have time to wait for you to figure it out, Hope. Protect your safety and Karl's, or protect your council job. You decide."

He gave final instructions and left.

STEP ONE: CASE THE JOINT for civilians. Rhys didn't use those exact words. For a mercenary, he was severely lacking in the requisite badass-itude . . . though the ache in Hope's ribs insisted that his bite was worse than his bark. If her own attitude seemed a little lacking in gravity, that was deliberate. It kept her thoughts from straying into territory that would reduce her from Cabal-fighting commando to quivering ditherer.

She couldn't think about Robyn, about Karl, about Irving Nast and what she'd do if she found him. Rhys made the choice sound so simple. End a lethal threat or keep her job, as if her council work was a part-time gig at McDonald's. But Hope's life and her council work were intertwined. It fed her chaos hunger in a way her conscience could live with. And if, in the last year, as that hunger grew, her council work had been steadily less effective? She couldn't consider that now.

Hope prayed she didn't find Irving Nast. If she did, she prayed Karl would be there to help her make the right choice.

RHYS SAID HE'D REPORTED COLM'S DEATH with an anonymous call to 911, so his son wouldn't be lying on the ground until employees tripped over him tomorrow morning. Any police presence, though, was gone before they arrived.

The parking lot was empty, which suggested the building was, too. Hardly ironclad proof, but they wouldn't have time to check. They needed to get in position and wait for the Cabal team, which *would* do a more thorough sweep. That's when they'd take them down, as they split up to search.

Hope managed to quickly skim one floor before a low strum of chaos told her the Cabal team had entered the building. She hurried to find a hiding place. As she passed a clinic waiting room, footsteps sounded in the hall, the brisk *click-click* of feminine footwear. Definitely not the SWAT team.

She backed into the room quickly. Too quickly. Her foot caught a chair leg, the metal yowling across the hard floor. She went still, gun raised. The footsteps continued, pace unchecked. She glanced over her shoulder. She was in a small room with four chairs and a door. She backed to the door and turned the knob. Locked.

A woman passed the door, heading the other way, her back to Hope. Carrying an armload of file folders, obviously putting in Sunday overtime, she was dressed in T-shirt, jeans and heels, her short hair spiked, loop earrings swaying as her head bopped to the beat from her earphones.

Her steps slowed and squeaked as she turned into a room. Another squeak, this time a chair. The whoosh of files dropping onto a desk. A third squeak, the chair being pulled in.

Hope eased from the corner, moving silently. She could still only see the woman's back now through an office door as she shuffled folders into piles.

Hope could hear her music, the distorted boom-screech-wail of heavy metal cranked full-blast. They could have a firefight in the hall and Hope doubted she'd notice. While it was tempting to leave it at that, it wasn't safe. Not for them, and not for the woman.

She positioned herself with the tranquilizer gun aimed at the woman's shoulder. Then she stopped. What made her so sure this was loaded with tranquilizers?

Rhys had asked where her paranoia came from. Maybe some of it was demon, some Karl, but most came from that loftiest of teachers: experience.

The deceptions and lies of society life were superficial, like saying "Oh, don't you look gorgeous. You're just the belle of the ball and I'm so happy for you," when what you really mean is "That dress makes you look like a cheap whore and if you ever show me up at my own party again, I will carve out your liver with a spoon and serve it as pâté." Of course, in the society world, no one's liver was in any actual danger. In the supernatural world? Don't bet against it.

Hope had been lied to and deceived and betrayed, then lied to and deceived and betrayed again. And no matter how strongly she believed in the innate goodness of mankind, eventually she'd noticed the "kick me" sticker on her butt, ripped it off and vowed never to let anyone replace it.

She might have tipped into paranoia, having leapt to wrong conclusions about Detective Findlay and Rhys. And she could be wrong questioning what was in this gun. But she wasn't shooting a bystander until she was sure. Rhys knew how sensitive the council was about killing. Why not hand her poison darts and say it was only a tranquilizer? She'd shoot, she'd move on and she'd never be the wiser.

Choices. Everyone had to make them. Some were uglier than others.

When she heard footsteps in the hall—heavy-booted ones—she saw her solution. She retreated into the waiting room, measured the distance between her and those footfalls. When they drew close, she counted to three, swung out and fired.

Hope got off two shots—the first a guess, the second aimed. Both hit the guy in the legs. He looked at her, blinking stupidly, then crashed to the floor.

The chair in the office squeaked. Hope flung herself against the wall and listened. Another squeak. Just her luck to drop the guy at a break between songs.

"Hello?"

No heel clicking accompanied the cautious greeting, and Hope pictured the woman standing beside her desk. She eased along the wall and dropped beside the Cabal guy. One hand checked his pulse while the other trained her gun on the office doorway.

A tentative click. Then another.

The man's pulse beat, thready, as if that second tranquilizer dart had been overkill. He'd be down for a while, but he'd recover.

"Hello?"

Three clicks. A shadow darkened the office doorway. The woman's hand appeared on the door. The shadow of her head moved forward, to peek.

"Hey!" Hope called.

Startled, the woman jumped back, her hands flying up, arms appearing. Hope's dart hit the back of her wrist. Hope dove through the nearest door before the woman saw her. A few seconds passed, then the *boom* of her body hitting the floor.

Hope was stepping out when the tramp of boots sent her scurrying back. Muted voices came from the stairwell.

Then, "He'll take her to the roof."

Karl's voice, slurred like he was drunk . . . not that she'd ever seen Karl drunk. The relief of hearing his voice lasted two seconds before she saw the advance guard sprawled across the hall, and heard those steps tramping closer to the landing.

She ran to the woman. A quick pulse check, then she pushed her back into the office and closed the door. She grabbed one of the guard's legs and heaved. His gun skidded across the floor. She froze. The footsteps continued, that same unhurried tramp.

She barely managed to drag the guard six inches before those footfalls thankfully passed the landing and continued up. She snatched his gun, put it in the office, then hauled the guard inside.

She was back in the hall—her own gun in hand—when footsteps pattered down the stairs.

"Take him up. I'll grab Rogers."

Irving Nast. Her breath stopped in her throat.

"Sir?" one of the team said.

Call him back. Tell him you'll get Rogers. Please, please—

"He was scouting the third floor," the man continued.

Irving thanked him and his footsteps continued. Hope shot into the office with the unconscious team member. The stairwell door creaked open before she had time to close hers. Her heel thumped the guard's arm. She carefully stepped over it and retreated into the shadows.

It was useless, of course. Nast was hunting for this missing guard. He'd see the body through the open doorway. He'd turn on the light and then . . .

Then what?

Did she have a choice?

Her heart battered her ribs, keeping double time with Irving's brisk, purposeful strides.

She gripped the tranq gun. A hair tickled her cheek, caught in an air current. It tickled back and forth, back and forth, making every inch of skin creep, every muscle tense, like a guitar tuner, cranking her nerves tighter and tighter.

Irving Nast's shadow passed the open door first. He strode past, eyes straight ahead, confident that his employee would come to him.

Hope watched him, her gaze fixed on his shoulder blade, gun trained on his upper arm. A perfect shot. Just pull the trigger.

She wasn't ready. Let him get past, while she took a moment to catch her breath, make a decision, yank that damn tickling hair out—

She fired.

Unprepared for the recoil, Hope was knocked back and, for a second, she thought she'd been shot. It was only as Nast faltered that she realized she'd pulled the trigger.

As he fell, she shuddered so hard she nearly dropped the gun. It wasn't chaos bliss but relief, so sweet it felt as good as chaos.

In pulling the trigger, she'd set her course. She'd shot him so now she had to follow through, had to kill him, as if in "accidentally" pulling that trigger, she'd absolved herself of responsibility for the rest. She had to go with the choice that she'd wanted to pick: their safety over the council.

To protect herself and Karl, Irving Nast had to die. That wasn't the demon talking. It was her, because all this talk of her and the demon was an artificial distinction that she knew in her heart was bullshit. There was no Hope and the demon. There was just Hope, and she wanted the threat of Irving Nast eliminated.

Then, as she pulled out the garrote wire, the zip of it slicing through the silence, she realized what she was about to do.

Rhys blamed the council for her reluctance to kill Irving, which proved that he understood Expisco demons as superficially as he did werewolves. It had nothing to do with laws. It was more than conscience, too.

Hope knew that taking a life was wrong. She felt that more deeply than Karl ever could. If she'd asked him why, when they needed to kill, he did it for them, he'd use that as an excuse: because he didn't mind and she did. The truth, as they both knew, was that the taking of a life was the one experience she'd denied the demon. Death was the demon's purest joy. A high like no other. If she *took* that life, would she find a new high? If so, could she live with that?

Enjoying death didn't have Hope wandering palliative care wards or racing to accident scenes. Her addiction was fed by serendipity— she took sustenance where she found it and never sought it out.

And yet . . .

Here was where Hope's drive to find her limits ended. Here she looked down from the precipice and saw the rest of her life consumed by a blaze of temptation and self-loathing.

She crouched beside Irving, garrote wire stretched between her hands. She knew she had to do it. Whatever the cost. Kill or be killed.

She pressed the wire against his throat. His skin whitened along it. She imagined that furrow filling with blood. Would he wake up at the last second, his windpipe severed, life-blood pumping out, gasping for breath, seeing her sitting there, patiently waiting for him to die?

Her bile rose. She swallowed it, burning down to her gut, adding to the roiling pit.

She couldn't do it. She couldn't. Not like this. Why a garrote? Why not a gun or a syringe of poison?

Was *that* what she wanted? A clean, quiet way to murder someone?

No, if she had to kill, it should be like this, messy and raw and undeniable.

She pushed down on the wire. A single spot of blood welled, then seeped along the wire.

Make it quick. If it's quick he won't wake—

Yes! If he didn't wake up, there wouldn't be any chaos.

Hope picked up the gun, ready to give Irving a second shot of the tranquilizer. Make sure he was out cold and then—

Her gorge rose again, bringing a fresh surge of bile. Sweat stung her eye; she swiped it back with a trembling hand.

She couldn't, couldn't, *couldn't*. Had to. Had to. *Had to*.

A crash from the stairwell sent Hope jetting to her feet. A thump, then another, the rapid *bump-bump-bump* of a body tumbling down stairs. A shout answered by a roar.

Another crash. Another *bump-bump-bump*. A vision flash came. Karl had turned on his captors, sending them flying into the stairwell walls and tumbling down. Hope grabbed the gun and the wire, the thread zipping back into its case as she flew down the hall.

She could say she was going to his aid, but she knew she wasn't. She was running, running as fast as she could. Running from Irving Nast to Karl, from the problem to the solution. Every pound of her feet drove a dagger of shame into her heart. But she kept running.

HOPE CLAMORED OVER THE BODY of one guard, then the second. The first was unconscious. The second? She didn't pause to check.

The air throbbed with residual chaos. Every pump pushed the shame of her cowardice deeper into memory, gone but not forgotten.

As she climbed to the roof, that chaos throb was like the faintest beat of a distant heart, that pulse coming stronger with every step, chaos reeling her in.

"Where is she?" Karl snarled.

"Put him down!" someone yelled.

"Oh, I intend to."

Hope threw open the door. Karl stood at the roof edge, one hand around Rhys's throat, holding him over the side. Two armed SWAT team members had their guns trained on Karl.

Rhys hung there, unmoving. He was fully conscious, just staying very, very still.

"Karl? I'm okay."

He turned. The Cabal team still shouted orders. But he ignored them. His gaze traveled up and down Hope, assessing, as if, should she be injured, he might not rethink his threat to drop Rhys.

The Cabal men—like good soldiers—gave her only the briefest glance, checking for weapons, then dismissing her. When they looked away she mouthed and pantomimed a message, telling Karl she'd come with Rhys, that he wasn't planning to harm her.

He turned away before she was certain he got the message.

"So your plan failed, did it?" he growled at Rhys. "Hope was smarter than you gave her credit for. Outwitted you and escaped. Don't expect me to give you another shot at her. That's not how I handle threats."

Rhys's eyes saucered, a choked "wait!" burbling up as Hope flew forward, shouting for Karl to stop. He spun . . . and threw Rhys at the nearest guard as he lunged at the other.

Rhys hit the first guard, bowling him down in a shower of gravel and dust. Karl knocked the second one flying. Hope ran for Rhys's gun, dropped near the door. She made sure it was loaded with darts, then shot both the Cabal men. It wasn't as easy as it sounded, but she managed . . . after missing once and lodging a second dart in Karl's pant cuff.

Afterward, as she held a torn scrap of Cabal SWAT uniform to Karl's newly re-split lip, she said, "Next time you plan a fake out, warn me."

"If I did, your reaction wouldn't be nearly as authentic."

Rhys returned from dragging the second guard behind the rooftop shed. "I'd appreciate a warning, too, though I'll settle for not being used as a missile."

Karl shrugged, committing to no such promise.

•   •   •

KARL AND RHYS HAULED UP THE MEN on the stairs—both unconscious and given a second shot to be sure they stayed that way. Then Hope told them about the woman and the guard on the third floor, and said, "Irving came down looking for the guard."

"And?" Rhys prompted.

"I tranquilized him."

"And?"

Karl's head whipping around. "What'd he ask you to do?"

Hope touched his arm. "I didn't. Rhys says Irving will come back after us, and he's right, but that's when I heard you, so I left him."

"Good. You two check for more guards. I'll look after Irving."

"I-I can. I should."

"No, you shouldn't. And you're not going to."

He strode off to take care of it for her . . . as always.

FINN

FINN HATED TO BE UNGRATEFUL. But if there were people with other supernatural powers, he couldn't help wishing he'd been blessed with a
more useful one, like teleportation. Having a phantom partner who
had to rely on public transit seemed rather mundane. And, under the
circumstances, rather frustrating.

He'd sent Damon on ahead with Adams and the man Robyn had
called Rhys. But when Finn lost their car in traffic, Damon had to bail,
then hitch rides back to the spot where he'd last seen Finn, find him
and tell him which direction Adams was traveling. Now they were
stuck canvassing the area, searching for the car.

Or, Finn should say, he and Robyn were searching. When Damon
got near his wife, he was as useless as a twelve-year-old boy with a
naked supermodel. He just sat there beside her in the backseat, staring and fidgeting, frustrated beyond reason, able to see and not touch.

"Did you get her shoulder checked?" Damon slid to the edge of the
seat and leaned over.

"Couldn't. She seems fine with it, though."

"Didn't I warn you that as long as Bobby's conscious, she'll say
she's fine? She needs to see a doctor."

"And she will, as soon as we're done. That's her decision."

When Finn had first started talking to Damon, Robyn would look
up sharply, listening just long enough to realize he wasn't speaking to
her, then nod and turn her attention back to the window. After a few
exchanges, she'd caught on to the tone he used with Damon and

stopped looking up. A fast learner. A fast adapter, too, already acting as if she'd spent her life around people who talked to ghosts.

"She looks good, don't you think?" Damon asked.

Finn looked at Robyn in the rearview mirror. She did look good. But a grunt seemed the safest answer.

"She seems to be getting back on her feet," Damon said.

Finn could agree with that, too. He had no idea what Robyn had been like before or after Damon's death, but the woman beside him—keenly watching out the window, stopping periodically to pepper him with questions—was far from the shell-shocked widow he'd expected.

"Hold on," Robyn said.

Finn hit the brakes.

She jolted forward, then gave a pained smile as she adjusted her lap belt. "I thought that would be less alarming than screaming 'Stop!' I was just going to say I recognize this area. Ahead is that bookstore I told you about, where we first saw the boy."

"Rhys's son."

"Why would he bring Hope—?" Her chin jerked up. "Hope was on the roof when his son jumped. She was trying to talk him down."

"But Rhys wasn't there."

"He's clairvoyant, remember?"

It took Finn a moment to make the connection. Apparently some people were adapting to this stuff slower than others. "That means he gets a, uh, vision of people. In the present. So he could have seen Hope."

"He did. He said as much in the motel. If he blames her for him jumping and he's taking her back there now . . ."

"Direct me."

She did.

ROBYN LED FINN to a medical office building. There were three vehicles in the lot. One was the car they'd been tailing. There was also a van and a car that Finn thought he'd seen earlier.

"Is that the van they put Marsten in?" he asked Damon.

"Uh . . ." Damon popped into the front seat for a better look. "Shit. Yeah. It is."

He parked at the far end of the lot. "Get closer and take a look."

When Damon left, Finn picked up the radio receiver.

"What are you doing?" Robyn said. "That's their car. They're inside the building."

"I know. I'm calling for backup."

"What?" She shot to the seat edge.

"I've just confirmed that's the van your friend Karl was in. That means we have a potential double hostage situation, possibly with two separate and hostile parties. I can't go in there alone."

"Fine." She grabbed the door handle and wrenched. "Unlock this."

"Calm down."

The moment the words left Finn's mouth, he knew they were the wrong ones. Now she turned her glare on him, her eyes flashing.

"I am calm, Detective Findlay. Calm enough to know that you're going to sit on your ass while my friend's life is in danger, and calm enough to know that I'm not going to do the same. Now open this door."

"I need backup. Standard—"

"—operating procedure." She twisted the words, wringing out a bucket of contempt. "Fine. You follow procedure, except on one point. You forgot to lock this door and I escaped."

"The longer you fight me, the longer it's going to take to make this call." Again, regret dogged the words. It was a perfectly logical thing to say, and it came out sounding perfectly condescending, like when a kid got frustrated and the teacher made him sit in the corner with a singsong "when you can behave, you can rejoin the class."

Robyn slid back in her seat. Her arms started to fold, then she thought better of it and let them fall by her sides. When Finn hesitated, watching her, she said, "Place your call, Detective."

Damon leapt into the passenger seat, making Finn jump.

"Put 'er in reverse and peel rubber," Damon said. "They're on the way out."

Finn backed from the lot.

Robyn shot forward again. "What the hell are you doing? They're still in there."

"Whoa, Finn," Damon said. "Talk to her."

Finn explained quickly as he found a spot to wait and watch.

"*Who's* coming out?" Robyn demanded.

"Hope, Karl and that guy," Damon said, and Finn relayed.

Damon climbed into the backseat. "What'd you do to her?"

"Nothing."

"You did something. She's furious."

"Are Adams and Marsten coming out as hostages?" he asked.

"Change the subject, huh? No. They appeared to be with him willingly. I think stopping here was a trap for those SWAT guys. They rescued Karl and disabled his captors."

"Disabled?"

"Knocked out. Tranquilizer guns." Damon's attention turned back to assessing his wife. Par for the course, but Finn had been with Damon long enough now to know he'd turned away a little too fast.

"What else?" Finn asked.

"I counted five guys in those SWAT uniforms, all unconscious now. There's one suit, too. And a woman. A bystander, I think, but she's okay."

"I meant what else did you find? What aren't you telling me?"

"Hmm?" He looked up. "That's it. I'm just . . . still processing, I guess. Tranquilizer guns. This is truly some weird shit going on, Finn . . . oh, there they are."

Through a stand of trees, Finn watched the trio head for a car.

"Robyn?"

"Hmm?" Polite, but cool. A petty grudge might be beneath her, but from her tone, Finn knew he'd slid from ally to enemy. Or at least obstacle.

"That guy." He pointed. "Is that Rhys?"

She moved along her seat to the window. "Yes."

"Da— Uh, David?"

"Nice save," Damon said, with a look that warned him against slipping again.

"Go with them," Finn said. "This time, if you lose me, keep going. Get their final destination, then rendezvous here."

HOPE

Once they'd gotten rid of the Cabal tail and Karl was free, Rhys apparently considered their partnership at an end. He assured Hope and Karl that he'd look after Adele and find a way to clear Robyn's name. Hope told him where he could shove his assurances—she wasn't leaving him until she had Adele.

It took some negotiating, but he finally agreed Adele could be tried by the council, as long as Hope and Karl played bodyguard on his kumpania visit, which she suspected was what he'd hoped for all along.

When they left the medical offices, Karl was behind the wheel, Rhys in the passenger seat, Hope in the back.

On the way Rhys finally decided to tell them about the kumpania. Maybe that had something to do with Karl pulling over on Mulholland Drive and demanding to know everything before he went any farther, the looming cliff edge an unspoken echo to his earlier threat.

"Kumpania," Rhys said. "It's a Romany name."

"Gypsy?" Hope asked.

"Right. The original members likely were, and the current bulibasha, Niko, claims to be a direct descendent."

"Bulibasha?"

"Leader. Romany again. Supposedly the kumpania started in the Old World and came to the New World fleeing the pogroms. The kumpania likes its mythology. No one much cares how accurate it is, as long as it's a good story."

"And everyone in the kumpania is a clairvoyant?"

He directed Karl to take the next turn. "A full clairvoyant manifesting powers. The kumpania was created for two express and interconnected purposes: preservation of the bloodline and preservation of the power. Preservation of power includes strengthening it through training and avoiding the curse of madness."

"Can they do that?"

He took off his ball cap and raked his fingers through his hair. "They've found that elusive happy medium, which works for most. And if it doesn't? The kumpania doesn't permit deviations from its core principles."

"You think they kill anyone who shows signs of going mad?"

"The kumpania presents itself as a community idealizing clairvoyant life. But they have more in common with a cult than with a commune, including strict indoctrination, severe restrictions on their members' movements and the willingness to kill to protect the community. Which is why Adele has no qualms about killing cops. It's the kumpania way. Preservation of self at all costs." He set his cap on the seat. "Which is not to excuse what she's done. The kumpania isn't a cult of murderers. In her case, it's merely a mitigating factor, something to consider."

"Which the council will."

He nodded and went quiet. That was all the information she needed and, she presumed, all they were getting. But after a moment, he went on.

"The second concern of the kumpania is the preservation of the bloodline. All kumpania children have two fully clairvoyant parents. That inbreeding, though, causes genetic problems, so they regularly infuse the bloodline with outside clairvoyants—durjardo. That's where I came in."

Karl had slowed as the road narrowed. Rhys waved for him to keep going.

"I joined the navy right out of high school," Rhys continued. "As a boy I was into Boy Scouts, Sea Cadets, the Junior Reserves . . . I had this fantasy of growing up to be a Navy SEAL, using my clairvoyance to protect my country. It didn't work out. That's when I met Neala, Colm's mother. Not a coincidence, as I figured out years later. The kumpania has ways of finding suitable candidates. I was ripe for the picking. A young man, angry and lost, meeting a pretty girl, another clairvoyant, who brought me home to this amazing group that welcomed me and promised a life of balance and sanity. You can't understand how important that can be."

Actually, Hope could. But she said nothing.

He went on. "People hear about cults and they can't believe anyone would join. But it's easy. Just offer what's missing in someone's life, what they want most. The first year was great. Yes, I was picked for Neala, but it wasn't like you'd think. I was in love; she was at least in like. I was happy. Twenty-one with a beautiful wife, a good job, a supportive community, a baby on the way . . ."

"Colm."

"No. Our first son was stillborn. Serious genetic defects. Bringing in fresh blood doesn't negate generations of cousin marriages. That's when it started falling apart for me, after he died. The kumpania was so fatalistic about it. Callous even. Neala was heartbroken, but the bulibasha told her to suck it in and try harder next time. She got pregnant right away, with Colm, and that helped her, but it was too late for me. I started asking questions and chasing answers. Young and naive, I thought if I confronted the group with what I knew, the general members would rise up against the phuri—the elders—and we'd fix things."

A pause, then, "Turn left up here, at the gravel road. We're almost there." He picked up his cap and ran the brim through his fingers. "Adele is where it really fell apart for me. She was another durjardo. She was five when she came. Colm had just been born and I was already on my mission, questioning everything. The phuri told Adele her mother gave her to the kumpania. Behind her back, but within earshot, they said her mother sold her."

"And she overheard?"

"She was supposed to. That was part of the brainwashing. To her face, they were loving and kind, shielding her from the awful truth. But they found ways to let her know her mother didn't want her. It . . . did things to her. Again, not an excuse. Mitigating circumstances."

"Did her mother sell her?"

He shook his head. "She brought Adele to the kumpania. She'd heard about them and followed the trail through her clairvoyant contacts. She thought they could both live with the kumpania. But her mother was a pale 'cido—a clairvoyant by blood only, no powers. To the kumpania, that made her a burden. A liability even."

"So they killed her."

He nodded.

"Does Adele know?"

"I doubt it. She thinks the big secret is that she was sold, not abandoned. Growing up, thinking your mother sold—" He shook his head. "Mitigating factors. Karl? That's it up ahead. Slow down so I can get a look, see what's changed."

Hope doubted anything had. The place looked like a commune out of the sixties. For the last ten minutes they'd been driving past large houses on lots of an acre or less. In this part of Southern California, those were considered palatial estates. She could only imagine how much the kumpania property was worth.

A fringe of forest hid the property from the neighbors, though it wasn't anything she'd suspect would offend them—a collection of buildings, neat and pretty, surrounded by flower and vegetable gardens. There was even a small, whitewashed barn with chickens and goats. Picture-perfect commune living. The neighbors probably found it quaint, drove their visitors by for a look, the way Pennsylvanians did with the Amish.

There was a metal gate—painted gleaming white and entwined with vines. From here, it seemed it could be opened by hand. When Hope said as much to Rhys, he nodded. "It's not locked. But there's a camera there, in the birdhouse. And an alarm will sound in the main house when the gate opens."

Hope was about to ask why clairvoyants needed a security camera. Then she answered her own question—their powers fixed on specific people, not locations or objects.

"So we're going in the front door?" she asked.

"I want to make this visit as civil as possible. I'm here to take Adele and tell the kumpania about her and the Cabal. That's it."

"Warn them and let them run."

"Most of the kumpania is exactly what they purport to be—a peaceful group dedicated to protecting and nurturing clairvoyants."

"And the rest . . . ?"

He adjusted his cap. "Someday I'll deal with that. I've been working on it for thirteen years, and it's not an institution I can dismantle today. For now I need to give them an escape route, so they don't panic. If things go wrong too fast, they have a predetermined course of action to follow, like most cults."

"Waco?"

"Jonestown."

Hope rubbed the goose bumps on her arms. In school, she'd read

a reference to Jonestown, and—being fascinated by the macabre—
had looked it up. She could still see the photographs, the halls and
rooms of corpses, the children, all the dead children. She stared at
those kumpania houses now and they didn't look nearly as quaint.

Karl turned into the drive.

"I'll get the gate," Rhys said. "Before I do, though, I need to warn
you again. As open and neutral as I try to make this meeting, we're
dealing with a lot of tension here and a lot of distrust. Hope, you have
that gun I gave you?"

Hope nodded.

"Absolute last resort," Rhys said. "The moment you pull that gun,
you've shut down negotiations, and there are more of them—with
many more guns. They'll be on edge already, seeing me after all these
years. A visit from the grave."

"They thought you were dead?"

He nodded and opened the door.

"That could help," Hope said. "A shock, yes, but a good shock."

"I don't think so." He got out and leaned his head back in.
"They're the ones who tried to kill me."

ADELE

Adele pulled the backpack from its hiding place in her bedroom, where she'd kept it packed since learning she was pregnant. She didn't really believe Rhys was on his way. He wasn't a fool. Maybe he would have come back someday, for his son, but Colm was dead and he'd never known about Thom. Rhys hadn't been part of the kumpania long enough to be trusted with the secret of the seers.

She'd always suspected the kumpania was behind Rhys's supposed death. Earlier, when she said she'd seen him, Niko had admitted it, saying she was old enough to know the truth, how they'd let this durjardo into their midst, given him one of their daughters, a job, a new life. Rhys had repaid them by trying to kidnap Adele and Colm and sell them to the Cabal. He was a monster, and they'd had to kill him.

All Adele remembered was Rhys coming to her late one night, Colm sleeping in his arms, telling her it was time. For weeks he'd promised to get her out and find her grandmama. It had been their secret.

Niko and the other men had caught him and hauled him before the phuri, while Colm and Adele were bundled back to bed. Then Rhys had been gone. The kumpania said he'd been exiled and, a few months later, died in a car accident—a fitting punishment from the gods.

Even when Adele had been old enough to suspect the kumpania had murdered Rhys, she'd cursed him. He'd promised her freedom and he'd failed. He was weak. He hadn't been willing to take chances, to make the bold moves.

Maybe he *had* planned to sell them to a Cabal. It didn't matter. Whatever happened thirteen years ago, Rhys would be a fool to return. Yet the phuri were convinced he was coming to see Neala now that their son was dead. Sentimental and silly. Why would you want to grieve with the wife who'd tried to kill you?

Unless . . .

If Rhys had escaped and the kumpania had been convinced he was dead, he couldn't have done it alone. Who would have helped him, if not Neala?

She remembered how Neala had acted when told her husband might still be alive. She'd been quick to protest. Too quick.

Adele straightened, backpack dangling from her arm.

If Neala had rescued Rhys from a death sentence, that would be treason. Prove it, and Adele would be rid of her enemy. She wouldn't need to run.

No, after what Adele had seen in Neala's face, she knew the woman wouldn't rest until Adele paid for Colm's death. Threat of exposure for treason wouldn't stop her. And now if Rhys was coming, if Neala told Rhys she thought Adele was responsible for Colm . . .

Time for Adele to settle her future as she should have done the moment she'd realized that killing Portia Kane hadn't solved her problem. Get out, contact Irving Nast and finish the negotiations. Don't let him know she was panicked. Use his greed to cut a fast deal.

The kumpania wouldn't come after her right away. They'd be too busy grieving for Colm and worrying about Rhys. They'd presume, in her own grief, she'd run. By the time they started their search, she'd be safely with the Cabal.

She heard Hugh shout outside. A car door slammed. She raced to the window.

It was Rhys. Worse, he'd brought Robyn Peltier's friends.

All three had their hands up—Rhys and the young woman holding theirs high, the dark-haired man's at chest level, a halfhearted effort as he surveyed his surroundings.

Rhys was talking. Adele cracked open the window. Someone answered—Bernard, she thought, but couldn't be sure. Hugh and whoever was with him were on the front porch, out of her sight line.

"Who're they?" Bernard demanded, turning to Rhys.

"Delegates from the interracial council."

The council? No *way*. Rhys was bluffing, and she had to run down there and warn—

How? The kumpania knew nothing about Robyn Peltier. Explaining that these were Robyn's friends would do no good.

"You brought the council here?" Niko—she'd know his voice anywhere. "On our property?"

"I left my gun in the car, Niko, not my brain. The council knows these two are with me. We've arranged to have the kumpania coordinates delivered to them in three hours if we don't make it back to L.A."

"And what's going to stop these two from bringing the council back?" Hugh said.

"When you hear what I have to say, that's going to be the least of your problems. Niko, you and I both know your bullshit about the council being part of the Cabals is just that. But regardless of who works for whom, you don't want either the council or the Cabal out here."

"We'll go inside," Niko said.

"No, we'll speak in the meeting—"

"Rhys!" Robyn's friend yelled.

Rhys spun as Hugh charged. Lily—stupid Lily—screamed in terror. The dark-haired man shot forward, grabbed Hugh by the arm and swung him off his feet. Swung the brawny young man up like he was a misbehaving child, then held him by the collar at arm's length. When Hugh struggled, the man only shook him.

"Before we talk, I should explain." Rhys pointed to the young woman. "She is an Expisco half-demon. You don't know what that is, I'm sure, but you just got a demonstration. She can read negative thoughts. If you try to attack, like Hugh did, she'll know before you make a move."

"And . . . that?" Lily had stepped off the porch and pointed at the dark-haired man.

Even from the window, Adele saw the man lift an eyebrow. "*That?* Hardly polite." He threw Hugh toward her. "What am I? Let's just say I won't fetch a stick for you. I won't beg for treats. And, no matter how nicely you ask, I will not roll over and play dead."

"A werewolf?" Lily squeaked, and for once, Adele didn't sneer at her terror.

If this man was a werewolf and the woman a half-demon—and whether they were or not, they were obviously supernaturals—then Adele had made a horrible, horrible mistake.

Robyn Peltier was no human, easily killed, quickly forgotten. She was a supernatural. Maybe even on the council herself. Or maybe being in L.A. meant she was part of the Nast Cabal. If so, then whatever deal Adele had with Irving Nast had evaporated the moment she set her sights on Robyn. Adele's imagination scampered about like a mouse caught with the lights on, running this way and that in a panic, imagining death in every corner.

Adele slammed her hand down on the heat register, the metal vent biting into her skin. By the gods, she was as bad as Lily, sniveling and cowering in fear. Yes, this was a problem, but it wasn't her fault. There was no way she could have known Robyn Peltier was a supernatural. The woman had tricked her, by hiding her powers and luring Adele in.

All that mattered right now was that those two were friends of Robyn's, meaning they were about to expose Adele.

She glanced at the window. Everyone had retreated elsewhere to talk. When they came for her, she had to be gone.

She took a few minutes gathering her money. Her brain still scampered and gibbered, and she couldn't concentrate, checking three past hiding places before remembering the latest.

She stuffed the cash into her pocket, down with the seer's room key she'd grabbed on her way over. She'd planned to visit Thom one last time, get a quick fix on Robyn Peltier, maybe on that detective too. No time for that now, but she would keep the key. One more problem to distract the kumpania. Tending the seers would be more important than hunting her.

She looked around. Did she have everything?

Footsteps tramped onto the porch. The front door squeaked open.

"Adele?" Hugh called. "Niko wants to talk to you."

She took a deep breath and shouldered her bag. Footsteps echoed across the floor below. Adele crept to the other window, the one overlooking the back porch.

She eased the window open and crawled out just as the stairs creaked. She closed the window all but an inch, stepped to the side and pressed against the wall, hidden under the leafy branches.

The bedroom door opened.

"She's not here," Bernard called.

"Check the closet," Hugh's distant voice replied.

Bernard's footsteps lumbered across the room. The door squeaked. A grunt. Another squeak as he shut it.

"Nope."

"Look in the other rooms. Niko says she came back here."

Adele thanked the gods that clairvoyants couldn't remote-view one another. She waited until Bernard's footsteps retreated. Then she climbed onto an overhanging limb, shimmied along it and down the trunk. She darted to a shadowy pocket beside the porch. A pause, listening intently before she leaned out.

All was clear.

She took a slow step, hunkering down, ready to sprint to the next house. Then Lily lunged from behind that house, waving wildly for Adele to stop. Hugh strode around the corner, heading for the main house. Adele jumped back out of sight. As soon as Hugh was gone, Lily leaned out and waved Adele over.

Adele didn't see a choice. If she went the other way, the stupid girl would probably draw Hugh's attention trying to attract hers.

When Adele reached her, Lily pulled her into a tight hug, trembling against her, voice cracking as she said, "They've gone mad, Adele. Everyone's gone mad. The things that awful man Rhys is saying about you. The lies. How can they believe him? I tried to defend you, but . . ." She sobbed. "Hugh told me to be quiet. Then he hit me, Adele. *Hit* me."

Too bad Adele missed that. She patted Lily's back and made suitable noises of sympathy.

Lily went on. "He's been so angry. Like it's my fault. Like I wanted the other men to . . . to . . ."

More pats as Adele peered over Lily's shoulder. The barn was a hundred feet away, and in it, plenty of implements to help rid her of this annoyance for good.

"Wherever you're going, Adele, I'm going with you. I'm going to help you escape." Lily sniffled and straightened. "We'll run to the barn. You can hide in there while I divert attention."

Adele tried not to smile. "Sure. The barn. Good idea."

With Lily watching her back, Adele ran to the next house. Lily caught up, then watched again as Adele made it to the barn. Adele walked into the dim interior, the bone-chilling dampness seeping through her clothes, the stink of beast and shit filling her lungs. By the gods, she'd be glad to get away from—

An ear-shattering *crack* made Adele stagger forward, the barn exploding in a blinding light. She dropped to her knees, arms flying up to protect her head. Another crack. Another explosion that left her ears ringing, her stomach pitching.

A bomb. Someone had rigged the barn with a—

A blow between Adele's shoulder blades knocked her face-first into the hay, the chaff filling her mouth and nose. She tried to cough, but her head pounded like it would split if she so much as whimpered.

Another blow, this one glancing off her shoulder. There was no bomb. Someone was beating her. She tried to push up. Her stomach lurched and she gagged, vomit dribbling out.

A kick in the ribs flipped her over and she saw her assailant, a featureless figure looming over her, shovel raised. That shovel swung down like a scythe. Lily's face appeared above it, contorted into a gargoyle mask of rage and hate.

Adele twisted out of the shovel's path. It struck her hip, fresh pain jolting through her, the shovel glinting as Lily swung it up again.

"That's enough, Lily," said a voice behind them. "For now."

Neala walked over and stood beside Lily. She looked down at Adele. Her eyes glowed, glittering orbs in a grinning death's head, pale skin tight over her sharp cheekbones and chin.

Adele flipped onto her stomach and grabbed fistfuls of hay, pulling herself along the floor, trying to escape.

"Did Lily tell you she got the results from Dr. Briar?" Neala said. "He was running tests, trying to understand why they couldn't conceive. Seems she was taking birth control pills. And it seems someone's been a very sweet sister lately, bringing Lily's coffee every morning."

Lily walked over and kicked Adele's ribs again, making her squeal like a spring piglet at the slaughter. "You think that hurts? It's nothing compared to what Hugh's going to do to you when he finds out."

"Hugh," Adele rasped. "It was his idea. The pills. He wanted to marry me, and if you couldn't have kids, you'd have to go to the kitchens, and he'd be free."

"Is *that* what happened?" Lily said sarcastically. "How can I ever repay you for telling me the truth? I know, I can let you go, right?"

"If you don't, he'll kill me. It's not my fault—"

"Nothing ever is, Adele," Neala said. "Lily, grab her other arm. We don't want the others to miss out on Adele's wonderful stories."

ROBYN

Robyn watched Detective Findlay walk along the gravel shoulder behind the compound where Hope, Karl and Rhys had gone. He was returning to the car after talking to the rest of the team. He had his gaze down, watching the ground intently, as if it teemed with scorpions, but when a can lay in his path, he stepped on it, giving a start when it crunched underfoot.

Frown lines creased his broad face. When the wind ruffled his hair, he shoved the strands back from his face, frown deepening, gaze returning to its intent study of his path.

Preoccupied, but not with ghosts. Robyn had already learned to recognize that look, that dreaminess, so jarring on his craggy face, like a cowboy wistfully gazing at the mountains, dreaming of a ranch of his own.

This current preoccupation seemed equally out of place, too intense, too angry. Deep in thought, and whatever those thoughts were, he didn't like them.

He climbed into the driver's seat and stared at a dead bug on the windshield, as if trying to commune with its spirit. She didn't expect him to speak. The tension between them had been stretching ever tighter since the medical offices.

She couldn't regret her reaction, nor shake the feeling that it had, under the circumstances, been the right one.

For Detective Findlay, though, this was a job, and she didn't expect him to put himself on the line for Hope and Karl, no more than she expected him to let her—his suspect—do the same. An irreconcilable clash of priorities that had settled into an irreconcilable war of intractability.

Even when Detective Findlay had finally managed to call for backup, it had only seemed to blacken his mood more. Apparently, he was stuck with a team from the sheriff's department, men he didn't know. He'd tried getting hold of a detective named Madoz, wanting him to be in on the takedown, and had been told he was on the way, but there was no sign of him yet.

She cleared her throat. "Detective Findlay—"

"You don't need to call me that."

"What's your name?"

He blinked, apparently having forgotten that somewhere between the gun showdown and the car chase, they'd failed to perform proper introductions.

"John," he said. "But everyone calls me Finn."

"Which do you prefer?"

He paused, as if it had been so long since anyone asked, he wasn't sure. "Finn's fine."

"Okay, so is the team ready to—"

A rap at the window. Finn lowered it. A beefy man leaned in too far, the invasion of space making the detective's shoulders square.

"Alvarez," the man said. "Just got here. My boys tell me you don't like my plan, Detective."

"I don't see any reason to put Ms. Peltier in further—"

"No danger, Detective. My boys are the best. I need her on-site to ID her friends, make sure we get them out."

"Out of what?"

"We don't know what we're facing in there. Our records show it's a multifamily residence. Some kind of commune, we think. We have to be prepared for the worst."

"Which is why Ms. Peltier shouldn't go in. I can ID her friends."

"We'd prefer her, for absolute confirmation."

"I want to speak to—"

"It's okay," Robyn said. "I'll go."

Finn didn't like that, lips tightening. Alvarez thumped the window sill and backed out. "All set then?"

He walked away without waiting for a response.

AS THEY TOOK UP POSITION in the woods surrounding the property, Finn only got moodier, snapping at the officers in a way that suggested he never snapped at anyone and didn't like hearing himself do it. But that didn't stop him either.

He seemed to be in communication with his spirit guide, but Robyn got the impression that at the moment, the ghost wasn't doing much guiding.

"I need you two over there." Alvarez pointed into the patch of woods bordering the property, then smacked binoculars into the detective's hand. "That's a safe distance. Have her pinpoint her friends and radio me with a full description of their location and apparel. Solheim here will go with you."

Alvarez marched off with his men, leaving an officer about Finn's age with a heavy brow and a heavier frown. He waved them into the forest and followed at their heels, rifle in hand. Every few seconds, Finn would glance back, as if being marched to a firing squad.

Robyn picked her way through the bush. When her feet got tangled, the detective pulled her up short and yanked wild grapevines from her ankles.

"Is this really necessary?" Finn said. "We can barely walk here."

"Cover," was all Solheim said.

When they were finally in deep enough, Solheim grunted for them to stop. Robyn could make out houses in the distance, and what looked like people moving between them, but it was so far away she doubted she would recognize Hope and Karl even with binoculars.

She glanced at Finn, who was squinting through them. She expected him to echo her thoughts, but instead he said, "How do you adjust these?"

Solheim grunted again, a sigh whispering through it this time. He set his rifle down and took the binoculars. Finn stepped back, behind Solheim, giving him a better vantage point. Robyn squinted, straining to see Hope's denim jacket.

"See this dial?" Solheim lifted the binoculars to his eyes. "You need to—"

A crack. Robyn spun to see Solheim falling, Finn behind him, gun raised.

As she stared in shock, Finn knelt beside the officer's body. "Out cold. Good. Now help me pull him—"

"You—you just knocked out a cop."

"He's not a cop, Robyn. None of them are."

"What?"

The detective rose, pushing his gun back into his holster. "I have no idea what's going on here, but I don't know any of these men—"

"Because they're from the sheriff's office!"

"Who we've been working with on this case, and I don't recognize a single name. Madoz is a no-show. I can't get through to my station. My cell phone is blocked. And look around. What are we doing out here?"

"You wanted me to be safe. This is—"

"They're sidelining us. Getting me out of the way. You gave them full descriptions of Adams and Marsten, down to what they're wearing. Why do you need to do that again?"

"You called for backup. On your police radio. I *saw* you. You can't tell me—"

"Something happened."

She took a slow step back. "Oh, I know what happened. You called for backup, expecting to get men you know, men you could control. Hope was right. You do work for that company."

"What? No. I—"

Robyn turned and ran. She felt his fingers brush her back, then an "oomph" as he stumbled in the undergrowth.

"Robyn!"

She reached into her jacket pocket for the gun, but it snagged and refused to come out.

"Robyn, just stop and listen—"

She ran faster, ducking to avoid a low branch, then, at the last second, grabbing it, pulling it as she ran, letting go, hearing it whip back, Detective Findlay cursing as he tripped again, trying to avoid it.

"Rob—Bobby!"

Grapevines seemed to snake from the ground, wrapping around her feet and she stumbled, twisting, hands flying up to ward him off.

"What did you say?" Her jaw wouldn't unhinge enough to let the words out properly, her fury so hot she could feel it, see it, white sparks exploding before her eyes.

"Bobby," he said. "Damon called you—calls you—"

"Don't you dare!"

He reached for her elbow, then drew back, glancing to the left with a gruff, "I know. I'm sorry," before turning back to Robyn. His lips twisted in what she supposed was a wry smile, but it looked like a grimace, and seeing it, she knew what he was going to say, what he was going to tell her, the lowest, cheapest ploy he could think of.

"Don't you dare."

"Rob—"

"If you tell me that Damon's here, helping you, I will— I will—" She could think of no threat great enough.

Detective Findlay stepped back, voice softening. "He says he calls you Bobby because he misread the place setting tags at Ava's wedding. It was a fancy script and he thought it said Bobby, and even after he knew your name was Robyn, he figured everyone must call you Bobby, so he kept using it, and it was months before anyone straightened him out."

The rage reignited, tears evaporating. "*Everyone* knows that story. They told it at our wedding, for God's sake. You and your people dug up everything they could, getting this lie ready to spring—"

"Fair," he said quickly, desperation flashing in his eyes. "He— Damon—said you like fairs. Yesterday when we went there, he was telling me how much you liked . . ." He trailed off, glancing to the side as if listening, then nodding emphatically. "Okay, okay. He says you two went to the fair last year with a couple of his college buddies. Damon threw up on the Tilt-a-Whirl and promised to do the housework for a month if you said *you* were the one who got sick."

The ground tilted as if, for a moment, she was back on that ride. They'd never told anyone that story, which was the point of course, saving Damon from endless razzing by his friends, who'd been on the other side of the ride and missed seeing which one of them threw up. Robyn teased him about it mercilessly, trying to blackmail extra chores for months.

If *she'd* never told anyone, and she knew *Damon* would never have told anyone . . .

Her gaze lifted to the spot beside Detective Finn's shoulder.

"Damon?" Again, that slow tilt of the world shifting, and it was like when she was eighteen, getting her wisdom teeth out, the anesthetic taking hold, a languorous wave of delicious warmth washing over her, her whole body relaxing and surrendering to it. She felt that again, swaying, muscles letting go as if she'd been holding them tight for six months and all she could do was stare at that spot, that empty spot, and say again, "Damon."

She closed her eyes, squeezing them shut, praying that when she opened them, she'd see him, see some part of him, if only a shimmer of light, something she could reach for.

She opened her eyes to dark forest. "What's he saying? Can he hear me?"

"He can, and he's saying that while he'd love to chat, you've got a psycho SWAT team on your tail, and you need to move your, uh, rear."

She hiccuped a laugh, hands flying up to stifle it. "Damon."

332 · KELLEY ARMSTRONG

"You're going to talk to him, Robyn. I promise." Finn stepped toward her, taking her by the elbows. "When this is over, I'll tell you everything he wants you to hear. But right now . . ."

"I need to move my ass."

He smiled, a genuine smile, the first she'd seen from him, his eyes crinkling. "Exactly. Now, if we go this way—"

He wheeled, head jerking up as if hearing something. Then he spun back, big hand slamming her between the shoulder blades, and hissing, "Down!" She hit the ground, her sore shoulder knocking against a tree trunk. She swallowed a gasp of pain as he dropped beside her.

"Isn't this where they're supposed to be?" a voice asked.

Another answered, more distant, muffled. Robyn tried to listen, but all she could think about was Damon, here, right here with her, watching her, and everything she wanted to say, and how much she'd give to hear his voice, just *hear* him. She squeezed her eyes shut. How greedy was that? Only hours ago she'd have given anything for *this* much—the chance to know he was truly and beyond doubt someplace, that he was okay, that they would get the chance they'd been denied that night on the highway, those last moments to say everything that hadn't been said, that it always seemed there'd be time—days, months, years—to say.

"Shit! It's Solheim. He's been knocked out."

That snapped Robyn back to the present. She tried to creep forward for a better look, but Finn laid his arm over her back, holding her down.

"Solheim, come on, wake up."

A groggy "Wha—?"

"Goddamn it, you were supposed to take care of them. You fucked up, didn't you? They saw you pull your sidearm."

"Wha—? No, I never— It's right here. I—I was looking through the binoculars, then . . ."

Robyn didn't catch the rest, her mind looping back to the first bit. Take care of them? Pull his sidearm? She remembered trudging through the forest, Finn glancing back at Solheim, her thinking he looked like a prisoner being led to a firing squad.

Because he was.

No, that was crazy. Why would—?

Why not? Finn was right. These men weren't police officers.

Running footsteps crashed through the forest. "Solheim, Barrett, Mac! Alvarez needs you up front. Something's going down." The footfalls stopped. "You took care of them, right?"

"They got away. We were just—"

"Shit! No. We need all hands up front. Their car is disabled, right? You managed that, I hope."

A chilly, "Yes, sir."

"Then, Solheim, scout the perimeter. Don't let them escape. Barrett, Mac, follow me."

When they were gone, Finn helped Robyn to her feet.

"We need to warn Hope and Karl," she said.

"I know. You still have the gun?"

She reached into her jacket. It slid out easily now. All in the angle, she supposed.

"Any idea how to use it?" he asked.

"I'll figure it out."

HOPE

After what Rhys told them about Adele, Hope supposed she should have been able to dredge up a few ounces of sympathy for her, growing up in a cult, believing she'd been sold by her mother.

But she'd given her "sister" birth control pills so she'd be forced into what Hope could only call group rape. She'd preyed on Colm's infatuation, then abandoned him, knowing he'd been conditioned to avoid capture with suicide. She'd murdered Portia Kane, Judd Archer, the bike officer and, if Rhys guessed right, an innocent bystander at the fair.

So as Hope stood in a garden and watched Adele—battered and bowed, her gun in the hands of the young woman she'd betrayed, her arm in the grip of the woman whose son she'd gotten killed—there was no mercy in her.

With each new accusation, Adele's terror spiked. And Hope guzzled it down.

"You have betrayed the kumpania," their leader, Niko, said. "You've maliciously interfered with your sister, Lily. You've caused the death of your brother, Colm. And you've committed the ultimate betrayal, conspiring with a Cabal—"

"No! It's not true. None of it. I—"

Neala cuffed the side of Adele's head. As Adele cried out, Neala's expression didn't change. When she'd first dragged Adele to the meeting place, delicious chaos vibes had danced around her, her grief mingled with the thrill of bringing her son's killer to justice.

Rhys said Neala had been a beautiful woman, but the years had been harsh, and she looked a decade older than him, her bright red hair pulled back tightly, making her appear all the more severe.

"The evidence has been presented and accepted, Adele," Niko continued. "I've rendered my judgment and now it's time to pass sentence. As our laws dictate, you will be stoned by those you betrayed—"

Adele's scream drowned out the rest, her terror so pure the demon gobbled it down and clamored for more, writhing in anticipation of such a gloriously chaotic death, such a—

Neala smacked Adele again and the girl blacked out, that momentary cutting of the chaos cord enough for Hope to fully realize what was going on.

"No," she said, stepping forward. "You can't execute her. She's going into council custody."

"Yes." Adele shot straight, steadying herself against a birdbath. "That's right. I claim council protection as a supernatural—"

"Adele?" Lily said. "Shut up."

"That's enough, Lily." Niko turned to Hope. "I'm sorry, but Adele is ours and we do not recognize the council's authority. We have the right to execute—"

"By what law? Not council, not Cabal, not human, and maybe you don't like to 'recognize' those, but you sure as hell better start. There's an innocent woman accused of Adele's crimes, who could go to jail if Adele vanishes off the face of the earth."

Karl moved up beside her. "Hope is right. We're taking—"

"No, you're not. I'm sorry about this woman, but she's not our concern. Adele is, and we're going to—"

"I'm pregnant," Adele blurted.

"Oh, gods," Lily muttered. "Here we go with the lies."

"It's not a lie. You have pregnancy tests in your room, don't you? Go get one. I'll take it right now and you'll see."

"The father." It took a moment to track the whisper to its source and even then, Hope didn't need to pinpoint the sound, just the face it came from—Neala's, a note of hope in her voice that wrung Hope's heart as no sob story from Adele ever could. "Is it Colm?"

Hearing that, Adele went still, like a predator catching a scent, and in her eyes Hope saw a beast less human than her demon, than Karl's wolf, stripped of humanity, only instinct remaining, eyes glittering with a cunning that could pass for intelligence.

"No, it's not Colm." She looked around and Hope swore those bloodied and swollen lips smiled. "It's Thom."

Niko strode forward, bellowing, "Blasphemy! How dare you ever suggest such a—"

"Because it's true." Now that curve in Adele's lips couldn't be mistaken for anything but a smile. "You can run any tests you want. I'm carrying Thom's child." She turned to Rhys. "Congratulations. It may not be Colm's, but you're still going to be a grandfather."

Silence. The chaos came in uncertain spurts.

"What?" Rhys said finally.

"Thom. Your—" Adele's horrible smile stretched. "Oh, that's right. You don't know. Really, Neala, now would be the time to tell him, ease the loss of one son by letting him know he still has another. His firstborn."

Rhys turned slowly. "Neala?"

Neala's pain hit Hope like an energy bolt. Karl grabbed her.

"You remember your firstborn, don't you?" Adele said. "The one Neala told you died? He didn't, but he's a retard. They keep him locked in a bomb shelter under the property, so they can use his powers."

"Neala?" A plea now, Rhys begging her to tell him this was another of Adele's lies.

Neala's pain hit Hope again, knocking her back into Karl's arms, her eyelids fluttering, seeing Neala step toward Rhys, her lips parting in an apology that Hope heard, over and over, in Neala's thoughts, but wouldn't reach her lips. Then, behind her, Adele spun, grabbing the gun from Lily's hand.

A scream. A shot. Neala staggered, eyes rounding, that apology stuttering in her head, desperately trying to find a way out, and then the chaos, the sweet, sweet chaos . . .

"Neala!" Rhys shot forward, grabbing her.

Hope tried to focus, but the chaos was so sweet, so perfectly sweet . . .

"Call an ambulance!" Rhys shouted.

It wouldn't help. Hope could feel Neala's life seeping away, her terror, chaos thundering all around, then a young man's voice yelling, "Niko! Niko!"

Footsteps pounded across the patio stones.

"Niko! Men—" Panting, gasping for breath. "Armed men. Guns. Hugh saw them. They're—they're all around—"

A scream cut him off. Then another.

Niko's voice rose above them. "No! It's all right. They aren't here to hurt us. Stay calm. Everyone stay—"

A shot. A crack. The peppery smell of tear gas. A long, keening scream. Then the smoldering pit of chaos detonated.

FINN

FINN GOT HIMSELF and Robyn close enough to see what was going on, but they couldn't hear it. He'd sent Damon for that. Damon hadn't been pleased; he wanted to watch over Robyn. Finn could have pointed out that if they were attacked, there was nothing Damon could do, but that would be cruel. Instead, he told Robyn they'd need to get closer, so they could listen in and, at that, Damon decided he could handle eavesdropping duty.

They were still in the small strip of woods bordering the property. Finn had caught a glimpse of Solheim, patrolling the fence. He was sticking to his post, though. His only task now was preventing Finn and Robyn from leaving.

As for who Solheim and the others really were and how they got here and where Madoz was, those were questions for later. With cell reception and the route to his radio blocked, he was on his own. As he watched the drama unfolding in the distance he had a feeling that being alone might be a good thing. Bringing in the law could turn a touchy situation into a tragedy. If Robyn was right, Adams and the others operated outside the law for good reason.

Adams, Marsten and Rhys stood in a garden between a cluster of four houses. Finn counted six people with them. There could be more standing at the perimeter, but his angle wasn't good, the houses partially blocking it.

He could clearly see Adams and Marsten, and that was the important thing. Together with Rhys, they were bookended by men with rifles, but those weapons dangled, a perfunctory threat. The only other gun he could see was held by a dark-haired girl, pointed at a young blonde whose face he'd never forget.

That face was now bloodied and battered, which brought a smile to Finn's lips. He felt a twinge of guilt at that, hearing his mother admonish him against ever taking pleasure in the misfortune of others. But it was a very small twinge.

Clearly Adele Morrissey's crimes had been exposed and now they seemed to be negotiating to turn her over to Adams and Marsten. And though they didn't seem to be in immediate danger from the commune people, he had to get a warning to them about *these* guys.

At a movement, he glanced over to see Damon jogging back. Perfect timing. He'd get a report on the whereabouts of the fake police squad, then—

"They're going to stone her!" Damon called, still running.

"Stone?" Finn said.

"A stone what?" Robyn said, popping out from behind the binoculars. A sheepish smile. "Sorry." She paused, then said hesitantly, "Is Damon back?"

Finn nodded. Her gaze traveled past him, searching for some sign of Damon. Disappointment flickered through her eyes, so sharp it was like an ice pick, a breathtaking jab of empathetic pain.

"Finn?" Damon waved his hands in front of Finn's face. "Could you stop staring at my wife and listen to me?"

Finn thought he heard a bite in Damon's voice, but when he glanced up, the ghost just looked impatient.

"I said they're going to *stone* Adele."

"You heard wrong."

"No, I did not. Her group, those people, they call themselves a company or something, they just held a trial. They convicted her of a whole pile of shit and sentenced her to be stoned by the whole group. Hope's arguing. She wants to take Adele back to that council and—"

A shot. A scream. Damon wheeled with a, "Holy shit!" Robyn lifted the binoculars, but Finn snatched them, ignoring her cry of protest and pushing her down to the ground as he lowered himself to his knees.

He swung the lenses to Adams and Marsten. Adams lay in Marsten's arms.

"Finn?" Robyn yanked on his sleeve. "What's happening?"

"They're down—taking cover," he added quickly. The lie came easier than any he'd ever told. "They're okay. Just—"

Another scream. Another shot. Armed gunmen rushed from behind the buildings, shouting orders. A mushroom cloud of tear gas exploded.

Finn shot to his feet. Robyn grabbed his pant leg. He put his hand on her head, keeping her down.

"Stay here."

"I'm not—"

He dropped to one knee, his face coming down to hers. "You need to stay here, Robyn. Please. Do you still have the gun?"

She nodded.

"Then *stay*. You aren't trained for this, okay?"

That did it—not safety issues but the reminder she wasn't qualified.

She lowered herself into the grass, then stopped, looking up. "Damon? Go with him. Help him."

Damon leaned down, kissing the top of her head. "I will, baby."

FINN CUT THROUGH THE FIELD, praying everyone was too busy to notice him. Damon ran ahead, ready to call back a warning if anyone took an interest. No one did.

The smoke floated out until Finn couldn't see, and moved by sound alone. After a moment, he recognized one of the shouting voices. Karl Marsten calling for Adams. When he ran toward the voice, he smacked into Marsten, who spun, lips curling in a snarl.

"I'm not working for the Nasts," Finn said quickly. "I—"

"I know. Find Hope," Marsten said, then was about to dive back into the smoke when Finn caught the back of his shirt.

"Is she shot?" he said. "I saw her fall—"

"No, that was—" He waved Finn off. "We—" A coughing fit cut him short. "We need to find her before she *gets* shot."

He turned again, but Finn still had a grip on his shirt. "That gas is going to knock us flat before we do."

Marsten's red-rimmed eyes blazed, and Finn thought he was going to deck him. Then his jaw flexed and he gave a curt nod. "We need gas masks. I thought I saw—"

A figure staggered out, bent double. Rhys. Marsten grabbed him, just long enough to recognize him—and recognize that he wasn't someone with a gas mask—then dropped him. Finn dove in to catch the man before he toppled.

"I thought I heard you," Rhys croaked, squinting up at Marsten. "Where's Hope?"

"That's what I'm trying to find out. They have gas masks, right?"

"What?" Rhys coughed so hard that blood flecked Finn's pants.

"Those men. They have gas masks, don't they?"

"I think so."

"Good."

Marsten strode back into the thick of it. Finn tried to grab him.

Rhys caught his hand. "If you like the current configuration of all your body parts, I wouldn't do that. He'll be fine."

"I'll cover him," said a voice behind Finn.

He turned to see Damon jog off after Marsten.

"Does he have a gun?" Finn asked.

"He doesn't need one. You're the detective who's after Adele, right?"

Finn nodded and looked in the direction Damon and Marsten had gone.

"He's fine. Really," Rhys said. "But if you want Adele, she's long gone. Last I saw, she was making a break for it."

"Robyn."

"What?"

Finn took off at a run. He'd left Robyn alone, without even Damon to watch her, and now Adele—the woman who wanted her dead, and who could find her anywhere—was on the loose.

He didn't slow until he reached the spot where he'd left Robyn. There, on the ground, lay the pair of binoculars.

HOPE

When the tear gas exploded, Karl knocked Hope to the ground. It wasn't necessary—she was already headed that way and grabbing for his arm to yank him down with her, the demon's hunger for chaos temporarily overridden by its hunger for continued life.

As Hope was twisting to pull him down, someone barreled into him. Hope rolled out of the way so he wouldn't drop on her and then . . .

She wasn't really sure what happened then. The demon decided they were out of danger long enough to enjoy a chaos snack before completing their escape. That interlude of euphoria ended when a foot crunched Hope's spine, she realized Karl wasn't beside her and the demon shouted at her to get the hell out of there.

She got on all fours, shut her eyes and crawled as fast as she could, ignoring the blows and kicks of people tripping over her. When she finally tasted a current of fresh air on the breeze, she opened her eyes. The chaos-laced smoke still eddied around them, but she could make out the shapes of buildings and people. One person in particular— Adele Morrissey racing across the field.

Hope scrambled to her feet and shot after Adele.

Hope started along a house, darting from bush to bush. But she quickly realized it wasn't necessary. Adele never glanced back, which told Hope she'd already been spotted. Adele must have caught a glimpse when Hope first started after her, and now she watched Hope's progress remotely, letting her think she hadn't noticed. Hope played the game, and kept her gun holstered, out of sight.

When Hope rounded the barn, she saw Adele's destination—a small outbuilding in the middle of a field. For an ambush or hiding place, she'd have chosen the barn, but Adele's trajectory put her on target for the shed and, sure enough, a moment later, she was inside it.

Hope darted to the door, then waited, ears and chaos sensors on full. A key clicked in a lock. Then a rhythmic *clang-clang*, growing distant until it faded. Hope slipped inside. One section of the hay-covered floor had been hastily cleared. Beneath it was a hatch, conveniently left open, should Hope not be clever enough to figure out where Adele had gone.

Beneath the hatch, a metal ladder descended into darkness. With a distant click, a dim light filled the bottom. The sound of one lock opening. Footsteps. The scrape of a key. The creak of a door. A blast of manic voices. Cartoons? The noise faded, and Hope dismissed it as shrieks from outside.

She climbed down the ladder, closing the hatch behind her so no one would follow her down. As she neared the bottom, she hunched down to get a better look at what she was descending into, but all she could see from her vantage point was an empty room with a door. She called on the demon to pick up any tremors of chaos. It reported negative. Hope still lowered herself as slowly as she could, knowing Adele could be waiting at the bottom.

She wasn't. She'd even left the door ajar for Hope.

Hope crept up to it, taking out her gun now, keeping it hidden under her jacket in case Adele was watching. Hope eased open the door. It led to a dimly lit tunnel and another door at the end, a sliver of light telling Hope it too was cracked open. She did a chaos check, then crept down the hall and pulled open the second door.

Adele stood right there, looking into the room, her back to Hope.

"Come in, Hope," she said. "It is Hope, isn't it?"

She spun, gun flying up . . . only to see Hope pointing at her. She looked at it. Blinked. And laughed, a high girlish laugh.

"The element of surprise is lost with us, isn't it?" She lowered her gun. "I'm not going to shoot you. Read my mind or whatever it is you do. You need to take me out of here alive. I want to leave alive, and the only way I'm doing that is in your custody."

She turned her back to Hope, a mind-blowing act of trust. Or, Hope suspected, arrogance. But she was right. Right now, their goals coincided. Still, Hope wasn't lowering her gun.

"Close the door," Adele said.

Hope did—she didn't want anyone sneaking up behind her.

"Might as well get comfortable. I have a plan to get us out, but until someone shows up to negotiate with, we're stuck."

Again, Hope had to agree. The property was swarming with armed men—cops or Cabal, she wasn't sure. Add the rifle-toting kumpania members, and she wasn't setting foot outside this bunker until someone granted her safe passage.

As for what they were in, *bunker* was the word that came to mind, but as she passed through the entryway into the main room, she had a vision . . . of a playground, the one she and Karl had been standing outside only hours ago. That's what this looked like: a day care, all bright colors and plush furniture. A TV flashed now—silent cartoons. There was even a crib pushed against the wall. Why would there be—?

" 'dele?"

"It's okay, sweetie," Adele said. "That's Hope. Oh, you like her, do you? You like pretty girls." Her voice was light, but a hard note crept into it, and the look she shot Hope was dagger-sharp.

Hope sidestepped to see around Adele. There was a boy in the chair and, for one jolting moment, she thought it was Colm. But it was a distorted view, as if the angle was skewed, something not quite right.

"Come meet Thom," Adele said. "I think he likes you." Her lips curved, but there was too much snarl in it to be mistaken for a smile.

As Hope moved forward she tried not to stare. The boy in the chair wasn't much older than Colm, with the same blue eyes and red hair, but his head was slightly oversized and misshapen, with plastic tubes running out of it—shunts, she realized.

Thom watched Hope. There was a keenness in his eyes, a probing curiosity.

Adele walked over, her arms going around his neck, lips to his bulging forehead.

"Yep, this is Thom. The proud daddy. Aren't you, sweetie?"

She snuggled against him, her breasts rubbing his face. When Adele had named her baby's father and called him "retarded," Hope had assumed she was lying, trying to shock the kumpania into outrage so she could escape. Now she saw the truth. Adele had seduced not only a fifteen-year-old boy, but his mentally handicapped brother, an act as horrific as molesting a child.

Adele pulled back, but not before squeezing his crotch. "You gave me a wonderful gift, didn't you, sweetie? One that will make my fortune." She looked at Hope. "When I told Irving I was carrying the child of a seer, I swear the old man got a hard-on just thinking about it."

"Seer?" Hope forced the word past her revulsion.

"Powerful clairvoyants who can project visions to others. Irving had heard stories about them—that's all most people hear, stories. But here they are, and Thom is the most valuable of them all."

"Them?"

Adele waved at the room and walked to a cupboard, taking down a bottle. Hope turned, slowly. Her gaze moved past the flashing TV to another chair, a recliner this time. In it, a hairless man stared vacantly at the cartoon.

"That's Melvin. Veggie Boy." Adele tapped her head. "No one's home. He's practically useless, but he's Niko's son, so they have to keep him alive."

Hope stepped sideways to see what Adele was doing. Filling a syringe.

Hope's hand tightened on her lowered gun. "What's that?"

"A sedative for Thom. He has a wicked temper. When the kumpania or the Cabal starts banging on that door, things will get ugly. I don't want him upset."

"When they do show up, let me do the talking. I'll negotiate—"

"With what?" Her look dripped disdain. "I'll do the talking. I know what we've got in here, and how to use it to our advantage."

"Adele, we—"

A noise behind Hope. A rustling. From the crib.

She'd forgotten the crib. Her knees locked, brain ordering her to stay where she was, not to look, that it wouldn't do any good.

And what good would it do to *not* look? Cover her eyes, plug her ears and whistle past the cemetery? When she got out, she had to do something about this, which meant she had to take the story back to the council. The full story.

Hope stepped to the crib, and a scream congealed in her throat. It wasn't a baby. It wasn't even human. It couldn't be. A doll. A prank. Adele's plan to shock Hope, distract her so she could get her gun.

It moved.

Hope's scream escaped in a strangled yelp.

Adele laughed. "That's Martha. Freaky, isn't she? Like a giant slug."

Once she said that, Hope couldn't shake the image, as hard as she tried to see what lay in that crib as human. It was a woman with long, tangled white hair. She was limbless and eyeless, her body so white it blended with her diaper. She writhed from side to side, mouth opening, mewling.

"She's probably hungry." A flat statement, carrying no sense of obligation to do anything about it. "She's the most powerful of them. But we can only pick up her visions—she can't communicate. That's why Thom's the most valuable. Aren't you, sweetie?"

Hope looked from Adele, pinging air bubbles from the needle, to Thom, watching Adele with that intent stare.

" 'dele," he said, the guttural word carrying the same edge as one of Karl's warning growls.

"Everything's okay, sweetie. I'm just giving you one of your shots, to calm you down."

"No."

"Oh, I know you don't like them. They make you feel all fuzzy, don't they?" She paused, head cocking. "Hear that, Hope? Seems they finally found us."

Hope caught the faint clink of metal. Someone descending the ladder.

"Don't worry. They can't get in." She took a key from the tabletop, waved it and dropped it into her pocket. "Once the door is closed, no one gets in or out without that. Of course, to get out, we're also going to need to get past them."

Adele lifted the needle to check the dose.

"You're going to hold the seers hostage," Hope said.

"It doesn't matter who's coming down those steps—Cabal or kumpania—for either one, these guys are the most valuable things on the property."

She started toward Thom. Chaos buzzed from him, fear muted by uncertainty, sensing danger but seeing only someone he trusted.

" 'dele . . ." He grabbed the arms of his chair, rising.

"I don't think that's necessary," Hope said. "He seems fine."

"Bold moves, Hope. You have to be willing to make the bold moves." She stopped in front of her. "When you see the options, there's always one that seems like it's too much. It goes too far. That's the one you need to take."

Hope tried to pick up a stray chaos vibe, a thought, anything to confirm her fears. Adele only looked at her, mind blank, face expressionless. But Hope knew. She knew.

The door clicked. They both looked over. The knob turned one way, the other, then stopped. Adele began to circle around Hope. She stepped into Adele's path.

"He doesn't need that shot," Hope said. "He's calm, and I'll make sure he stays that way. You negotiate. Thom will be my responsibility."

Adele tried sidestepping. When Hope countered, Adele's lips tightened in annoyance. "I'm just going to give him a sedative, let him sleep this out."

"No, you're not. This isn't a bold move, Adele. It's craz—premature. We haven't even opened negotiations."

She hesitated. Reconsidering? After a moment, she sighed. "We have to enter from a strong position. Don't you see that? Start by proving we aren't making idle threats."

"But Thom—"

"—is the most valuable seer. A huge loss. Enter from that position, and we'll have them scrambling to save the other two."

She sidestepped again. Hope raised her gun.

Adele laughed. "You aren't going to use that. You need me."

"Not badly enough to let you kill anyone else."

She stepped past Hope. "I gave you a story. Stick with that."

Hope turned the gun on Adele. "Put the needle down."

"Relax, Thom." Adele laid her hand on his chest, pushing him back into his seat. "You're just going to take a nap, okay, sweetie?"

He resisted her push, but didn't shove back, staying on the edge of his seat, fear tempered with confusion, sensing danger, seeing only Adele.

Hope raised the gun, to her head. "Adele, put down—"

"Oh, please." She moved the syringe to Thom's arm. "Bold moves, Hope. You have to be willing to make—"

Hope fired.

ROBYN

Robyn saw Hope and Adele run from the tear gas fog, Adele escaping, Hope giving chase. She leapt up from her hiding place, thinking, "I have to tell Finn."

Then she'd seen the gun clutched in her hand and thought *what the hell am I thinking?*

Hope deserved someone who knew how to *fire* a gun, but at this moment, Robyn was the only person close enough to help. So after one last look around, hoping for a glimpse of Finn or Karl, Robyn gave chase.

FOLLOWING HOPE WASN'T EASY. They had a huge head start and Robyn would have lost them if Adele's goal hadn't been obvious—a building in the field. By the time Robyn reached it, Hope and Adele were inside. Robyn pulled another mystery show move, sliding along the wall toward the door, her nerves eased by thinking how Damon would get a laugh if he could see her and maybe, just maybe, he could.

Robyn cracked open the door and peered in. It was a tiny shed, empty, no place to hide. She slipped in. When her eyes adjusted, she noticed a bare spot in the hay and, beneath it, a trapdoor. She opened it, listened and descended.

There was a second door below. Closed, but not locked, it led into a darkened hall. She made her way carefully down it, gun at the ready. It led to another door. This one was closed *and* locked. Beyond it, she made out the murmur of voices. One was Hope's. The other, female, presumably Adele's. Robyn caught a word here and there, but not enough to decipher the conversation.

She pressed her ear against—

A blast from the room sent Robyn reeling back. She caught her balance, then replayed what she'd heard. A bang. A crash. Something falling. She told herself it was some*thing* falling not some*one,* but she'd heard those sounds too often in the last few days to mistake it for anything.

A gunshot and a body dropping.

She flew to the door, grabbing the knob.

"Hope! Hope!"

She screamed her name until she couldn't, until her throat was raw, and still she whaled on the door, yanking and yanking and yanking, her shoulder blazing.

When Damon died, everyone said, "I'm here for you, Rob. Just let me know what you need." Hope never said that. She was just there, making a meal or doing her laundry or working silently at her kitchen table while Robyn sobbed in the bedroom, thankful to be alone yet not alone. Hope hadn't asked whether Robyn wanted her to come out to L.A. She'd shown up. She didn't ask whether Robyn needed Portia's murder solved. She just did it.

And now, when Robyn could have helped her, she'd failed.

She kept banging and shouting and then, finally, between pounds, soft as a whisper. "Rob?"

Her hand jerked back from the door. The gun fell. She let it, and swayed there a moment, before pressing her hands to the cold metal and leaning in until her ear rested against it.

"Hope?"

It could be a trick, the voice was too low to say with any certainty that it was Hope's or that it was a voice at all and not just a sound she'd willfully misheard.

"Rob?"

"Hope! Yes, it's Robyn. Open the door."

Silence.

Robyn hammered the door. "Hope? Open the door, Hope!"

It was a trick. Had to be. Why else wouldn't she—?

Robyn remembered what Hope had said about the boy, Rhys's son, that if she saw a vision of his death, that's all she'd see. She'd be lost in it. How much worse would it be to witness a death live?

Karl would know what to do. She'd get Karl, and he'd snap her out of it or break this door down—

If she walked away now, there was no guarantee she'd get back before someone else did. Someone just as dangerous as Adele.

"Hope? I need you to open this door."

Robyn kept repeating it, as calmly and firmly as she could. After a minute, the door quavered under her hands, jerking back and forth.

"It . . . it won't open." Hope's voice, but still with that chillingly flat affect, as if she really didn't care whether she got the door open or not.

"Are there keys?"

A pause. "What?"

"Keys, Hope. Did Adele have keys?"

"Adele . . . I shot— I had to."

That's good, Robyn thought, but said, "That's okay. Did she have a key?"

"Key? Yes. She . . . Hold on."

Getting that key seemed to take forever. Robyn was tempted to bang on the door again. Then a key turned in the lock. The door opened. Robyn pulled Hope out and caught her up in a hug. Hope returned the embrace only a moment, then pulled back with a tired chuckle.

"No time for that," she said. "I'm guessing the situation hasn't resolved itself up there?"

"Probably not."

Hope rubbed her eyes. "Okay. Let's get out of here before someone finds us."

"Is Adele . . . ?"

Hope nodded.

"You had to," Robyn said.

"Yes, I did." There was no emphasis in her voice, no need to justify.

"Is there another exit?" Robyn started reopening the door to look inside.

Hope backed into the opening and held the door fast. "No."

"What is—?"

"No. Really, Rob." She looked up at her. "On this one, trust my call."

Robyn stepped back. Hope seemed about to follow, then held up a finger, slid back into the room and closed the door before Robyn could stop her.

A moment later, she heard Hope's voice. She leaned forward to say she couldn't hear her, but Hope was murmuring, as if talking to someone else. Was Adele still alive?

Hope came out and lifted her gun. "Almost forgot this. I grabbed Adele's, too. For you."

"I've got one." Robyn retrieved hers from the floor.

"Armed to the teeth, aren't we?" Another tired smile. "Who'd have thought?"

Hope closed the door.

"Is someone . . ." Robyn began. "I thought I heard you talking."

"Hmm? Oh, muttering to myself. Still a bit confused. Don't worry, it's passing."

Hope checked the door, making sure it was locked, then headed for the ladder.

FINN

"KARL'S IN THE BARN," Damon called as he raced to Finn, striding through the wooded border, Rhys at his heels.

Finn was about to say, with all respect to Karl Marsten, that he didn't give a rat's ass where the man was. Then Damon caught up and continued. "He's trying to get to Bobby and Hope."

"Where are they?"

"Hold up a minute so I can show you. Man, you're as bad as that guy from *The Fugitive*. You've caught Bobby and now you're not about to let her get away, huh?"

Was there a twist of sarcasm to those words? Before Finn could comment, Damon directed his attention to a tool shed fifty feet behind the barn . . . and a pair of fake cops standing guard between the buildings.

"What the hell are they doing in there? Of all the hiding places—"

"It's a bomb shelter."

"What?"

"It leads to an underground shelter. Bobby and Hope were coming out when they noticed those guys making a beeline for the shed. They ducked back down. Those two took a peek inside and didn't see the hatch. But that seems to be their assigned post so they aren't budging. And Karl's getting tired of waiting."

"Guide us in."

• • •

"THIS WAY," Damon said as they slipped into the barn.

Rhys stepped in the other direction, toward the dark stalls.

"No!" Damon said. "Stop him."

"What?"

Rhys motioned that he wanted to check the rest of the barn, be sure it was clear.

"Tell him I already got it," Damon said. "He doesn't need to—"

Rhys was already disappearing into the stalls.

"Shit! Call him back, Finn."

Finn wasn't about to raise his voice. He jogged after Rhys, rounding the corner to see the other man dropping beside a woman lying in the hay. Finn picked up his pace.

It was a couple, a man beside the woman, arms around her, her face against his chest.

"The gas," Finn whispered. "It must have knocked them out."

"No." Rhys rose and extended his hand. In it lay two small vials.

Finn strode over for a closer look. There were no lights in the barn, but a sliver of sunlight through the beams illuminated the face of the young man on the floor. His features were contorted in agony. The woman's face was hidden against him, but Finn recognized her dark hair and blue dress. The girl who'd held a gun on Adele.

"Hugh and Lily," Rhys murmured, his voice thick.

Damon murmured he'd go check on the women. As Rhys took off his ball cap, Finn looked around. Deep in the shadows he could make out two more bodies. Rhys hadn't noticed them, and Finn wasn't about to point them out. Whatever Rhys's connection to this place, these people weren't anonymous victims to him.

Rhys looked up sharply. "The others. I have to—"

"You have to get Hope, Robyn and Adele Morrissey." Marsten appeared from nowhere. "As for the rest? What's done is done."

Harsher than Finn would have put it, but Rhys only pulled his ball cap back on and straightened. Then he dropped the vials and crushed them under his shoe.

"Those are stashed all over the property," he said. "Anyone who hasn't been captured will have already done what they were taught. They'll presume it's a Cabal."

"But these people had rifles," Finn said. "They could have fought back."

Rhys shook his head. "Then some could be captured. They wouldn't risk that."

"It's the Nasts, isn't it?" Marsten said, keeping his voice low. "I believe I suggested we switch cars in case they'd planted a tracking unit."

"And I said that my car has a device to scramble the signal. They'd be in North Hollywood by now."

"Whoever is here, I think it's my fault," Finn said. "I called for backup, and this is what I got. I have no idea how or why—"

"They diverted calls from your radio," Rhys said.

"That's not poss—"

"Believe me, it is. Cabal technology. Almost certainly the Nasts. As for why . . . I have my suspicions—"

"Unimportant." Marsten walked back from peering out the window. "We have a rescue to launch. Hope, Robyn and Adele's trail seems to lead to that building behind the barn. But the guards have already checked in there, so—"

"They're underground." Finn explained what Damon told him, as quickly and quietly as possible.

"Don't worry about Adele," Damon said as he returned. "There was a situation. Hope took her down. Shot her."

Again, Finn relayed. Seeming less pleased with that than Finn would have expected, Marsten frowned and walked to the window.

"What we'll do then is create a distraction," Finn began.

Marsten didn't turn from the window. "At this point, I'm not looking for a humane course of action, Detective. It's too risky."

As Rhys answered, Finn thought he saw a movement behind the dead couple. He peered into the shadows. A hand moved across the hay. A ghost? Finn took a step toward it. The ghost lay facedown, as if too shocked to stand. His hand was moving toward a rifle. The straw crackled and shifted under the man's fingers . . . and told Finn this was no ghost.

Finn slipped up over the man, bent and pressed his gun to his skull. "Stop right there."

Running footsteps pounded the concrete pad outside the barn. Finn looked up sharply, but the stall blocked his view. Rhys wheeled, gun rising. Two pairs of hands lifted over the stall. Women's hands. Rhys lowered his gun as Marsten strode over.

"There's a guy in the hay. He's—" Hope saw Finn with his gun trained on the man. "You found him. Good. Rob and I were running beside the barn when I caught a stray thought."

"Niko?" Rhys strode over, kicked the rifle aside and hauled the middle-aged man to his feet. "Playing possum, were you?"

"Th-the poison," Niko said. "It didn't work for me."

Rhys cold-cocked Niko and sent him flying into the hay pile.

"I'm not going to fight," Niko said, struggling up. "I claim sanctuary." His gaze swung to Hope. "With the council."

"The same council you've always sworn was in league with the Cabals?"

"You don't understand, Rhys. You never did. To give clairvoyants the community they need, we lie. It's a blueprint created by bulibashas long before my time."

"Lies? Like the one about hiding from the Cabals? Protecting the kumpania from them?"

"We *do* protect—"

"You brought the Cabal here, Niko. When Adele told you the Cabal chased her and Colm earlier today, you knew she was wrong. The Cabal wouldn't do that because they *own* the kumpania. It's not a safe haven. It's a clairvoyant farm."

"That's—"

"I've been following the trail for ten years now, and finally figured out where it ended. You tried to stop this—" He waved to the dead young couple. "—from happening by telling the kumpania not to worry, not to panic."

"Of course, I didn't want—"

"Because if they killed themselves, it would be your fault. You alerted the Cabal. You told them about me. They somehow linked it all to Detective Findlay's investigation—"

"Because he visited the Nast offices today," Hope said. "He met with Sean, who went digging for information on clairvoyants to help me, which must have triggered an alert. They found out about Detective Findlay's visit, and put it together."

"And the Cabal wouldn't want the police descending on their kumpania. They rerouted Detective Findlay's calls, and probably all emergency calls from that motel."

"Because they wanted to *protect* us!" Niko said. "As they have always protected us, Rhys. That protection comes with a price. One clairvoyant every ten years. A pittance to pay. But you couldn't leave well enough alone. And look what happened." He pointed to the couple.

"The Cabal swooped in because of Adele," Rhys said. "Adele was your creation, Niko. Her actions brought everyone to your doorstep—"

"Uh, guys?" Damon ran in. Rhys and Niko were still arguing. Damon leapt between them. "Finn, get them to shut up. *Now.* We've got—"

Marsten strode in. "They've figured out where we are. Process of elimination or he—" A chin jerk toward Niko. "—alerted them. We have eight armed men heading this way, led by one old man—"

"Rhys Vaughan? Hope Adams? Karl Marsten?" a voice boomed. "This is Thomas Nast. We have the building surrounded."

"Come out with your hands raised," Hope muttered, sounding surprisingly calm.

"Split up," Finn said. "Take the windows. How many guns—?"

"No, Detective," Hope said. "Fortunately for us, this isn't going to end in a hail of bullets."

"We can negotiate," Rhys said.

Hope took a deep breath. "Okay, as the council representative and chaos-sensing half-demon, I should be the one—"

"No." Marsten grabbed her arm. "Rhys wanted to go this alone. I think it's time we let him."

"Really?" Rhys said. "And I thought you were about to volunteer. Silly me."

"Stop it." Hope brushed off Marsten's hand. "I'm—"

"Bobby!" Damon shouted.

Finn spun to see Robyn disappearing out the barn doors, armed men closing in, eight guns trained on her. Finn broke into a run.

"Mr. Nast?" she said. "We'd like to declare a truce."

HOPE

This was one of those cases that happens more often than anyone cared to admit, where the council and the Cabal were not on opposite sides. The council wanted to stop Adele. The Cabal wanted to protect its kumpania. Killing Adele had accomplished both. Now they just needed to tidy the loose ends. So they negotiated.

It helped that neither side had taken casualties. Even Irving Nast wasn't dead. Karl had tied him up and locked him in a closet, figuring that once they were done at the kumpania, they could notify the Nasts that he'd kidnapped a Pack wolf. The threat of diplomatic fallout would have the Nasts scrambling to punish Irving, a minor and relatively inconsequential family member.

With Adele dead, there was no way to pin the murders on her, not without the danger of exposing the clairvoyants. The Nasts vowed Robyn's name would be cleared, at their expense—lawyers, bribes, whatever it took.

In return, the Nasts got Niko, two of the seers and the remnants of his kumpania. Five members were dead, including Neala. Niko would regroup and spin lies, and the kumpania would carry on. Rhys wasn't happy with that, but it was a fight for another day. The Nasts granted him custody of Thom, and that was all that mattered for now.

Rhys had been right about the Cabal operating the kumpania. That was the real reason he'd taken the job with Irving Nast—hoping to prove his theory. The Nasts and the kumpania had been linked from the beginning, centuries ago in Europe. It was a secret pact between the bulibasha and the Nast CEO, which is why neither Sean nor Irving knew about it, leading Irving to negotiate with Adele.

The Nasts protected the kumpania from threats, including other Cabals. In return the kumpania provided them with clairvoyants. In fact, they'd been negotiating to provide one in the next year. The last clairvoyant had been a disappointment, so Niko had promised Thomas Nast the brightest star of the new generation: Adele Morrissey.

DETECTIVE FINDLAY TOOK ROBYN to the station. Hope stayed with her as long as she could. The detective swore Robyn would be fine and he'd get her to the hospital as soon as he could.

When Hope and Karl left the station, Rhys was outside waiting.

"I'll walk with you to your car," he said, falling in beside them.

"How's Thom?" Hope asked.

"Confused. Angry. I had to sedate him." He shoved his hands into his jacket pockets. "It'll be a big adjustment for both of us. We're flying tonight to a supernatural hospital. I wanted to touch base with you two before I left. First, Karl, I didn't get a chance to say it earlier, but you were right to leave Irving Nast alive. A better plan than mine."

Rhys braced, as if expecting Karl to sarcastically thank him for his approval, but Karl only nodded, knowing Rhys's admission wasn't easy—or necessary.

"Also, I have a business proposition for Hope. Well, for both of you, since I assume it's a package deal. All the better, because I know I'd never have a chance of hiring you otherwise, Karl." They turned the corner before he continued. "Earlier today you called me a mercenary, Hope. I could argue the nuances of that, but it is, in essence, what I am."

"I already—"

"—work for the council. I respect that. I respect the council and what they do, though I meant what I said about them not being as effective as the supernatural world needs. That's the nature of the beast. A body of justice cannot afford to slide into gray areas. That's the arena of other organizations."

"Like yours?"

"I'd like the chance to make my case, Hope." He handed Hope a card with a phone number. "A pressure-free pitch. What you're doing for the council is great, but I think you can do more." His eyes met hers. "I think you might need to do more."

KARL AND HOPE STOOD on their hotel room balcony. She leaned against the railing, watching the line of cars below, a parade of lights slow-marching to the beat of overamped music and horn blasts. Two motorcycles weaved through the traffic, leaving glowing trails like lightning bugs.

"I have a decision to make, Karl. A tough one."

"I know."

"I'm not sure that the council is where I belong anymore."

"I know."

Hope crossed her arms, still leaning against the railing, face averted, fists balled where he couldn't see them.

"Karl . . . ?"

"Hmm?"

"About us . . ."

She felt him tense, a jolt of chaos escaping before he reined it in.

She turned around. "Karl, I need . . ." Her throat closed there, refusing to let the next words out, only letting her reverse and repeat. "I need . . . I need . . ."

He took a slow step toward her, struggling to keep those chaos vibes in check, hands lifting as if he wanted to stop whatever she was going to say. A foot from her, he halted, hands going into his pockets.

"Hope . . . whatever . . ." A surge of chaos, then he blurted, "We'll work it out."

"I-I hope so."

A rush of breath. "All right then. Tell me what you need."

"You." Hope's voice was barely audible even in the silence. "I need you. Too much."

He put his arms out and she moved into them, his hands going to her back, her cheek against his chest, and that was easier, so much easier, resting there, listening to his heart, where she could feel his response but didn't have to see it. Cowardly, maybe. But it was the only way she'd get through this.

"I need to go back to the council and explain what happened. Then I need to make some hard decisions and . . ." A deep breath. "You can't fix this for me, Karl. And if you're here, you'll want to. I know you try not to, but you do, and I let you, and I don't think either of us is happy about it."

He went quiet and she braced for him to argue, to say he'd give her space, and she knew he'd try, maybe succeed, but she wouldn't. Even if she managed not to ask his advice, she'd take her decisions to him, watch his face and monitor his chaos vibes. If they didn't support her choice, she'd change it.

She trusted Karl more than she trusted herself. That had to change. Time to grow up. But it was one thing to hint she needed time alone. Another to insist. She didn't think she could do that.

"There's a job in Australia," he said finally. "I wasn't going to do it, because it would take more than my usual two weeks and I certainly don't need the money, but . . ."

She pulled back to look at him. "How long are we talking?"

"Six weeks at least. Probably closer to two months."

"Two months?"

"If you need more—"

"No, I was just thinking . . . two months. That's . . . long. But, yes. I might not like it . . ."

"But you need it." He put his hands on her hips and turned her around, backing to rest against the railing. "I can't stop wanting to help, and by 'help,' I really mean guide, and by 'guide' I mean protect. That has nothing to do with you and whether you can take care of yourself. It's about me and what I want, which is to make life easier for you, because I know it isn't easy and it's only getting harder, and I'm scrambling madly to smooth those rough edges before you get hurt."

"I'm going to get hurt, Karl."

His hands tightened on her hips, as if the very idea was a threat to fight and defeat. After a moment, he said, "I know."

"I need to know I'll be okay, Karl. That I can do this on my own. That as much as I appreciate your help, I don't *need* it."

They were quiet for a minute.

"Two months . . ." she whispered.

"And then I'll be back. You know that."

"I think that's part of it. Yes, I know you'll be back, and yet . . ."

"You don't quite trust it. You can't help thinking that I'll meet some glamorous Aussie at the opera house, seduce her for her jewels and decide this 'life mate' business isn't what I want after all." He looked down at her. "I know we don't discuss my past and I'm glad of it. But my past means I know exactly what else is out there, what I'm 'missing,' and I don't miss it at all."

"But don't you . . . get tired of it? My endless angst, my issues . . ."

"And don't you get tired of mine? Overly protective. Overly territorial. Ambivalent about the Pack. And forget the werewolf issues— I'm a jewel thief. I have enough money, so why don't I settle down, get a nice office job so you don't have to lie to your friends and family—"

Hope cut him off with a kiss. "I understood from the start that's what you are, what you need to be. I bought the whole package."

"As did I." He shifted her aside. "Wait here."

He went inside. A minute later, he returned.

"Put out your hand."

She smiled. "Do I have to close my eyes?"

"Of course."

She did. Something small and cold dropped into her palm. She opened her eyes to see what looked like a figure-eight charm. When she held it by the ring, though, the eight lay on its side. The symbol for infinity.

"I considered a ring, but feared that might be pushing my luck. A more abstractly symbolic gesture seemed appropriate. I'd have hung it on your charm bracelet, but I don't know where you've put it."

"Some thief you are."

"I could take a look . . ."

She caught his sleeve, closed her hand around the charm and lifted her arms to his neck.

He caught her wrist. "There's an inscription."

She found it. Three words, repeated on the front and back. *No matter what.*

"Yes," Karl said. "Quite possibly the least poetic inscription ever written."

"No it's . . ." She clasped the charm. "It's perfect."

"And I mean it, Hope. I'm here for you, no matter what. I always will be. You can never do anything that will scare me away. No matter how hard you try."

She laughed, the tears jolting free. He wiped them away.

"You're right," he said. "You have decisions to make and I shouldn't be a part of that. I don't *need* to be. You'll make the right choice, and whatever you decide is fine with me . . . as long as it doesn't involve handing back my condo keys."

"It won't."

"Then, I meant what I said the other day. I'm just along for the ride. Council, Cabal, mercenary, I don't care. I come willingly, and it's not about following you or protecting you. I enjoy it. You aren't the only one who's finding that what satisfied those 'uncivilized urges' in the past isn't doing the job the way it used to. So consider your options, make your choice and call me home."

"I will."

FINN

NO ONE THOUGHT IT WOULD WORK.

Hope Adams had put Finn in touch with a necromancer named Jaime Vegas. Finn thought the name sounded familiar, though he wasn't sure where from.

She'd promised to walk him through it over the phone, but warned him the task was difficult enough for experienced necromancers, let alone one who'd never actively practiced the art. As Damon would say, he didn't have the juice.

From what little Finn had learned so far, most necromancers saw ghosts all the time, not sporadically at murder sites. Of course, no one—not even Damon—suggested Finn lacked the power to pull it off. They were just very, very cautious in their optimism.

Finn had passed those warnings on to Robyn and she'd been quicker than anyone to assure him that she understood, that if it didn't work, that was okay. Which wasn't true. Yes, she'd understand. But it wouldn't be okay. Not for her. Not for Damon. Not for Finn.

They tried it in Robyn's apartment, just the three of them: Finn, Damon and Robyn. He'd followed the ritual and then . . . A flicker of images, like a film strip on fast forward. It lasted only a second or two, and when his vision cleared, he was in a strange apartment, sitting in a leather beanbag chair.

Finn touched the chair. He could see his fingers make contact, but couldn't feel the leather. He poked it. His fingers passed through, the leather still smooth.

From the other room, he heard . . . his voice. Singing. A song he didn't recognize, in a timbre he didn't recognize. A sob. Then a cry that he knew—even if he couldn't make it out—was Robyn saying a name. Damon's name.

He pictured Robyn leaping from her chair, her face . . .

The apartment next door went silent, and he imagined her throwing herself toward him. His arms outstretched. Robyn in them. Robyn kissing him. But not him. Not really him.

He imagined it and . . .

He stopped imagining it.

As he sat there, trying not to eavesdrop, an idea wriggled up from the deepest part of his brain. It had been burrowing there since he'd first realized he might be able to let Damon into his body.

It wasn't so much an idea as an impulse. One that if he decided to follow through on, he knew he couldn't think too much about. Do it or don't.

He pushed to his feet. At the door, he reached for the knob. His fingers passed through. He paused a moment, staring at it. From the next room came a chuckle, then a snuffle—a laugh breaking off in a sob. Finn squared his shoulders and stepped through the door.

Down the hall. He paused outside the elevator, but had no idea how that would work, and wasn't about to shimmy down elevator cables. To the stairwell then. To the lobby. Out the front doors.

He stopped in the doorway. Did he want to do this? It felt like the right thing to do, and he supposed that was what counted. As for what *he* wanted, he honestly didn't know anymore. It had been too long since he'd considered it.

He did know one thing. He was tired. Tired of being in Los Angeles. Tired of solving cases no one seemed to care about. Tired of the whispers, the looks, the laughs. Tired of being different. Tired of being alone.

A shoe squeaked behind him. Before he could turn, a man walked through him, striding down the sidewalk, briefcase swinging.

Finn made it a dozen steps before a voice called, "And where do you think you're going?"

Finn turned. To his left was an abstract sculpture. A woman in jeans, boots and a T-shirt sat on it, reclining against a curved piece of steel, her face in shadow.

"I'm talking to you, Detective," she said.

She stretched and stood and, for a moment, Finn saw the girl from the photograph in Sean Nast's office. Nast's little sister. But this woman was older—at least Finn's age, with dark eyes, not bright blue. Still, the resemblance was uncanny.

"I asked where you think you're going." The woman walked toward him, her foot passing through a discarded soda bottle. A ghost.

"It's okay," he said, because it was all he could think of. A polite nod, then he turned to head on his way.

"Actually, it's not okay." The woman walked in front of him and turned around. "You can't leave Damon in your body. An insanely noble gesture, Detective Findlay, but you can't. The Fates let you pull off the body switch, but it's temporary. I'm here to make sure of that. And neither of us, I'm afraid, has any say in the matter."

Finn stepped to the side. The woman put out her hands and murmured something. The air between her hands glittered, then shimmered, a sword taking form. A huge one, with glowing symbols etched into the metal.

"Pretty, huh? Being a necro, you know what this is, right?"

Finn shook his head.

The woman sighed. "It's the outfit, isn't it? I know, they keep trying to make me wear the uniform, but those wings are just so damned uncomfortable. Have you ever tried sitting with wings stuck to your shoulders? And the halo? Does nothing for me."

"An . . . angel?"

"Don't sound so skeptical. You'll hurt my feelings." She lifted the sword. "Point is, this baby has a point. A very sharp one. And you do not want to feel it. So we're doing this the easy way. We let Damon and Robyn have their reunion, and you go back into your body, and nobody gets hurt. Got it?"

Finn said nothing.

"Damn, you're stubborn, aren't you?" She stepped closer. With the boots, she was almost as tall as Finn. "You're going back, Detective. That's not an option. If you get away from me, I hunt you down and introduce you to the sword. And don't ask me to look the other way and let you go, because it won't help. In minutes, they'll have another angel here to dump you back into your body before Damon's allotted hour is up, and I'll get my ass kicked for screwing up. No one will thank you for that, least of all me. So you are going back."

"Can I—?"

"No. Whatever the question is, the answer is no. Your life isn't over, you have to finish it. That's not up for negotiation. The most I can do is extend Damon's visit a little. Take you for a walk, get caught up in the chitchat, give him a couple of hours . . ."

Finn could tell arguing would do no good. He did hesitate, though, enough to make the angel sigh and lean on her sword, toe tapping. Then he nodded.

"Good man. We'll go this way. I thought I saw a park. If we catch a mugging in progress, I might be able to use my sword. Not a full-fledged soul-chopping, mind you. But a little nick that'll sting like a son of a bitch. Always fun."

They turned onto the sidewalk.

"I hear you met Sean the other day."

Finn glanced at her.

"Sean Nast."

"Right . . ."

"Did he seem okay to you? His dad has been worried. Well, we both have actually. Sean's a good kid, but he really doesn't belong in the Cabal and Kris hates seeing . . ."

ROBYN

Robyn was burning her scrapbook.

It was a grand symbolic gesture that should, she admitted, have an equally grand setting—curled up by a massive fireplace, feeding pages into the blaze. In an apartment, it wasn't nearly so grand . . . or so simple. She had a metal garbage can by the open patio doors, a fan blowing the smoke out and wet towels draped over the smoke detectors. And she had to remove the newspaper clippings from the plastic pages before lighting them. But she did have a glass of wine beside her, which helped the atmosphere.

It took nearly an hour to go through the scrapbook, back to front. Then, finally, she held the first clipping. Damon's death notice. She looked at it, at his unsmiling face, at the cold harsh facts of his death . . . and she held the lighter to the corner.

As she watched the article crumble into black ash, she smiled. She'd kept that article as her last memory of him . . . and now it wasn't. She had a new one—of Damon right here, in this room, holding her, talking to her, singing to her.

It had been strange at first, seeing him in Finn's body. But all she'd had to do was close her eyes and it was Damon. His voice, his touch, his kiss and, most of all, his words.

She'd envied people who had last moments with their loved ones, a chance to say final words before they passed. But even then there would be things they hadn't realized they wanted to say until it was too late. She'd gotten that chance and she would never forget what a blessing it was, no more than she'd forget who'd given it to her.

Even just telling her Damon was still "alive" in some way, that he still lived, still existed, had been an amazing gift. Relaying his words to her would have been wonderful. But Finn had done more. And he'd paid the price, exhausted and weak, still dragging himself into work the next morning, determined not to hand her case off to another detective.

When the doorbell rang, Robyn dropped the last corner of the article into the garbage can and hurried to the door. No one had buzzed from downstairs, so it must be Hope, having forgotten to stick the apartment key on her ring again.

Hope had moved in yesterday. Robyn had invited her to stay with her for the rest of her work exchange. There was nothing keeping Robyn in L.A.—once the issues with the case were resolved, she could return to Philadelphia and get a new job there. But Hope had come here for her, and now she'd stay for Hope. Hope insisted Karl was just on a business trip, but Robyn got the feeling there was more to it and that her friend could really use the company.

When she checked out the peephole, though, it wasn't Hope.

"The landlord let me in," Finn said when she opened the door. "I brought those papers you need to sign."

"I'd have come to the station," she said, taking them.

He shrugged. "I was in the area."

"Do you have time for a coffee?"

Finn hesitated. "He's not with me."

"I know that."

She stepped back and waved him in. He paused another moment, then followed.

THEY HAD THEIR COFFEE on the patio. Robyn hadn't used it since she'd arrived—couldn't even remember opening the door until today—so they'd had to drag out chairs from the kitchen. Now she sat there, enjoying the sun and realizing, to her shock, that she had an amazing view. Patio chairs were going on the shopping list. Maybe even a table.

As they drank, Robyn said she'd decided to go with Hope to the council meeting that weekend. She'd told Hope she wanted to meet the delegates to assure them they weren't in any danger with her knowing their secrets. And maybe they could use a little PR assistance, someone to advise them and craft cover-up stories. Being non-supernatural herself, she was the perfect person to help them navigate exposure threats from the human world.

She hadn't told Hope that part of the plan. It seemed a bit foolish. Presumptuous, maybe. Now she bounced it off Finn, and he said it sounded like a good idea. So maybe it wasn't so crazy after all.

"About this meeting," he said, setting his mug on the railing. "Is it open to any . . . supernaturals? I was just thinking, maybe I should go to one. Introduce myself. Offer my help. See about getting some help myself from other . . . necromancers." He stumbled over the word, clearly not comfortable with it yet. "That Jaime Vegas woman I talked to is supposed to be a delegate of this council."

"Then she'll be there. And I'm sure you're welcome. It's in Portland. You can come up with us, if you like."

He nodded and sat there, still nodding, gazing out over the city for at least a minute before saying, "It would just be me, Robyn."

"What? No Damon? Forget it then. You're uninvited." She gave him a look. "I know Damon will still be spending some time with you, helping on cases. I know that's what he's supposed to be doing when he's here, helping *you*, not visiting his wife. I know he's supposed to have only minimal contact with me, so we can both move on with our lives, and if he starts using his time here to hang out with me, he loses his day passes. You explained all this to me, Finn."

"I know but—"

"But now every time I ask you in for coffee, you're going to wonder if I'm really asking you, or I'm asking the guy who keeps me connected to my dead husband." She sighed and cupped her mug between her hands. "I guess, then, maybe this isn't such a good idea, us trying to . . ." She shrugged. "Stay in contact, whatever. Of course I wouldn't mind keeping that connection with Damon. But to invite you along on our trip, just to—"

"You wouldn't do that. I know. Sure, ask Hope about the meeting. If it's okay with everyone, I'll come along."

He took his mug, lifted it to his lips, then frowned, as if just realizing it was empty.

"Got time for another?" she asked. When he hesitated, she took his mug. "I'll refill it anyway."

HOPE

Hope had returned to work at *True News* on Monday morning as if the last few days had never happened. That wasn't easy. She'd dropped Karl at the airport that morning, wanting to run after him like a scared little girl, screaming "Don't go! Don't go!"

She reminded herself of how many other times she'd dropped him at an airport . . . and picked him up again when he came home. In two months, she'd do the same and she'd have booked that promised cabin in the woods for them, and everything would be as it was. Better than it was. But still she worried. They both did.

On the weekend, Hope was supposed to appear before the council and explain what had happened with Adele and the kumpania. With Irving alive and the Cabal not making any complaints, there was little threat of a full inquiry, but that worry had forced her to consider whether it was time to move on.

She'd never abandon the council. Whatever path she chose, she was keeping her job at *True News*, and if she caught a whiff of an exposure threat, it would go to the council. But maybe, for her, working for the council was like taking regular-strength Tylenol for migraines, and it was time to admit the remedy was no longer strong enough.

Today she was meeting Rhys. He was flying in to have lunch and pitch his proposal. She wanted to tell him about Neala's last thoughts, her final, unspoken apology. Maybe it would help. Maybe it wouldn't. But he should know she'd wanted to say it. Hope had news for him, too. News she hoped he'd already heard, because she hated to be the one to break it.

Adele Morrissey was still alive.

In the aftermath at the kumpania, no one had questioned her death. Hope had blown a hole through her head. It hadn't occurred to her to check for a pulse.

Sean Nast had called last night with the news. Adele was brain dead, but being kept alive in a Cabal hospital until her baby reached full term.

Sean said rumors of it were already flying through the Cabal world. Whispers of a clairvoyant of unsurpassed power, gestating in a Nast laboratory. Another story to add to the others, omens and portents that already had supernaturals whispering and eyeing the skies uneasily. Even those who scoffed at such superstitious nonsense had begun to admit the recent rate of "unnatural" occurrences in their world was . . . discomfiting.

Twins born to two werewolf parents, the first known full-blooded werewolves.

Humans cracking the code of magic, conducting horrible experiments with child sacrifice.

A previously unknown supernatural race fully evolving in a few generations.

Coincidences easily dismissed, all of them. Nervous minds seeing correlations where none existed, viewing the world through the limits of time and experience, and mistaking rare events for unprecedented ones.

There had been female werewolves before, so surely there had been full-blooded werewolves. The cases just weren't documented or preserved.

Humans had experimented with magic for centuries and small breakthroughs *had* been documented. This greater success only suggested latent supernatural blood in the caster.

Supernatural races did evolve and die out—they already knew that. Jaz and his brother had been genetic anomalies, not signs of an accelerated evolutionary pace.

Adele Morrissey's child might not be a functioning clairvoyant, much less an über-powerful one. And even if he was, his conception was the result of twisted ambition and adolescent hormones, not divine—or demonic—intervention.

And yet . . .

Hope knew it might just be her overly active imagination. Maybe exhaustion and stress were making her see connections where none existed. Or maybe her demon blood knew—just knew—that all this meant something, that change was coming, that she would have a role to play.

A role for the good? She hoped so. But she couldn't shake the feeling that when the time came, the choice might not be hers to make. And that scared her more than anything.